GODSLAYER

TOR BOOKS BY JACQUELINE CAREY

Godslayer
Banewreaker

Kushiel's Avatar
Kushiel's Chosen
Kushiel's Dart

GODSLAYER

Volume Two of The Sundering

𝔍𝔞𝔠𝔮𝔲𝔢𝔩𝔦𝔫𝔢 𝔈𝔞𝔯𝔢𝔶

TOR®

A TOM DOHERTY ASSOCIATES BOOK
NEW YORK

GODSLAYER

This book is printed on acid-free paper.

Map by Ellisa Mitchell

A Tor Book
Published by Tom Doherty Associates, LLC.
175 Fifth Avenue
New York, NY 10010

www.tor.com

Tor® is a registered trademark of Tom Doherty Associates, LLC.

Library of Congress Cataloging-in-Publication Data

Carey, Jacqueline, 1964–
     Godslayer / Jacqueline Carey.—1st ed.
         p. cm.—(The sundering ; v. 2)
     "A Tom Doherty Associates book."
     ISBN 0-765-31239-5 (acid-free paper)
     EAN 978-0-765-31239-6
     1. Title.

   PS3603.A74G63 2005
   813'.54—dc22

                                                                    2005041728

First Edition: August 2005

Printed in the United States of America

0   9   8   7   6   5   4   3   2   1

DRAMATIS PERSONAE

SEVEN SHAPERS
Haomane, Lord-of-Thought
Arahila the Fair
Satoris the Sower
Neheris-of-the-Leaping-Waters
Meronin the Deep
Yrinna-of-the-Fruits
Oronin the Glad Hunter

DARKHAVEN'S FORCES
Tanaros Blacksword—General, one of the Three
Ushahin—Dreamspinner, one of the Three
Vorax—Glutton, one of the Three
Hyrgolf—Fjel field marshal
Carfax—Staccian captain
Skragdal—Fjel squadron commander
Speros—Midlander, recent arrival
Meara—madling, attendant to Cerelinde

HAOMANE'S ALLIES
Malthus the Counselor—Haomane's emissary
Ingolin the Wise—Lord of the Rivenlost
Cerelinde—Lady of the Ellylon
Aracus Altorus—heir to Kingdom of the West
Blaise Caveros—Aracus' second-in-command, member of
Malthus' Company
Fianna—the Archer of Arduan, member of Malthus' Company
Peldras—Ellyl, member of Malthus' Company
Lorenlasse of Valmaré—Leader of the Host of the Rivenlost
Dani—Yarru, the Bearer
Thulu—Yarru, Dani's uncle and guide

OTHERS
Lilias—Sorceress of the East
Calandor—dragon, one of the Eldest
Calanthrag—dragon, the Eldest
Grey Dam—ruler of the Were

Now conscience wakes despair
That slumber'd,—wakes the bitter memory
Of what he was, what is, and what must be
Worse.

John Milton, *Paradise Lost*

GODSLAYER

ONE

ALL THINGS CONVERGE.

In the last Great Age of the Sundered World of Urulat, which was once called Uru-Alat after the World God that gave birth to it, they began to converge upon Darkhaven.

It began with a red star rising in the west; Dergail's Soumanië, a polished stone that had once been a chip of the Souma itself—that mighty gem that rested on the sundered isle of Torath, the Eye in the Brow of Uru-Alat, source of the Shapers' power.

Satoris the Shaper took it for a warning, a message from a sister who had loved him, once upon a time; Arahila the Fair, whose children were the race of Men. His enemies took it as a declaration of war.

Whatever the truth, war ensued.

Haomane, First-Born among Shapers, long ago uttered a Prophecy.

"When the unknown is made known, when the lost weapon is found, when the marrow-fire is quenched and Godslayer is freed, when a daughter of Elterrion weds a son of Altorus, when the Spear of Light is brought forth and the Helm of Shadows is broken, the Fjeltroll shall fall, the Were shall be defeated ere they rise, and the Sunderer shall be no more, the Souma shall be restored and the Sundered World made whole and Haomane's Children shall endure."

It began with the rising of Dergail's Soumanië. Cerelinde, the Lady of the Ellylon, a daughter of Elterrion's line, plighted her troth to Aracus Altorus. It was the first step toward fulfilling Haomane's Prophecy; Arahila's Children and Haomane's conjoined, their lines inextricably mingled. But in Lindanen Dale, their nuptials were disrupted.

Bloodshed ensued.

It was a trap; a trap that went awry. It seemed at first that all the pieces fell into place. Driven by vengeance, the Grey Dam of the Were spent her life in an attack, and the half-breed Ushahin Dreamspinner unleashed madness and illusion. Under its cover, Tanaros Blacksword abducted the Lady Cerelinde and took her to Darkhaven.

Haomane's Allies were misled. Pursuing a rumor of dragons, under the command of Aracus Altorus, they raised an army and launched an assault on Beshtanag and Lilias, Sorceress of the East. And there the trap went awry. The Ways were closed, and the Army of Darkhaven was turned back, their company's leadership scattered. In Beshtanag, Haomane's Allies took to the field.

There, they prevailed.

They were not supposed to do so.

They were coming; all of them.

They came on foot and on horseback and by sailing ship, for the Ways of the Marasoumië had been destroyed. Lord Satoris had done this in his wrath. The Dragon of Beshtanag was no more, slain by the Arrow of Fire; the lost weapon, found. Bereft of her Soumanië, the Sorceress of the East was nothing more than an ordinary woman; Lilias, mortal and powerless. The Were had struck a bitter bargain with Aracus Altorus, ceding to his terms; defeated ere they rose. Aracus was coming, his heart filled with righteous fury, knowing he had been duped.

Malthus the Wise Counselor, trapped in the Ways, had vanished beyond the sight of even Godslayer itself . . . but rumor whispered of a new figure. The Galäinridder, the Bright Rider, whose words bred fear in the hearts of Men, inspiring them to betray their ancient oaths to Lord Satoris.

But Haomane's Allies had not won yet.

On the westernmost verge of the Unknown Desert, Tanaros Blacksword, Commander General of the Army of Darkhaven, made camp alongside a creek. There he slaked the thirst of his long-parched flesh and made ready to rally his surviving troops and set his face toward home. Immortal though he was, he could have died in the desert. Thanks to a raven's gratitude, he lived.

When he dreamed, he dreamed of the Lady Cerelinde.

On the back of a blood-bay horse, Ushahin Dreamspinner rode the pathways between waking and dreaming, plunging into the Midlands and leaving a trail of nightmares in his wake. A wedge of ravens forged his path, and on either side, a riderless horse flanked him; one a spectral grey, the other as black as coal.

If he had dreamed, which he did not, he would dream of the counsel of dragons.

Vorax the Glutton, muttering over his stores, awaited them in Darkhaven.

The immortal Three were soon to be reunited.

Haomane's Prophecy was yet to be fulfilled.

In the mighty fortress of Darkhaven, where the Lady Cerelinde endured imprisonment and fought against a rising tide of doubt, the marrow-fire yet burned. Within it hung the dagger, Godslayer; ruby-red, a Shard of the Souma. Once, it had wounded Satoris; the wound that would not heal. Godslayer alone could end a Shaper's life; the life of Lord Satoris, the life of any of the Shapers. And while the marrow-fire burned, no mortal hand could touch it. None but a Shaper would dare.

Only the Water of Life, drawn from the Well of the World, could extinguish the marrow-fire. The Water had been drawn, but its Bearer was lost.

Thrust out of the Ways by Malthus the Counselor in a desperate gambit, abandoned and lost, Dani of the Yarru wandered the cold lands of the Northern Harrow, deep in Fjeltroll territory, with only his uncle to guide him. Together, they sought to follow the rivers, the lifeblood of Urulat, to Darkhaven.

And they, too, were being hunted. . . .

Led by Skragdal of the Tungskulder, the Fjel were on the hunt. Their loyalty to Lord Satoris was beyond question. Haomane's Prophecy promised them nothing but death. No matter where it led them, they would not abandon their quest. They would succeed or die trying.

All things converge.

NEHERINACH WAS A GREEN BOWL cradled in the mountain's hands. Here and there, small boulders breached its surface; elsewhere, a half dozen small hillocks arose, covered in flowering ivy. A small river, spring-fed, wound through the center of it, meandering westward to sink belowground. Low mountains, sloping upward with a deceptively gentle grade, surrounded it. Patches of gorse offered grazing to fallow deer, shelter to hare that crouched in the shadow of small crags.

It was a peaceful place, and a terrible one.

On the verges, the Kaldjager scouts waited, glancing sidelong out of yellow eyes to watch the others' straggling progress. Skragdal, leading them, knew what the Kaldjager felt. This was where it had begun.

They assembled in silence on the field of Neherinach. The green grass was soft beneath their feet. Water sparkled under the bright sun. Birds stirred in the trees, insects took flight from grass stems.

"Come," Skragdal said quietly.

They crossed the field together, and the grass flattened beneath their approach, springing back once they had passed. It smelled clean and sweet. Skragdal felt his talons breach the surface of the soil beneath, rich and crumbling. It filled him with an ancient fury. There was old blood in that soil. Thousand upon thousand of Fjel had died in this place, fighting without weapons against a vast army of Men and Ellylon, attacked without quarter for the crime of giving shelter to the wounded Shaper who had taught them the measure of their own worth. The ivy-covered hillocks that dotted the field marked the cairns of Fjel dead; one for each of the six tribes.

In the end, they had won; by treachery and stealth, according to the songs of Haomane's Allies. It was true, they had laid traps, but what was treachery to a people invaded without provocation? It had been a bitter victory.

Near the riverbank, where the ground was soft enough to hold an impression, they found a trace of old hoofprints. Skragdal frowned. Only Men and Ellylon rode horses, and he did not like the idea of either despoiling Neherinach.

"A rider," Thorun said.

"Aye.

"The earl's Galäinridder?"

"Perhaps."

Led by the Kaldjager, they followed the tracks to their origin. At the northern tip of Neherinach, a node-point of the Marasoumië had lain buried in a hollow place. Now, a great crater had been gouged from the earth. Splintered rock thrust outward in every direction. Whatever had emerged had done so with great force. The innermost surfaces of the granite were smooth and gleaming, as if the rock itself had become molten. It had not happened all that long ago. There were fresh scratches on the rock, and the remnants of hoofprints were still visible on the churned ground.

"That's not good," Thorun said.

"No." Staring into the hole, Skragdal thought of Osric's Men gossiping in the tunnels, and of Osric in Gerflod Hall, grinning his dead grin at the ceiling. The ragged hole gaped like a wound in the green field of Neherinach, exposing the ashen remains of the node far below. Earl Coenred's final words echoed in his memory, making his hide crawl with unease. *Dead, and you don't even know it!* "It's not."

He thought about changing their course, setting the Kaldjager to track the Galäinridder; but General Tanaros had told them, again and again, the importance of obeying orders. It was important to obey orders, even those Lord Vorax had given. Anyway, it was already too late. Gerflod Keep lay a day behind them, and the Rider had some days' start. Not even the Gulnagel could catch him now.

But they could warn Darkhaven.

"Rhilmar," he said decisively. "Morstag. Go back. If General Tanaros has returned, tell him what we have seen here. Tell him what happened in Gerflod. If he is not there, tell Lord Vorax. And if he will not listen, tell Marshal Hyrgolf. No; tell him anyway. He needs to know. This is a matter that concerns the Fjel."

"Aye, boss." Rhilmar, the smaller of the two, shivered in the bright sun. In this place of green grass, sparkling rivers, and old bones, fear had caught up to him; the reek of it oozed from him, tainting the air. "Just . . . just the two of us?"

One of the Kaldjager snorted with contempt. Skragdal ignored it. "Haomane's Allies didn't fear to send only two, and smallfolk at that," he said to Rhilmar. "Go fast, and avoid Men's keeps." He turned to the Kaldjager. "Blågen, where is the nearest Fjel den?"

The Kaldjager pointed to the east. "Half a league." His yellow eyes gleamed. "Are we hunting?"

"Aye." Skragdal nodded. "We follow orders. We will spread word among the tribes until there is nowhere safe and no place for them to hide. Whoever—whatever—this Galäinridder is, he did well to flee Fjel

territories and put himself beyond our reach." Standing beside the des-
ecrated earth, he bared his eyetusks in a grim smile. "Pity the smallfolk
he left behind."

THEY SPENT AN ENTIRE DAY camped beneath the jack pines, reveling in
the presence of water and shade. Red squirrels chattered in the trees,
providing easy prey for the Gulnagel. Speros, ranging along the course
of the creek, discovered a patch of wild onion. Tanaros' much-dented
helmet, having served as bucket and shovel, served now as a makeshift
cooking pot for a hearty stew.

By Tanaros' reckoning, they had emerged to the southeast of Darkhaven. Between them lay the fertile territories of the Midlands, then
the sweeping plains of Curonan. It was possible that they could locate
an entrance to the tunnels on the outskirts of the Midlands, but there
was still a great deal of open ground to cover. It would be an easy
journey by the standards of the desert; but there was the problem of
the Fjel. Two Men traveling in enemy territory were easily disguised.

Not so, three large Gulnagel.

"We'll have to travel by night," Tanaros said ruefully. "At least we're
well used to it." He eyed Speros. "Do you still remember how to steal
horses?"

The Midlander looked uncertain. "Is that a jest, sir?"

Tanaros shook his head. "No."

They passed a farmstead on the first night and stole close enough
to make out the shape of a stable, but at a hundred paces the sound of
barking dogs filled the air. When a lamp was kindled in the cottage
and silhouetted figures moved before the windows, Tanaros ordered a
hasty, ignominious retreat, racing across fields, while the Gulnagel accompanied them at a slow jog.

Not until they had put a good distance between themselves and the
farmstead did he order a halt. Back on the dusty road, Speros doubled
over, bracing his hands on his thighs and catching his breath. "Why . . .
not just . . . kill them? Surely . . . farmers wouldn't be much trouble."

Tanaros cocked a brow at him. "And have their deaths discovered?
We've leagues to go before we're in the clear, and all of the Midlands
standing on alert. You were the one served in the volunteer militia,
Speros of Haimhault. Do you want one such on our trail?"

"Right." Speros straightened. "Shank's mare it is, General."

They walked in silence for several hours. After the desert, Tanaros reflected, it was almost pleasant. Their waterskins were full, and the fields provided ample hunting for the Gulnagel. The air was balmy and moist, and the stars overhead provided enough light to make out the rutted road. On such a night, one could imagine walking forever. He thought about the farmstead they had passed and smiled to himself. While his motive for having done so was reasoned, there was a luxuriant pleasure in having spared its inhabitants' lives. Such choices seldom came his way. He wondered what story they would tell in the morning. They'd pass a sleepless night if they knew the truth. Likely the scent of the Gulnagel had set the dogs to barking; better to send Speros alone, next time. He wondered if Fetch, who had flown ahead, might be able to scout a likely candidate for horse-thievery.

"It's funny, isn't it?" Speros remarked. "I never could have imagined this."

"What's that?"

"*This.*" The Midlander waved one hand, indicating the empty road, the quiet fields. "Us, here. Tramping across the country like common beggars. I'd have thought . . . I don't know, Lord General." He shrugged. "I'd have thought there'd be more *magic.*"

"No." Tanaros shook his head. "There's precious little magic in war, Speros."

"But you're . . . one of the Three, sir!" Speros protested. "Tanaros Blacksword, Tanaros . . ." His voice trailed off.

"Kingslayer," Tanaros said equably. "Aye. An ordinary man, rendered extraordinary only by the grace of Lord Satoris." He touched the hilt of his sword. "This blade cannot be broken by mortal means, Speros, but I wield no power but that which lies in reach of it. Are you disappointed?"

"No." Speros studied his boots as he walked, scuffing the ruts in the road with cracked heels. "No," he repeated more strongly, lifting his head. "I'm not." He grinned, the glint of starlight revealing the gap amid his teeth. "It gives me hope. After all, Lord General, *I* could be you!"

As Tanaros opened his mouth to reply, one of the Gulnagel raised a hand and grunted. The others froze, listening. Motioning for silence, Tanaros strained his ears. Not the farmsteaders, he hoped. Surely, they had seen nothing. There had been only the warning of the dogs to disturb their sleep. Like as not, they had cast a weary gaze over the empty fields, scolded the dogs, and gone back to sleep. What, then? The Fjel had keener ears than Men, but all three wore perplexed expressions. Speros, by contrast, bore a look of glazed horror.

Tanaros concentrated.

At first he heard nothing; then, distantly, a drumming like thunder. Hoofbeats? It sounded like, and unlike. There were too many, too fast—and another sound, too, a rushing, pulsating wind, like the sound of a thousand wings beating at once. It sounded, he realized, like the Ravensmirror.

"Fetch?" Tanaros called.

"Kaugh!"

The fabric of the night itself seemed to split beneath the onslaught as they emerged from the dreaming pathways into the waking world; ravens, aye, a whole flock, sweeping down the road in a single, vast wing. There, at the head, was Fetch, eyes like obsidian pebbles. And behind them, forelegs churning, nostrils flaring . . .

Horses.

They emerged from darkness as if through a doorway, and starlight gleamed on their sleek hides. All around them, the ravens settled in the fields; save for Fetch, who took up his perch on Tanaros' shoulder. Their iron-shod hooves rang on the road, solid and real, large bodies milling. There were three of them; one grey as a ghost, one black as pitch, and in the middle, a bay the color of recently spilled blood.

And on its back, a pale, crooked figure with moonspun hair and a face of ruined beauty smiled crookedly and lifted a hand in greeting.

"Well met, cousin," said Ushahin Dreamspinner. "A little bird told me you were in need of a ride."

"Dreamspinner!" Tanaros laughed aloud. "Well met, indeed." He clapped one hand on Speros' shoulder. "I retract my words, lad. Forgive me for speaking in haste. It seems the night holds more magic than I had suspected."

Speros, the color draining from his desert-scorched skin, stared without words.

"I have ridden the wings of a nightmare, cousin, and I fear it has brushed your protégé's thoughts." Ushahin's voice was amused. "What plagues you, Midlander? Did you catch a glimpse of your own mortal

frailties and failings, the envy to which your kind is prey? A rock, per-
chance, clutched in a boyish fist? But for an accident of geography,
you might have been one of *them*." His mismatched eyes glinted,
shadows pooling in the hollow of his dented temple. "Are you afraid
to meet my gaze, Midlander?"

"Cousin—" Tanaros began.

"No." With an effort of will, Speros raised his chin and met the half-
breed's glittering gaze. Clenching one hand and pressing it to his
heart, he extended it open in the ancient salute. His starlit face was
earnest and stubborn. "No, Lord Dreamspinner. I am not afraid."

Ushahin smiled his crooked smile. "It is a lie, but it is one I will
honor for the sake of what you have endured." He nodded to his left.
"Take the grey. Do you follow in my footprints, within the swath the
ravens forge, she will bear you in my wake, Tanaros." He pointed to
the black horse. "You rode such a one, once. Here is another. Can
your Gulnagel keep pace?"

"Aye," Tanaros murmured, his assent echoed by the grinning Fjel.
He approached the black horse, running one hand along the arch of
its neck. Its black mane spilled like water over his hand, and it turned
its head, baring sharp teeth, a preternaturally intelligent eye glimmering.
Clutching a hank of mane low on the withers, he swung himself astride.
Equine muscle surged beneath his thighs; Fetch squawked with dis-
pleasure and took wing. Using the pressure of his knees, Tanaros
turned the black. He thought of his own stallion, his faithful black, lost
in the Ways of the Marasoumië, and wondered what had become of it.
"These are Darkhaven's horses, cousin, born and bred. Where did you
come by them?"

"On the southern edge of the Delta."

Tanaros paused. "My Staccians. The trackers?"

"I fear it is so." There was an unnerving sympathy in Ushahin's expression. "They met a . . . a worthy end, cousin. I will tell you of it,
later, but we must be off before Haomane's dawn fingers the sky, else
I cannot keep this pathway open. Night is short, and there are . . .
other considerations afoot. Will you ride?"

"Aye." Tanaros squeezed the black's barrel, feeling its readiness to
run, to feel the twilit road unfurling like a ribbon once more beneath
its hooves. He glanced at Speros and saw the Midlander, too, was

astride, eyes wide with excitement. He glanced at the Gulnagel and saw them readying themselves to run, muscles bunching in their powerful haunches. "Let us make haste."

"Boss?" One held up Tanaros' helmet. "You want this?"

"No." Thinking of water holes, of shallow graves and squirrel stew, Tanaros shook his head. "Leave it. It has served its purpose, and more. Let the Midlanders find it and wonder. I do not need it."

"Okay." The Fjel laid it gently alongside the road.

Tanaros took a deep breath, touching the sword that hung at his side. His branded heart throbbed, answering to the touch, to the echo of Godslayer's fire and his Lordship's blood. He thought, with deep longing, of Darkhaven's encompassing walls. He tried not to think about the fact that *she* was there. A small voice whispered a name in his thoughts, insinuating a tendril into his heart, as delicate and fragile as the shudder of a mortexigus flower. With an effort, he squelched it. "We are ready, cousin."

"Good," Ushahin said simply. He lifted one hand, and a cloud of ravens rose swirling from the fields, gathering and grouping. The blood-bay stallion shifted beneath his weight, hide shivering, gathering. The road, which was at once like and *unlike* the road upon which they stood, beckoned in a silvery path. "Then let us ride."

Home!

The blood-bay leapt and the ravens swept forward. Behind them ran the grey and the black. The world lurched and the stars blurred; all save one, the blood-red star that sat on the western horizon. Now three rode astride, and two were of the Three. The beating of the ravens' wings melted into the drumming sound of hoofbeats and the swift, steady pad of the Gulnagel's taloned feet.

And somewhere to the north, a lone Rider veered into the Unknown Desert.

In the farmsteads and villages, Midlanders tossed in their sleep, plagued by nightmares. The color of their dreams changed. Where they had seen a horse as white as foam, they saw three; smoke and pitch and blood.

Where they had seen a venerable figure—a Man, or something like one—with a gem as clear as water on his breast, they saw a shadowy face, averted, and a rough stone clenched in a child's fist, the crunch of bone and a splash of blood.

Over and over, it rose and fell.

Onward, they rode.

LILIAS WAS SEASICK.

She leaned over the railing of the dwarf ship *Yrinna's Bounty* and spewed her guts into the surging waves. When the contents of her belly had been purged to emptiness, her guts continued to churn. There was no surcease upon these lurching decks, this infernal swell. The waves rose and fell, rose and fell, a constant reminder that the world she knew had vanished. Lilias retched and brought up bile until her very flesh burned with dry, bitter heat. It was no wonder she failed to hear the approach of the Ellyl behind her.

"Pray, steady yourself, Sorceress." A cool hand soothed her brow, and there was comfort and sweet ease in the touch. " 'Tis but Meronin's waves that do disturb those accustomed to the solid ground of Uru-Alat."

"Get away!" Lilias, straightening, shoved him. "Leave me alone."

"Forgive me." The Ellyl took a graceful step backward, raising his slender hands; Peldras, one of Malthus' Companions. The one with the damnable shadow of sorrow and *compassion* in his gaze. "I meant only to bring comfort."

Lilias laughed, a sound as harsh as the calling of gulls. Her mouth was parched and foul. She pushed strands of dark hair, sticky with bile, out of her face. "Oh, comfort, is it? Can you undo what is done, Ellyl? Can you restore Calandor to life?"

"You know that such a thing cannot be." The Ellyl did not flinch, and the sorrow in his gaze only deepened. "Lady Sorceress, I regret the deaths at Beshtanag. Even, yes, perhaps even that of the Eldest. It grieves me to have come too late. Believe me, if I could have prevented them, I assure you, I would have. I did seek to do so."

"So." Lilias shrugged and glanced across the deck toward where Aracus Altorus bent his head, listening to the Dwarf captain, who was the picture of ease upon the pitching decks, with his short stature and his root-gnarled legs astraddle. She was unsure how or why Yrinna's Children had stood ready at Port Eurus to ferry Haomane's Allies over the waters. "You failed."

"Yes." Peldras bowed his head, fair, gleaming hair falling to curtain his somber brow. "Lady Sorceress," he said softly, "I do not think your heart is as black as it has been painted. I would speak to you of one I met, Carfax of Staccia, an agent of the Sunderer's will who by Arahila's mercy became a Companion in truth at the end—"

"*No.*" Gritting her teeth and swallowing hard, Lilias pushed past him. "I don't want to hear it, Ellyl. I don't want your cursed pity. *Do you understand?*"

He took another step backward; avoiding her foul breath, no doubt. Once, even one of the Rivenlost would have stood awed in her presence. Now, there was nothing to her but bile and decay. This foulness, this mortality, it rotted her from the inside out. The stench of it bothered her own nostrils. "Forgive me, Sorceress," he breathed, still reaching out toward her with one pale, perfect hand. "I did not mean to offend, but only to offer comfort, for even the least of us are deserving. Arahila's mercy—"

"—is not something I seek," Lilias finished brusquely. "And what did Arahila the Fair know of *dragons?*"

It was something, to see one of the Ellylon at a loss for words. She took the image with her as she stumbled toward the cabin in which she had been allotted space. Haomane's Children, scions of the Lord-of-Thought. Oh, it gave them such pleasure to imagine themselves wiser than all other races, than all of the Lesser Shapers.

The air was hot and close inside the narrow cabin, but at least it blocked out the sunlight that refracted blindingly from the waves, making spots dance in her vision. Here it was mercifully dark. Lilias curled into a Dwarf-size bunk, wrapping herself around her sick, aching belly into a tight bundle of misery.

For a few blessed moments, she was left in solitude.

The door cracked open, slanting sunlight seeping red through her closed lids.

"Sorceress." It was a woman's voice, speaking the common tongue with an awkward Arduan inflection. The cool rim of an earthenware cup touched her lips, moistening them with water. "Blaise says you must drink."

"Get away." Without opening her eyes, Lilias slapped at the ministering hand; and found her own hand stopped, wrist caught in a strong, sinewy grip. She opened her eyes to meet the Archer's distasteful gaze. "Let *go!*"

"I would like to," the woman Fianna said with slow deliberation, "but I have sworn a vow of loyalty, and it is the will of the King of the West that you are to be kept alive. It is also the will of our Dwarfish hosts that no *Man* shall accompany one of our gender in closed quarters. So . . . drink."

She tilted the cup.

Water, cool and flat, trickled into Lilias' mouth. She wanted to refuse it, wanted to flail at the life-sustaining invasion. The Archer's hard gaze and the calloused grip on her wrist warned her against it. And so, with resentful gulps, she drank. The cool water eased the parched tissues of her mouth and throat, rumbling in her belly. Still, it stayed where it was put.

"Good." Fianna sat back on her heels. "Good."

"You should wish me dead," Lilias rasped. "Aracus is a fool."

"You know his reasons. As for me, I do." The Archer's voice was flat, and there was no burdensome compassion in her mien, only hatred and steady distrust. "Would you say elsewise of me?"

"No." Lilias drew herself up until her back touched the wall of the cabin. "Oh, no. I would not."

"Then we understand one another." She refilled the cup. "Drink."

Lilias took it, careful to avoid contact with the Archer's fingers. Those were the hands that had nocked the Arrow of Fire, those the fingers that had drawn back the string of Oronin's Bow. She did not want to feel their touch against her skin ever again. "Indeed, we do." She sipped at the water, studying Fianna's face. "Tell me, does Blaise Caveros know you are enamored of him?"

A slow flush of color rose to the Archer's cheeks; half-anger, half-humiliation. "You're not fit to speak his name!" she spat, rising swift to her feet.

Lilias shrugged and took another sip. "Shall I tell him?"

For a moment, she thought the other woman would strike her. Fianna stood, stooped in the tiny cabin, her hands clenching and unclenching at her sides. At length, the habit of discipline won out, and she merely shook her head. "I pity you," she said in a low voice. "I shouldn't, but I do. You've forgotten what it means to be a mortal woman." She regarded Lilias. "If, indeed, you ever even knew. And it's a pity because it's all that's left to you, and all that ever will be."

"Not quite." Lilias gave a bitter smile. "I have my memories."

"I wish you the joy of them!"

The door slammed on the Archer's retort. Lilias sighed, feeling her tense body uncoil. If nothing else, at least the confrontation had distracted her from her misery. It felt as though she might survive the sea journey after all. Aracus' will, was it? Well, let him have his way, then. It was nothing less than the Son of Altorus demanded. "I wish you the joy of it," Lilias whispered.

Finishing the water, she curled onto her side and slept.

When she awoke, it was black as pitch inside the cabin, and stifling hot. Somewhere, the sound of breathing came from another bunk, slow and measured. Was it the Archer? Like as not, since the Dwarfs maintained a prohibition on men and women sharing quarters.

The thought of it made her stomach lurch. Moving silently, Lilias clambered from the bunk and made her way to the door. It was unlatched and opened to her touch. She exited onto the deck, closing the door quietly behind her.

Outside, the sea breeze blew cool and fresh against her face, tasting of salt. She took a deep breath, filling her lungs. For a mercy, her stomach settled in the open air. It was almost pleasant, here beneath the vault of night. The stars seemed to shine more brightly than ever they did in the mountains, and the waxing moon laid a bright path on the dark waves. Here and there, lanterns were hung from the ship's rigging, lending a firefly glow. Dwarfish figures worked quietly by their light, tending to this and that, ignoring her presence.

It was bliss to have no keeper for the first time since Beshtanag. Lilias made her way to the prow of the ship, finding its swaying no longer discomforted her as it had earlier. To her chagrin, she found she was not alone; a tall figure stood in the prow, gazing outward over the water. His head turned at her approach, moonlight glinting on the gold fillet that encircled his brow.

She halted. "My lord Altorus. I did not mean to intrude."

"Lilias." He beckoned to with one hand. "Come here. Have you ever seen Meronin's Children?"

She shook her head. It was the first time he had addressed her thusly, and it felt strange to hear her name in his mouth. "No, my lord. Until this morning, I had never even seen the sea."

"Truly?" Aracus looked startled. "I would have thought . . . ah, 'tis of no mind. Come then, and see. Come, I'll not bite." He pointed as she came hesitantly to stand beside him. "See, there."

In the waters beyond the ship's prow, she saw them; a whole gathering, graceful forms arching through the waves in joyous leaps. Their sleek hides were silvery beneath the stars and there was a lambent wisdom in their large, dark eyes, at odds with the merry smiles that curved their slim jaws.

"Oh!" Lilias exclaimed as one blew a shining plume of spray. "Oh!"

"Wondrous, aren't they?" He leaned pensively on the railing. "It seems, betimes, a passing pleasant way to live. The world's strife does but pass across the surface of their world, leaving no trail. Though they will never be numbered among the Lesser Shapers, perhaps Meronin was wise to Shape his children thusly. Surely, they are happier for it."

" 'And Meronin the Deep kept his counsel,' " Lilias quoted.

Aracus glanced at her. "You know the lore."

"Does it surprise you so?" She gazed at the graceful figures of Meronin's Children, describing ebullient arcs amid the waves. "I have never seen the sea, but I have lived for a thousand years on my mountain, Aracus Altorus, and the counsel of dragons is as deep as Meronin's."

"Perhaps," he said. "But it is false."

Lilias eyed him. "Do you know, my lord, that dragons number Meronin's Children among the Lesser Shapers? They say their time is not come, nor will for many Ages. Still, they say, Meronin has planned well for it. Who benefited most when the world was Sundered?"

He frowned at her. "You know well it was the Sunderer himself."

"Was it?" She shrugged. "Haomane First-Born says so, but Lord Satoris has lived like a fugitive upon Urulat's soil with ten thousand enemies arrayed against him. Meanwhile, Meronin's waters have covered the Sundered World, and his Children multiply in peace." Lilias nodded at the leaping forms. "Meronin the Deep keeps his counsel and waits. It may be that one day he will challenge the Lord of Thought himself."

"You speak blasphemy!" Aracus said, appalled.

"No." She shook her head. "Truth, as I know it. Truth that is not found in scholars' books or Shapers' prophecy. Whatever I may be, I am Calandor's companion, not Haomane's subject. You spoke of lore. There is a great deal I know."

"And much you will not share." His voice turned blunt. "Why?"

Lilias shivered and wrapped her arms around herself. "You speak of the Soumanië? That is another matter, and my lord knows *why*."

His gaze probed hers. "You understand a woman's life is at stake?"

"Yes." She met his gaze without flinching. "Would you believe me if I told you Satoris will not kill her?"

He raised his brows. "Surely you cannot pretend to believe such a thing."

She sighed. "I can, actually. Once upon a time, Satoris Third-Born, too, was much given to listening to the counsel of dragons; aye, and speaking with them, too. For good or ill, I know something of his nature. Although it is twisted, there is nobility in it—and pride, too. A Shaper's pride. He will not slay her out of hand."

"No." Aracus debated, then shook his head. "No!" Beneath the dull, emberless stone of the Soumanië, his face was set. "Do you see *that*?" With one stabbing finger, he pointed unerring at the red star that rode high overhead in the night skies. "It is a declaration of war, Sorceress. I saw the innocent dead at Lindanen Dale. I witnessed my betrothed wrenched away in vile captivity, and followed into a trap that would have slain us all, save for Haomane's grace. If the Sunderer spoke to you of mercy, he has ensnared your thoughts in his lies."

"No," Lilias said gently. "*You* declared war upon Satoris, my lord Aracus, when you pledged yourself to wed the Lady of the Ellylon. The red star merely echoes that deed. I do not absolve him of his actions, any more than I ask absolution for mine. Only . . . what else did you expect him to do?"

"It is Haomane's Prophecy." His hands gripped the railing until his knuckles whitened, and he stared over the waters, watching Meronin's Children disport themselves with a mix of unconscious envy and fresh unease. "I did not *ask* for this destiny."

"I know." Lilias watched him. "But you accepted it nonetheless." Moonlight cast faint shadows in the lines worry and weariness had etched into his features. He was young, yes; but he was a Man, and mortal. How would it be to watch his beloved endure, unaging, while his flesh withered and rotted? She, who had replaced scores of pretty attendants in her own ageless time, had the strangest urge to smooth his furrowed brow.

"What choice had I?" He turned his wide gaze upon her, filled with that compelling combination of demand and *trust*. "Truly, what had I?"

All things must be as they are, little sssister. All thingsss.

"I don't know, my lord," Lilias whispered, tears blurring her vision. Lifting one hand, she touched his cheek, laying her palm against it and feeling the warmth of his skin, the slight rasp of red-gold stubble. On his brow, the Soumanië pulsed with a brief, yearning glow at her nearness. It made her heart ache. "Tell me, do you love her?"

"Yes." His fingers closed on her wrist. "I do."

There were a thousand things he could have said; how Cerelinde's beauty put the stars to shame, how her courage made him curse his inadequacy. How he understood the sacrifice she had made for the Rivenlost, and how terrible the cost would be. Aracus Altorus said none of them, and yet all were present in his simple, blunt words, in his wide-set, demanding gaze. He was a warrior; oh, yes.

One who loved the Lady of the Ellylon.

"Well, then." Lilias opened her hand, letting him steer it away, deflecting her touch harmlessly. "You had no choice, did you?"

He stared at her. "You trouble me, Sorceress."

"Good." She smiled through her tears. "You *should* be troubled, my lord Altorus." Wrenching her hand free, she took a stumbling step away from him. "Thank you for sharing your vision of Meronin's Children with me. Whether or not it was true, it was a pleasant dream."

The disinterested Dwarfs watched her progress, and Aracus' stare followed her back to her cabin, until she closed the door onto stifling darkness and the Archer snoring in the second bunk.

Lilias closed the door, and wept.

TWO

FOR DAYS, THEIR PATH HAD taken them westward on an arid course
through the Northern Harrow, following an underground branch of
the Spume River.

Thulu led the way, probing with his digging-stick and listening,
listening to the lifeblood coursing through Uru-Alat's veins, deep below
the surface. Dani did not question his uncle's guidance. All children of
the Yarru-yami were taught to follow the deep veins of Uru-Alat, but the
skill was honed by age and practice, and this was a task for which the
Yarru elders had trained his uncle for many years.

Although it was a hardship, at least it was one to which the Yarru
were suited. Dani and his uncle sipped sparingly from their waterskins, their bodies accustomed to eking the most from every precious
drop. When ordinary folk would have faltered, the Yarru pressed onward with only a touch of discomfort.

They kept to low ground, to dry gorges and valleys. Away from the
leaping rivers there was scant sign of any other living thing, save the
tall spruce that dotted the mountainsides. It was a mercy, for it meant
they saw no sign of Fjeltroll. Here and there, Uncle Thulu found a tiny
spring, like an unexpected gift of Neheris, a sparkling trickle of water
darkening a narrow cleft amid the rocks.

Where there were springs, there was small game; hare and ptarmigan. Using Yarru-style slings Thulu had made with strips of hide, both
of them took turns shooting for the pot. It was harder to get a clean
shot than it was in the open desert, but to his pleasure, Dani found his
keen eye held him in good stead as a marksman.

After clambering amid the mountain peaks, it was almost easy going. Their feet, already hardened by the desert, grew accustomed to the harsh terrain. The nights were cool, but nowhere near as chill as they had been in the heights. After some debate, they gauged it safe to build a brisk fire, which dispelled the worst of the cold; for the rest, they shared their wool cloaks and huddled together, doubling their warmth.

On the morning of the seventh day, they heard a distant roar. Uncle Thulu, leaning on his freshly sharpened digging-stick, turned to Dani with a grin. "That's it, lad. That's our river!"

The trail wound through a torturous series of switchbacks, and it was an afternoon's hard tramping before they reached the source, standing upon a promontory of rock and beholding what lay below.

When they did, Dani gazed at it with awe.

The Spume River burst out of the side of a mountain, plunging in a mighty cascade to the churning riverbed below. At close range, the sound of it was deafening. It was like a living thing, foam-crested and green-thewed, boiling around the boulders that dared disrupt its course. On the edge of the near bank, the barren limbs of a half-fallen spruce tree struggled desperately against the current.

"We're going to follow *that*?" Dani asked, agape.

"Aye, lad!" Uncle Thulu widened his nostrils and inhaled deeply. He shouted his reply. "Can't you smell the taint of it? One way or another, it will lead us to Darkhaven!"

Opening his mouth to respond, Dani gazed past his uncle and paused. Forty yards downriver, hunkered on a ledge, a squat figure was watching them.

At a passing glance, it looked like a boulder, perched and stolid, the color of dull granite; then it flung out one massive arm to point at them, its barrel chest swelled and swelled, increasing vastly in girth, and its mouth gaped to reveal a cavernous gullet.

The roar of a Tordenstem Fjel split the gorge.

Dani's blood ran cold.

It was a wordless roar, and it echoed between the walls of the gorge, drowning out the sound of the river, impossible though it seemed. Dani clapped both hands over his aching ears, his insides reverberating like a struck gong. His teeth, the very marrow of his bones, vibrated at the cacophonous howl.

"Fjeltroll!" he shouted unnecessarily.

Again the roar sounded, making his innards quiver. And, oh, worse, even worse! On the ridge above it, other heads popped up, silhouetted against the sky; inhuman heads, misshapen and hideous. There were at least a score of them. The sentry repeated its deafening howl and the Fjeltroll began to descend with horrible speed, jamming talons into narrow fissures and swarming down the cliffs.

"Dani!" He could see Uncle Thulu's mouth shaping his name as he pointed toward the banks of the churning river. "This way!" Without waiting, Thulu plunged downward, slithering through a gap in the rocks.

"Don't leave me!" Fighting panic, Dani scrambled after his uncle. It was hard to hold a thought while his insides churned, and he could scarce feel his fingertips. The paralyzing roar sounded again. Glancing behind him, Dani saw the Fjel drawing closer. They wore nothing over their coarse hide, and their leathery lips were drawn back to reveal long tusks. Small yellow eyes glinted with ruthless cunning under their bulging brows. "Uru-Alat," he whispered, freezing.

"Come on!" Uncle Thulu shouted. At the bottom of the gorge, he had made his way to the fallen spruce and was wrenching at its uppermost branches, breaking them loose. "Dani, come on!"

Half-sliding, half-falling, the Water of Life banging against his chest in its clay flask, Dani made the descent. The plunging Spume boiled like a cauldron, then snarled and raged in its narrow bed, spitting geysers in his path. He stumbled across rocks slick with spray to his uncle's side.

"Hold these." Sparing a quick glance up the gorge, Thulu thrust a load of spruce branches into his arms. "No, like so. Good lad."

"Are they . . . ?" Dani clenched his jaw to still his chattering teeth.

"Aye. Fast." As calm as though he were braiding thukka-vine in the desert, Thulu wove a length of rabbit-hide rope amid the branches, deftly knotting and tightening. "We have to try the river, Dani. It's our only chance." He met Dani's gaze. "Whatever happens, hold tight to the branches. They'll keep you afloat."

Dani nodded, understanding.

"Good lad." With a single, quick motion, Thulu stooped and grabbed his digging-stick, shouldering past Dani. "Now go!"

The Fjeltroll were on them.

The path was narrow, and even the sure-footed Fjel could only attack two at a time. Uncle Thulu fought like a tiger at bay, wielding his stick in a blur. The unarmed Fjel hissed in fury, swiping with their terrible talons, unable to get within reach. The largest among them barked a guttural order, and two pair split away, clambering up the gorge in order to flank the older Yarru on his left. Dani, clutching his makeshift float, stared in horror. The one who had given the order grinned, a malicious intelligence in his yellow eyes.

"What are you waiting for?" Thulu shouted over his shoulder. "Go, Dani! *Go!*"

"No." Deep within him, an unexpected wave of fury surged. Dani dropped the spruce bundle and reached for his sling. "Not without you!"

Busy fighting for his life, Uncle Thulu grunted.

It was a clean rage, clearing Dani's head and making the blood sing in his ears. Somehow, although fear was still present, it seemed distant and unimportant. He reached into his pouch and withdrew a smooth stone, fitting it into the sling. He spun it, taking careful aim at the nearest Fjeltroll approaching on the left. Uru-Alat, but they were hideous! With a grimace, the Fjel pointed at the flask on his chest with one grimy talon, saying something in its harsh tongue. Dani let fly with the sling.

His aim was true. Clasping one hand over its right eye, the Fjeltroll roared and staggered. Grabbing a handful of stones, Dani flung a barrage in quick succession, driving the Fjel several paces backward. The others regrouped, watching. "Leave us *alone!*" he shouted at them.

It was a brief respite. Lowering their heads, the uninjured Fjel renewed their approach, grimacing as Dani's sling-flung rocks bounced from their tough hides, from the dense ridge of bone on their brows. In a few seconds, they would reach him.

On his right, he heard rather than saw it; Thulu's sharp exclamation of pain, then a grunt of effort and a heavy thud. A Fjel voice roared in agony. An arm clamped hard about Dani's waist, wrenching him off-balance. *"Now,* lad!"

And then he was falling.

The river smacked him like a mighty fist. It *was* like a living thing; a malevolent one that sought his life at every avenue, seeking to extinguish the spark of vital fire that made his heart beat and his lungs draw breath. Water filled his eyes and ears and nose and mouth, more water then he had known in a lifetime. Dani flailed and the river rolled him over like a piece of debris, driving him into its depths.

If not for his uncle, he would surely have drowned. It was Thulu's strong arm around his waist that hauled him up until his head broke water and he gasped for air. With his other arm, Uncle Thulu held tight to the spruce-branch float, his fingers wedged under the hide ropes. "Hold on!" he shouted above the river's din. "Hold on to the branches!"

Dani did.

It was barely large enough to let them keep their heads above water. The river spun them and Dani saw the Fjel on the banks, arguing amongst themselves. One lay fallen and motionless, Uncle Thulu's digging-stick jutting from its torso. On the ledge above the gorge, the lone sentry howled in fury, receding quickly from view.

The biggest Fjel, the one who had given the orders, gave pursuit.

"Uru-Alat!" Clinging to the float, Dani watched the Fjel race along the narrow path, using all four limbs, scrambling and hurdling. His heart sank. Its mouth was open and panting hard, but it was outpacing the very current. "Can they swim?"

"I don't know." His uncle grimaced. Glancing at him, Dani saw trails of blood winding through the foam that churned around his submerged chest.

"You're injured!"

"A scratch." Thulu pointed with his chin toward a bend in the river. "Here he comes. Kick with your legs, Dani! I don't think he *can* swim. If we can swing wide left, maybe the current will carry us past him."

There where the bend created a shallow apron of shoreline and the current slowed a fraction, the Fjel was fording the river, wading with dogged persistence to intercept their course. Water parted to surge around the mighty thews of its thighs, around its waist. The force of it would have swept anything else off its feet.

Not the Fjel.

Step by step, it continued its steady advance.

Dani kicked frantically, felt the float's course shift. His uncle grunted, beating at the river with one arm. The trails of red in the foam surrounding him spread and widened. Almost . . .

Neck-deep in the river, the Fjel raised one dripping arm and reached out with a taloned hand to catch a branch of their float, halting its progress. It had to tilt its chin to keep its mouth clear of the river's surface. It was close enough that Dani was staring into its slitted yellow eyes, mere inches away.

It said something in the Fjel tongue.

"Go *away*!" Dani kicked at it.

The Fjel grinned and said something else, reaching with its other hand for the clay flask that hung about his neck. Water surged all around them on every side. Its taloned hand closed around the flask . . .

. . . and dropped, sinking below the surface of the river as though it held a boulder in its grasp. The Fjel sank, its head vanishing beneath the river. Its grip was torn loose from the float, and the current restaked its claim. Dani choked, feeling the thong tighten around his neck and burn his skin; then that, too, eased as the Fjel let go.

The float rotated lazily as it cleared the bend, its passengers clinging for dear life. Behind them, a column of bubbles broke the surface. The big Fjel rose, dripping, and staring after them.

Too late.

They had rounded the bend.

Struggling to stay afloat, Dani watched it until it was out of sight and wondered what the Fjel had said. And then the river's course took a steep drop and it turned once more to a white-water torrent, and he obeyed his uncle's desperate, shouted orders and clung to the float and thought of water and how to stay alive in it and nothing else, until the raging current flung them hard against a boulder.

Something broke with an inaudible snap, and Dani felt an acute pain in his shoulder and a dull one in his head. As the world went slowly black in his vision, he worked one hand free to fumble at the clay vial around his throat. It was intact.

It was his last conscious thought.

THE ROAR OF THE TORDENSTEM Fjel echoed through Defile's Maw, scattering the ravens into a circling black cloud, setting the shrouded webs of Weavers' Gulch to trembling, welcoming them back to Darkhaven.

Speros glanced at the figures crouching on the heights, remembering all too well his ungentle reception at their hands. He ran his tongue over his teeth, probing the gap where a front one was missing.

"Last chance, Midlander." General Tanaros drew rein beside him, an unfathomable expression in his dark eyes. "I mean it. Turn around now, and ride away without looking back. You can keep the horse."

Speros shook his head. "No."

"You know what's coming?"

"Aye, Lord General." He kept his gaze steady. "War."

Tanaros sighed. "If you had an ounce of sense, you'd take my advice and go."

"Where, sir?" Speros shook his head again. "There's no place for me out there. Should I join Haomane's Allies and ride against you? I would sooner cut off my right arm." Alarm squeezed his chest. "Do you seek to be rid of me? Is it because of what happened with the Yarru? I promised, I'll not fail you again. And I *did* help, after all; you'd not have gotten the Well sealed without my aid."

"Aye." The General's strong hand rested on his shoulder. "You're a good lad, Speros. I do you no kindness in accepting your loyalty."

"Did I *ask* for kindness?" Anger mixed with the alarm. "Sir?"

"No." The General lifted his gaze, watching the ravens circle overhead. An errant lock of hair fell over his brow. Behind his austere features was a shadow of sorrow. "Perhaps it is a piece of wisdom that you do not."

Something in Speros' heart ached. The General feared for him. His family had reckoned him shiftless, an idler whose goals would never amount to aught. They had never showed as much concern for his well-being as the General did. They cared nothing for the ideas that fired his imagination. He had met their expectations accordingly and paid the price for it.

General Tanaros was different. He had believed in Speros, taken a chance on him. He knew, in a wordless way, that he would do anything to see General Tanaros smile, to see his expression lighten with approval.

Even if it led to defeat, it would be worthwhile.

"I'm staying." Setting his heels to his mount's flanks, he shook off Tanaros' hand and jogged ahead before the Lord General could say aught else to dissuade him. One of the trotting Gulnagel grinned at him, and Speros grinned back, his sense of alarm fading. These were his comrades, his companions. One had given his life for him. They had given him the honor and respect his own family had denied him. They had labored side by side together, laying the dead to rest. How could he think of leaving?

He would find a way to prove himself to General Tanaros.

Ahead of him, Ushahin Dreamspinner rode astride, swaying as his blood-bay mount picked its way along the path of the Defile. Hearing Speros approach, he glanced languidly over his shoulder. "Weavers' Gulch, Midlander." He waved a crabbed hand at the sticky strands crossing the vast loom of the Defile, the scuttling weavers that spun the warp and weft of it. "Does it evoke fond memories for you?"

"Not especially, Lord Dreamspinner." Speros eyed the hanging veils of webbing and swallowed hard. He touched his bare neck, remembering the sharp sting of a spider's bite and awakening trussed and bound. "Not especially."

Ushahin gave his lopsided smile. "The ones who come to *me* pass through untouched. Such is the protection I afford them in the purity of their madness. Still, I think you must be a little bit mad to attempt it at all."

Speros shivered and fell back, following in the half-breed's wake, though it was no longer necessary now that they traveled by ordinary day, and not on the path between dreaming and waking that had carried them through the Midlands and across the plains of Curonan. "Perhaps," he said.

"Oh, I think it is more than *perhaps*." Amid the ghostly veils of webbing, Ushahin smiled once more. "Tanaros Blacksword might disagree, but he's a little bit mad, too, isn't he? We will see, in time."

They made steady progress through the Defile. The Gulnagel breathed deeply through widened nostrils, inhaling the odor of the ichor-tainted waters, the welcome scent of home. Beyond the Weavers' Gulch, the Defile Gate and its flanking towers loomed amid the vast, encircling wall. Alerted by the Tordenstem, teams of Fjel were already at work opening the gate. Overhead, the ravens circled in grim triumph. The walls were crowded with Fjel, armed to the teeth, waving axes and maces in the air, shields held high. They were shouting.

"Tan-a-ros! Tan-a-ros!"

"Go on, cousin." Ushahin nodded. *"You're* the one they've been awaiting."

Giving him a deep look, General Tanaros nudged his mount forward. He lifted one hand as he rode between the gates, acknowledging the cries. He looked weary, Speros thought. And why not? He had done a hero's work, carrying out his Lordship's bitter orders, keeping them alive in the desert. He had earned a rest.

"You love him, don't you?" Ushahin asked in a low voice.

"No," Speros said automatically, then thought of the General's shoulder beneath his arm, urging him to keep going, step by torturous step. The General's hands, cradling his head, placing the drought-fruit to his lips. The General, stooping under the starlight, scooping sand in a battered helmet, helping dig a grave for poor Freg. "Aye!" he said then, defiant. "I have a care for him. Why shouldn't I, after all? My own Da never did half as much for me as the Lord General's done."

"Ah, well, then." The Dreamspinner's mismatched eyes glittered. "There's a little piece of madness for you."

Speros flung his head back. "What would *you* know of it, my lord?"

"Love?" the half-breed mused. He shook his head, fair hair shimmering. "Not much, Speros of Haimhault. What love I had, I have betrayed. The Grey Dam Vashuka will attest to that. But heed my advice, and make a good job of it." He nodded at Tanaros. "There's a hunger in him for the son he never had. And there's a hunger in him for the woman whose love he lost. One, it would seem, is greater than the other. But who knows? If it comes to a choice, you may find yourself an unexpected fulcrum."

With that, Ushahin took his leave, passing through the Defile Gate. Speros stared after him while the Gulnagel who had accompanied them passed him by on either side. With a start, he touched his heels to his mount's flanks. It stepped forward, the color of smoke, obedient to his will.

The Gate closed behind them.

He was home.

IT FELT STRANGE TO BE alone in his quarters. They had been tended, and recently; that much was clear. His dining table gleamed with hand-rubbed beeswax, the floors had been swept clean and the carpets beaten. The lamps were lit and a fire was laid. Hot water steamed in the tub in his bathing-chamber, but not a madling was in sight.

Tanaros hadn't been truly alone since he had birthed himself from the Marasoumië and climbed up the well-shaft of the Water of Life. The silence, the absence of another's heartbeat, was deafening. He found himself wishing Fetch had stayed with him, but the raven had rejoined his own kin.

Piece by piece, he removed his dirty, dented armor. The straps were stiff with grime. He placed each piece carefully on the stand, then unbuckled his sword belt and propped the sword in the corner. There was no scratch at the door, no madling coming to beg to touch the black blade tempered in his Lordship's blood. Tanaros frowned and sat on the low stool to pry off his boots.

It wasn't easy to get them off and it wasn't pleasant once he did. For a time, he simply sat on the stool. All the weariness of the long, long journey he had endured settled into his bones. There was no part of him that did not ache; save for his branded heart, which no longer tugged like a yearning compass toward the fortress of Darkhaven. He was home, and he was grateful beyond telling that his Lordship had given them a night's respite before requiring their report.

"Truly, my Lord is merciful." He spoke the words aloud, half-listening for a murmured chorus of agreement.

No one answered.

With an effort, Tanaros levered himself upright and padded to the bathing-chamber, where he peeled off clothing so filthy it defied description. From one pocket, he withdrew the *rhios* Hyrgolf had given him, setting it gently upon a shelf. Everything else he left in a stinking pile on the tiled floor.

Beneath the clothing, his naked body was gaunt. The Chain of Being only stretched so far; privation had taken its toll. His ribs made ridges along the sides of his torso. Skin that had not seen daylight for weeks on end was shockingly pale, grey as a ghost. Tanaros sank into the tub, watching the water turn cloudy.

A long, long time ago, when he would return from a hard day's labor of training Roscus Altorus' troops, Calista had drawn his bath with her own hands. At least, she had always made a show of pouring the last bucket of steaming water, smiling at him under her lashes. *See what I do for you, my love?* And then she would draw a stool alongside the tub so she might sit beside him and scrub his back and add a few drops of scented oil to the water. It had smelled like . . . like vulnus-blossom, only sweet and harmless.

The memory made his eyes sting. Tanaros ducked his head underwater and came up dripping. He grabbed a scouring cloth and a ball of soap and set to work mercilessly on his grimy skin. The water in which he sat grew murkier. Grey skin turned grub-white, in marked contrast to his strong, sun-scorched hands. He had wrapped those hands around her throat.

Slayer. The Yarru Elder Ngurra's voice stirred in his memory, prompted by the odor of vulnus-blossom. Dark eyes in a creased face, filled with wisdom and sorrow, beneath the hanging shadow of a black sword. Old men, old women, hanging back and clinging to one another's hands. *You do not have to choose this.*

Tanaros scoured harder.

He wished he were Vorax. It would be simpler, thus. He would have come home to a bevy of Staccian maidens and reveled in it. Simple pleasures. The Staccian asked nothing more and never had. Only to enjoy them in abundance, forever. It was a good way to live. Even Ushahin had his madlings . . . oh, yes, of course.

That was where *they* were. Rejoicing in the return of their own particular master, in the camaraderie of souls twisted out of true. Settling back into the warm water, Tanaros closed his eyes. Since he was alone, he might as well indulge in his memories.

The bath-oil had smelled like vulnus-blossom . . .

He tried to summon it; the rage, the old, old anger. Calista's gaze meeting his as she lay in her birthing-bed, eyes stretched wide with guilty fear as she held the babe with red-gold hair close to her breast. Roscus, looking surprised, the hand he had extended so often in false brotherhood clutching uncomprehending at the length of steel that had pierced his belly. Remembering the scent of vulnus-blossom, Tanaros tried to summon the bitter satisfaction that moment had engendered.

It wouldn't come.

Too far away, and he was tired, too tired for rage. There was too much to be done, here and now. Calista had been dead for a long, long time; aye, and Roscus, too. Somewhere, somehow, the fearsome womb of the Marasoumië, the blazing sands and merciless sun of the Unknown Desert, had rendered their ghosts into pallid shadows. It was the living who commanded his attention. One, more than others.

Since the comfort of anger was denied him, he sought to turn his mind to matters at hand, to the report he must make on the morrow to

Lord Satoris and the preparations for battle to come; but the odor of vulnus-blossom wove a distracting thread through his thoughts. He shied away from the memory of Ngurra's uplifted face and the old Yarru's words. Why was there such pain in the memory, enough to displace the murder of his wife? His thoughts fled to the moon-garden and he saw *her* face, luminous and terrible with beauty. The Lady of the Ellylon.

What did you see? he had asked her.

You. I saw you . . .

"No." Shaking his head, scattering droplets of water, Tanaros arose. He stepped dripping from the tub and toweled himself dry, donning a dressing-robe. Despite the fire laid in his hearth, he shivered. She was here in Darkhaven, separated from him only by a few thick walls, burning like a pale flame. Alone and waiting. Had she heard word of his return? Did she care if he lived or died? Or did she think only of Aracus Altorus? Gritting his teeth, he willed himself not to think of it. "Ah, no."

There was a crisp knock at the door to his chambers.

He padded barefoot to answer it, feeling the luxury of Rukhari carpets beneath his feet. Meara was there when he opened the doors, eyes downcast. Another madling accompanied her, carrying a tray. Savory odors seeped from beneath the covering domes.

"Meara!" His mood lightened. "'Tis good to see you. Come in." He opened the doors wider, inhaling deeply. His stomach rumbled in sympathy, hunger awakening in his starved tissues. It had been a long time since he had allowed himself a proper meal. "What have you brought? It smells delicious."

"Squab, my lord." Her tone was short. "And other things." She watched the second madling lay the table with care. "Forgive us, Lord General, that we cannot stay. Others will return in time to tend to everything."

Tanaros frowned. "Does the Dreamspinner demand your presence, Meara? Or is it that I have offended you in some way?"

She lifted her gaze to his. "Does my lord even remember?"

He did, then; her weight, straddling him. The smell of her; of womanflesh, warm and earthy. Her teeth nipping at his lip, her tongue probing. His hand, striking her face, hard enough to draw blood. Tanaros flushed to the roots of his hair.

He had forgotten.

"Aye." Meara nodded. "That."

"Please." He made a deep courtier's bow, according her the full measure of dignity any woman deserved. "Allow me to apologize again, Meara. Forgive me, for I never meant to strike you."

"Oh, and it's *that* you think demands apology the most, my lord?" She put one hand on her hip. "Never mind. I forgave you *that* from the beginning."

"What, then?" Tanaros asked gravely. "Tell me, and I will make amends."

"No." Gnawing her lip, she shook her head. "I don't think so, my lord. Not if you have to ask. Some things cannot be mended. I know, I am one of them." Meara shivered and gripped her elbows, then gave a harsh laugh. "Ask the Lady, if you want to know. She's heard word of your return. She is waiting, although she does not say it."

"Is she?" He kept his voice polite.

"Oh, yes." She eyed him. "She does not fear you as she does the others. I think she has seen some kindness in you that she believes might be redeemed. Be wary, my lord. There is danger in it."

Tanaros shrugged. "She is a hostage, Meara. She can do no harm."

The bitten lips curved in a mirthless smile. "Go to her, then. One day, you will remember I warned you. I did from the first. It was a mistake to bring her here." She beckoned to her companion and turned to depart.

"Meara," Tanaros called after her.

"I have to go, my lord." She walked away without looking back. "Use the bellpull if you have need of aught else."

He stared after her a moment, then closed the doors. The aroma of his supper called him to the table. Despite the accumulated hunger of weeks of privation, he delayed for a moment, savoring her words.

Cerelinde was waiting for him.

USHAHIN DREAMSPINNER SAT CROSS-LEGGED ON a high chopping block.

All around him, his madlings pressed and swarmed, jostling for position, reaching out to touch his knee or his foot in reassurance. He sat and waited for all of them to assemble—not just the cooks and servants, but the launderers, the maids, the stable lads. All of the folk who tended to his Lordship's glorious fortress.

His people.

Darkhaven's kitchens were roasting hot and greasy, redolent of cooking odors. For the madlings, it was a safe haven, one of the few places in the fortress in which they enjoyed the comfort of domestic familiarity. Here, they established their own society, their own hierarchy. Cooks possessed by mad culinary genius worked cheek by jowl with half-witted assistants and found common ground. All took pride in their labor, knowing that Darkhaven could not function without them; and the kitchens represented the pinnacle of that pride.

Ushahin did not mind being there. The atmosphere soothed his aching joints, reminding him of the moist, fecund air at the heart of the Delta. The belching ovens might have been Calanthrag's nostrils. The thought gave him pleasure, though he hid it from his madlings.

Their mood, at once ebullient and penitent, disturbed him. It came as no surprise, in light of what Vorax had told him. Sifting through the endless tangle of their waking thoughts, Ushahin saw a single image repeated: Cerelinde, the Lady of the Ellylon.

He kept a stern visage until all were assembled. When Meara and the lad who accompanied her returned from their errand, he raised one hand for silence. With whispers and broken murmurs, a sea of madlings obeyed. Their twitching faces were raised to listen, gleaming gazes fixed upon him.

"My children," Ushahin addressed them. "I have labored long and hard, through countless dangers, to return to you. And now I find Lord Vorax is wroth. How do you account for yourselves in my absence?"

A hundred faces crumpled, a hundred mouths opened to shape a keening wail of guilt. It surged through the kitchens, echoing from the grease-blackened rafters and the bright copper pots and kettles, scoured to an obsessive shine. Some went to their knees, hands outstretched in a plea for forgiveness.

"So." Ushahin nodded. "You know of what I speak. Did you bring her *here*?"

A wail of protest rose in answer. Heads shook in vehement denial, matted hair flying. No, no. They had not brought her here.

"Where?" he asked.

The wailing trickled into shuffling silence. Ushahin waited.

"A place." One of them offered it in a mutter, eyes downcast. "A place behind the walls, lord, that we made bigger."

Another looked up, pleading. "You said those were *our* places, lord!"

"The spaces in between." Ushahin nodded again. "I did. Those are the places we occupy, my children; those of us whom the world has failed to claim. No one knows it better than I. And I entrusted those places to you, with Lord Satoris' blessing. Why, then, did you bring the Ellyl woman there?"

The hundredfold answer was there in the forefront of their thoughts, in their hungry, staring eyes. None of them gave voice to it. It didn't matter; he knew. Lives of happy normalcy, wives and husbands, sons and daughters. An honest livelihood filled with the myriad mundane joys of living. *What-might-have-been.*

Oh, yes, Ushahin Dreamspinner knew.

" 'Tis a bittersweet joy," he said softly, "is it not? What might have been. I, too, have wondered, my children. What might *I* have been, had my Ellyl kin claimed me?" He lifted his gnarled hands, gazing at them, then at his madlings. "A bridge, perhaps, with limbs straight and true, built to span the divide between Haomane's Children and Arahila's. Instead"—he shook his head—"I am the abyss. And when they seek to gaze into the spaces in between and stake a claim there, they will find *me* gazing back at them. I am the dark mirror that reflects their most fearful desires. I am the dark underbelly of Haomane's Prophecy."

The madlings were silent, rapt.

"Never forget." Ushahin's voice hardened. "It was the *Ellylon* who rejected me, who wanted no part of a child of mixed blood, gotten in violence and tainted—*tainted*, they say—by Lord Satoris' Gift. I am the very future they court in fear and loathing. I am the shadow that precedes the children of the Prophecy they seek to fulfill. And who can say that they will not despise their own offspring? For they, too, will carry the taint of Lord Satoris' Gift with them."

Someone hissed.

Ushahin smiled. "Oh, yes," he said. "For they despise his Lordship above all else; always and forever. They may grieve at your pain, and they may offer pleasant visions, but they are Haomane's Children, and they will not lift one finger"—he raised one crooked finger—"to aid you unless Haomane profits by it."

The kitchen erupted in indignant rage. Ushahin rode their anger like a wave, letting them seethe and rant until they subsided, turning toward him with expectant eyes, waiting to hear what he would say next. His madlings knew him. They understood him. He had been broken and had risen triumphant nonetheless; he bore the badges of his breaking—his uneven face, his twisted limbs—in painful solidarity with their aborted lives and shattered minds. It was for this that they loved him.

A vast tenderness infused his heart, and he wondered if Shapers felt thusly toward their Children. It seemed it might be so.

"It is well that you remember this," he told them, "for war comes upon us. And we may put faces to those enemies we know, but 'tis harder to put faces to the enemies among us. Who among you would betray Lord Satoris?"

No one, no one, arose the cries; at once both true and not-true. Somewhere, the seeds of betrayal had already taken root. Listening to the madlings' protestations, Ushahin thought of Calanthrag the Eldest and the things of which she had spoken. A shadow of sorrow overlay the tenderness in his heart. The pattern was fixed and inevitable. He could only serve his Lordship as best he might and pray that these spreading roots would not bear fruit for many generations to come. The Eldest herself had borne the same hope. He remembered her words, uttered in her knowing, sibilant hiss: *Yet may it come later than sssooner for ssuch as I and you.*

"Well done, my children," Ushahin said to his madlings. "Keep faith, and hope. Remember that it is his Lordship's mercy that protects us here." He held up his hand to quiet them and made his voice stern once more. "Now, who will speak to me of the hole that pierces the bowels of Darkhaven? How is it that a gap has opened onto the marrow-fire itself?"

This time, the silence was different.

"We didn't do it, my lord!" It was one of the stable lads who spoke, near the exits. He ducked his head with a furtive blush. "It was just *there.*"

Madlings glanced at one another, catching each other's eyes. The question was asked and answered. There were nods and murmurs all around. Each time, it was the same. They had had naught to do with it.

A cold finger of fear brushed the length of Ushahin's crooked spine. He thought of how Darkhaven had been built, of how Lord

Satoris had used the power of Godslayer to raise the mountains that surrounded the Vale of Gorgantum and laid the foundation of Dark-haven itself. What did it mean if the foundation was crumbling? What did it mean if Lord Satoris himself had allowed it to happen—or worse, was unaware?

For all things mussst be as they musst.

"No." He caught himself shaking his head, saying the word aloud. With an effort, Ushahin willed himself to stillness, breathing slowly. The madlings watched him with trepidation. "No, never mind, it's all right." He forced a lopsided smile. "You did no wrong, then. It is nothing that cannot be mended. All is well."

A collective sigh of relief ran through his madlings. With a final nod, Ushahin gave them license, permitted them to shuffle forward, a sea of humanity surging against the small island promontory of his chopping-block dais. He gave them his broken hands to clutch and stroke, offering no false promises nor comfort, only the sheltering shield of his stubborn, enduring pain.

"Oh, lord!" It was a young woman who spoke, eyes bright with emotion. She kissed his fingertips and pressed his hand to her cheek. "I tried, my lord, I did. Forgive me my weakness!"

"Ah, Meara." Bending forward, Ushahin caressed her cheek. He touched the surface of her thoughts and saw the shadow of Tanaros' face therein. He grasped a little of what it betokened and pitied her for it. What was love but a little piece of madness? "All is well. I forgive you."

She caught her breath in a gasping laugh. "You shouldn't. I brought her there. We are weak. *I* am weak." She cradled his hand, gazing up at him. "You should kill her, you know. It would be for the best."

"Yes." Ushahin grew still, hearing his own thoughts echoed. "I know." For a moment, they remained thusly. Then his heart gave a twinge beneath the branded skin that circumscribed it, and he shook his head ruefully and withdrew his hand. "I cannot, little sister. I am sworn to his Lordship, and he would see her live. I cannot gainsay his will. Would you have it otherwise?"

"No." Unshed tears pooled like diamonds in her eyes.

"Remember what you are," he said gently to her, "and do not dwell on what-might-have-been. Remember that *I* love you for that-which-is."

"I will!" Her head bobbed, overbrimming tears forging swathes down her sallow cheeks. Meara sniffled and scrubbed at her tears. "I will try, lord."

"Good." Ushahin gazed past her at the faces of the madlings still awaiting his regard. "Well done, my child." So many of them! How had their numbers come to swell so large? Their pain made his heart ache. He understood them, understood their weaknesses. What-might-have-been. A rock, clutched in a boy's hand, descending. What if it had never fallen? A trader's shadow, darkening the alley before withdrawing; his father, a tall shadow, turning away with averted face. What if someone—anyone—had intervened? It was a dream, a sweet dream, a bittersweet dream.

He understood.

And as for the other thing . . .

Ushahin shuddered, thinking of the foundations of Darkhaven giving way beneath him. The passages were too narrow to allow the Fjel masons access, and any patchwork Vorax's Staccians had done was merely a stopgap. If the foundation crumbled, it was symptomatic of things to come. Only his Lordship could root out this decay—if he retained the will and the power and the sanity to do so. Ushahin would speak to him. He prayed his Lordship would hear his words and act upon them, for if he did not . . .

"May it come later than sooner," he whispered, opening his arms to his throng. "Oh, please, may it!"

THREE

ON THEIR SECOND DAY ON land, Haomane's Allies compared notes as they rode along the coastal road that lay between Harrington Bay, where the dwarf-ship *Yrinna's Bounty* had deposited them, and Meronil, the Rivenlost stronghold whence they were bound.

All of them had been plagued by strange visions in the night.

The Borderguardsmen spoke of it in murmurs, clustering together in their dun cloaks, bending their heads toward one another. Even the Ellylon spoke of it, when the tattered remnants of Malthus' Company found themselves riding together on the broad road.

"'Twas as if I dreamed," Peldras mused, "or so it seems, from what Men have told me; for we do not lose ourselves in sleep as Arahila's Children do. And yet it seemed that I did wander therein, for I found myself watching a tale not of my own devising unfold. And a great wind blew toward me, hot and dry as the desert's breath, and I beheld him emerge from it—the same, and not the same, for the Wise Counselor was somehow *changed*."

"Yes!" Fianna breathed, her face aglow. "That's what *I* saw!"

"'Twere as well if he were," Lorenlasse of the Valmaré said shortly, coming abreast of her. "For all his vaunted wisdom, Haomane's Counselor has led us into naught but folly, and we are no closer to restoring the Lady Cerelinde."

Nudging his mount, he led the Rivenlost past them. Sunlight glittered on their armor and their shining standards. Peldras did not join his fellows, but gazed after them with a troubled mien. At the head of the long column of Allies, Aracus Altorus rode alone and spoke to no one. His dun cloak hung down his back in unassuming folds, but his bright hair and the gold circlet upon it marked him as their uncontested leader.

"What did *you* see?" Blaise Caveros asked Lilias abruptly.

Bowing her head, she studied her hands on the reins—chapped for lack of salve, her knuckles red and swollen. She preferred to listen, and not to remember. It had been an unpleasant dream. "What do my dreams matter?" she murmured. "What did *you* see, Borderguardsman?"

"I saw Malthus," he said readily. "I saw what others saw. And you?"

Lifting her head, she met his dark, inquisitive gaze. What *had* she seen, dreaming beside the fire in their campsite? It had been a restless sleep, broken by the mutters and groans of Men rolled in their bedrolls, of Ellylon in their no-longer dreamless state.

A Man, or something like one; venerable with age. And yet . . . there had been something terrible in his eyes. Lightning had gathered in folds of his white robes beneath his outspread arms, in the creases of his beard. There was a gem on his breast as clear as water, and he had ridden into her dreams on the wings of a desert sirocco, on a horse as pale as death.

And he had raised one gnarled forefinger like a spear, his eyes as terrible as death, and pointed it at *her*.

"Nothing," Lilias said to Blaise. "I saw nothing."

On that night, the second night, the dream reoccurred; and again on the third. It kindled hope among the Men and unease among the Ellylon, and discussion and dissent among members of both races.

"This is some trick of the Misbegotten," Lorenlasse announced with distaste.

"I do not think he would dare," Peldras said softly. There were violet smudges of weariness in the hollows of his eyes. "For all his ill-gained magics, Ushahin the Misbegotten has never dared trespass in the minds of Haomane's Children."

On orders from Blaise Caveros, the Borderguard sent scouts to question commonfolk in the surrounding territories. They returned with a confusion of replies; yes, they had seen the Bright Rider, yes, and the other Rider, too, the horses the colors of blood, night, and smoke. A wedge of ravens flying, a desert wind. A stone in a child's fist, crushing bone; a clear gem, and lightning.

They were afraid.

Lorenlasse of Valmaré listened and shook his fair head. "It is the Misbegotten," he said with certainty. Others disagreed.

Only Aracus Altorus said nothing. Weariness was in the droop of his shoulders; but he set his chin against the weight of the Soumanië as he rode and glanced northward from time to time with a kind of desperate hope.

And Lilias, whom the visions filled with terror, watched him with a kind of desperate fear.

"You know more than you say, Sorceress," Blaise said to her on the fourth day.

"Usually." Lilias smiled with bitter irony. "Is that not why I am here?"

He studied her. "Is it Malthus?"

She shrugged. "Who am I to say? You knew him; I did not."

Blaise rode for a while without speaking. "Is it Ushahin Dreamstalker?" he asked at length, adding, "You knew him; I did not."

"I met him," Lilias corrected him. "I did not *know* him."

"And?" He raised his eyebrows.

"What would you have me do?" she asked in exasperation. "You are a courteous enough keeper, Blaise Caveros, but I am a prisoner here. Would you have me *aid* you, my lord? After you destroyed my life and rendered me"—Lilias held up her wind-chafed, reddened hands—"*this?*"

"What?" Leaning over in the saddle, Blaise caught her wrist in a strong grip. Their mounts halted, flanks brushing. "Mortal? A woman?" His voice softened. "It is the lot to which you were born, Lilias of Beshtanag. No more, no less. Is it so cruel?"

Ahead of them, the Rivenlost rode in glittering panoply, ageless features keen beneath their fluttering pennants. "Yes," Lilias whispered. "It is."

Blaise loosed his grip and retrieved his dropped rein, resuming their pace. "I do not understand you," he said flatly.

"Nor do I expect you to," she retorted, rubbing her wrist.

He stared across at her. "Did we not show you mercy?"

Unwilling laughter arose from a hollow place within her. "Oh, yes!" Lilias gasped. "As it suited you to do so. Believe me, you'll regret *that*, my lord!" She laughed again, a raw edge to the sound. "And the great jest of it is, I find that being forced to continue living, I have no desire to cease. I am afraid of dying, Blaise."

He looked away. "You, who have sent so many to their death?"

"Not so many." She considered his profile, stern and spare. "Beshtanag was left in peace, mostly. The Regents were afraid of Calandor. Do you think me a monster?"

"I don't know." Blaise shook his head. "As you say, I have met you, Sorceress. I do not *know* you. And of a surety, we are agreed: I do not understand you." He rode for a time without speaking, then asked, "What was he like?"

"Calandor?" Her voice was wistful.

"No." He glanced at her. "Ushahin."

"Ah." Lilias gave her bitter smile, watching her mount's ears bob and twitch. "So you would pick over my thoughts like a pile of bones, gleaning for scraps of knowledge."

He ignored her comment. "Is it true it is madness to meet his gaze?"

"No." Lilias thought about her meeting on the balcony, the Soumanië heavy on her brow, and her desire to Shape the Dreamer into wholeness, taking away his bone-deep pain. And she remembered how he had looked at her, and her darkest fears had been reflected in his mismatched eyes. Everything he had seen had come to pass. Another hysterical laugh threatened her. "Yes, perhaps. Perhaps it is, after all."

Blaise watched her. "Have you met others of the Three?"

"The Warrior." Seeing him look blank, she clarified, "Tanaros Kingslayer. Your kinsman, Borderguardsman."

"And?" His jaw was set hard.

"What do you wish me to say, my lord?" Lilias studied him. "He is a Man. Immortal, but a Man. No more, and no less. I think he gives his loyalty without reserve and takes betrayal hard." Out of the corner of her eye, she saw Fianna the Archer watching them with distaste and smiled. "And he does not understand women. You are much like him, Blaise Caveros."

Blaise drew in a sharp breath to reply, wrenching unthinking at the reins. His mount arched its neck and sidled crabwise.

But before he could get the words out, the fabric of the world ripped.

A hot wind blew across the coastal road, setting the dust to swirling. Haomane's Allies halted, their mounts freezing beneath them, prick-eared. Borderguardsmen shielded their eyes with their hands; Ellylon squinted. At the head of the column, Aracus Altorus lifted his chin.

A clap of lightning blinded the midday sun.

Out of the brightness, a figure emerged; the Galäinridder, the Bright Rider, astride a horse that shone like sea-foam in starlight. The horse's broad chest emerged like the crest of a wave, churning onto the world's shoals. The Rider's robes were white and his white beard flowed onto his chest. Nestled amid it was a gem as clear as water, as bright as a diamond, so bright it hurt to behold it.

"Borderguard!" Aracus' voice rang as his sword cleared its sheath. "Surround him!"

They moved swiftly to obey, dun cloaks fluttering in the breeze as they encircled the shining Rider, who calmly drew rein and waited. Blaise nodded at Fianna as he moved to join them, entrusting Lilias to her care. At a gesture from Lorenlasse, the Rivenlost archers strung their bows, moving to reinforce the Borderguard.

"How is this, Aracus?" The Rider smiled into his beard. "Am I so changed that you do not know me?"

"I pray that I do." Aracus nudged his mount's flanks, bringing him within striking range. His voice was steady, the point of his blade leveled at the Rider. "And I fear that I do not. Are you Malthus, or some trick of the Sunderer?"

The Rider opened his arms. "I am as you see me."

Sunlight dazzled on the clear gem. Lilias flinched. On her right, Fianna unslung Oronin's Bow and nocked an arrow, pointing it at Lilias' heart.

No one else moved.

Aracus Altorus broke into an unexpected grin. "That's a wizard's answer if ever I've heard one." He sheathed his sword, leaning forward to extend his hand. "Welcome back, my lord Counselor! We feared you dead."

"Ah, lad." Malthus' eyes crinkled as he clasped Aracus' hand. "I'm harder to kill than that."

The Borderguard gave a cheer, unbidden. There was no cheering among the Rivenlost, but they lowered their bows, returning arrows to their quivers. Turning her head, Lilias saw that Fianna kept an arrow loosely nocked, aimed in her direction. There was lingering distrust in her gaze.

"How?" Aracus asked simply.

"It took many long days," Malthus said, "for I spent my strength in maintaining the spell of concealment that hides the Bearer from the Sunderer's eyes. What strength remained to me, I lost in my battle with his Kingslayer. When the Sunderer destroyed the Marasoumië, I was trapped within it, scarce knowing who I was, let alone where. And yet, in the end, I won free." He touched the white gem on his breast, his face somber. "I fear the cost was high, my friends. As I am changed, so is the Soumanië. It is a bright light in a dark place, one that may illuminate Men's souls, but no longer does it possess the power to Shape."

A murmur of concern ran through the ranks of Haomane's Allies.

"Is that all?" Aracus Altorus laughed, and removed the gold fillet from his head. A gladness was in his manner for the first time since Cerelinde had been taken from him. "Here," he said, offering it. "The spoils of Beshtanag. It's useless to me. I'd thought to ask you teach me how to wield it, but it's better off in your hands, Malthus. I'm a warrior, not a wizard."

Toward the rear of the company, Lilias made a choked sound.

"Ah, lad." Malthus gazed at the fillet in Aracus' palm, the gold bright in the sunlight, the Soumanië dull and lifeless. "Truly," he murmured, "you have the heart of a king. Would that the gem could be given as easily. No." He shook his head. "It is not truly yours to give, Aracus. The Soumanië must be inherited from the dead or surrendered freely by a living owner. Until that happens, I can wield it no more than you."

Aracus frowned. "Then—"

"No one can wield it." Malthus lifted his head, and his gaze was filled with a terrible pity. With one gnarled forefinger, he pointed at Lilias, who sat motionless, conscious of the Archer's arrow pointed at her heart. "Not so long as the Sorceress of Beshtanag lives."

DANI OPENED HIS EYES TO see a dark blot swimming in a pool of light hovering above him. His head ached and the bright, blurred light made him feel nauseated. He blinked and squinted until his vision began to clear, and the dark blot resolved itself into the worried face of his uncle, silhouetted against the blue Staccian sky.

"Dani!" Thulu's face creased into a grin. "Are you alive, lad?"

There seemed to be a stone upon his chest. He tried an experimental cough. It hurt in a number of places. "I don't know," he whispered. "Are you?"

"Barely." Thulu sat back, nodding at him. "You can let go of it now, lad. It's safe enough."

"What?" He realized his right hand was clutching the flask containing the Water of Life so hard it ached, pressing it hard against his flesh. His fingers had cramped frozen, and it took an effort to open them. The pressure on his chest eased when he released the flask. He tried to sit and floundered, finding his left arm bound and useless.

"Careful." Uncle Thulu moved to assist him. "There you go."

"What's that for?" Sitting upright, Dani looked at his left arm in bewilderment. It was secured in a damp makeshift sling torn from one of their cloaks, knotted around his neck. He tried moving it. A jolt of pain shot through his shoulder. "Ow!"

"Careful," Thulu repeated. "What do you remember, lad?"

"The river." He could hear it roaring nearby. The sound of it cleared some of the mist from his thoughts. "The Fjeltroll. We were attacked." He blinked at his uncle, remembering red blood swirling in the river foam. "You were wounded."

"Aye." Uncle Thulu showed him the gashes, three lines gouged across his chest. He had packed them with clay from the riverbank to stop the bleeding. It had worked, but his skin had a greyish cast. "I had a time getting you out of the river."

"We hit a rock." Dani felt at his head, finding a painful lump. It throbbed beneath his fingertips. He winced.

"*You* hit a rock," his uncle corrected him. "*I* fished you out." He padded out of sight and returned to hand Dani a much-battered bowl. "Here. Drink."

Dani sipped broth, made from strips of dried hare boiled in river water, and felt a measure of warmth in his belly, a measure of strength return to his limbs. He glanced around the makeshift campsite. It was sparse, little more than a sheltered fire and a few garments drying on the rocks. Their pine-branch float was nowhere in sight. He shifted his shoulders and felt the pain lance through him. It was bad, but bearable. "How badly am I hurt?"

"I don't know." Thulu's gaze was unflinching. "I think you broke a bone, here." One calloused finger brushed Dani's collarbone on the left side. "I bound it as best I could. How's your head?"

"It hurts." Dani squinted. "We're not safe here, are we?"

"No." A deep compassion was in his uncle's gaze, as deep as the Well of the World. "They're after us, lad. They'll follow the river. It won't be long. If you mean to continue, we'll have to flee." He opened his empty hands. "Across dry land, those places the Fjel do not believe sustain life."

"You lost your digging-stick!" Dani remembered seeing it, the length of peeled baari-wood jutting from the rib cage of a Fjel corpse. It had saved his life. "Can you still find water's path beneath the earth?"

"I believe it." His uncle stared at his empty palms, then clenched them into fists. "We are Yarru-yami, are we not?" He bared his teeth in a grin made fearful by the loss of fatty flesh, his face gaunt and hollow. "As Uru-Alat wills, I am your guide, Dani. Though we cross dry land, and our enemies pursue us, we will survive. We will flee, cunning as desert rats, until we come to the source of illness. If it is your will to follow the veins of Uru-Alat, I will lead you."

"It is, Uncle." In a gesture of trust, Dani set down his bowl and laid his right hand open like an upturned cup over his uncle's clenched fists. The radiating lines that intersected his pale palm formed a half a star. "Lead, and I will follow."

Thulu nodded, swallowing hard. The apple of his throat moved beneath his skin, and tears shone in his dark eyes. "Finish your broth," he said gently, "then gather yourself. We dare not wait. The Fjeltroll will not be far behind."

"Aye, Uncle." Dani nodded and picked up the bowl, finishing the last of his broth. With his free hand, he levered himself to his feet. For an instant, the world swam around him—then it steadied, anchored around the pain in his left shoulder, and the weight that hung suspended from his throat. He drew a deep breath. "I am ready."

"All right, then." Rising from a squat, his uncle scattered the fire with one well-placed kick of a calloused heel. Seizing their lone cooking-pot, he trampled on the coals, grinding them beneath his feet, then kicked pebbles and debris over the site until nothing of it remained. The River Spume surged past, heedless. Thulu exhaled, hard, and doubled over, catching at his chest. Bits of clay mingled with blood flaked loose. "All right," he said, straightening. "Let's go, lad."

They went.

SKRAGDAL ROARED.

The Fjel under his command kept silent and out of his way, keeping to the walls of the Nåltannen moot-hall. A Tungskulder in a rage was a thing to be avoided. Skragdal stormed in a circle, stomping and roaring, waving his arms in an excess of rage. The Nåltannen Elders glanced uneasily at the trembling stalactites on the ceiling of their den's central chamber. The Gulnagel runner who had brought news of the sighting crouched and covered his head, waiting for Skragdal's fury to pass.

Eventually, it did.

The blood in his frustrated veins cooled from anger's boiling-point. Skragdal willed himself to stillness and drew a deep breath. Rationality seeped back into his thoughts, the cool battle logic that General Tanaros had tried so hard to instill in him, that Field Marshal Hyrgolf had entrusted him to maintain.

"Tell me again," he rumbled.

Obliging, the Gulnagel stood and repeated his story. The smallfolk had been sighted in the southwestern verge of the Northern Harrow, where the Spume River reemerged from its journey underground. A Tordenstem sentry had given the alarm, and a pack under the command of Yagmar of the Tungskulder had cornered them beside the river. The smallfolk had held them off long enough to make an escape down the river.

"That," Skragdal said ominously, "is the part I do not understand."

The Gulnagel raised his hands in a shrug. "Who expects a cornered rabbit to fight? It was a narrow path and Yagmar's folk were taken by surprise. Besides"—he eyed Skragdal's plated armor, the axe and mace that hung at his belt, "they were not armed by Darkhaven."

"Still," Skragdal said. "They are Fjel."

"Yes." The Gulnagel shrugged. "It happened swiftly. Yagmar followed. He caught them where the river bends. He told them if they gave him the flask you seek, he would let them go. They paid him no heed."

Skragdal closed his eyes. "They are Men," he said softly. "Smallfolk from the desert. They do not speak Fjel."

"Oh!" The Gulnagel considered. "Some Men do."

"Staccians, yes." Skragdal opened his eyes. "These are not. And Yagmar should not have tried to bargain. His Lordship's orders are to kill them."

"Yagmar stood this deep," the Gulnagel said, placing the edge of one hand against his throat. "The river runs fast." There was a murmur of comprehension among the gathered Fjel. They appreciated the power of the northern rivers, which Neheris-of-the-Leaping-Waters had Shaped herself. Some could be forded; not all, not even by a Tungskulder. And none of them could swim. The density of their body-mass would not permit it.

Skragdal sighed. "So Yagmar tried to take the flask."

"Yes." The Gulnagel nodded. "And although it was no bigger than his thumb, it make him sink like a stone."

"Where are they now?" Skragdal stared at the messenger.

"Fled." The Gulnagel grimaced. "Away from the river, back into the dry mountains. It is what I am sent to tell you. Yagmar found their trail, but it leads away from water. After a day and a half, he had to turn back." He pointed at the waterskin slung from Skragdal's belt. "Neheris' bounty provides. We do not carry tools for hunting far from her rivers, where only small prey dwells."

"We are hunting small prey," Skragdal growled.

The Gulnagel gave another shrug. "What would you have us do?"

Skragdal considered the smaller Fjel, then glanced around at his companions. They returned his gaze impassively. None of them would dare advise him; not even Thorun, on whom he relied as a fellow Tungskulder. Dim light filtering through the air-shafts of the moot-hall glinted on their armor and weapons. This was the third den they had visited since leaving Neherinach. It felt strange to be among free-living members of his own people. They seemed vulnerable to him. It was not only the lack of arms, but the simplicity, the innocence. They remembered Neherinach—but that had been before Haomane had sent his Wise Counselors, armed with the Soumanië. Skragdal remembered what had happened in the Marasoumië, and the blasted node-point

they had found, the carnage in Earl Coenred's hall. Those of Neheris'
Children who did not serve Darkhaven had no idea of the forces arrayed against them.

He wished, very much, to be one of them.

The thought made him turn to the Nåltannen Elders. They were
gathered in a group, watching and waiting to hear what he would decide. Skragdal bowed his head and addressed Mulprek, who was se-
nior in this den. She was a female, her withered dugs giving testament
to the myriad pups she had born. Her mate, he knew, was some years
her junior. "Old mother," he said humbly. "Give me your counsel."

"Does the great warrior seek advice?" Mulprek wrinkled her lip and
bared dull, yellowing eyetusks. She shuffled forward to peer up at
him, laying a hand on his forearm. Her worn talons gleamed like steel
against his hide, and she smelled of musk. Despite her age, her eyes
were keen and bright. "This is a hunt, not a battle. Your prey has left a
trail. You know where they are bound." She nodded at the Kaldjager
Fjel in his company. "Use the Cold Hunters. Flush the prey, and herd
them. Lay a trap. So we have always done. So I say."

It was good advice.

Skragdal nodded. "Let all the tribes remain vigilant," he said. "All
hands may be needed for this." He turned to Blågen, whom he knew
best among the Kaldjager. "Can your lads do this thing?"

"Aye. If you don't mind losing your scouts." The Kaldjager's eyes
gleamed yellow. He slapped his waterskin. It made a heavy, sloshing
sound. "We've no fear of dry land. If the Gulnagel will lead us to the
trail, we'll hunt. We'll kill them if we can and herd them if we can't.
Where do you want the smallfolk?"

The image of a green field dotted with vine-laced barrows rose in
his mind. It lay on their route, and it would be a fitting place to make
an end to it. Why these desert smallfolk had chosen to oppose his
Lordship, he could not fathom. Already, they had paid a terrible price
for their folly.

But it didn't matter, only that the thing was done.

"Neherinach," Skragdal said grimly. "Bring them to Neherinach."

A RIVER OF WINGS FILLED the Tower of Ravens, black and beating.
     Flying in a circle.

Tanaros stood outside himself, watching through Fetch's eyes. He was part and parcel of the endless river, riding the silent current. Curving along the basalt walls. Wings, overlapping like scales, glossy feathers reflecting the blue-white flicker of the marrow-fire. He saw his brethren, bright eyes and sharp beaks. It was important that the wings overlap, beating in intricate layers.

His Lordship had summoned the Ravensmirror.

There he stood, at its center. A core of looming darkness, darkness visible. The Ravensmirror revolved around him. He had spoken the words in the ancient Shapers' tongue. His blood was a tang in the air.

Through doubled eyes, Tanaros beheld him; and the Three. He saw Vorax, who stood sturdy as a bulwark in the raven's gaze. To his eyes, the Staccian looked tired and worn. The news out of Gerflod had taken its toll. He saw Ushahin, who shone like a beacon in Fetch's eyes. Tanaros saw a feverish glitter in the half-breed's mien. There was power there, gathering and unspent. Where, he wondered, did it come from?

He saw himself.

A circling vision, glimpsed in the round. A pale face upraised, tracking the ravens' progress. A furrowed brow, a lock of hair falling, so. A pair of hands, strong and capable, gentle enough to cup a scrap of life wrought of hollow bones and feathers, a quick-beating heart. The fingers of one hand curled tenderly about the hilt of his black sword, holding it like a nestling.

Tanaros blinked, clearing his doubled vision. He tightened his grip on his sword-hilt, knuckles whitening.

Lord Satoris uttered the word. *"Show!"*

Around and around the ravens surged, and images formed in the reflection of their glossy wings.

None of them were good.

The last time Lord Satoris had summoned the Ravensmirror, it had shown armies of Haomane's Allies gathering. Now, they were on the move. In every quarter of Urulat, they had departed. In Pelmar, the Five Regents had assembled a massive delegation; they issued forth like a stream of ants, bent on honoring the pacts made at the overthrow of Beshtanag. In Vedasia, long trains of knights wound along the orchard-lined roads, flanked by their squires and attendants. A corps of archers marched forth from the tiny nation of Arduan. Along Harrington Inlet, the Free Fishers drew lots to determine who would stay, and who would fight. On the ruffled waters of the bay, ships hurried toward Port Calibus, where Duke Bornin of Seahold awaited with the foot soldiers under his command, returning from the Siege of Beshtanag.

Vorax cleared his throat. "They're coming here this time, aren't they?"

"Soon." Lord Satoris stared at the Ravensmirror. "Not yet." He turned his unblinking gaze on Vorax. "Shall we see what transpires in the north, my Staccian?"

The Ravensmirror tilted, images fragmenting, reforming in the shape of mountains and pines, leaping rivers. Where they bordered Fjel territory, the stone fortresses of Staccia were sealed tight in adamant defense. To the southwest, along a narrow swath . . .

Vorax grunted at the sight of Staccian lordlings arming themselves for battle, preparing to venture southward. "Too long," he said. "It has been too long since I went among them and reminded them of our bargain, and the peace and prosperity it has garnered Staccia."

"Do not despair." Tanaros watched the unfolding vision as it veered farther north. All across the peaks and valleys Neheris had Shaped, Fjel hunted; a collection of tough hide and bared eyeteeth, seeking their quarry. There were too many, and the territory too vast, for the ravens of Darkhaven to encompass, but it showed enough for hope. "The Fjel are loyal. If this Bearer is to be found, they will find him."

"But *Staccia*—"

"No." Ushahin shook his head. "Do not blame yourself, cousin. The Galäinridder made that path, bursting from the field of Neherinach, if my vision and the Fjel's tale holds true. I felt him as I rode, sifting through the dreams of Men."

Lord Satoris clenched his fists. "Malthus!"

The Three exchanged a glance.

"Where *is* he?" Tanaros asked aloud. "I thought him trapped and done." He bent his gaze on the shifting Ravensmirror. "Where's Aracus Altorus? Where are the Borderguard? Where are the *Rivenlost*?"

The fragmented visions shattered like a dark mirror, reforming to show something new. Wings beat and whispered, flitting among a copse of trees along the road, keeping a careful distance and staying hidden. The Arrow of Fire was spent, but the Archer's gaze endured. It was best to be wary. A group; a small group, measured against the numbers they had been shown, but a doughty one. There was the Borderguard of Curonan, in their dun-grey cloaks. There were the Rivenlost, tall and fair, radiant in silver armor. They were leaving Seahold behind them, with all its pennants flying. Toward Meronil they rode, the stronghold of Ingolin the Wise, steeped in Ellylon magic.

Tanaros drew in his breath in a hiss.

At the head of the company rode two Men; one mortal, with a Soumanië dull and ashen on his brow. He knew him, knew that demanding, wide-set gaze. And the other—the other it hurt to behold, robes rustling like a storm, a diamond-bright gem nestled in his white beard. Tanaros knew him, too. He remembered the shock that had resonated through his arms when the black blade of his sword had bitten deep into the old one's staff and stuck there. So close, it had been.

And then the Marasoumië had exploded.

"Malthus," he whispered, watching. "Would that I had killed you." The Counselor rode a mount as white as foam, and something in the arch of its neck, the placement of its hooves and the silvery fall of its mane, made his heart ache. Tanaros remembered it differently, cast in hues of night, as willful as this mount was tranquil. "That's my *horse!* What have you done to it?"

"What, indeed?" Lord Satoris' smile was like the edge of a knife. "Ah, Malthus! It is a violent resurrection you performed to escape entombment in the Ways. I did not believe it could be done. But it came at a price, did it not? Not dead, but almost as good."

Ushahin squinted crookedly at the vision in the Ravensmirror. "He's spent its power, hasn't he? The Soumanië. He's spent it all."

"Not all." The Shaper studied his adversary. "But that which remains is a brightness cast by the Souma, even as matter casts shadow. My Elder Brother's weapon Malthus no longer has the power to Shape matter, only the spirit."

"Dangerous enough," Tanaros murmured, thinking of the Staccian exodus they had witnessed, the tale Skragdal's Gulnagel had brought of Earl Coenred's betrayal. "Where the spirit wills, the flesh follows."

"Yes." Lord Satoris nodded. "But no longer is Malthus the Wise Counselor capable of bringing down the very gates of Darkhaven."

Vorax stirred. "He had such power?"

"Oh, yes, my Staccian." In the center of the tower room, the Shaper turned to him. "Malthus had such power, though not enough to defeat me in the bargain." His words hung in the darkling air. "For that, he would need an army."

"My Lord, he has an army," Vorax said bluntly. "And another Soumanië."

"Yes." Lord Satoris gave his knife-edged smile. "Useless to him, now. None can use it, unless its living holder surrenders it, or dies. It will be a fascinating thing to see, how my Brother's weapon deals with this dilemma." He turned back to consider the swirling visions, forgetful of the presence of his Three. "What will you do, Malthus?" he asked the Counselor's image. "Will you let the Sorceress live, seek to sway her heart, and endure the consequence if you fail? Or will you see her judged and condemned to death for her crimes?" The Shaper laughed aloud, a sound that made the foundations of Darkhaven vibrate. "Oh, it would be an amusing thing if it were the latter!"

A shudder ran over Tanaros' skin. He glanced sidelong at the Ravensmirror, where Aracus Altorus still rode alongside Malthus. There, farther back in the train, he saw her: Lilias of Beshtanag, the Sorceress of the East. She was much changed from the woman he had met in Beshtanag; pale and haggard, with fear-haunted eyes. Tanaros was aware of his heart beating within his branded chest, a solid and endless pulse.

He wondered what it would be like to have that stripped away after so long, to know, suddenly, that his heartbeats were numbered, that each one brought him a step closer to death.

In the Ravensmirror, the company of Malthus drew farther away, their image dwindling. They were passing the copse, into a stretch of open road. Among the ravens, a shared memory flitted from mind to mind: Arrow, arrow, arrow! Bodies tumbling from the sky. The ravens of Darkhaven dared not follow.

"Enough."

Lord Satoris made an abrupt gesture, and the Ravensmirror splintered into myriad bits of feathered darkness, scattering about the tower. Black eyes gleamed from every nook and cranny, watching as the Shaper paced in thought.

"It is bad, my Three," he said in time. "And yet, it is better than I feared. We have strong walls, and the Fjel to withstand their numbers. Malthus' power is not as it was. What we have seen is not enough to destroy us." He halted, a column of darkness, and tilted his head to gaze out the window toward the red star of Dergail's Soumanië. "It is what we have not seen that troubles me."

"The Bearer," Ushahin said.

"Yes." The single word fell like a stone.

"My Lord." Tanaros felt a pang of love constrict his heart. "The Fjel are hunting. He will be found, I swear it to you."

The Shaper bent his head toward him. "You understand why this thing must be done, my General?"

"I do, my Lord." Tanaros did not say it aloud; none of them did. The Prophecy hovered over them like a shroud.

"Perhaps the lad's dead." Vorax offered the words hopefully. "The travails of the Marasoumië, a hard journey in a harsh land—they're desert-folk, they wouldn't know how to survive in the mountains." He warmed to the idea. "After all, think on it. Why else would the damnable wizard head south, if his precious Bearer was lost in the northlands?"

"Because Malthus cannot find his Bearer, my Staccian." Grim amusement was in Lord Satoris' voice. "The lad is hidden by the Counselor's own well-wrought spell—from my eyes, and the eyes of Ushahin Dreamspinner. Now that the Soumanië is altered, Malthus cannot breach his own spell. And so he trusts the Bearer to the workings of my Elder Brother's Prophecy and goes to Meronil to plot war, and because there is a thing there he must retrieve."

No one asked. After a moment, Ushahin sighed. "The Spear of Light."

"Yes." Lord Satoris returned to the window, gazing westward. "I believe it to be true." His shoulders, blotting out the stars, moved in a slight shrug. "It matters not. Malthus has ever had it in his keeping."

Tanaros' mouth was dry. "What is your will, my Lord?"

The Shaper replied without turning around. "Send the runners back to Fjel territory, accompanied by as many Kaldjager as you can spare. The hunt must continue. Once they have gone, set a team to blocking the tunnels. Too many in Staccia know the way, and traitors among them. Tell the Fjel to return overland when they have succeeded." He did turn then, and his eyes glared red against the darkness. "Tell them to bring me the Bearer's head. I want to see it. And I want to see Malthus' face when it is laid at his feet."

Tanaros bowed his head. "My Lord."

"Good." The Shaper moved one hand in dismissal. "The rest you know, my Three. They are coming. Prepare for war."

They left him there, a dark figure silhouetted against darkness. Wet darkness seeped from his unhealing wound, trickling steadily to form a gleaming pool around his feet. Twin streaks of shadow streamed past his massive shoulders into the night as Ushahin bid the ravens to leave the Tower. Watching them go, Tanaros had an urge to call Fetch back, though he didn't.

"Well." Descending the winding stair, Vorax exhaled heavily and wiped his brow. "That's that, then."

"War." Ushahin tasted the word. "Here."

"Aye." Vorax grunted. His footsteps were heavy on the stairs. "I still think there's a fine chance that little Charred lad may be dead, and this a lot of fuss over nothing. It would be like that damnable wizard to play us for fools." He nudged Tanaros. "What do you say, cousin? Are the Charred Folk that hard to kill?"

Tanaros thought of the boy he had seen in the Ways, with a clay vial at his throat and a question in his eyes. He thought of the Yarru elders; of Ngurra, calm and sorrowful beneath the shadow of his black sword.

I can only give you the choice, Slayer.

"Yes," he said. "They are."

After that, the Three continued in silence. What his companions thought, Tanaros could not guess with any certitude. They had never spoken of what would befall them if Haomane's Allies were to prevail.

It had never seemed possible until now.

FOUR

THE VALLEY IN WHICH THE Rivenlost haven of Meronil lay was a green cleft shrouded in mist. By all appearances, it filled the valley to the brim, moving in gentle eddies, sun-shot and lovely, a veil of rainbow droplets.

Lilias caught her breath at the sight of it.

Blaise Caveros glanced at her. "I felt the same when I first saw it."

She made no reply, watching as Aracus Altorus and Malthus the Counselor rode to the valley's edge, peering into the mists. There, they conferred. Aracus inclined his head, the Soumanië dull on his brow. Mist dampened his red-gold hair, making it curl into ringlets at the nape of his neck.

He needs a haircut, Lilias thought.

Aracus didn't look at her. She wished that he would, but he hadn't. Not since the day the Counselor had appeared before them, pointing his gnarled finger at her, and spoken those fateful words.

Not so long as the Sorceress of Beshtanag lives.

It was Aracus Altorus who had placed his hand on the Counselor's forearm, lowering his pointing finger. It was Aracus who had raised his voice in a fierce shout, bidding Fianna the Archer to lower her bow. And it was Aracus who had brought his mount alongside hers, fixing her with his wide-set gaze. All the words that had passed between them were in that gaze. He was not a bad man, nor a cruel one. He had extended trust to her, and mercy, too.

"Will you not release your claim upon it, Lilias?" he had asked her simply.

In the back of her mind there arose the image of Calandor as she had seen him last; a vast mound of grey stone, the crumpled shape of one broken wing pinned beneath him, the sinuous neck stretched out in death. To join him in death was one thing; to relinquish the Soumanië willingly? It would be a betrayal of that memory. While she lived, she could not do it. Tears had filled her eyes as she shook her head. "I cannot," she whispered. "You should have let me die when you had the chance."

Aracus had turned away from her then, giving a curt order to Blaise to ensure her safety. There had been dissent—not from Blaise, but among the others, and the Archer foremost among them. Arguing voices had arisen, calling for her death. In the end, Aracus Altorus, the would-be King of the West, had shouted them down.

"I will not become like our Enemy!"

Throughout it all, Malthus the Counselor had said nothing; only listened and watched. A horrible compassion was in his gaze, and Lilias flinched when it touched her. It had done so all too much since he had rejoined them. She wished he would turn his gaze elsewhere.

Now, on the edge of the valley, Malthus turned in the saddle, beckoning to the commander of the Rivenlost, Lorenlasse of the Valmaré. The clear gem at Malthus' breast flashed as he did so, making the mist that filled the valley sparkle.

Lorenlasse rode forward, placing the mouthpiece of a silver horn to his lips.

A single call issued forth, silvery and unsubstantial.

For a moment, nothing happened; then an echoing call arose from the valley's depths, and the mists parted like a veil, revealing that the paved road continued onward in descent. Below them lay the cleft green valley, divided by a gleaming river that widened as it flowed toward the sea harbor, spanned by an intricate series of bridges that joined fanciful towers spiring on either side. It was white, white as a gull's wing. White walls curved to surround both hemispheres, and the city itself was wrought of white marble, structures more delicate than Men's arts could compass.

Through it all ran the Aven River, toward the silvery sea. Sunlight gilded its surface, broken into arrowing ripples by the low, elegant boats being poled here and there. And on an island in the center of the river stood the Hall of Ingolin the Wise, his pennant flying from

the highest tower, depicting the argent scroll of knowledge on a field
of sage green. A trio of white-headed sea eagles circled the spire in a
lazy gyre, borne aloft on broad wings.

"Meronil." There was deep satisfaction in Blaise's voice. "Have you
ever seen anything so lovely?"

Lilias remembered Calandor alive and the majesty of his presence.
How he had looked perched on the cliff's edge; sunlight glittering on
his bronze scales, the glint of his green-gilt eyes, filled with knowledge. Love. A trickle of smoke, twin plumes arising in the clear air.
The moment when he launched his mighty form into flight, the gold
vanes of his outspread pinions defying the void below. So impossible;
so beautiful.

"Perhaps," she murmured.

In the valley below, a company of Ellylon warriors emerged from
the eastern gate, riding forth to meet them. They wore Ingolin's livery
over their armor, sage-green tunics with his argent scroll on the breast.
Their horses were caparisoned in sage and silver, and their hooves
beat a rhythmic tattoo on the paving stones as they drew near.

The leader inclined his head. "Lord Aracus, Lorenlasse of Valmaré,"
he said, then inclined his head toward Malthus. "Wise Counselor. Be
welcome to Meronil. My Lord Ingolin awaits you."

With a gesture, he turned his mount and his men fell into two lines,
flanking their guests to form an escort. With Aracus, Lorenlasse, and
Malthus at the head, the company began the descent.

Lilias found herself in the middle of the column; behind the Rivenlost, but at the forefront of the Borderguard of Curonan. She twisted in
the saddle to look behind her, and Blaise, ever mindful, leaned over
to claim her mount's reins. Riding at her immediate rear, Fianna the
Archer gazed at her with smoldering distrust. Lilias ignored her, watching what transpired. As the last Borderguardsman cleared the lip of the
valley, the pearly mist arose. Dense as a shroud, it closed behind the
last man. Once again, the green valley was curtained; and yet, overhead the sky was clear and blue, the sun shining upon Meronil.

There was magic at work here she did not understand; Ellylon
magic. What was true Shaping, and what was illusion? She could not
tell, only that she was captive within its borders. Lilias shuddered.
Without thinking, she lifted one hand to feel her brow, keenly aware
of the Soumanië's absence.

"Are you well, Sorceress?" Blaise asked without looking at her.

"Well enough." Lilias dropped her hand. "Lead on."

They completed their descent. There was fanfare at the gate. Lorenlasse blew his silvery horn; other horns sounded in answer. The leader of their escort spoke courteously to the Gate's Keeper; the Gate's Keeper replied. Rivenlost guards stood with unreadable faces, crossing their spears. Aracus sat his mount with his jaw set and a hard expression in his eyes. The Gate's Keeper inclined his head. Malthus the Counselor smiled into his beard, fingering the bright gem at his breast. Fianna the Archer scowled, trying hard not to look overwhelmed by Ellylon splendor. Blaise conferred with his second-in-command, delegating. The bulk of the Borderguard withdrew to make camp in the green fields outside Meronil's eastern gate.

All of it gave Lilias a headache.

The Gate's Keeper spoke a word, and there was a faint scintillation in the air. The gate opened. They rode through, and the gate closed behind them.

They had entered Meronil.

The Rivenlost had turned out to see them. They were Ellylon; they did not gape. But they stood along their route—on balconies, in doorways, upright in shallow boats—and watched. Male and female, clad in elegant garb, they watched. Some raised their hands in silent salute; others made no gesture. Their age was unknowable. They were tall and fair, with grave eyes and a terrible light in their faces, a terrible grief in their hearts. Their silence carried a weight.

There should have been music playing.

Meronil was a city made for music, a symphony in architecture, its soaring towers and arching bridges echoing one another, carrying on a dialogue across the murmuring undertone of the Aven River.

Instead, there was only mourning silence.

In the city, Lorenlasse of the Valmaré dismissed his company. They parted ways, returning to their homes; to regroup, to await new orders. Lorenlasse bowed low to Aracus Altorus before he took his leave, promising to see him anon. Was there mockery in his bow? Lilias could not say.

Then, they were few. Haomane's Allies; Malthus' Company. There was Aracus and Malthus, and Blaise and Fianna, keeping watch over Lilias. Among the Ellylon, only Peldras accompanied them. Ingolin's escort led them across a wide bridge toward the island, while the River Aven flowed tranquilly below and the denizens of Meronil watched. No longer hidden amid a large party, Lilias shrank under their regard, feeling herself small and filthy beneath it, aware of the stain of her own mortality.

She imagined their disdain.

So this *is the Sorceress of the East?*

She reclaimed her reins from Blaise and concentrated on holding them, fixing her gaze upon her own reddened, chapped knuckles. It was better to meet no one's eyes. The Bridge's Keeper granted them passage. The company alighted on the island. When the doors to the Hall of Ingolin were thrown wide open, Lilias kept her gaze lowered. She dismounted at Blaise's quiet order and bore out the exchange of courtesies, the embraces given and returned, with little heed. None of it mattered. She wished she were anywhere in the world but this too-fair city.

"Sorceress."

A voice, a single voice, speaking the common tongue, infused with deep music and bottomless wisdom, a host of magic at its command. It jerked her head upright. Lilias met the eyes of Ingolin the Wise, Lord of the Rivenlost.

He was old; so old, though it was not in his features, no. Or if it was, it was not in such a way that mortal Men understood. It was true, his hair was silver-white, falling like a shining river past his shoulders. Still, his shoulders were broad, and his features unlined. Time's footprints did not touch the Ellylon as they did the rest of the Lesser Shapers. But his eyes . . . ah!

Fathomless and grey, eyes that had seen the world Sundered.

They met hers, measured and *knew* her. They saw the hopeless tangle of grief and envy knotted in her heart. Ingolin was not called the Wise for nothing. He bent his head a fraction in acknowledgment of the status she had once held. "Lilias of Beshtanag. We welcome you to Meronil as our guest."

Others watched her; Aracus, with the dead Soumanië on his brow, filled with longing. Fianna, seething with resentment. Malthus and the Ellyl Peldras, both with that awful compassion. And Blaise; what of Blaise? He sat his mount quietly, scarred hands holding the reins, avoiding her eyes.

Lilias drew a deep breath. "You put a pleasant face upon my captivity, Lord Ingolin."

"Yes." Ingolin offered the word simply. "You know who you are, Sorceress; what you have been, what you have done. You know who we are and what we seek." He indicated the open door. "You will be granted hospitality within these walls; and sanctuary, too. Of that, I assure you. No more, and no less."

Lilias' head ached. There was too much light in this place, too much whiteness. She rubbed at her temples with fumbling fingers. "I don't want it."

There was no pity in his face, in the eyes that had beheld the Sundering of the world. "Nonetheless, you shall have it."

"IT'S *HIM*!" MEARA HISSED.

Cerelinde's heart clenched in a spasm of fear. She willed herself to a semblance of calm before glancing up from the embroidery in her lap. "Has Lord Satoris summoned me, Meara?"

"Not his *Lordship*!" The madling grimaced and jerked her head at the doorway. "General Tanaros. He's *here*."

This time, it was a surge of gladness that quickened her heart. It was more disturbing than the fear. Cerelinde laid aside her embroidery and folded her hands. "Thank you, Meara. Please make him welcome."

She did, muttering to herself, and made a hasty exit without apology.

And then he was there.

He was taller than she remembered; or perhaps it was the gauntness his travail had left that made him seem so. The room seemed smaller with him in it. Muted lamplight reflected dimly on the glossy surface of his ceremonial black armor. He bowed, exacting and courtly. "Lady Cerelinde."

"General Tanaros." She inclined her head, indicating the empty chair opposite her. "Will you sit?"

"Thank you." Encased in unyielding metal, Tanaros sat upright, resting his hands on his knees. He regarded her in silence for a moment, as though he'd forgotten what he'd come to say. "I trust you are well?"

"As well as I may be." Cerelinde smiled faintly. "Meara has obtained materials that I might indulge in needlework to alleviate the tedium. His Lordship has not permitted Lord Vorax to kill me."

"Vorax?" The straps of Tanaros' armor creaked as he shifted. "He wouldn't."

"He would like to."

"He won't."

Another silence stretched between them. Cerelinde studied him. He looked tired, his face bearing the marks of sun and wind. The hollows of his eyes looked bruised, and beneath the errant lock of dark hair that fell across his brow, there were furrows that had not been there before. It stirred pity in her heart, an emotion she sought to repress. He was Tanaros Kingslayer, one of the Three, Lord General of the Army of Darkhaven.

Still, he was here, sitting in her well-appointed prison cell, and he was the only sane person she had seen in this place who did not appear to wish her dead.

"In Haomane's name," she said quietly, "or any you might honor, will you please tell me what is happening?"

"War." Tanaros held her gaze without blinking. "Not yet, but soon. Even now, they are gathering in Meronil to plot strategy. They are coming for you, Lady."

Cerelinde nodded once. "Do they have a chance?"

He shrugged, making his armor creak. "Do I think they can take Darkhaven? No, Lady, I do not. But nothing in war is certain save bloodshed."

"It could be averted."

"By letting you go?" Tanaros gave a short laugh. "To wed Aracus Altorus?"

She made no reply.

"Ah, Lady." His voice roughened. "Even if your answer were no . . . how long? One mortal generation? Ten? How long do you suppose it will be until another scion of Altorus is born who sets your heart to racing—"

"Enough!"

"—and makes the blood rise to your cheeks?"

"Enough, my lord," Cerelinde repeated, flushing. "There is no need to be vulgar."

Tanaros raised his brows. "Vulgar?"

She opened her mouth, then closed it.

Tanaros sighed and rumpled his hair with one hand. "In the end, it matters naught. I do not think Haomane's Allies would ever be willing to forgo the Prophecy. And I am quite certain, in this instance, that his Lordship is not interested in negotiating."

"He could relent," Cerelinde said in a low, impassioned voice. "I have said it before, and it is still true. He could relent and surrender to Haomane's will. There is that. There is *always* that."

"No." Tanaros shook his head. "No, Lady, I don't think there is. I don't think there ever was."

"Why?" she asked steadily.

He shrugged again. "Ask *him*, if you truly want to know. Perhaps the answer lies in what-might-have-been."

"You heard of that?" Cerelinde flushed a second time. "I meant to speak to you of the incident. It is a small gift, a small magic. Vorax was wroth, but I did not mean to disturb, only to bring comfort. It eases them, to glimpse the paths they might have walked." She considered Tanaros and added softly, "I could show you, if you wished."

"No!" The word exploded from his lips. He took a slow breath, bracing his hands on his knees. "No," he repeated more gently. "Do you think I don't know, Lady? An ordinary cuckold's life, with all the small shames and painful sympathies attendant upon it. Believe me, I know what I abandoned."

"Perhaps. Perhaps not." Cerelinde looked at his braced hands, then raised her gaze to his face. "Is that why you killed her?"

"No." Tanaros lifted his hands, examining them in the dim lamplight. "I was angry." He met her gaze. "I held her hand through the birth. I wept tears at her pain. It was only afterward, when I saw the babe. I saw his red hair, and I remembered. How she and Roscus had smiled at one another. How they had fallen silent when I entered a room. A thousand such incidents, meaningful only now. I asked her, and she denied it. Lied. She lied to me. It was not until my hands were at her throat that she confessed. By then, my anger had gone too far." He paused. "You don't understand, do you?"

"No." She shook her head. "Neither portion, I fear."

"It is said the Ellylon cannot lie," he mused. "Is it so?"

"We are Haomane's Children," Cerelinde said, perplexed. "The

Lord-of-Thought Shaped us. To think is to speak; to speak is to be. How can we speak a thing that is not true? We might as well unmake ourselves. It is not a thing I can fathom."

"Ah, well." Tanaros gave her a twisted smile. "We are Arahila's Children, and the truth of the heart does not always accord with that of the head. Be mindful of it, Lady, since you propose to wed one of us. If I am wrong, and we lose this coming war, it may matter."

"Aracus would not lie," she said certainly.

"Perhaps," he said, echoing her words. "Perhaps not."

Silence fell over the room like a shroud.

"Tanaros Kingslayer," Cerelinde said aloud. "Do you lay that death, too, at anger's doorstep? For it seems to me you must have loved him, once, for him to have wounded you so deeply."

For a long time, he was silent. "Yes," he said at length. "Anger, and love. It is the one that begat the other's strength, Cerelinde. He was my liege-lord; and for many years, like unto a brother to me." His mouth quirked into another bitter smile. "Do the Ellylon understand *betrayal*?"

"Yes." She did not tell him what was in her mind; that the Ellylon had known betrayal at the hands of Men. So it had been, since before the world was Sundered. From the dawning of the Second Age of Urulat, Arahila's Children had coveted the Gifts of Haomane's. And they had made war upon the Ellylon, believing in their folly that a Shaper's Gift could be wrested away by force. "We do."

"So be it." After considering her words, Tanaros give himself a shake, like a man emerging from a dream. He cleared his throat. "Forgive me, Lady. I did not come here to speak of such things."

"What, then?" Cerelinde asked simply.

His dark gaze was steady and direct. "To assure you that I continue to vouch for the safety of your well-being. No more, and no less."

She inclined her head. "Thank you."

"Well." Tanaros flexed his hands upon his knees. He made to rise, then hesitated. "Lady . . . if it might please you, there is something I might show you outside the walls of Darkhaven proper. On the morrow, perhaps?"

Outside.

For the third time in the space of an hour, Cerelinde's heart leapt. "Oh, yes," she heard herself whisper. "Please."

Tanaros rose, executing another crisp bow. "On the morrow, then."

Like a good hostess, she saw him to the door. He paused only briefly, searching her face. Something haunted was in his gaze, something that had not been there before. Then he took his leave, averting his eyes. The Fjeltroll on duty saluted him in passing, closing the door upon his departure.

It locked with an audible sound, sealing Cerelinde into her quarters.

Left alone, she placed her hand upon the ironwood door, contemplating her outspread fingers.

"ALL TOGETHER, NOW," SPEROS SAID encouragingly. "That's right, you've got it, lean on the lever. One, two, three . . . *yes!*" He let out a triumphant whoop as the great boulder settled into place with a resounding crash. "Oh, well *done*, lads!"

On the crude ramp, one of the Tordenstem let loose a reverberating howl, lofting the heavy, pointed log that had served as a lever. Delighted in their achievement, the others echoed his cry until loose pebbles rattled and the very air seemed to tremble.

Despite his aching eardrums, Speros grinned. "Hold on!" he shouted, prowling around the wooden rick on which the boulder rested. "Let's be sure it will hold."

It would. The thick branches groaned and the ropes lashing them together creaked, but in time they settled under the boulder's weight, ceasing their complaint. They would hold. High atop the crags above the Defile, Speros lay on his belly, squirming forward on his elbows, inching onto the overhanging promontory until he could peer over the edge.

Far, far below him lay the winding path that led along the desiccated riverbed. The mountains that Lord Satoris had erected around the Vale of Gorgantum were impassable, except perhaps to a determined Fjeltroll. With the tunnels blocked, the path was the only way into the Vale. If Haomane's Allies sought to penetrate Darkhaven's defenses, they would have to traverse it.

It would be difficult. Speros meant to make it impossible.

"Right." He squirmed backward and got to his feet. "We'll need to pile it high, with as much as it can hold. If we can get enough weight to take off the edge of this crag . . ." He made a chopping gesture with one hand. "It will block the path. But first we need to get our fulcrum in place." He glanced around, seeking a smallish boulder. "How about that one?"

"Aye, boss!" A Tordenstem Fjel padded cheerfully down the log ramp. It dipped under his heavy tread. He splayed his legs and squatted, lowering his barrel chest near to the ground, and wrapped powerful arms around the rock. It came loose in a shower of pebbles. "Where do you want it?"

"Here." Speros pointed to the spot.

The Fjel grunted and waddled forward. There was a second crash as he set down his burden at the base of the wooden rick. "There you are, then."

"That's done it. Shall we see if it will work?" Speros reclaimed the lever and tested it, lodging the pointed tip of the log beneath the mammoth boulder they had first moved. He positioned the midsection over the rock intended to serve as the fulcrum and leaned all his weight on the butt.

"Careful, boss," one of the Tordenstem rumbled.

"Don't worry." Speros bounced on the lever. Nothing so much as shifted. "Can *you* move it, Gorek?"

The Fjel showed the tips of his eyetusks in a modest smile. "Like as not." He approached the lever, taloned hands grasping the rough bark, and pushed.

It shifted, and the entire structure groaned.

"All right!" Speros said hastily. "One, then; or two of you at the most. We'll work it out later. Come on, lads, let's load the rick."

Hoofbeats sounded along the path that led from Darkhaven proper as the Fjel formed a chain, piling the wooden rick high with loose rocks and stones. Speros went out to meet the approaching rider. And there was Tanaros, clad in black armor, all save his helmet, astride the black destrier he had claimed in the Midlands, surveying his—*his*—accomplishments.

"Lord General!" Speros felt his face split in another grin. "Do you see what we've done here?"

"Indeed." Tanaros drew rein and took it in; the rick, the boulders, the lever, the Tordenstem padding their way up the crude ramp to deposit heavy stones. Dismounting, he strode to the edge of the promontory and gazed at the path below, gauging the trajectory. The wind stirred his dark hair. "Would it block the path entirely?"

"Long enough to give them trouble. There's another site that may work as well." Watching the General stand on the verge of the abyss gave Speros an uneasy feeling in the pit of his stomach. "Careful, my lord. There's not much holding that ledge up."

Tanaros raised his brows. "That's the point, isn't it?"

"Aye." Speros swallowed nervously.

"Don't worry. I've lived too long to die falling off a cliff." Tanaros came back to place a hand on Speros' shoulder. "Well done, Midlander. This was a fine thought you had."

"Thank you, sir!" His anxiety vanished in a surge of pride. "It came to me after we rode through the Defile. Why not use the strength of the Tordenstem to greater effect? It was filling in the Well of the World that gave me the idea. You recall how—"

"Yes." A shadow of sorrow crossed the General's face.

"—we used skids and levers . . ." Speros stopped. "Forgive me."

"No matter." Tanaros shook his head.

"I know, I failed you in the desert." Speros took a deep breath. "Believe me, Lord General, I have sworn an oath. I have said it before and will say it again. A thousand times, if need be. It will never happen—"

"Speros!" The General's grip on his shoulder tightened until it hurt. "Enough," he said quietly. "You will speak no more of it. I bear you no blame for what happened with the Yarru. What happened there . . ." He sighed and released Speros' shoulder, gazing out across the gorge of the Defile. "It will be good to fight an enemy who comes seeking a battle."

"Aye, sir." Speros followed the General's gaze uncertainly.

"Not *yet*, lad!" His mood shifting, Tanaros smiled at him. "They'll come soon enough. And I thank you for making us that much the readier for it."

"Aye, sir!" Speros smiled back at the General.

"You're a good lad, Speros of Haimhault." With another clap on the shoulder, Tanaros left him, striding across the stony ground to greet the Tordenstem. He knew them all by name. In another moment, he was gone, swinging astride the black horse and heading back toward the fortress, his figure dwindling beneath the dull grey sky.

Watching him go, Speros retained a lingering vision of the General standing on the edge of the cliff, the wind tugging at his dark hair, a specter of sorrow haunting his eyes. He wished there was something he could do or say to dispel that shadow.

He wished it *was* his own failure that had put it there.

It wasn't, of course. In his heart of hearts, he knew it. That was his own specter, the ghost of his father's voice, his family's disapproval. It had nothing to do with General Tanaros. That was something else altogether. He had heard what the old Yarru had said about the General's choice, and he had heard the General's reply, his final, agonized shout: *Give me a reason not to make it!*

But he hadn't. The old man had just stood there. *Choose*, he'd said; as if his people hadn't sent one of their own off upon a quest to fulfill Haomane's Prophecy, to destroy Lord Satoris and everything General Tanaros held dear. And what had followed afterward, the black blade flashing, the dull thud of Fjeltroll maces and blood sinking into the sand . . .

"What else was he supposed to do?" Speros asked aloud.

"Boss?" One of the Tungskulder glanced quizzically at him.

"Nothing." He squared his shoulders. There was one thing, at least, he could do. "Come on, lads, let's move. We've got another one of these to build before Haomane's Allies come a-calling."

FJELTROLL WERE HUNTING THEM AND Uncle Thulu was sick.

He had denied it for days; and long, thirsty, grueling days they were. After the first Fjeltroll to follow them had turned back, Dani had dared to hope. They worked their way slowly westward, avoiding all save the smallest water sources, concealing their trail as they went. It was slow and laborious, and he was increasingly worried about his uncle's condition, but at least they were spared the threat of Fjel.

Then they had seen another.

Dani had spotted it in the distance. It wasn't like the others that had attacked them. This one traveled alone, moving swiftly and silently. It worked its way back and forth across the terrain in purposeful arcs, pausing at times to lift a narrow, predatory head and scent the air. If it hadn't been for the glint of sunlight on its armor, he might have missed it.

Armor.

The Fjel hunting them was armed; worse, it carried a waterskin. Dani choked out a warning. Uncle Thulu clamped a hand over his mouth, casting around wildly for a place to hide.

Uru-Alat be thanked, he had found one—a cave, scarce more than a shallow depression, its opening partially hidden by pine branches. Uncle Thulu shoved Dani into it, scrambling after him and dragging the branches back in place. He stripped off a handful of needles as he did, grinding them hard between his palms.

"Here," he whispered, pressing half of the damp wad into Dani's good hand. "Rub it on your skin. It will help mask our scent."

Dani obeyed awkwardly, hampered by the cloth that bound his left arm. "I don't think he saw us," he whispered back. "Can they track by scent like the Were?"

"I'm not sure." Thulu peered through the branches. "But I suspect it's live prey rather than a cold trail he's sniffing after. If it wasn't, he'd be on us already." He settled back, adding grimly, "We'll find out soon enough, lad."

Pressed close to his uncle, Dani could feel the dry, feverish heat of his skin and hear the faint rattle in his chest as he breathed. Offering a silent prayer to Uru-Alat, he touched the clay vial at his neck like a talisman.

They waited.

The Yarru-yami were good at waiting. It took patience to survive in the desert. Many a time, Dani had squatted in front of a crevice in the rocks, a rock in his sling, waiting for hours for a lizard to emerge. He had never thought until now how much worse it must be for the lizard, hidden in darkness, unable to see or smell beyond the walls of its shelter, making the tentative decision to emerge without knowing whether a predator awaited it.

Dani strained his ears for the sound of heavy Fjel feet crunching on the rocks, the scrape of talons. Surely something that large could not move in total silence? Perhaps; perhaps not. There was no sound but the rattle of his uncle's breath. It seemed to be growing louder. His own mouth grew dry and parched. Dani sucked on a pebble to relieve the dryness and waited.

Beyond the spray of pine needles that curtained their hiding place, shadows moved across the ground. They stretched long and black, slanting toward twilight, before Uncle Thulu gauged it safe to investigate.

"I'll do it." Dani moved before his uncle could argue, parting the branches and wriggling out of the shallow cave and into open air.

With his heart in his throat, half-anticipating a blow, he scrambled to his feet and glanced around wildly.

There was nothing there, for as far as the eye could see. Only the slanting shadows; rocks and pine trees, and a mountain thrush warbling somewhere in the branches. Overhead, the sky was turning a dusky hue.

Dani laughed with relief. "He's gone, Uncle!"

The pine branches curtaining the cave rustled, then went still. Dani waited for a moment with a dawning sense of alarm. When Thulu failed to emerge, he wrenched the branches aside with his right hand, admitting light into the cavern.

"Uncle!"

The older Yarru squinted at him. "Sorry, boy. Thought the rest . . . do me good, at least." He made an effort to rise and grimaced. "Seems not."

A cold hand of fear closed around Dani's heart. In the lowering light of sunset, Uncle Thulu looked *bad*. His eyes were fever-bright and his face was drawn and haggard. His lips were dry and cracked, and his ashen skin seemed to hang loose on his bones.

Dani took a deep breath, touching the clay vial in an instinctive gesture. He willed his fear to subside. Without meaning to, he found himself thinking of Carfax the Staccian, who had found the courage to save him at the end, when the Were had attacked them. It seemed like a very long time ago.

Still, he found courage in the memory.

"Let me see." He knelt beside his uncle, untying the laces on the front of his woolen shirt. Folding back a corner to lay bare his uncle's chest, he hissed involuntarily through his teeth. The three gashes left by a Fjel's talons were angry and red, suppurating. Proud flesh swelled in ridges on either side, and a yellowish substance oozed from them.

"It's nothing." Uncle Thulu fumbled at his shirt. "I can go on, lad."

"No." Dani sat back on his heels. "No," he said again more strongly. "You can't." He nodded, mostly to himself. "But we're going to stay here until you can."

FIVE

IT FELT GOOD TO HUNT with the Kaldjager.

Skragdal had shed his armor for the hunt; set aside his shield, un-buckled the leather straps to remove the unwieldy carapace of steel, laid down his battle-axe and his mace. Without them, he felt light as a pup, almost giddy with lightness.

Beyond the western outskirts of Drybone Reach, where the small-folk had fled, ash trees grew and the White River tumbled from the heights in measured stages. Water gathered in foaming pools, a shin-ing ribbon spilling over a worn granite lip only to gather and spill on-ward, lower and lower. In this fashion did it make its way to the field of Neherinach, several leagues hence.

It was beside one such pool that Skragdal crouched amid the roots of a tall ash, his talons digging into the rich loam. He was glad he had chosen to dally here. A cool breeze played over his exposed hide. He widened his nostrils, inhaling deeply.

There.

The odor of blood, living blood. A beating heart and the rank odor of fear, the distinctive scent of lanolin. He felt a keen hunter's smile stretch his mouth. Late summer, when the young males among the mountain sheep vied for precedence and territory, staking their claim for the winter to come.

The Kaldjager were driving one his way.

Lifting his head, he saw it. A ram, descending in bounds. Its coat was shaggy and greyish-white. A pair of ridged horns rose from its brow in looping, massive curves, as thick as a Tungskulder's forearm.

It saw him and froze.

And there were the Kaldjager, emerging from their pursuit, one on either side. They moved quickly and efficiently, sealing off the young ram's avenue of retreat. One of them saw Skragdal as he rose from his crouch, stepping from beneath the shadow of the ash tree. Even at a distance, his yellow eyes glinted. He hunched his shoulders, opening one hand in an overt gesture. *Tungskulder, the prey is yours.*

Skragdal spread his arms gladly. They felt so *light* without armor.

Beside the pool, the ram halted, setting its forelegs and planting its cloven hooves. It was breathing hard. It lowered its head, the heavy, curling horns tilting as it glanced behind it to either side, catching sight of the grinning Kaldjager.

There was no way out.

Skragdal lowered his head and roared.

Everything else went away when the ram charged. It came hard and fast, its scent filling his nostrils. At the last moment, it rose upon its hind legs. For an instant, the ram's head was silhouetted against the sky. He took in its amber-brown eyes, filled with determined fury of the will-to-survive, its narrow, triangular nostrils and oddly Man-like mouth set in a slender muzzle, the heavy, ridged spirals of its horns. It was for these moments that Fjel lived in the wild.

The ram descended.

Skragdal met it head-on; head to head, brow to brow. It made a clap like thunder breaking. The shock of it reverberated through the thick ledge of bone protecting his brow, through his whole body. His shoulders sang with echoing might. Digging his taloned feet into the loam, he reached out with both arms, filling his hands with lanolin-greasy wool.

They grappled, swaying.

And then the ram's legs trembled. Its amber-brown eyes were dazed. With another surge of strength, Skragdal roared and wrenched sideways, breaking its neck. He swiped at the ram's throat as he flung it to the ground. Red furrows gaped in the wake of his talons. The ram lay without moving, blood seeping slowly over the rocks without a beating heart to pump it.

Truly, Neheris had Shaped her Children well.

Skragdal grinned as the wild Kaldjager approached. "My thanks, brethren. That is how the Tungskulder hunt," he said to them. "What do the Kaldjager say?"

They eyed his kill with respect. "We say it is well done, Skragdal of Darkhaven," one of them said. "Our clan will feast well tonight; aye, and your lads, too. As for the rest?" He nodded to the east. "One comes. One of yours."

Skragdal straightened, feeling the tug of absent armor on his shoulders where the straps had worn his hide smooth and shiny. It was Blågen, coming at a trot, his arms and armor jangling, a half-empty waterskin sloshing at his belt. He was unaccompanied.

"Boss," Blågen said briefly, saluting as General Tanaros had taught them.

Everything that had gone away came crashing back. He was not free from the constraints of command. Skragdal sighed and pulled at the pointed lobe of one ear, willing the act to stimulate words, thoughts. "Where are they?"

"We lost their trail in Drybone Reach."

Skragdal stared at him. "How?"

Blågen shrugged, glancing sidelong at the dead ram. "It is a large area. They are Arahila's Children, cunning enough to hide and let us pass. Ulrig and Ruric have gone back to begin at the beginning. We will find them." He glanced then at the other Kaldjager and showed the tips of his eyetusks. "We could use the aid of our brethren if they are willing to undertake a different kind of hunt."

The wild Kaldjager exchanged slow smiles.

Skragdal considered them. "How many of you?"

"Twelve," one replied. He nodded at Blågen's waterskin. "If we had those. Twelve and your three would be enough to sweep the Reach. Your smallfolk could not hide." He pointed at the dead ram. "You see how we herd our prey."

Others from Skragdal's company began to arrive, straggling; Gulnagel, Nåltannen, the strapping young Tungskulder Thorun. Not taking part in the hunt, they had retained their arms, and their gear rattled and sloshed about them. Skragdal suppressed another sigh. He had hoped it would have ended sooner, more simply, but was not to be. He squinted at the sun, which seemed so *bright* after the Vale of Gorgantum. Although he misliked entrusting the task to Fjel he had not seen trained himself, too much time had passed to equivocate.

Anyway, old Mulprek was right. There were no better hunters than the Kaldjager. Although they were not as swift as the Gulnagel nor as strong as the Tungskulder, they were swifter and stronger than any of the other tribes. Kaldjager were strange and solitary for Fjel, living in roaming clans instead of proper dens, but they were unflagging in the chase, and utterly ruthless. Not even General Tanaros could improve upon their skills. If the Cold Hunters could not do it, it could not be done.

"All right, then." Stooping, Skragdal picked up the ram's corpse and slung it over his shoulder. Its head lolled, blood gathering to fall in slow drops from its gashed throat. It had seemed like a gift, this fine, clean kill, and now it was spoiled. Feeling obscurely cheated, he glared at the other Fjel. "Why is it so hard to kill these smallfolk?"

For a long moment, no one answered.

"Don't worry, boss." Blågen broke the silence with the fearless insouciance of the Cold Hunters. "We'll find them."

"You had better," Skragdal said grimly. "It is the only thing his Lordship has asked of us." He held Blågen's gaze until the Kaldjager blinked. "Back to the clan's gathering-place," he said. "We will share out our gear there."

"Then we hunt?"

"Yes." Skragdal grunted, shifting the ram's corpse on his shoulder. "And we go to Neherinach to lay a trap."

THEY WERE WAITING FOR HER in the great hall.

Sunlight blazed through the tall windows that surrounded it, glistening on the polished amber wood of the long table and the marble floor with its intricately laid pattern of white and a pale, veined blue. In the center of the table was a gilded coffer inlaid with gems. Between the windows, pennants hung from gilded poles. The clear windows were bordered with narrow panes of sea-blue glass, and the slanting sunlight threw bars of cerulean across the room.

It looked, Lilias thought, like a beautiful prison-chamber.

Ingolin the Wise presided at the head of the table, with Malthus the Counselor at his right hand and Aracus Altorus at his left. The others were Ellylon. Lorenlasse of Valmaré she knew; the others, she did not, although their faces were familiar. All of it was familiar. One of the Ellylon was a woman, with features so lovely at close range that Lilias could have wept.

Instead, under the combined weight of their regard, she froze in the doorway.

"Go on." Blaise prodded her from behind. He pointed to an empty chair on one side of the table, isolated from the rest. "Take your seat."

Lilias took a deep breath and entered the room, crossing through the bars of blue light. She drew out the chair and sat, glancing back at Blaise. He had positioned himself like a guard beside the tall doorway. High above him, on the pediment that capped the entrance, was the room's sole imperfection: a shattered marble relief that had once depicted the head of Meronin Fifth-Born, Lord of the Seas.

The memory evoked pain—the splintering pain she had endured when the sculpture had been demolished—but it evoked other memories, too. Lilias raised her chin a fraction, daring to face the assembly.

"Lilias of Beshtanag," Ingolin said. "You have been brought here before us that we might gain knowledge of one another."

"Am I on trial here, my lord?" she inquired.

"You are not." His voice was somber. "We seek the truth, yes. Not to punish, but only to know. Willing or no, you are a guest in Meronil and I have vouched for your well-being." He pointed at the ruined pediment. "You see here that which was once the work of Haergan the Craftsman. I think, perhaps, that it is not unfamiliar to you, Sorceress. Did you speak to us in this place using Haergan's creation, claiming that the Lady Cerelinde was in Beshtanag?"

"Yes." She threw out the truth. Let them make of it what they would. Around the table, glances were exchanged. Aracus Altorus gritted his teeth. She remembered how he had reacted when she had made Meronin's head speak words he despised, leaping onto the table, hurling an Ellylon standard like a javelin.

"How did you accomplish such a thing?" Ingolin frowned in thought. "It is Ellyl magic Haergan wrought, and not sympathetic to Men's workings. Even the Soumanië should not have been able to command matter at such a distance."

"No, my lord." Lilias shook her head. "I used Haergan's mirror."

"Ah." The Lord of the Rivenlost nodded. "It was in the dragon's hoard." Sorrow darkened his grey eyes. "We have always wondered at Haergan's end. It is a difficult gift to bear, the gift of genius. A dangerous gift."

"To be sure," Lilias said absently. Although she did not know the details of Haergan's end, Calandor's words echoed in her thoughts, accompanied by the memory of his slow, amused blink. *I might not have eaten him if he had been more ussseful.*

"Why?" It was the Ellyl woman who spoke, and the sound of her voice was like bells; bells, or silver horns, a sound to make mortal flesh shiver in delight, were it not infused with anger. She leaned forward, her lambent eyes aglow with passion. *"Why would you do such a thing?"*

Her words hung in the air. No one else spoke. Lilias glanced from face to face around the table. Plainly, it was a question all of them wanted answered; and as clearly, it was an answer none of them would understand.

"Why do you seek to fulfill Haomane's Prophecy?" she asked them. "Tell me that, and perhaps we may understand one another."

"Lilias." Malthus spoke her name gently. "These things are not the same, and well you know it. Urulat is Sundered from itself. We seek that which Haomane the Lord-of-Thought himself seeks—to heal the land, so restore it to the wholeness and glory to which it was Shaped, and which Satoris Banewreaker has perverted."

"Why?" Lilias repeated. They stared at her in disbelief, except for Malthus, who looked thoughtful. She folded her hands on the table and met their stares. "I ask in earnest, my lords, my lady. Was Urulat such a paradise before it was Sundered?"

"We had the light of the Souma!" Lorenlasse of Valmaré's voice was taut with fury, his bright eyes glittering. "We are Haomane's Children and we were torn from his side, from all that sustained us." He regarded her with profound contempt. "You cannot possibly know how that feels."

"Lorenlasse," Ingolin murmured.

Lilias laughed aloud. There was freedom in having nothing left to lose. She pointed at the lifeless Soumanië on Aracus' brow. "My lord Lorenlasse, until very recently, I held a piece of the Souma itself. I stretched the Chain of Being and held mortality at bay. I had power to Shape the very stuff of life, and I could have twisted your bones like jackstraws for addressing me in such a tone. Do not speak to me of what I can or cannot know."

"My lord Ingolin." The Ellyl woman turned to the Lord of the Rivenlost. The rigid lines of her body expressed her distaste. "It seems to me that there is naught to be gained in furthering this discussion."

"Hold, Lady Nerinil." Malthus lifted one hand, forestalling her. "There may yet be merit in it. Lilias." He fixed his gaze upon her. Seated among Ellylon, he looked old and weary. "Your questions are worthy ones," he said. "Let me answer one of them. Yes, Urulat *was* a paradise, once. In the First Age, before the world was Sundered, when the world was new-made and the Shapers dwelled among us." Malthus smiled, gladness transforming his face. "When Men had yet to discover envy and delighted in the skills of the Ellylon; when the Were hunted only with Oronin's blessing and the Fjeltroll heeded Neheris, and the Dwarfs tilled the land and coaxed forth Yrinna's bounty." On his breast, the clear Soumanië blazed into life. "That is the world the Lord-of-Thought shaped," he said quietly. "That is the world we seek to restore."

Lilias blinked, willing away an onslaught of tears. "It may be, Counselor. But that world was lost long before Urulat was Sundered."

"Through folly," Aracus said unexpectedly. "Men's folly; *our* folly. What Haomane wrought, we unmade through covetousness and greed."

"Men did not begin the Shapers' War," Lilias murmured.

"I am not so sure." Aracus shook his head. "It was Men who made war upon the Ellylon, believing they withheld the secret of immortality from us. If we had not done so, perhaps Haomane First-Born would not have been forced to ask the Sunderer to withdraw his Gift from us."

Ingolin laid a hand upon Aracus' arm. "Do not take so much upon yourself. The House of Altorus has never been an enemy to the Ellylon."

"Perhaps not," Aracus said. "But I would atone for the deeds of my race by working to see Haomane's Prophecy fulfilled. And then perhaps, in a world made whole, we might become what once we were."

A silence followed upon his words. Even Lorenlasse of the Valmaré was respectful in the face of Aracus' passion.

Malthus smiled at Lilias. White light flashed in the depths of his transfigured Soumanië, casting scintillating points of brightness around the room. "Is your question answered in full, Lilias of Beshtanag?"

"Yes, Counselor." Lilias rubbed at the familiar ache in her temples. "Your point is made. I understand the purpose of this meeting. You may now ask me once more to relinquish the Soumanië."

"I do not ask on my own behalf." Resonant power filled Malthus' voice, making her lift her head to meet his eyes. "I ask it on behalf of the Lady Cerelinde, who suffers even as we speak. I ask it on behalf of the Rivenlost, who endure the pain of separation, dwindling year by year. I ask it on behalf of those noble Men who would atone for the misdeeds of their race. I ask it on behalf of all Urulat, that this vision we share might come to pass. And I ask it, yes, on behalf of those poor souls who have fallen into folly, through the lies of Satoris Banewreaker, that they might know redemption. The Soumanië that Aracus Altorus bears was Shaped by Haomane himself, carried into battle by Ardrath the Wise Counselor, who was like unto a brother to me. Lilias of Beshtanag, will you release your claim upon it?"

"No." The word dropped like a stone from her lips. Despite the welling tears and the ache in her head, Lilias laughed. "It is a pleasant fiction, Counselor. But there is a problem with your story. You are Haomane's Weapon, Shaped after the world was Sundered. How can you claim knowledge of the First Age of Urulat?"

At the head of the table, Ingolin stirred. With a frown creasing his brow, the Lord of the Rivenlost bent his gaze on Malthus. "How do you answer, old friend?"

Something deep shifted in Malthus' eyes, and it was as if a veil had been withdrawn, revealing ancient and terrible depths. "I am as the Lord-of-Thought Shaped me," he said softly. "And I possess such knowledge as he willed. More than that, Sorceress, I cannot say, nor may I."

Lilias nodded. "Can you tell me, then, why Haomane refused when Satoris offered his Gift to Haomane's Children?"

"Because such a thing was not meant to be." Malthus shook his head, and the semblance of age and weariness returned to his mien. "Thus was the will of Uru-Alat, which only the Haomane First-Born, the Lord-of-Thought, sprung from the very brow of the world, grasps in its fullness."

"Except for dragons, of course. But perhaps it wasn't Haomane's will that you possess *that* knowledge." Lilias pushed back her chair and stood, gazing at their silent, watching faces. Her vision was blurred with the weak, foolish tears she couldn't seem to suppress. "You should have tried to woo me," she said to Aracus. "It might even have worked." Thick with tears, her voice shook. "I am a proud woman, and a vain one, and if you had begged me for the Soumanië

I might have relented. But although I am flawed, I have lived for a very long time, and I am *not* a fool." She dashed at her eyes with the back of one hand, a choking laugh catching in her throat. "I'm sorry, Counselor," she said to Malthus. "It must disappoint you to learn that your Soumanië has not illuminated my soul."

"Yes." There was no mockery in Malthus' tone, only abiding sorrow. He gazed at her with profound regret. "It does."

"Yes, well." Lilias took another shaking breath. "Perhaps I am protected by the claim I have not relinquished, or perhaps this place suffers from a surfeit of brightness already. Perhaps, after all, my soul is not so black as it has been painted." She stood very straight, addressing all of them. "I know who I am and what I have done. I have endured your compassion, your mercy, your righteous outrage. But you should not have brought me here to humiliate me with your *goodness.*"

"Such was not our intention, Sorceress," Ingolin murmured. "If that is your feeling—"

"No." She shook her head. "You claimed to want knowledge, Ingolin the Wise, but all you truly wanted was my repentance. And the Soumanië." Lilias smiled through her tears and spread her arms. "And yet, I cannot gainsay what I know. All things must be as they are. For the price of my life, the Soumanië is yours. Will you take it and be forsworn?"

The Lord of the Rivenlost exchanged glances with Aracus and Malthus. "No, Sorceress," he said with terrible gentleness. "We will not."

"Well, then." Lilias swallowed, tasting the bitter salt of her tears. "Then I will keep my claim upon it until I die of uselessness and shame." She turned to Blaise. "Will you take me back to my quarters, please?"

Blaise looked to Aracus, who gave a curt nod. Without a word, Blaise opened the door. She followed him through it.

Behind her, the silvery voices arose.

THE LADY CERELINDE SMILED AT him. "General Tanaros."

"Lady." He bowed in greeting, thinking as he straightened that perhaps it had been a mistake to come here. The impact of her presence was always greater than he remembered. "Are you ready?"

"I am."

Out of the courtly habit he had kept for over a thousand years, Tanaros extended his arm to her as he escorted her from her chamber. Cerelinde took it as she had done the night he brought her to the moon-garden, her slender, white fingertips resting on his forearm. He had forgone his armor, wearing only the black sword belted at his waist, and he could feel her touch through the velvet sleeve of his austere black doublet. Clear and distinct, each fingertip, as though she were setting her own brand upon him through some forgotten Ellyl magic; as powerful as Godslayer, yet more subtle.

What would it be like, that delicate touch against bare skin?

The thought came before he could quell it, and in its wake arose a wave of desire so strong it almost sickened him, coupled with a terrible yearning. It was a nameless emotion, its roots as old as mortality; covetous envy thwarted, manifesting in the desire to possess something so other, so *fine*.

"Are you all right?" There was concern in her voice.

"Yes." Standing in the hallway outside her door, Tanaros caught the eye of the leader of the Havenguard quartet he had assigned to accompany them. The sight of the Mørkhar Fjel looming in armor steadied him. He touched the *rhios* that hung in a pouch at his belt, feeling its smooth curves, and willing his racing pulse to ease. "Krognar," he said. "This is the Lady Cerelinde. Your lads are escorting us to the rookery."

"Lady," Krognar rumbled, inclining his massive head.

"Sir Krognar." She regarded him with polite, fascinated horror. Tanaros could feel the tremor that ran through her. "This way, Lady," he said.

The quartet of Mørkhar Fjel fell in behind them as he led her through the winding corridors of Darkhaven. The marble halls echoed with the heavy pad and scritch of their horny, taloned feet, accompanied by the faint jangle of arms.

"You needed no guard the night you brought me to see Lord Satoris' garden," Cerelinde said presently. Although her voice was level, her fingers clenching his forearm were tight with fear.

"The moon-garden lies within the confines of Darkhaven," Tanaros said. "The rookery does not. I am responsible for your security, Cerelinde."

She glanced briefly at him. Despite her fear, a faint smile touched her lips. "Do you fear I will use Ellyl magic to effect an escape?"

"Yes," he said honestly. "I do. I fear enchantments of the sort you invoked in Cuilos Tuillenrad. And I fear . . ." Tanaros took a deep breath. "I fear I do not trust myself to resist your beseechment, should you seek to beguile me. It is best that the Havenguard are here."

Color rose to her cheeks, and her reply was unwontedly sharp. "I did not *beseech* you to do this, Tanaros!"

"True." He disengaged his arm. "Shall we go back?"

Cerelinde hesitated, searching his face. "Is it truly *outside?*"

"Yes." He answered without hesitating, without pausing to consider the pleasure it gave him to answer her with the truth. "It is outside. Well and truly, Cerelinde."

She turned away, averting her gaze. Strands of her hair, as pale as corn silk, clung to his velvet-clad shoulder. "Then I would fain see it, my lord Blacksword," she murmured. "I would walk under the light of Haomane's sun."   .

Tanaros bowed. "Then so you shall."

They exited Darkhaven through the northern portal, with its vast doors that depicted the Council of the Six Tribes, in which the Fjeltroll Elders had voted to pledge their support to Lord Satoris; he to whom they had given shelter, he who had sought to teach the Fjel such Gifts as Haomane had withheld. Tanaros wished that Cerelinde had noticed the depiction and inquired about it. There was much he would have liked to discuss with her, including the quixotic nature of Haomane's Gift, the gift of *thought*, which only Arahila's Children shared.

But beyond the doors, there was daylight.

"Ah, *Haomane!*" Cerelinde breathed the word like a prayer. Relinquishing his arm, she ran on ahead with swift, light steps; into the daylight, into the open air. Although the sky was leaden and grey, she opened her arms to it, turning her face upward like a sunflower. And there, of a surety, was the sun. A pale disk, glimpsed through the clouds that hovered over the Vale of Gorgantum. "Tanaros!" she cried. "The *sun!*"

"Aye, Lady." He was unable to repress a smile. " 'Tis where you left it."

Her face was alight with pleasure. "Mock me if you must, Tanaros, but the light of the sun is the nearest thing to Haomane's presence, without which the Rivenlost fade and dwindle. Do not despise me for taking joy in it."

"Lady, I do not." It seemed to him, in that moment, he could never despise her. "Shall we proceed?"

He escorted her down the paths that led into beechwood. Although the wood lay within the vast, encircling wall that surrounded Darkhaven, the dense trees blotted out any glimpse of its borders. Were it not that the trees grew dark and twisted, their trunks wrenched around knotted boles, they might have been anywhere in Urulat.

Once they were beneath the wood's canopy, Tanaros gave way, allowing Cerelinde to precede him, wandering freely along the trail. The Mørkhar padded behind them, heavy treads crunching on the beech-mast. Autumn was approaching and the leaves were beginning to turn. Elsewhere, they would have taken on a golden hue. Here in Dark-haven, a splotch of deepest crimson blossomed in the center of the jagged spearhead of each leaf, shading to dark green on the outer edges.

Cerelinde touched them, her fingertips trailing over glossy leaves and rutted, gnarled bark. "There is such pain in the struggle," she wondered aloud. "Even their roots groan at their travail. And yet they adapt and endure. These are ancient trees." She glanced at him. "What has done this to them, Tanaros? Is it that Lord Satoris has stricken them in his wrath?"

"No, Lady." He shook his head. "It is his blood that alters the land in the Vale of Gorgantum, that which flows from his unhealing wound. For thousands upon thousands of years, it has seeped into the earth."

"A Shaper's blood," she murmured.

"Yes." He watched her, his heart aching. In the muted, blood-shot light beneath the beech canopy, the Lady of the Ellylon shone like a gem. How finely they were wrought, Haomane's Children! No wonder that Haomane loved them so dearly, having taken such care with their Shaping. "Come, it is this way."

She paused for a moment as they entered the rookery, where a hundred ragged nests adorned the crooked trees, absorbing the sight in silence. The wood was alive with ravens, bustling busily about their messy abodes, sidling along branches and peering at the visitors with bright, wary eyes. When she saw the small glade and the table await-ing them, Cerelinde turned to him. "You did this?"

"Aye." Tanaros smiled. "Will you join me in a glass of wine, Lady?"

Another faint blush warmed her cheeks. "I will."

The table was laid with dazzling white linens and set with a simple wine service; a clay jug and two elegantly turned goblets. It was Dwarfish work, marked by the simple grace that characterized their labors. How it had made its way to Darkhaven, Tanaros did not know. Beneath the glowering light of the Vale, table and service glowed alike, filled with their own intrinsic beauty. And beside the table, proud and upright in plain black livery, stood Speros, who had undertaken the arrangements on his General's behalf.

"Speros of Haimhault," Tanaros said. "This is the Lady Cerelinde."

"Lady." Speros breathed the word, bowing low. His eyes, when he arose, were filled with tears. In the desert, he had expressed a desire to behold her. It was a wish granted, this moment; a wish that made the heart ache for the beauty, the *fineness*, that Arahila's Children would never possess. "May I pour you a glass of wine?"

"As you please." Cerelinde smiled at him, taking her seat. The Mørkhar Fjel dispatched themselves to the four quarters of the glade, planting their taloned feet and taking up patient, watchful stances. "Thank you, Speros of Haimhault."

"You are welcome." His hand trembled as he poured, filling her cup with red Vedasian wine. The lip of the wine-jug rattled against her goblet. With a visible effort, he moved to fill his General's. "Most welcome, Lady."

Tanaros sat opposite Cerelinde and beheld that which made the Midlander tremble. He pitied the lad, for a wish granted was a dangerous thing; and yet, Ah, Shapers, the glory of her! It was a light, a light that shone from within—it was Haomane's love, shining like a kiss upon her brow. It was present in every part of her; bred into the very fineness of her bones, the soaring architecture of the flesh. All at once, it enhanced and shamed its surroundings.

And she was pleased.

In all his prolonged years, he had never seen such a thing. One of the Ellyl; pleased. Her heart gladdened by what Tanaros had done. It was reflected in the gentle curve of her lips. It was reflected in her eyes, in the limitless depths of her pupils, in the pleated luminosity of her irises, those subtle colors like a rainbow after rain. And although her mood had not yet passed, it would. The thought filled him with a prescient nostalgia. Already he longed to see it once more; yearned to be, in word and deed, a Man as would gladden the heart of the Lady of the Ellylon and coax forth this brightness within her. Who would not wish to be such a Man?

"Cerelinde." He hoisted his goblet to her.

"Tanaros." Her smile deepened. "Thank you."

"*Kaugh!*"

Tanaros startled at the sound, then laughed. He extended an arm. In a flurry of black wings, Fetch launched himself from a nearby branch, alighting on Tanaros' forearm. "This," he said fondly, "is who I wanted you to meet." He glanced at Speros, feeling an obscure guilt. "Or *what*, I should say."

The Lady of the Ellylon and the bedraggled raven regarded one another.

"His name is Fetch," Tanaros said. "He was a late-born fledgling. Six years ago, I found him in his Lordship's moon-garden, half-frozen, and took him into my quarters." He stroked the raven's iridescent black feathers. "He made a fearful mess of them," he added with a smile. "But he saved my life in the Unknown Desert; mine, and Speros', too. We are at quits now."

"Greetings, Fetch," Cerelinde said gravely. "Well met."

Deep in his throat, the raven gave an uneasy chuckle. He sidled away from her, his sharp claws pricking at Tanaros' velvet sleeve.

"My apologies." Tanaros cleared his throat in embarrassment as Fetch scrambled to his shoulder, clinging to the collar of his doublet and ducking beneath his hair to peer out at Cerelinde. "It seems he is shy of you, Lady."

"He has reason." Her voice was soft and musical. "My folk have slain his kind for serving as the Sunderer's eyes, and the eagles of Meronil drive them from our towers. But it is also true that the Riven-lost do not begrudge any of the small races their enmity." Cerelinde smiled at the raven. "They do not know what they do. One day, perhaps, there will be peace. We hope for it."

Shifting from foot to foot, Fetch bobbed his tufted head. His sharp beak nudged its way through the dark strands of Tanaros' hair, and his anxious thoughts nudged at Tanaros' mind. Opening himself to them, Tanaros *saw* through doubled eyes a familiar, unsettling sensation. What he saw made him blink.

Cerelinde ablaze.

She burned like a signal fire in the raven's gaze, an Ellyl-shaped woman's form, white-hot and searing. There was beauty, oh, yes! A terrible beauty, one that filled Fetch's rustling thoughts with fear. Her figure divided the blackness like a sword. And beyond and behind it, there was a vast emptiness. The space between the stars, endless black and achingly cold. In it, as if through a crack in the world, stars fell; fell and fell and fell, trailing gouts of white-blue fire, beautiful and unending.

Somewhere, there was the roar of a dragon's laughter.

Tanaros blinked again to clear his vision. There was a sudden pressure upon his shoulder as Fetch launched himself, soaring with outspread wings to a nearby branch. The raven chittered, his beak parted. All around the rookery, his calls were uneasily echoed until the glade was alive with uneasy sound.

"Perhaps I am unwelcome here," Cerelinde said softly.

"No." At a loss for words, Tanaros quaffed his wine and held out his goblet for Speros to refill. He shook his head, willing the action to dispel the lingering images. "No, Lady. You are a guest here. As you say, they are fearful. Something happened to Fetch in the desert." He furrowed his brow in thought, pondering the strange visions that flitted through the raven's thought, the recurrent image of a *dragon*. Not just any dragon, but one truly ancient of days. "Or before, perhaps. Something I do not understand."

"It seems to me," said the Lady of the Ellylon, "many things happened in the desert, Tanaros." She gazed at him with the same steady kindness she had shown the raven, the same unrelenting pity with which she had beheld the madlings of Darkhaven. "Do you wish to speak of them?"

Speros, holding the wine-jug at the ready, coughed and turned away.

"No." Resting his elbows on the dazzling white linen of the tablecloth, Tanaros fiddled with the stem of his goblet. He studied the backs of his hands; the scarred knuckles. It had been a long, long time since he had known a woman's compassion. It would have been a relief to speak of it; a relief so deep he felt the promise of it in his bones. And yet; she was the Lady of the Ellylon, Haomane's Child. How could he explain it to her? Lord Satoris' command, his own reluctance to obey it. Strength born of the Water of Life still coursing in his veins, the quietude of Stone Grove and Ngurra's old head lifting, following the rising arc of his black blade. His refusal to relent, to give a reason, any reason. Only a single word: *Choose.* The blade's fall, a welter of gore, and the anguished cry of the old Yarru's wife. The blunt crunch of the Fjel maces that followed. These things, she would not understand. There was no place for them here, in this moment of civilized discourse. "No," he said again more firmly. "Lady, I do not."

"As you please." Cerelinde bowed her head for a moment, her features curtained by her pale, shining hair. When she lifted her head, a nameless emotion darkened her clear eyes. "Tanaros," she said. "Why did you bring me here?"

All around the rookery, ravens settled, cocking their heads.

"It is a small kindness, Lady, nothing more." Tanaros glanced around, taking in the myriad bright eyes. There was Fetch, still as a stone, watching him. A strange grief thickened his words. "Do you think me incapable of such deeds?"

"No." Sorrow, and something else, shaded her tone. "I think you are like these trees, Tanaros. As deep-rooted life endures in them, so does goodness endure in you, warped and blighted by darkness. And such a thing grieves me, for it need not be. Ah, Tanaros!" The brightness returned to her eyes. "There is forgiveness and Arahila's mercy awaiting you, did only you reach out your hand. For you, and this young Man; yes, even for the ravens themselves. For all the innocent and misguided who dwell beneath the Sunderer's shadow. Is it asking so much?"

He drew breath to answer, and the rookery burst into a flurry of black wings as all the ravens of Darkhaven took flight at once, a circling stormcloud. Without thinking, Tanaros found himself on his feet, the black sword naked in his fist. The Mørkhar Fjel came at a thundering run, bristling with weapons. Speros, unarmed, swore and smashed the Dwarfish wine-jug on the edge of the table, shattering its graceful form to improvise a jagged weapon. Red wine bled in a widening stain on the white linen.

"Greetings, cousin." Ushahin stood at the edge of the glade; a hunched form, small and composed. Above him, the ravens circled in a tightening gyre, answering to him as if to one of the Were. His uneven gaze shifted to Cerelinde. "Lady."

"Dreamspinner." Her voice was cool. She had risen, standing straight as a spear.

"Stand down." Tanaros nodded to Speros and the Fjel and shoved his sword back into its sheath. His hand stung and his chest felt oddly tight, as though the brand over his heart were a steel band constricting it. "What do you want, Dreamspinner?"

"I come on his Lordship's orders. 'Tis time to send the ravens afield again." Ushahin gave his tight, crooked smile. In Cerelinde's presence, he looked more malformed than ever. Here was the beauty of the El-lylon rendered into its component parts and poorly rebuilt, cobbled together by unskilled hands. "But there is a matter of which I would speak to you, cousin. One that concerns the safety of Darkhaven." He paused, and in the silence, Fetch descended, settling on his shoulder. "A matter of corruption."

He said no more, waiting.

Tanaros inclined his head. A moment had passed; an axis had tipped. Something had changed, something was lost. Something bright had slipped away from him, and something else had settled into place. Its roots were deep and strong. There was a surety, a knowledge of self, and the course he had chosen. Beneath its brand, his aching heart beat, each beat reminding him that he owed his existence to Lord Satoris.

A vast and abiding love.

He touched the pouch at his belt, feeling the contours of Hyrgolf's *rhios* through it, letting himself be humbled by the awesome loyalty of the Fjel. The Fjel, to whom it seemed Arahila's forgiveness did not extend. On the far side of the glade, Ushahin's eyes glittered as if he knew Tanaros' thoughts.

Perhaps he did.

"Permit me to escort the Lady Cerelinde to her quarters," Tanaros said to the half-breed. "Then I am at your disposal." Turning to Cerelinde, he extended his arm. "Lady?"

Cerelinde took his arm. "Thank you," she whispered, "for this glimpse of sun."

"For that, Lady, you are welcome." Tanaros heard the unsteadiness in his voice and despised it. He crooked his arm, capturing her fair, white fingers against his torso and made his voice harsh. "Now, come with me."

She went, making no protest.

Behind them came the padding footfalls of the Havenguard, crunching upon the beech-mast. And all the way, Tanaros felt the combined gaze of Ushahin and the ravens of Darkhaven upon him. On his arm, Cerelinde's touch burned; on the outer edges of his sight, Fetch's vision burned, a raven's fitful thoughts, backed by a dragon's roar, and the gleam in Ushahin's mismatched eyes.

Somewhere between the two, lay his path.

So be it, Tanaros thought, conscious of the steady throb of his beating heart, and all that he owed, every breath drawn, to Lord Satoris.

A matter of corruption?

No. Never.

SIX

FROM HIS PERCH HIGH ATOP a pine tree, Dani saw the Fjel.

It was the fourth time that day he had clambered up the tree, using it as a vantage point to survey the barren reach. Each time, he whispered a prayer to Uru-Alat, praying to find the landscape empty as it had been the day before, and the day before it.

On the third day, his luck ran out.

Although it was hard to tell from so far away, they appeared to be the same kind he had seen before—lean and predatory, with smooth, grey hides that were blended into the rocky terrain. If he hadn't been keen-sighted, he might have missed them. But, no, there it was again—a steely flash in the distance, the northern sunlight glinting on armor plate. Clinging to the pine's trunk with his good right arm, he stared intently at the direction of the Fjel. There were more of them this time, though only one wore armor. Save for the waterskins strapped over their torsos, the rest were unadorned.

They were traveling in a pack and they were traveling swiftly. For a moment, Dani watched, mesmerized by their steady, tireless lope. Even at a distance, an awful grace was in it.

Then fear returned in a rush, the sour taste of it in his mouth. Using both feet and the one hand, Dani descended the pine tree in awkward haste, heedless of the prickling needles and rough bark, and hurried into the hidden cave.

"Fjeltroll?" Uncle Thulu's voice was faint and thready.

"Aye." He met his uncle's feverish gaze. "A dozen at least."

"Did they see you?"

"No." Dani shook his head. "They're pretty far south of us and moving fast, all in a pack. It doesn't even look like they're hunting. I think they'll miss us," he added hopefully. "Maybe they're not even looking."

"No." Uncle Thulu coughed weakly and wheezed, one hand scrabbling at his chest. In the dim light, his shirt was stained dark with seeping fluids. Despite Dani's best efforts to clean and tend them, his wounds continued to fester. Yesterday, they had begun to slough dead flesh and the small space stank of it. "Help me sit."

With alacrity, Dani eased him into a sitting position, propped against the cavern wall. "Better?"

"Aye," Uncle Thulu whispered, licking his dry, cracked lips.

"Here." Moving deftly and quietly, Dani made his way to the mouth of the cave. There, in a shallow depression to one side, was a cache of moss he had gathered. It had sustained them during the past three days. Grasping a smooth stone, he ground the spongy moss into a damp paste. Scooping up a handful, he returned to squat beside his uncle. With gentle care, he spread the paste on the elder Yarru's parched lips. "Try to eat."

Uncle Thulu's mouth worked with difficulty, his sluggish tongue taking in the moss paste. Blinking back tears, Dani spread another fingerful on his lips. There was moisture in it, not much, but enough to live on. It was the only thing he had been able to find within half a day's journey of their hiding place. And if he had not seen a single lost elk grazing on it, he might never have thought to try the moss. It was all that had kept his uncle alive.

And barely, at that.

"Enough." Uncle Thulu grasped Dani's wrist with urgent strength and drew in a deep, rattling breath. "Dani, listen to me."

"Yes, Uncle." His chest ached with fear and love.

"They're starting over. That's why they're moving in a hurry. They're going back to pick up our trail from the beginning. And if they've added to their numbers, they're not going to miss us this time." Thulu's eyes were overbright in his wasted face. "Dani, you have to go. *Now.*"

"I won't." He refused to hear what Thulu was saying. "Not without you."

His uncle said it anyway. "I'm dying, Dani."

"What if we went back?" The thought struck him like an offer of salvation. "We could wait for them to pass, then head south! They wouldn't hunt for us once we passed out of Fjel territory, and the Staccians . . . well, they're just Men, we can hide from Men, Uncle! And get you home, where—"

"Dani." Uncle Thulu's grip tightened on his wrist. "I'm not going anywhere," he said gently. "Do you understand? This is where the journey ends for me. I'm sorry, lad. You've got to go on without me."

"No!" Pulling away, Dani clutched the clay vial around his neck. "For what?" he asked angrily. "For *this*? It's not worth it! It's not *fair*, uncle!" He yanked at the vial with all his strength. For a moment, the braided cord on which it was strung burned the skin of his neck; then it parted with a faint snap. Dani held the vial in one hand. Hot tears burned his eyes, and his voice trembled. "I didn't *ask* to be the Bearer! What's Satoris ever done to the Yarru-yami, anyway, that we should seek to destroy him? It's not *his* fault Haomane's Wrath scorched the desert, he was just trying to *hide* from it! And if he hadn't . . . if he hadn't, we wouldn't have found the Water of Life! We wouldn't be the keepers of Birru-Uru-Alat. We wouldn't even be what we *are*!"

The ghost of a smile moved Thulu's cracked lips. "These are fitting questions for the Bearer to ask," he whispered. "But you will have to answer them alone."

Dani unclenched his hand, staring at the vial. It lay on the starry, radiating lines of his grimy palm; a simple object, fragile and crude. Clay, gathered from a scant deposit at one of the Stone Grove's water-holes, fired with baari-wood and dung in a pit dug into the desert's floor.

Inside it was the Water of Life, water he had drawn from the Well of the World and dipped from the bucket, holding it in his cupped palms as old Ngurra had told him to do, filling the vial with care. The lifeblood of Uru-Alat, the World God; the secret the Yarru-yami held in trust. A gift only the Bearer could draw; a burden only the Bearer could carry. A choice in the making.

In the apple orchards of Malumdoorn, while the sun slanted through the trees and the Dwarfs stood watching, a single drop had caused a dead stick to burst into green life; planting roots, sprouting leaves and blossoms.

A dawning certainty grew in him. For the first time, Dani saw

clearly the divided path before him and understood that the choice between them was his, and his alone, to make. Not for the sake of
Malthus, whose impassioned words had swayed him; not for the sake
of Carfax, who had given his life to save him. Not even for his uncle,
who would gainsay it. The choice was his, and his alone. This, and not
the Water itself, was the Bearer's true burden.

Dani lifted his head. "No, Uncle. Not just yet."

"Ah, lad!" There was alarm in Thulu's weak voice. "The Water of
Life is too precious to waste—"

"Am I the Bearer?" Dani interrupted him. "You keep telling me it is
my right to choose, Uncle, and yet you give me no guidance, no hint
as to which choice is *right*. Well, I am choosing." With one thumbnail,
he pried at the tight cork, working it loose. The faint scent of water,
life giving and mineral-rich, trickled into the small cavern. With his
heart hammering in hope and fear, Dani bent over his uncle and
smoothed his brow, putting the vial close to his lips. "I choose for you
to live."

Uncle Thulu exhaled one last, long, rattling breath and closed his
eyes in surrender. "May it be as Uru-Alat wills," he whispered.

At close range, the stench of his suppurating wounds vied for dom-
inance with the odor of water. Dani ignored it, concentrating on tilting
the flask. Under his breath, he chanted the Song of Being, the story of
Uru-Alat and how the World God died to give birth to the world. It
was an act of prayer; a Yarru prayer, the oldest prayer, a story learned
and told in the deep places of the earth, where the veins of life pulsed
and the Yarru had hidden from Haomane's Wrath. It was an old story;
older than the Shapers. It was as old as dragons, who were born in the
deep places from the bones of Uru-Alat and carried a spark of
marrow-fire in their bellies.

A single drop gathered on the clay lip of the vessel. It gathered and
swelled; rounding, bottom-heavy. It shone like a translucent pearl,
glimmering in the shadowy cavern, reflecting all the light in the world.

Beneath it were his uncle's parted lips. Dark flesh, fissured and
cracked, smeared with moss-paste. The tip of his tongue, a pink sup-
plicant lying quiescent on the floor of his thirsting mouth.

Dani tilted the vial.

One drop; two, three!

They fell like stars through the dark air into the mortal void of

Uncle Thulu's waiting mouth. And, oh, Uru-Alat! A sweet odor burst forth as they fell, redoubled in strength; a scent like a chime, like the sharp clap of a pair of hands.

It happened almost too quickly for sight to follow. Uncle Thulu's eyes sprang open, wide and amazed. His chest heaved as he drew in a great, whooping gasp of air. Dani cried aloud in astonishment, scrambling backward and nearly spilling the Water of Life. He shoved the cork into the clay flask, then shoved his knuckles into his mouth, fearful that his outcry would draw the Fjeltroll.

"Ah, Dani, lad!" Uncle Thulu sat upright. The brightness in his eyes owed nothing to fever—it was the brightness of sunlight on clear waters, a promise of life and health. "If this is folly, what a glorious folly it is!" He grinned, showing strong white teeth, and yanked his shirt aside to expose his chest. "Tell me what you see!"

Beneath the foul-crusted wool, Thulu's skin was smooth and dark, gleaming with health. In the dim light, Dani could barely make out three faint lines, pale threads like long-healed scars. He sighed with relief. "They're well and truly healed, aren't they?"

"More than healed!" His uncle's voice reverberated joyously from the cavern walls. "Ah, lad! I've never felt better in my life! Why, I could—"

"Shhh!" Dani laid one hand over Thulu's lips. "The Fjeltroll."

"Right." His uncle nodded. "Aye, of course."

"I'll go look." Without waiting for Thulu to argue, Dani turned to wriggle out of the cavern's narrow opening. With the vial in one hand and the dirty sling still tied around his left arm, it was awkward going. He inched beneath the concealing pine branches and into the open, crawling on his belly until he had a clear view.

There, to the southeast, a moving smudge on the landscape; a dull glint of steel. He didn't even need to climb the tree to spot them. The Fjel had already passed them. They were moving fast . . . and they would be returning fast, too.

"Have they gone?"

Dani winced at the sound of his uncle's voice. Glancing over his shoulder, he saw Thulu standing in front of the cave. "Aye, barely. Uncle, get down, *please*!"

"Sorry, lad." Thulu drew a shuddering breath and dropped to a squat. In the open light of day, he looked even more hale—unnervingly hale. The muscles in his sturdy thighs bunched and twitched with vigor. "It's just . . . I don't know if I can explain, but it's like a fire in my veins, Dani. I can't hold still." He rubbed his face with both hands. "Just as well, isn't it? We've no time to waste."

"You'll have to sit for a minute." Dani sat in a hunched pose and concentrated on splicing the broken thukka-vine thong on which the vial was strung, braiding the strong fibers. "We're not going anywhere until those Fjeltroll are long out of sight."

"And where shall we go when we do, Bearer?" Despite it all, Uncle Thulu put the question to him gently, remembering the words Dani had spoken in fear and anger. "It seems, against the odds, that I am still here to guide you. Where is it you would go?"

Dani bowed his head, his coarse black hair hiding his expression. "Darkhaven," he murmured. "We go to Darkhaven, Uncle."

"You're sure?"

"Aye." He stroked the pit-fired clay vessel with one fingertip. "I made a choice, Uncle. I'm responsible for it now. And if there are questions the Bearer should ask . . ." He shrugged. "Perhaps I should ask them in Darkhaven."

Uncle Thulu watched him. "It is Darkhaven's agents who seek your life."

"I know." Dani tested the spliced thong's strength and gauged that it would hold. Raising his good arm, he slipped the vial around his neck, feeling it nestle into place against his chest. "I have given them reason."

"You know, lad." Uncle Thulu nodded at Dani's left arm, bound in its sling. "I know what I said before. But we've a long way to go, and Fjeltroll to outrun. Whatever questions you might ask, it's not going to alter their orders; not here and now. A single drop from that flask—"

"No." Dani shook his head. Fear had passed from him; in its wake, he felt tired and resigned. "You were right, Uncle. It *is* too precious to waste. And how terrible might we become if the Bearer chose to use it thusly? No," he said again. "It was my choice to use it to save your life. It is enough." He glanced behind him, surveying the horizon. There was no glint of sunlight on steel; the moving smudge had gone. "Shall we go?"

"Aye, lad." Uncle Thulu sprang to his feet, then paused. He fumbled at his chest with blunt fingertips, finding no wound, but only the pale ridges of long-healed scars. An expression of perplexity crossed his broad face. "What was I saying? It was a folly of some sort, I fear. Something has changed here, Dani, has it not? I should be dead, and yet I live. And you, you . . ."

"I am the Bearer," Dani finished softly. For the first time, he had a glimmering of what the words meant, and it made him feel very, very alone. With an effort, he used his good arm as a lever, clambering upright. Once standing, he touched the clay vial at his throat, aware of his burden. "Will you be my guide, Uncle?"

"I will," said his uncle. And he bowed, low. "Aye, lad, I will."

THE WALL WAS LIKE A dragon's spine, coiled and sinuous. It stretched for league upon league around Darkhaven, clinging with determination to every sinking valley and rising ridge in the Vale that surrounded Lord Satoris' fortress.

It was taller than the height of three men, and broad enough for four horsemen to ride astride atop it; or four Fjel to run at a trot. Within its confines lay all that Darkhaven encompassed. There, to the north, were the mines where the Fjeltroll labored, digging iron from the earth. There, closer, were the furnaces where it was smelted, the forges where it was beaten into steel. The Gorgantus River made its sluggish way beneath a pall of grey-black smoke, tapped by the cunning of Speros of Haimhault, who had built a waterwheel and made it serve Darkhaven's purposes.

There was the training-field, the expanse of beaten ground where Tanaros drilled his army, day upon day. And there, southward, were the pastures where Staccian sheep grazed on dark, wiry grass, fattening to fill Fjel bellies, drinking tainted water from the Gorgantus River and thriving upon it. From their blood the foul-smelling *svartblod*, dearly loved by the Fjel, was fermented.

And there, far to the west—a gleam in the distance—was the shoreline of the Sundering Sea, where Dergail the Counselor had met his death at the hands of the Were. Beyond it, somewhere in the shining sea-swell of the distance, lay Torath, the Crown of Urulat, home of the Souma, where the Six Shapers dwelled and Haomane First-Born ruled over them.

It was all visible from the wall, interrupted at regular intervals by the watchtowers, manned by the faithful Havenguard, who kept a watch over the whole of Lord Satoris' empire.

On an empty stretch of wall between towers stood Tanaros Blacksword, who was gazing at none of it. A brisk breeze whipped at his dark hair, lashing it against his cheeks. He was one of the Three, and he was dangerous. Lest it be forgotten, one hand hovered over the hilt of his black sword.

"Tell me," he said to his companion, "of this *corruption*."

His look and his tone would have intimidated any sane comrade. Ushahin Dreamspinner sighed and hugged himself instead, warding off the autumn chill. His thin arms wrapped about his torso, his sharp elbows protruded. Cold seemed to bite deeper since his time in the Delta. It had not been his choice to meet on the wall. "Tell me," he said to Tanaros, "what you know of Darkhaven's construction."

"What is there to know?" Tanaros frowned. "Lord Satoris caused it to be created. After the Battle of Curonan, he retreated to the Vale of Gorgantum and raised up these mountains, using Godslayer's might. And he conceived of Darkhaven, and the Fjel delved deep into the earth and built high into the sky, building it in accordance with his plan. So it was done, and we Three were summoned to it."

"Yes." Ushahin extended one crooked hand and waggled it in a gesture of ambivalence. "And no. Darkhaven was not built by Fjel labor alone, and it is made of more than stone and mortar. It is an extension of its Shaper's will. It exists here because it exists in his Lordship's mind. Do you understand?"

"No," Tanaros said bluntly. "Do you say it is illusion?" He rapped his knuckles on the solid stone ramparts. "It seems solid enough to me, Dreamspinner."

Ushahin shook his head. "Not illusion, no."

"What, then?" Tanaros raised his brows. "Is it Fjel craftsmanship you question, cousin? I tell you, I am no mason, but I would not hesitate to pit their labors against the craftsmanship of Men; aye, or Ellylon, either."

"Then why is it that in two thousand years the Fjel have never built anything else?" Ushahin asked him.

Tanaros opened his mouth to reply, then closed it, considering. "Why would they?" he asked at length. "The Fjel are delvers by nature, not builders. They built Darkhaven for *him*, for his Lordship, according to his design. I say they made a fine job of it, cousin. What is it that you say?"

Ushahin shrugged. "You are too much of one thing, Tanaros, and not enough of another. It is not a matter of questioning the Fjel, but a matter of what causes Darkhaven to *be*. There are places that exist between things; between waking and sleep, between being and not-being. Darkhaven is such a place."

"Perhaps. And perhaps you spend too much time among your madlings, cousin." Tanaros eyed him. "What has this do with corruption?"

"Come," said Ushahin. "I will show you."

He walked with Tanaros along the wall, past the watchtowers where the Fjel saluted them, descending the curving stair at the inner gates of the keep. By the time they reached the entryway, Ushahin's bones ached fiercely with the cold. It was a relief to enter Darkhaven proper, to hear the bronze-bound doors close with a thud and the bar drop into place, the clank and rattle of the Havenguard resuming their posts. The black marble walls shut out every breath of wind, and the flickering blue-white veins of marrow-fire warmed the halls and lit them with an eldritch gleam that was gentle to his light-sensitive gaze.

"This way." Ushahin led Tanaros toward the section of the fortress in which his own austere quarters were housed. Madlings skittered from their approach. Although their fealty was unquestioned, he seldom brought anyone this way and it made them wary—even of the Lord General.

"If you wanted to meet in your quarters—" Tanaros began.

"Here." Ushahin halted in front of a niche. The arch that framed it rose almost to the vast ceiling above. On the back wall of the niche was a sculpture depicting the Wounding of Satoris, standing out in high relief, the outer limbs reaching across the arch into open air to engage one another.

Two figures were in opposition, tall enough to dwarf even a Fjel onlooker; Oronin Last-Born, the Glad Hunter, and Lord Satoris, Third-Born among Shapers. They grappled like giants, both figures shimmering with a fine network of marrow-fire. Satoris' hands were raised to parry a blow, one catching Oronin's left wrist; Oronin's right leg was extended, indicating how he had slipped as he lunged, planting the Shard of the Souma in Satoris' thigh with his right hand. Where

Godslayer's haft stood out from his Lordship's marble flesh, a node of marrow-fire shone, brighter than the rest, and a bright vein trickled down his thigh.

"Forgive me, Dreamspinner," Tanaros said. "It is a mighty piece of work, but I don't understand—"

"Look closely." Ushahin waited patiently as Tanaros examined the niche. It was not easy to spot the opening, a low, narrow doorway hidden in the recesses and rendered almost invisible by the deep shadow cast by the bright figures.

"Ah." Tanaros saw it at last. "One of your madlings' passageways?"

"Yes."

"What would you have me say?" Tanaros shrugged. "I would that there were none, cousin, but they do no harm as long as they are confined within the inner walls. Indeed, forbid it be so, but were Darkhaven ever to face invasion, they might serve a purpose. Did not Lord Satoris himself cede you such rights?"

"Yes," said Ushahin. "To the spaces in between, where creatures such as I belong. But Tanaros, who built the passageways?" Watching the other's expression, he shook his head. "They were not here when I was first summoned, cousin. My madlings did not build them; others, yes, but not one such as this, built into the very structure of the wall. It would require inhuman strength."

"The Fjel . . ."

Ushahin pointed at the narrow gap, accessible only between the braced legs of the two Shapers' figures. "What Fjeltroll could fit in that space? I have asked and the Fjel have no knowledge of it, not in any generation. It was not there, and then it was. Darkhaven *changes*, Tanaros; its design shifts as his Lordship's thoughts change. This is what I seek to tell you."

"Ah, well." Tanaros gazed at the sculpted face of Lord Satoris. The Shaper's expression was one of agony, both at Godslayer's plunge and the greater loss. Oronin's blow had dealt him his unhealing wound, that which had stolen his Gift. "He is a Shaper, cousin. Is it such a surprise?"

"No, Blacksword. Not *this*. I've known about *this* for centuries." Ushahin shook his head in disgust. Ducking beneath Oronin's outstretched arm, he opened the hidden door onto the passageways between the walls. "Come with me."

Once behind the walls, he led with greater confidence, following a
winding path with a shallow downward slope. The air grew closer and
hotter the farther they went, then leveled once more. Tanaros followed without comment, his footsteps crunching on rubble. When
they reached the rough-hewn chamber the madlings had claimed
for their own, Tanaros paused. The madlings had not gathered here
since the day Vorax had found them with the Lady of the Ellylon, and
his Staccians had cleared much of the debris, but the evidence of their
presence remained—scratched gibberish on the walls, overlooked
candle-butts wedged into crevices.

Tanaros sighed. "Will you tell me this is his Lordship's doing? I have
spoken with Vorax, cousin; and I have spoken with Cerelinde, too. I
know what happened here."

"Oh, I know you've spoken with *Cerelinde*, cousin." A dark tone
edged Ushahin's voice. "No, it's not this. Further."

They squeezed through a narrow portion of the passage. A few
paces beyond it, the level path dropped into a sharp decline. Ushahin
led them onward, down and down, until a blue-white glow was visible ahead, as bright and concentrated as the sculpted node of Godslayer's dagger.

"Do you see it?" he asked.

"Aye." Tanaros' jaw was set and hard. "It is no more than Vorax
told me."

A roaring sound was in the air, and an acrid odor, like the breath of
dragons. Ushahin grinned, his mismatched eyes glittering with reflected
marrow-light. "Come see it, then."

They descended the remainder of the way with Ushahin leading,
sure-footed on the pathways that were his own, his aching joints at ease
in the hot, stifling air. There, all the way to the bottom of the decline.

A new chasm had erupted.

There was the old one, patched over by Vorax's Staccians. They
had made a fair job of it for mortal Men. The old path was clearly visible, scuffed with gouges where a slab of stone had been dragged with
great effort, capping the breach. It was braced by beams that had been
soaked in water, already faintly charred by the heat of the marrow-fire,
but holding. Rocks and rubble had filled the gaps.

And there, to the left of it—a gaping wound, emitting a violent, erratic light. Above it, a vaulted hollow soared. At the bottom, far, far below, the Source of the marrow-fire blazed and roared like a furnace. Heedless of danger, Tanaros stood at the edge and looked downward.

The sides of the sheer drop beneath his feet were jagged and raw. The marrow-fire was so bright it seared his eyes. He gazed upward, where his shadow was cast large and stark, flickering upon the hollow chamber of the ceiling. It, too, appeared new, as though hunks of rock had been sheared away.

Tanaros frowned. "There is some fault in the foundation that causes this. Small wonder, cousin, when it is built upon *this*." He turned to Ushahin. "Have you spoken of it to his Lordship?"

"Yes," Ushahin said simply.

"And?"

In the stifling heat, Ushahin wrapped his arms around himself as if to ward off a chill. His voice, when he answered, held an unwonted note of fear. "His Lordship says the foundation is sound."

Tanaros returned his gaze to the fiery, seething depths of the chasm. For a long moment, he was silent. When he spoke, it was without turning. "I will ask again, Dreamspinner. What does this have to do with *corruption*?"

"There is a canker of brightness at the core of this place," Ushahin said quietly. "Even as it festers in the thoughts of my madlings, even as it festers in your very heart, cousin, it festers in his Lordship's soul, gnawing at his pride, driving him to stubborn folly. There is no fault in the structure, Blacksword. Lord Satoris *is* the foundation of Darkhaven. How plainly would you have me speak?"

"You speak treason," Tanaros murmured.

"He caused rain to fall like acid."

The words, filled with unspoken meaning, lay between them. Tanaros turned around slowly. His dark eyes were bright with tears. "I know," he said. "I *know*. He had reason to be wroth, Ushahin!" He spread his arms in a helpless gesture. "There is madness in fury, aye. No one knows it better than I. Everything I have, everything I am, his Lordship has made me. Would you have me abandon him *now*?"

"No!" Ushahin's head jerked, his uneven eyes ablaze. "Do not mistake my meaning, cousin."

"What, then?" Tanaros stared at him and shook his head. "No. Oh, no. This is not *Cerelinde's* fault. She is a pawn, nothing more. And I will not gainsay his Lordship's orders to indulge your hatred of the Ellylon, cousin."

"It would preclude the Prophecy—"

"No!" Tanaros' voice rang in the cavern, echoes blending into the roar of the marrow-fire. He pointed at Ushahin, jabbing his finger. "Do not think it, Dreamspinner. Mad or sane, *his* will prevails here. And, aye, his pride, too!" He drew a shaking breath. "Would you have him become *less* than Haomane? I will not ask his Lordship to bend his pride, not for your sake nor mine. It has kept him alive this long, though he suffers agonies untold with every breath he takes. Where would any of the Three be without it?"

"As for that, cousin," Ushahin said in a low voice, "you would have to ask the Lady Cerelinde. It lies in the realm of what-might-have-been." Bowing his head, he closed his eyes, touching his lids like a blind man. "So be it. Remember, one day, that I showed you this."

Turning, he began to make his way back toward the upper reaches.

"I'll bring Speros down to have a look at it," Tanaros called after him. "He's a knack for such things. It's a flaw in the *structure*, Dreamspinner! No more and no less. You're mad if you think otherwise!"

In the glimmering darkness, Ushahin gave his twisted smile and answered without pausing, the words trailing behind him. "Mad? Me, cousin? Oh, I think that should be the least of our fears."

LILIAS SAT BESIDE AN OPEN window.

The chambers to which she was confined in the Hall of Ingolin were lovely. The parlor, in which she sat, was bright and airy, encircled with tall windows that ended in pointed arches; twin panes that could be opened or closed, depending on whether one secured the bronze clasps that looked like vine-tendrils. The Rivenlost did love their light and open air.

A carpet of fine-combed wool lay on the floor, woven with an intricate pattern in which the argent scroll insignia of the House of Ingolin was repeated and intertwined. It gave off a faint, sweet odor when she walked upon it, like grass warmed by the sun.

In one corner of the parlor was a spinning-wheel. A bundle of the

same soft, sweet-smelling wool lay in a basket beside it, untouched. Ellylon noblewomen took pride in their ability to spin wool as fine as
silk.

There had been a spinning-wheel in Beshtanag. In a thousand
years, she had scarce laid a hand to it.

On the southern wall was a shelf containing half a dozen books,
bound in supple leather polished to a mellow gleam. They were
Rivenlost volumes—an annotated history of the House of Ingolin, the
Lost Voyage of Cerion the Navigator, the Lament of Neherinach—crisp
parchment pages inscribed with Ellylon characters inked in a flowing
hand. Although Calandor had taught Lilias to speak and read the Ellylon
tongue, she hadn't been able to bring herself to read any of them.

It was clear that these rooms were designed to house a treasured
guest, and not a prisoner. Still, a lock was on the outer door, and beyond her lovely windows awaited a drop of several hundred feet.

The rooms were at the top of one of the outer towers. From her
seated vantage point, Lilias could watch the sea-eagles circling the
central spire. Their wings were as grey as stormclouds, but their heads
and underbellies were pristine white, white as winter's first snowfall
on Beshtanag Mountain.

Every thirty seconds, they completed another circuit, riding the up-
drafts and soaring past on vast, outspread wings. They made broad circles, coming so close it almost seemed she could touch them as they
passed. Close enough to see the downy white leggings above their
yellow feet, talons curved and trailing as they flew. Close enough to
make out the fierce golden rings encircling the round, black pupils
of their eyes. She felt their gaze upon her; watching her as she
watched them. Like as not it was true. The Eagles of Meronil served
the Rivenlost.

"And why not?" Lilias said, addressing the circling sea-eagles. "That
is what we do, we Lesser Shapers. We impose our wills upon the
world, and *shape* it to our satisfaction. After all, are you so different
from the ravens of Darkhaven?"

The sea-eagles tilted their wings, soaring past without comment.

"Perhaps not." Since the eagles did not deign to reply, Lilias answered her own question, reaching out one hand to touch the glass
panes of the open window. It felt cool and smooth beneath her fingertips. Far below, the Aven River beckoned, a silvery ribbon dividing

to encompass the island upon which the Hall of Ingolin was built, winding its way toward the sea. "In the end, it is a question of who chooses to use you, is it not?"

There was a scraping sound; in the antechamber, the outermost door to her quarters was unlatched, swinging open.

"Lady Lilias."

It was an Ellyl voice, fluted and musical. There was much to be discerned from the layering of tones within it. That was one of the hardest parts of her captivity; enduring the unspoken disdain and muted hatred of those Rivenlost whom Ingolin had assigned to attend her. "Lady," yes; after a thousand years of rule, they would accord her that much. Not "my lady," no. Nobleborn or no, she was none of *theirs*. Still, it was better than their compassion. Her words in the great hall had put an end to that particular torment. Lilias got to her feet, inclining her head as her attendant entered the parlor.

"Eamaire," she said. "What is it?"

Her attendant's nostrils flared. It was a very fine nose, chiseled and straight. Her skin was as pale as milk. She had wide-set, green eyes, beneath gracefully arching brows. The colors of her irises appeared to shift, like sunlight on moving grasses, on the rustling leaves of birch-trees. "There is a Man here to see you," she said.

Blaise Caveros stood a few paces behind her. "Lilias."

"Thank you, Eamaire," Lilias said. "You may leave us."

With a rigid nod, she left. Lilias watched her go, thinking with longing of her quarters in Beshtanag with their soft, muted lighting, a warm fire in the brazier, and her own attendants, her pretty ones. If she had it to do over, she would do it differently; choose only the willing ones, like Stepan and Sarika, and her dear Pietre. No more surly charms, no.

No more like Radovan.

It hurt to remember him, a flash of memory as sharp and bright as the gleam of a honed paring-knife. On its heels came the crash of the falling wall and Calandor's voice in her mind, his terrible brightness rousing atop Beshtanag Mountain.

It is time, Lilias.

With an effort, she pushed the memory away and concentrated on Blaise. "My lord Blaise." She raised her brows. "Have you come to make one last plea?"

"No, not that." He looked ill at ease amid the graceful Ellylon furnishings. "I don't know, perhaps. Would it do any good?"

"No," Lilias said quietly. "But you could sit and talk with me all the same."

"You're a stubborn woman." Blaise glanced away. "I don't know why I came, Lilias. I suppose . . . I feel a responsibility for you. After all, I kept you from taking your life." He smiled bitterly. "You did try to warn me that I would regret it."

"Do you?"

"Yes." He met her eyes, unflinching. "Perhaps not entirely for the reasons you believe."

Lilias tilted her head, considering him. "Will you not sit and tell me why?"

He sat in one of the parlor's four chairs, which were wrought of a pale, gleaming wood that seemed not to have been carved so much as woven, the slender branches wrought into an elegant form with arms like the curled ends of a scroll. The chair, made for an Ellyl's slighter weight, creaked beneath him. Blaise ignored it, waiting for her.

She took her seat by the window. "Well?"

"It was something you said." He cleared his throat. "That you had the right to seek death in defeat. That I wouldn't have denied you a clean death on the battlefield if you had been a man."

"Nor would you," Lilias murmured.

"No." Blaise picked restlessly at a loose thread on the knee of his breeches. "There was a man I wanted to kill," he said abruptly. "A Staccian, Carfax, one of the Sunderer's minions. His men attacked us outside Vedasia. Malthus . . . Malthus handled the others. Him, we took prisoner. I thought he was too dangerous to live, especially . . ."

"In company with the Bearer?" Lilias suggested. She laughed tiredly at his wary glance. "Ah, Blaise! Did you think I didn't know?"

"I wasn't sure."

"So you let him live."

He nodded. "On Malthus' orders. And in the end . . . do you know that, too?"

"Yes." Lilias swallowed against the sudden swelling in her throat. Brightness, falling. All the brightness in the world. "I know all that Calandor knew, Blaise. I know it all, even unto the cruel end." She rubbed the tears from her eyes, contempt shading her voice. "Will you tell me now what lesson lies within your tale? How even I am not so far gone that Arahila's mercy cannot redeem me?"

"No." He shook his head. "That wasn't my purpose."

"What, then?"

Blaise shrugged. "To say . . . what? Although I maintain poison is an unclean death, I do regret depriving you of the dignity of your choice. It was unfairly done; perhaps, even, at cross-purposes with Haomane's will. Who can say?" He smiled crookedly. "If Malthus had not maintained that Carfax of Staccia had the right to choose, we would not be having this conversation."

"No," Lilias said quietly. "We wouldn't."

Blaise sighed and rumpled his hair. "I raised the hackles of your pride, Lilias; aye, and your grief, too. I know it, and I know what it has cost us. I know the Counselor's words in the great hall stroked you against the grain. I knew it when he spoke them. I am here to tell you it was ill-considered."

Lilias glanced out the window. The Eagles of Meronil soared past on tilted wings, watching her with their gold-ringed gazes. "Do you suppose any of this will change my mind?" she asked.

"No. Not really, no." There were circles around his eyes, too; dark circles, born of weariness and long effort. "Lilias . . ." He hesitated. "Did you know that Darkhaven's army wasn't coming?"

There must, she thought, be a great sense of freedom in riding the winds' drafts; and yet, how free were they, confined to this endless gyre? Lilias thought about that day, during the siege, when she had dared the node-point of the Marasoumië beneath Beshtanag and found it blocked, hopelessly blocked.

"Yes," she said. "I knew."

"Why didn't you surrender, then?" Blaise furrowed his brow. "That's the part I don't understand. The battle was all but lost. You could have *told* us that the Lady Cerelinde was in Darkhaven. And if you had—"

"*I know!*" Lilias cut him off, and drew a shuddering breath. "I would still be a prisoner, but Calandor would live. *Might* live. How many other things *might* have happened, Borderguardsman? If you had arrived a day later, Calandor would have prevailed against Aracus' army. Or we might have escaped together, he and I. Did you never wonder at that?" They could have fled; they could have hidden. *For a time, Liliass. Only that.* The too-ready tears burned her eyes. "Aye, I regret it! Is that what you want to hear? A few months, a few years. Would that I had them, now. But you had reclaimed the Arrow of Fire. Could it have ended otherwise?"

"No." Blaise Caveros murmured the word, bowing his head. A lock of dark hair fell across his brow. "Not really."

"Ask yourself the same question," Lilias said harshly. "What is it worth, this victory? Aracus could buy peace for the price of his wedding vows."

"Aye." He ran both hands through his dark, springing hair to push it back, peering at her. "For a time, Lilias. And then what? It begins anew. A red star appears on the horizon, and the Sunderer raises his army and plots anew to destroy us. If not in our lifetimes, then our children's, or their descendants'. You heard Malthus' words in the council, Lilias. You may disdain his methods, but it is a true dream; Urulat made whole, and the power to forge peace—a lasting peace— in our hands. Aracus believes it, and I do, too."

"Malthus . . ." Lilias broke off her words, too weary to argue. "Ah, Blaise! Satoris didn't raise the red star."

He stared at her, uncomprehending. "What now, Sorceress? Do you claim it is not Dergail's Soumanië?"

"No." Outside her window, the sea-eagles circled while the Aven River unfurled beneath them, making its serene way to the sea. She sighed. "Dergail flung himself into the Sundering Sea, Blaise. It was never Satoris who reclaimed his Soumanië."

There was genuine perplexity in his frown. "Who, then?"

"This is the Shapers' War," Lilias said in a gentle tone. "It has never been anything else. And in the end, it has very little to do with *us*."

"No." Blaise shook his head. "I don't believe it." Something mute and intransigent surfaced in his expression. "Aracus was right about you. 'Tis dangerous to listen to your words." He heaved himself to his feet, the chair creaking ominously under his weight. "Never mind. You've made your choice, Sorceress, insofar as you were able. In the end, well . . ." He gestured around her quarters. " 'Tis yours to endure."

Lilias gazed up at him. "Aracus said that?"

"Aye." He gave her a wry smile. "He did. I'm sorry, Lilias. Would that I could have found words that would make your heart relent. In truth, it's not why I came here today. Still, I do not think it is a choice you would have regretted."

"Blaise." Lilias found herself on her feet. One step; two, three, closing the distance between them. She raised her hand, touching the collar of his shirt. Beneath it, his pulse beat in the hollow of his throat.

"Don't." He captured her hand in his, holding it gently. "I am loyal to the House of Altorus, Lilias. It is all I have to cling to, all that defines me. And you have seen that brightness in Aracus, that makes him worthy of it." Blaise favored her with one last smile, tinged with bitter sorrow. "I have seen it in your face and heard it in your words. You find him worthy of admiration; perhaps, even, of love. If I understand my enemy a little better, I have you to thank for it."

"Blaise," she whispered again; but it was a broken whisper. Lilias sank back into her chair. "If you would but *listen*—"

"What is there to say that has not been said?" He gave a helpless shrug. "I put no faith in the counsel of dragons. Without them, the world would never have been Sundered."

It was true; too true. And yet, there was so much to explain. Lilias struggled for the words to articulate the understanding Calandor had imparted to her. From the beginning, from the moment the red star had first risen, he had shared knowledge with her, terrible knowledge.

All things musst be as they musst.

The words did not come; would never come. Fearful mortality crowded her thoughts. A void yawned between them, and the effort of bridging it was beyond her. "Go," she said to him. "Just . . . go, and be gone from here."

Blaise Caveros bowed, precise and exacting. "You should know," he said, hesitating. "The Soumanië, *your* Soumanië—"

"Ardrath's Soumanië," Lilias said wearily. "I know its provenance, Borderguardsman. Have you listened to nothing I say?"

"Your pardon." He inclined his head in acknowledgment. "You should know, having once possessed, having *still* possession of it—it is being set into a sword. It was Aracus' choice," he added, "with Malthus' approval. 'Tis to be set in the hilt of his ancestral sword, as a pommel-stone. Malthus is teaching him the use of it, that he might draw upon its power should your heart relent. Does it not, Aracus will carry it into battle against the Sunderer nonetheless."

"How men do love their sharp, pointy toys. I wish him the joy of it." Lilias turned her head to gaze out the window. "You may go, Blaise."

After a moment's hesitation, he went. "Good-bye, Lilias."

Although he did not say it, she knew he would not return. He would go forth to live or die a hero, to find love or squander it among others who shared the same fierce, hard-edged certainty of his faith. And so it would continue, generation upon generation, living and dying, his children and his children's children bound to the yoke of the Shapers' endless battle, never reckoning the cost of a war not of their making. She would tell them, if only they had ears to hear. It was not worth the cost; nor ever would be. But they would never hear, and Lilias, who had lived a life of immortality surrounded by mortals, was doomed to spend her mortality among the ageless.

Outside her window, the sea-eagles soared, tracing an endless parabola around the tower. Beyond her door, the sound of his receding footsteps began to fade.

Already, she was lonely.

SEVEN

PEERING INTO THE CHASM, SPEROS gave a low whistle. The brilliant flicker of the marrow-fire far below cast a masklike shadow on his face. "*That's* what this place is built on?"

"That's it," Tanaros said. "What do you think? Is there aught we can do?"

The Midlander glanced up at raw rock exposed on the ceiling, then back at the chasm, frowning. "It's beyond my skills, Lord General. I can make a better job of patching it than Lord Vorax's Staccians did, but it's only a matter of time."

"Where does the fault lie?"

Speros shrugged. "There's no fault, not exactly. Only the heat of the marrow-fire is so intense, it's causing the rock to crack. Do you feel it? There's no forge in the world throws off that kind of heat. I'd wager it's nearly hot enough to melt stone down there at the Source."

Tanaros' brand itched beneath his doublet. He suppressed an urge to scratch it. "Aye, and so it has been for a thousand years and more. Why does it crack *now*?"

"I reckon it took that long to reach the breaking point." Speros stamped on the stony floor. "This is hard rock, Lord General. Or it may be . . ." He hesitated. "Hyrgolf said there was a rain that fell while we were away, a rain like sulfur."

"Aye," Tanaros said quietly. "So I heard."

"Well." The Midlander gave another shrug. "Rain sinks into the earth. It may have weakened the stone itself." He glanced at Tanaros.

"Begging your pardon, Lord General, but why is it that Lord Satoris chose to erect Darkhaven above the marrow-fire?"

"Gorgantum, the Throat, the Pulse of Uru-Alat." Tanaros favored him with a grim smile. "You have heard of the dagger Godslayer, have you not, Speros of Haimhault? The Shard of the Souma?"

"General Tanaros!" Speros sounded wounded. "What manner of ignorant fool do you take me for? I know the stories well."

"I know what they say in the Midlands," Tanaros said. "I am telling you that the legends are true, lad. It is Godslayer that wounded his Lordship. It is Godslayer, and Godslayer alone, that holds the power to destroy him. And it is *that*"—he pointed into the flickering depths—"which protects it."

"From whom?" Speros gazed into the bright void.

"Anyone," Tanaros said harshly. "*Everyone.* Godslayer hangs in the marrow-fire in the Chamber of the Font because his Lordship placed it there. And there, no mortal hand may touch it; no, nor immortal, either. Believe me, lad, for I know it well. Your flesh would be burned to the bone simply for making the attempt, and your bones would crumble ere they grasped its hilt. So would any flesh among the Lesser Shapers."

"Even yours?" Speros asked curiously. "Being one of the Three and all?"

"Even mine," Tanaros said. "Mine, aye; and Lord Vorax's, and Ushahin Dreamspinner's. Godslayer's brand does not protect us from the marrow-fire." His scar burned with new ferocity at the searing memory. "Even the Lady Cerelinde, lest you ask it. Not the Three, not the Rivenlost. Another Shaper, perhaps, or one of the Eldest, the dragons." He shook his head. "Elsewise, no one."

"Ah, well." The Midlander tore his gaze away from the marrow-fire. "I can't imagine anyone being fool enough to try. I wouldn't, not if I had a hundred buckets of that cursed water."

"The Water of Life." Tanaros remembered the taste of the Water in his mouth; water, the *essence* of water, infusing him with vigor. If the Well of the World were before him now, he would dip his finger into it and sooth the burning tissue of his brand. "Did you taste it?"

"Are you mad?" Speros' eyes widened. "The cursed stuff nearly killed me. I wouldn't put it in my mouth for love nor money!" He laughed. "I can't imagine what those poor little Yarru folk think to do with it. Haomane's Prophecy doesn't exactly say *how* they're to use it, does it?"

"No," Tanaros murmured. "It doesn't."

"Well, then." Speros shrugged. "If you ask me, Lord General, I think you worry too much. This is a problem, aye, but you see that?" He pointed to the ceiling. "By my gauge, there's a good twenty fathoms of solid rock there. At this rate, it ought to hold until Aracus Altorus is old and grey. And by *that* time, Haomane's Allies may as well call off the siege—and make no mistake, Lord General, Darkhaven can hold out that long, fortified as it is!—because now that I've seen her with my own two eyes, I don't see the Lady Cerelinde taking some doddering old mortal relic into her bed, Prophecy or no. So then it's too bad for them, try again in another generation or three, and meanwhile Lord Satoris can pluck Godslayer out of the marrow-fire and put this right. Do you see?"

Tanaros laughed. "Clear as day. My thanks, lad."

"Aye, sir." Speros grinned at him. "So what would you have me do here?"

"Seal the breach," Tanaros said. "If it is all we can do, we will do it."

BY THE SECOND DAY, IT seemed to Dani that his entire life had consisted of running, stumbling and exhausted, across a barren grey landscape. It was hard to remember there had ever been anything else. The sun, rising in the east and moving westward, meant nothing. Time was measured by the rasp of air in his dry throat, by one foot placed in front of another.

He would never have made it without Uncle Thulu. What vigor the Water of Life had imparted, his uncle was determined not to waste. He was Yarru-yami, and he knew the virtue of making the most of water. His desert-born flesh, accustomed to privation, hoarded the Water of Life. When Dani flagged, Uncle Thulu cajoled and exhorted him. When his strength gave way altogether, Thulu gathered moss while Dani rested, grinding it to a paste and making him eat until he found the will to continue.

On they went, on and on and on.

The terrain was unforgiving. Each footfall was jarring, setting off a new ache in every bone of Dani's body, every weary joint. His half-healed collarbone throbbed unceasingly, every step sending a jolt of pain down his left arm. On those patches of ground where the moss cushioned his steps, it also concealed sharp rocks that bruised the tough soles of his feet.

When darkness fell, they slept for a few precious hours; then there was Uncle Thulu, shaking him awake.

"Come on, lad." Rueful compassion was in his voice, coupled with a reserve of energy that made Dani want to curl up and weep for envy. "You can sleep when you're dead! And if we wait, the Fjeltroll will see to it for you."

So he rose and stumbled through the darkness, clutching a hank of his uncle's shirt and following blindly, trusting Thulu to guide him, praying that no Fjel would find them. Not until the sky began to pale in the east could Dani be sure they were traveling in the right direction.

On the third day, it rained.

The rain came from the west, sluicing out of the sky in driving grey veils. And while it let them fill their bellies and drink to their heart's content, it chilled them to the bone. It was a cold rain, an autumn rain. It rained seldom in the reach, but when it did, it rained hard. Water ran across the stony terrain, rendering moss slippery underfoot, finding no place to drain in a barren land. And there was nothing, not hare nor ptarmigan nor elk, to be found abroad in the downpour.

"Here, lad." Uncle Thulu passed him a handful of spongy moss. They had found shelter of a sort; a shallow overhang. They stood with their backs pressed to the rock behind them. Rain dripped steadily from the overhang, a scant inch past the end of their noses. "Go on, eat."

Dani thrust a wad of moss into his mouth and chewed. The more he chewed, the more it seemed to expand; perversely, the rainwater he had drunk made the moss seem all the drier, a thick, unwieldy wad. The effort of swallowing, of forcing the lump down his throat, made the clay vial swing on its spliced thong, banging at the hollow of his throat.

Uncle Thulu eyed it. "You know, Dani—"

"No." Out of sheer weariness, he closed his eyes. With his right hand, he felt for the vial. "It's not *for* that, Uncle. Anyway, there's too little left." Though his lids felt heavy as stones, Dani pried his eyes open. "Will you guide me?"

"Aye, lad," Thulu said gruffly. "Until the bitter end."

"Let's go, then." Still clutching the clay vial, Dani stumbled into the rain and Uncle Thulu followed, taking the lead.

After that, it was one step, one step, then another. Dani kept his head down and clung to his uncle's shirt. The rain, far from relenting, fell with violent intent. It plastered his black hair to his head and dripped into his eyes. Overhead, clouds continued to gather and roil, heaping one upon another, building to something fearful. The dull grey sky turned ominous and dark.

Since there was no shelter, they kept going.

They were toiling uphill; that much, Dani could tell. The calves of his legs informed him of it, shooting protesting pains with every step he took. Still, he labored. Above them, the roiling clouds began to rumble with thunder. Lightning flickered, illuminating their dark underbellies. What had been a steady downpour was giving way to a full-fledged storm.

Beneath his feet, the steep incline was beginning to level. Although he could see nothing in the darkness, Dani's aching calves told him that they had reached the hill's crest. He began to breathe a bit easier.

"Still with me, lad?" Uncle Thulu shouted the words.

"Aye!" Dani tossed the wet hair from his eyes. "Still with you, Uncle!"

Thunder pealed, and a forked bolt of lightning lit up the sky. For an instant, the terrain was revealed in all its harsh glory. And there, looming in the drumming rain, was one of the Fjeltroll.

Its lean jaw was parted in a predator's grin. In the glare of the forked lightning, its eyes shone yellow, bifurcated by a vertical pupil. Rain ran in sheets from its impervious grey hide. It said something in its own tongue, reaching for him with one taloned hand.

Dani leapt backward with a wordless shout, grasping the flask at his throat. Beneath his bare feet, he felt the hill's rocky crest crumble. And then it was gone, and there was nothing but a rough groove worn by flooding and him tumbling down it, the afterimage of the horrible Fjel grin seared into his mind.

"Dani!"

Borne by sluicing water, he slid down the hill, his uncle's shout echoing in his ears, vaguely aware that Thulu had plunged after him. It was worse than being caught in the rapids of the Spume. Beneath the torrent of rainwater, rocks caught and tore at his flesh, tearing away the makeshift sling that had held his left arm immobilized. He grunted at the pain, conscious only of his momentum, until he fetched up hard at the base of the hill. There he lay in the pouring rain.

"Dani." Uncle Thulu, illuminated by flickering lightning, limped toward him. Reaching down, he grabbed Dani under the arms and hoisted him to his feet. Beyond them, a dark figure was picking its way down the slope. "Come on, lad, run. Run!"

He ran.

It was no longer a matter of pain. Pain was a fact of existence, a familiar sound in the background. His limbs worked, therefore no new bones were broken. The clay vial was intact, bouncing and thumping as he ran. For the first half a league, sheer terror fueled his flight. Then his steps began to slow.

It was a matter of exhaustion.

As hard as his lungs labored, Dani couldn't get enough air into them. He gasped convulsively. Lurid flashes of lightning lit the sky, blinding him, until he could see nothing in the pouring rain but scintillating spots of brightness everywhere. Pain blossomed in his side, a keen shriek piercing the chorus of aches. Though he willed himself to ignore it, he couldn't stand upright. Hunched and dizzy, he staggered onward until Uncle's Thulu's hands grasping his shoulders brought him to a halt.

"Dani."

He peered under his dripping hair and fought to catch his breath. Blinking hard, he could make out his uncle's face. "Yes, Uncle?"

"Don't argue with me, lad."

Before Dani could ask why, the last remaining air was driven from his lungs as Uncle Thulu hoisted him like a sack of grain and flung him over his shoulder. Without hesitating, Thulu set off at a steady trot.

In the darkness behind them, loping through the falling rain, the Kaldjager Fjel grinned and gave its hunting cry. Across the reach, its brethren answered, passing on the cry, until all had received the word.

Their prey was found.

MERONIL WAS FILLED WITH SONG.

A vast contingent of Haomane's Allies would be departing on the morrow. For the past two days, delegates from other nations had met in the great hall of Ingolin the Wise. Seahold, the Midlands, Arduan, Vedasia, Pelmar, the Free Fishers—all of them had sent pledges. Their armies were on the march.

They would converge on the southern outskirts of the plains of Curonan, and there their forces would be forged into a single army under the command of Aracus Altorus, the would-be King of the West. From there, they would march to Darkhaven.

While they would march under many banners, two would fly above all others. One was the Crown and Souma of Elterrion the Bold, and it would be carried by the host of the Rivenlost. Ingolin the Wise would command them himself, forgoing his scholar's robes for Ellylon armor, and the argent scroll of his own house would fly lower than that of Elterrion's.

The other banner was that of the ancient Kings of Altoria, a gilt sword upon a field of sable, its tangs curved to the shape of eyes. It would be carried by the Borderguard of Curonan, for their leader, Aracus Altorus, had sworn that he would take up the banner of his forefathers the day he led the Borderguard against Satoris Banewreaker. So it would be carried, as Aracus would carry the sword of his ancestors; the sword of Altorus Farseer, with its gilded tangs shaped like eyes and a Soumanië set as its pommel-stone. And at his side would be Malthus the Counselor, whose Soumanië shone bright as a diamond, who carried the Spear of Light, the last of Haomane's Weapons.

Tomorrow, it began.

Tonight, Meronil was filled with song.

It began as darkness encroached from the east and Haomane's sun settled in the west in a dwindling blaze of golden splendor. As the last rays faded like embers, purple dusk settled over Meronil, turning its ivory towers and turrets, its arching bridges, to a pale lavender that darkened to a violet hue.

At her lonely window, Lilias sat and watched.

Throughout the city, lights were kindled. Tiny glass lights, smaller than a woman's fist, burning without smoke. The Rivenlost placed them in fretted lamps; hung from doorways, in windows, on bridges, carried by hand. A thousand points of light shone throughout the city, as though Arahila the Fair had cast a net of stars over Meronil. And as the lamps were kindled, Ellylon voices were raised in song.

She had been right, it was a city meant for music. The sound was inhumanly beautiful. A thousand voices, each one as clear and true as a bell. Lilias rested her chin on one hand and listened. She was not alone. Even the Eagles of Meronil ceased their vigilant circling and settled on the rooftops to listen, folding their wings.

A city of Men would have sung war songs. Not the Ellylon. These were laments, songs of loss and mourning, songs of remembrance of passing glory. From each quarter of Meronil, a different song arose; and yet, somehow, they formed a vast and complex harmony. One melody answered another in a deep, resonant antiphony; the simple refrain of a third wound between the two, stitching them together and making them part of the whole. A fourth melody soared above the rest, a heartbreaking descant.

"And Haomane asks us not to envy them," Lilias whispered.

One by one, the melodies died and faded into silence. In the lucid stillness that followed, she saw the first barge glide onto the Aven River and understood. The Pelmaran delegates had brought more than a pledge of aid in the coming war. Traveling in the wake of Aracus and his swift-moving vanguard, they had come more slowly, bearing wagons in their train. They had brought home the casualties of the last war, the Ellylon dead of Beshtanag.

There were only nine of them. The Host of the Rivenlost was a small company, but a doughty one. They had fought bravely. Only two had been slain by her Beshtanagi wardsmen. Their faces were uncovered, and even from her tower chamber, Lilias could see that they were as serene and beautiful in death as they had been in life. The bodies of the Ellylon did not wither and rot with mortality as did those of Men.

Three barges, three dead to a barge. A single lamp hung from the prow of each vessel, their light gleaming on the water. The barges glided on a river of stars, moved by no visible hand. The bodies of the nine lay motionless. Seven of them were draped in silken shrouds, their forms hidden, their faces covered.

Those would be the ones Calandor had slain with fire.

Alone at her window, Lilias shuddered. "Why couldn't you just leave us *alone?*" she whispered, knowing it was a futile question, at once false and true. They had come to Beshtanag because she had lured them there. The reason did not alter their deaths.

A fourth barge glided into view, larger than the others. It was poled by Ellyl hands and it carried a living cargo. In the prow stood Malthus the Counselor, distinguished by his white robes and his flowing beard, holding a staff in one hand. On his right stood Aracus Altorus, his bright hair dimmed by darkness, and on his left stood Ingolin the Wise. Others were behind them: Lorenlasse of Valmaré, kindred of the slain. There was a quiet liquid murmur as the Ellylon polemen halted the barge.

Malthus raised his staff and spoke a single word.

It was no staff he bore, but the Spear of Light itself. As he spoke, the clear Soumanië on his breast burst into effulgence, radiating white light. It kindled the Spear in his hand. Tendrils of white-gold brilliance wrapped its length, tracing images on the darkness. At the tip, its keen blade shone like a star. By its light, all of Meronil could see the retreating sterns of the three barges making their silent way down the Aven River, carrying their silent passengers. The barges would carry them all the way to the Sundering Sea, in the hope that the sea would carry them to Torath, the Crown, where they might be reunited in death with Haomane First-Born, the Lord-of-Thought.

A voice, a single voice, was lifted.

It was a woman's voice, Lilias thought; too high, too pure to be a man's. The sound of it was like crystal, translucent and fragile. No mortal voice had ever made such a sound nor ever would. It wavered as it rose, taut with grief, and Lilias, listening, was caught by the fear it would break. It must be a woman's voice, for what man had ever known such grief? It pierced the heart as surely as any spear. Who was it that sang? She could not see. The voice held the anguish of a mother's loss, or a wife's.

Surely it must break under the weight of its pain.

But it held and steadied, and the single note swelled.

It soared above its own anguish and found, impossibly, hope. The hope of the dwindling Rivenlost, who longed for Haomane's presence and the light of the Souma. The hope of Aracus Altorus, who dreamed of atoning for Men's deeds with a world made whole. Hope, raised aloft like the Spear of Light, sent forth like a beacon, that it might give heart to the Lady Cerelinde and bid her not to despair.

Other voices arose, one by one. A song, one song. Raising their clear voices, the Ellylon sang, shaping hope out of despair, shaping beauty out of sorrow. Three barges glided down the Aven River, growing small in the distance. In the prow of the fourth barge, Malthus the Counselor leaned on the Spear and bowed his head, keeping his counsel. Ingolin the Wise, who had watched the Sundering of the world, stood unwavering. Aracus Altorus laid one hand on the hilt of his ancestors' sword, the Soumanië dull in its pommel.

Around and above them, the song continued, scaling further and further, ascending impossible heights of beauty. Inside the city, delegates from the nations of Men listened to it and wept and laughed. They turned to one another and nodded with shining eyes, understanding one another without words. In the fields outside Meronil's gates, the Borderguard of Curonan heard it and wept without knowing why, tears glistening on cheeks weathered by wind and sun. The Rivenlost of Meronil, grieving, made ready for war.

In her lonely chamber, Lilias of Beshtanag wept, too.

Only she knew why.

EIGHT

"Tell me again."

The Shaper's voice was deep and resonant, with no trace of anger or madness. It loosened something tight and knotted in Ushahin's chest, even as the warmth of the Chamber of the Font eased his aching joints. The blue-white blaze of the Font made his head ache, but the pulse of Godslayer within it soothed him. Between the heat and the sweet, coppery odor of blood, the Chamber was almost as pleasant as the Delta. Ushahin sat in a high-backed chair, both crooked hands laced around one updrawn knee, and related all he had seen and knew.

Armies were making their way across the face of Urulat.

His ravens had scattered to the four corners and seen it. It would be better to recall them and summon the Ravensmirror, but they were yet too far afield. Still, Ushahin perceived their flickering thoughts. He could not render their multitude of impressions into a whole, but what glimpses they saw, he described for his Lord. Pelmarans, marching like ants in a double row. Vedasian knights riding astride, encased like beetles in steel carapaces. Arduan archers in leather caps, accorded a wary distance. Midlanders laying down their plows, taking up rusted swords.

A company of Rivenlost, bright and shining, emerging from the vale of Meronil. Behind them were the Borderguard of Curonan, grim-faced and dire. Above them flew two pennants; the Crown and Souma, and the gilt-eyed Sword of Altorus Farseer. And among the forefront rode Malthus the Counselor, who carried no staff, but a spear whose blade was a nimbus of light.

Lord Satoris heaved a mighty sigh. "So he has brought it forth. Ah, Malthus! I knew you had it hidden. Would that I dared pluck Godslayer from the marrow-fire. I would not be loath to face you on the field of battle once more."

Sitting in his chair, Ushahin watched the Shaper pace, a vast moving shadow in the flickering chamber. There was a question none of them had dared to ask, fearful of the answer. It had been on the tip of his tongue many times. And when all was said and done, the fears of Ushahin Dreamspinner, who had made a friend of madness, were not like those of other men. This time, he asked it. "Will it come to that, my Lord?"

"It will not." The Shaper ceased to pace and went still. Shadows seethed in the corners of the chamber, thickening. Darkness settled like a mantle on Satoris, and his eyes shone from it like twin coals. "For if it came to that, Dreamspinner—if it became necessary that I must venture onto the field of battle myself—it would mean we had already lost. It is not the defense I intended, nor have spent these many years building. Do you understand?"

"Perhaps, my Lord," Ushahin offered. "You have spent much of yourself."

"Spent!" Lord Satoris gave a harsh laugh. "Spent, yes. I raised Darkhaven, I bound it beneath a shroud of clouds! I summoned my Three and bent the Chain of Being to encompass them! I bent my Brother's weapon to my own will and tuned the Helm of Shadows to the pitch of my despair. I brought down the Marasoumië! I am a Shaper, and such lies within my reach. It is not what I have spent willingly that I fear, Dreamspinner."

The blue-white glare of the Font gleamed on the trickle of ichor that bled down the black column of the Shaper's thigh. At his feet, a dark pool was beginning to accumulate, spreading like ink over the stone floor. How much of the Shaper's power had his unhealing wound leached from him over the ages?

"My Lord." Ushahin swallowed, the scent of blood thick in his throat. "I spoke to you of my time in the Delta. There is power there, in the place of your birth. Might you not find healing there?"

"Once, perhaps." Satoris' voice was unexpectedly gentle. "Ah, Dreamspinner! If I had fled there when Haomane's Wrath scorched me, instead of quenching my pain in the cool snows of the north . . .

perhaps. But I did not. And now it is Calanthrag's place, and not mine. The dragons have paid a terrible price for taking part in this battle between my brethren and I. I do not think the Eldest would welcome my return."

"She—" Ushahin remembered the endless vastness behind the dragon's gaze and fell silent. There were no words for it.

"You have seen."

Not trusting his voice, he nodded.

"All things must be as they must," the Shaper mused. "It is the one truth my Brother refuses to grasp, the one thought the Lord-of-Thought will not think. Perhaps it is easier, thus. Perhaps I should have spent less time speaking with dragons when the world was young, and more time among my own kind."

"My Lord?" Ushahin found his voice. "All of Seven . . . each of your brethren, they Shaped Children after their own desires, yet you did not. Why is it so?"

Lord Satoris, Satoris Third-Born, who was once called the Sower, smiled and opened his arms. In his ravaged visage, beneath the red glare of his eyes and his wrath-scorched form, there lay the bright shadow of what he had been when the world was young. Of what he had been when he had walked upon it and ventured into the deep places his brethren feared, and he had spoken with dragons and given his Gift to many. "Did I not?" he asked softly. "Hear me, Dreamspinner, and remember. *All* of you are my Children; all that live and walk upon the face of Urulat, thinking thoughts and wondering at them. Do you deny it?"

There was madness in it; and there was not. The madness of Shapers could not be measured by the standards of Men—no, nor Were, nor Ellylon, nor any of the Lesser Shapers. The foundations of Darkhaven shifted; the foundations of Darkhaven held. Which was true?

All things must be as they must.

Ushahin shuddered and glanced sideways, his gaze falling upon Godslayer. There it hung in the glittering Font, beating like a heart. A Shard of the Souma, its rough handle a knob of rock. It would fit a child's hand, such a child as might raise it and bring it crashing down, heedless of what it crushed. Heedless of what it pierced. The pattern, the Great Story, was present in every pulse of light it emitted.

Let it come later than sooner.

Tears made his vision swim, spiked the lashes that framed his uneven eyes. "Ah, my Lord! No, never. I would not deny it."

"Ushahin." There was tenderness in the Shaper's voice, a tenderness too awful to bear. "These events were set in motion long ago.
Perhaps there was a better course I might have chosen; a wiser course.
Perhaps if I had tempered my defiance with deference, my Elder
Brother's wrath would not have been so quick to rouse. But I cannot
change the past; nor would it change the outcome if I could. My role
was foreordained ere the death of Uru-Alat birthed the Seven Shapers,
both its beginning and its ending—and though I grow weary, when
that will come, not even Calanthrag the Eldest can say with surety.
Thus, I play my role as best I might. I honor my debts. I must be what
I am, as long as I may cling to it. And when I cannot, I will not. Do
you understand?"

Ushahin nodded violently.

"That is well." Satoris, moving without sound, had drawn near. For
a moment, his hand rested on Ushahin's brow. It was heavy, so heavy!
And yet there was comfort in it. Comfort, and a kind of love. "You see
too much, Dreamspinner."

"I know," he whispered.

"Tell me, then, what you see to the north." The hand was withdrawn, the Shaper resumed his pacing. Where he had stood, the
stones drank in his ichor and the dark pool vanished. Another portion
of him had become part of Darkhaven. "Have your ravens found the
Bearer? Have my Fjel dispatched him yet?"

"No." Ushahin shook his head. "Many of your Fjel gather in Neherinach. That much, my ravens have seen. I suspect the hunt is afoot.
More, I cannot say." He hesitated. "There is another thing, my Lord."

The red glare of the Shaper's eyes turned his way. "Say it!"

"Staccians." Ushahin cleared his throat. "Those we saw in the
Ravensmirror, arming, those along the path the Galäinridder forged . . .
I have touched their dreams, and they make their way to the plains of
Curonan, for it is the place toward which all the armies are bound.
And yet the Staccians, they were the first to set out. By now they may
have reached the outskirts."

Lord Satoris laughed. It was an unpleasant sound. "Might they?"

"Aye." Ushahin glanced involuntarily at the Helm of Shadows,
sitting in its niche. Darkness filled its eyeholes like the promise of

anguish. "I could learn more if you would give me leave to walk the plains—"

"No." Lord Satoris raised one hand. "No," he repeated. "I do not need to know what lies in the hearts of these *Men,* who beheld the flight of Malthus the Counselor and his colorless Soumanië, that is so strange and altered. Still, I may use them as an example. Let Staccia see how I deal with oath-breakers, and Haomane's Allies how I deal with those who would destroy me." He smiled. It was not a pleasant sight. "Go, Dreamspinner, and send General Tanaros to me. Yes, and Lord Vorax, too."

"As you will," Ushahin murmured, rising.

"Dreamspinner?" The Shaper's voice had altered; the unlikely gentleness had returned.

"My Lord?"

"Remember," Lord Satoris said. "Whatever happens. All that you have learned. All that you have *seen.* It is all I ask."

Ushahin nodded. "I will."

SOMEWHERE IN THE MIDDLE OF the night, Uncle Thulu's strength began to wane.

Dani felt it happen.

He had done his part; he had not argued. Once he had regained his breath, they had come to an accommodation. If Uncle Thulu would lower him from his shoulder, Dani would suffer himself to be carried on his uncle's back.

He had wrapped his legs around his uncle's waist, clinging to his neck. Uncle Thulu resumed his steady trot. It made Dani feel like a child again; only this night was like something from a child's nightmare. What did the desert-born know of rain? After the storm passed, it continued to fall, endless and drumming, soaking them to the skin. It was cold. He had not known it was possible to be so cold, nor so tired. Dani rested his cheek against Uncle Thulu's shoulder. The vial containing the Water of Life was an uncomfortable lump pressing into his flesh. Still, through the rough wool of his shirt, he could feel the warmth rising from his uncle's skin, warming him. It was one of the gifts the Water of Life had imparted.

When it began to fade, he felt that, too. Felt the shivers that raced through his uncle as coldness set into his bones. Felt his steps begin to falter and stagger. Slight though he was, Dani was no longer a child. His weight had begun to tell.

"Uncle." He spoke into Thulu's ear. "You must put me down."

It took another handful of staggering steps before his uncle obeyed. Dani slid down his back, finding his feet. His limbs had become cramped and stiff, and his right arm did not quite work properly. Every inch of flesh ached, bruised and battered by his flood-borne tumble down the rocky slope. Still, he was alive, and he had recovered enough strength to continue unaided.

"Can you go on?" he asked.

Uncle Thulu was bent at the waist, hands braced on his knees, catching his breath. At Dani's question, he lifted his head. A dull grey light had begun to alleviate the blackness of the eastern skies behind them. It was enough to make out the rain dripping steadily from his face, into his open, exhausted eyes.

"Aye, lad," he said roughly. "Can you?"

Dani touched the clay vial at his throat. "Yes."

Once more, they set out at a slow trot.

Several hundred yards behind them, the watching Kaldjager chuckled deep in their throats and fanned out behind their prey.

IN THE DIM GREY LIGHT that preceded dawn, Tanaros rose and donned his armor, piece by piece. Last of all, he settled his swordbelt and the black sword in its scabbard around his waist. There were to be no survivors. His Lordship had ordered it so.

He had misgivings at the thought of leaving Darkhaven unattended; though it wouldn't be, not truly. There was Ushahin Dreamspinner and his field marshal Hyrgolf, with whom Tanaros had spoken at length. And, too, there was Speros. Though the Midlander was loath to be left behind, he was grateful to be entrusted with a special task: ensuring the safety, in Tanaros' absence, of the Lady Cerelinde.

The sojourn would be brief; a quick strike, and then back to Darkhaven. The return journey would afford him a chance to check the perimeter of the Vale, to make certain that any tunnels leading beneath it were well and truly blocked. It would ease his mind to see it firsthand.

In the end, it didn't matter. Lord Satoris had ordered it; Tanaros would go.

And it felt good, after so long, to be *doing* and not waiting. He had slept deeply that night, nurturing the coal of hatred that burned at the core of his heart. This was a simple task, an *easy* task. The Staccians who had chosen to follow Malthus had betrayed their ancient accord. They were warriors. They had reckoned the price of their betrayal, as surely as they had reckoned the price of their fealty. It should be easy to kill them.

A ruddy light was breaking in the eastern skies when they assembled.

Vorax was there, splendid in his gilded armor. He rode a mount big enough to bear him, his thick thighs wrapped around its barrel. An uncanny awareness was in his mount's eyes, echoed in the others'. Fifty mounted Staccians followed his lead, all of them riding the horses of Darkhaven. He grinned at Tanaros, his teeth strong and white in the thicket of his ruddy beard. "Shall we go a-hunting, cousin?"

"Aye." Tanaros glanced at the throng of Gulnagel that surrounded him, the muscles of their haunches twitching with eagerness. "Let us do so." He gave the command. "Open the gate!"

They made good time on the narrow path of the Defile. Tanaros rode with the ease of long familiarity, glorying in the freedom. There was the Weavers' Gulch; he ducked his head, laying his cheek alongside the black's neck. The heavy feet of the Gulnagel pounded along the rocks, their talons scoring stone. Here and there, the little weavers scuttled along their vast loom, repairing the torn veils, disapproval in the angle of their poisoned fangs. Behind him, Vorax and his Staccians thundered.

Overhead, the Tordenstem sentries roared. Though vibration of their voices displaced showers of rocks, it was a sound of approval. If it had not been, they would be dead. Tanaros craned his neck as he rode, noting the position of the Midlander's carefully laid traps with approval.

After the narrow paths came the plains.

"Go," Tanaros whispered, flattening himself on his mount's back. Pricked ears twitched backward, laying close to its skull. It heard, and ran. Long grass parted like the sea. Tanaros looked left and right. To either side, he saw the Gulnagel, running. They surged forward in great bounds, tireless. Behind them, the Staccian contingent pounded. Vorax, at their head, was shouting a battle-paean.

There should have been scouts. Ever since Altoria had fallen—ever since Tanaros had led forth an army, the Helm of Shadows heavy on his shoulders—there had been scouts. The Borderguard of Curonan, keen-eyed and deadly in their dun cloaks.

There were none.

There had been none since they had ridden to attend their leader Aracus Altorus upon his wedding in Lindanen Dale. As the sun moved slowly across the unclouded sky, they rode, unchallenged. All of the armies of Haomane's Allies were spread across the face of Urulat, moving slowly toward this place. Now, it was empty. The ghosts of Cuilos Tuillenrad lay still, only whispering at their passage.

Those who betrayed Lord Satoris would pay.

AT SUNRISE, THE RAIN CEASED.

Dawn broke with surprising glory over the reach, golden light shimmering on the wet rocks, turning puddles of standing water into myriad, earthbound suns. Where the moss grew, it brought forth an abundance of delicate white flowers.

It revealed another surprise, one that Dani hailed with a low cry of joy. They had come to the western verge of the empty reach. Ahead lay a craggy decline in which green trees grew in profusion, and mountains rising to the north. Somewhere, there was birdsong and the sound of rushing water.

Uncle Thulu summoned a weary smile. "That's our river, lad. Shall we find it?"

"Aye." Dani took a deep breath. "Give me a moment." He turned behind him to gaze at the sun with gratitude. Although his sodden clothes made him shiver, the sun's first warmth dispelled some of the chill. The sky overhead was pale gold, the underbellies of the dispersing clouds shot through with saffron.

And there . . .

Dani froze. "Fjeltroll," he whispered.

They were coming, a long, ranging line of them. Distance made the figures small, but they were drawing steadily nearer, moving at the effortless lope that had not diminished in the slightest. Sunlight glinted on their hides, still wet from the night's rainfall; on a few, it glinted on armor. One of them hoisted a waterskin, raising it as if in mocking salute, then tilted it to drink deep. Its pace never faltered.

Uncle Thulu swallowed audibly. "Run!"

They ran.

At a hundred paces, they reached the verge and began scrambling down the crags. Dani used hands and feet alike, ignoring the scraping pain in his palms and soles. Something gave way with a tearing sound near his right shoulder and a fresh jag of pain wrenched at him. He ignored that, too.

"This way!" Thulu plunged into the trees at the base of the decline. Checking the clay flask at his throat, Dani ran after him. Behind him, he could hear the sound of talons on rocks and the hunting cries of the Fjel.

Under the canopy of trees, it was cool and green. The loamy ground was soft, muting their footfalls. Gilded shafts of sunlight pierced the green. Drops of gathered rain slid from the leaves overhead, shining as they fell. Over the sound of water and birdsong and the harsh breath rattling in his lungs, Dani could hear the calls of the Fjel as they spread out through the woods. He found a burst of new energy in fresh terror.

They ran.

"Come on." Uncle Thulu panted grimly, veering northward toward the sound of rushing water. "Maybe the river . . ." He slowed, saving his breath as they rounded the trunk of a massive ash tree and came upon it; the White River, plunging down from the mountains in a series of cataracts. Water gathered in pools, spilling downward. "Maybe . . ."

Dani stifled a shout and pointed.

Beside one of the pools, one of the Fjel crouched on its powerful haunches, grey and motionless as a boulder. Its yellow eyes gleamed in its narrow visage. The intelligence in them was almost human. It shook its head slowly, baring its eyetusks in a predator's grin.

"Go!" Thulu shoved Dani back the way they had come. "Go, lad, go!"

They fled due west, straining their ears for the sounds of pursuit. If any was forthcoming, it was inaudible over the river-sound and their own labored breathing. Dani, running hard, felt the sharp stitch of pain return in his left side.

"South," Uncle Thulu gasped. "We'll cut south and pick up the river later!"

For a time it seemed it would work. They ran unimpeded. The ground rose sharply, but the path ahead was clear. Dani ran half-doubled with pain, clamping his left elbow hard against his ribs. It eased the stitch, but a bolt of pain shot through his right arm with every stride. He grabbed his right elbow with his left hand and staggered onward, hugging his rib cage. He had to lower his head to make the incline, bare toes digging into the loam, step by exhausted step.

Near the top, Uncle Thulu loosed a wordless cry and grabbed his arm. Dani lifted his head wearily.

One of the Fjeltroll awaited them, sitting in an easy crouch, loose-limbed and ready. It pointed west with one taloned hand and said something in its guttural tongue, smiling a terrible smile. Its tongue lolled in its mouth, grey-green and pointed.

"Back, back, back!" Thulu suited actions to words, scrambling backward down the incline, heedless of the dirt that smeared his skin.

Dani followed, breathing hard. "Can we get behind them?"

His uncle nodded grimly. "Let's try."

It was no good.

They doubled back, retracing their steps; there was another Fjeltroll, two Fjeltroll, stepping out from behind the massive tree-trunks. There was a cunning light in their yellow eyes; almost amused. One spoke to the other, and both laughed. Sunlight glinted on their eye-tusks. They pointed westward.

Westward they ran; zigging and zagging to the north and south, fleeing like coursing hares. As they ran, cries resounded through the wood. And at the end of every avenue of flight that did not run true west along the rushing course of the White River, they found one of the Fjeltroll waiting. Looming among the leaves. Waiting, and pursuing at leisure.

All the same kind, with smooth grey hide, yellow eyes, and a predator's smile.

All pointing west with infinite patience.

"Uncle." In the middle of the woods, Dani staggered to a halt. The golden light of dawn had given way to the sinking amber hues of sunset. Under the leafy canopy, insects whined and flitting birds uttered high-pitched calls. Keeping his arms wrapped tight around his aching midsection, he lifted haunted eyes to meet his uncle's gaze. "I think we are being driven."

"Aye." Uncle Thulu nodded heavily. "I think you are right, lad."

"Well, then." The giddiness of despair seized Dani. Somewhere to his right, to the north, the White River was running, burbling over rock and stone. Around them, unseen, the Fjeltroll were closing, making ready to drive them farther westward. "There's no point in running, is there?"

"No." Thulu shook his head with sorrow. "No, lad. No point at all."

Dani touched the vial at his throat. "Then we won't."

Together, they began to walk.

NINE

THE STACCIAN TRAITORS HAD ESTABLISHED a tidy campsite on the southern outskirts of the plains of Curonan. One of the wide-ranging Gulnagel spotted it first in the late afternoon of their second day. Tanaros gave the order for the halt, lifting the visor of his helm and staring across the waving sea of grass. Shouts of alarm were borne on the wind, high and faint, as the Staccians caught sight of the attackers.

"Why do you delay?" Vorax drew alongside him. Through the slits in his visor, his face was flushed with betrayal and battle-rage. "Did you not hear what happened in Gerflod? I say we strike *now*, Blacksword, before they are ready!"

"No." Tanaros thought of the news out of Gerflod; of Osric and his men slain out of hand. He weighed it against the memory of Ngurra, the Yarru Elder, unarmed beneath the shadow of his sword. "They are warriors. We will give them a warrior's death."

Vorax made a sound of disgust. "They are dogs and deserve to die like dogs."

Tanaros looked hard at him. "Do you contest my command, cousin?"

"Not yet." Vorax wheeled his mount, taking his place at the head of his Staccians. "Your word you'll give me first strike!" he called.

"My word." Tanaros nodded.

Here and there, figures ran among the hide tents, racing to don armor. The Staccians had staked their horses some distance from their campsite, strung in a long line that each might have ample room to graze. Tanaros frowned and wondered what they had been thinking.

Had they supposed they would be safe here on the plains? Had they expected Malthus to be here waiting, offering his protection? Did they believe Darkhaven would not take the risk of striking against them?

If so, they had made a grave error in judgment.

Perhaps, he thought, they had had no choice at all. Malthus the Counselor had ridden past them like the wind, cutting a swath through Staccia; the Galäinridder, risen from the ruined depths of the Marasoumië, the Bright Rider with a gem on his breast that shone like a star. It no longer held the power to Shape matter; only spirit. Which was more terrible? Had they chosen to betray Lord Satoris and their old bargain? Or had they merely been caught in the net of Malthus' power, compelled to follow Haomane's Weapon as the tides followed Arahila's moon?

"Boss?" One of the Gulnagel interrupted his thoughts. "They're in formation, Lord General, sir."

Tanaros blinked. "Krolgun," he said, remembering. Hyrgolf had assigned to this task all three of the Gulnagel who had accompanied him during their awful trek through the Unknown Desert. He laid a gauntleted hand on the Fjel's bulky shoulder. "We'll do this for Freg, eh?"

"Aye, boss!" Krolgun gave a hideous, delighted grin. "He'd like that, he would!"

"First strike to Lord Vorax and his lads," Tanaros reminded him.

"Aye, Lord General!"

"And keep your shields *up*."

"Aye, Lord General, sir!" There was a rattle along the ranks of the Gulnagel as their shields were adjusted. Some hundred and fifty yards away, the enemy had mounted, forming a dense wedge, bristling with spears. There were nearly two hundred of them, outnumbering Vorax's company four to one. Even counting the forty Gulnagel, the treasonous Staccians held the advantage in numbers. Still, it was a mistake, Tanaros thought. Numbers did not tell the whole tale. He had gauged this task's needs with care. Better for them if they had formed a circle and made ready to fight back-to-back.

Then again, what did the Staccians know? They may have skirmished against unarmed Fjel in the wilds. They had never fought a unit of Fjel trained by *him*.

"Blacksword!" Vorax's voice was impatient. He had his men in a wedge formation, too. Behind their visors they were grim-faced, ready to avenge the affront to their own loyalty. They, too, had lost comrades since the red star had risen. "Will you take all day, cousin?"

Hatred. Hatred was clean. It swept aside doubt. Tanaros thought about Osric of Staccia, dying in the Earl of Gerflod's banquet hall, an unsuspecting guest. He thought about the Gulnagel Freg, carrying Speros' weight and staggering to his death in the desert. Malthus the Counselor had caused these things. If these Staccians wished to follow him, let them die for him. They were Arahila's Children, and Haomane First-Born had given them the Gift of thought. Whether they used it or not, they had *chosen.*

His sword rang clear of its sheath as he gave the signal. "Go!"

Vorax roared, clapping his heels to his mount's flanks. He was a formidable figure; sunlight glittered on his gilded armor. He, too, had long been kept idle. His men streamed after him, hair fluttering beneath steel helms. At a hundred yards, the Staccian leader gave the command. The plains of Curonan shuddered beneath pounding hooves as the two wedges surged toward one another.

"Traitors!" Lord Vorax's bellow rose above the fray as the two forces collided. *"Traitors!"*

Tanaros watched as Vorax's company plunged into the Staccian wedge, sowing chaos and turning the neatly ordered formation into a disordered melee. These were not men who had trained together on the drilling field, day after day. Riders milled across the plains, trying in vain to regroup and bring their short spears to bear on the enemy that had split their ranks. Vorax's men thundered through them and past, swinging wide, their wedge still intact. The horses of Darkhaven held their heads high and contemptuous as Vorax brought his company around for a second assault.

"Let's go, lads," Tanaros said to his Fjel. *"Go!"*

With great, bounding strides and shields held high, the Gulnagel raced into battle. The long grass parted in their wake; some of them swung their axes like scythes, shearing grass out of an excess of high spirits as they ran. Twenty to one side, twenty to the other. The Staccian traitors turned outward in alarm, too late; Vorax and his men were back in their midst. And now there was no time to regroup. There was no guarding their backs, where spears and swords were waiting to thrust, finding the gaps in their armor. No guarding their fronts, where the Gulnagel wielded axe and cudgel, using their shields to parry, ducking with ease on their powerful thighs, bounding to strike from unexpected angles. They fought with concerted, trained efficiency. Their axes slashed at Staccian spears until they drooped like broken stems of grass, heavy-headed. Their cudgels dented steel with mighty blows.

Horses fell, shrieking beneath the onslaught. There were broken limbs, spouting arteries. Astride his black mount, Tanaros pounded into the fray, laying about him with his black sword. This battlefield, any battlefield, was his home. For a thousand years, he had been honing his skills. There was no blow he could not parry, no contingency he failed to anticipate. The blood sang in his veins and a clean wind of hatred scourged his heart. Where he struck, men died. His sword had been tempered in the blood of Lord Satoris, and it sheared through steel and flesh alike.

He wondered if Cerelinde knew. He wondered if she worried. The thought quelled his battle-ardor, leaving a weary perplexity in its wake.

"You." Tanaros came upon the Staccian leader; unhorsed, dragging himself through the long grass, blood seeping under his armpit. He pointed with the tip of his sword. "Why?"

The man fumbled at his visor, baring a grimacing, bearded visage. "You are dead, Darkling!" he said, and spat bloody froth onto the plains. "So the Bright Paladin told us. Dead, and you don't even know it!"

A sound split the air. The butt-end of a short spear blossomed from the Staccian's chest. Its point, thrown with furious force, had pierced his breastplate. He stared unseeing at the sky.

Tanaros looked sidelong at Vorax.

"Not so dead as him," Vorax said impassively. "Are we done here, cousin?"

"Aye." Tanaros drew a deep breath and glanced around him. "Very nearly."

They left no survivors. It went quickly, toward the end. A few of the Staccians threw down their arms and pleaded, begging to surrender. Tanaros left those to Vorax, who shook his head, steady and implacable. His Staccians slew them where they knelt, swinging their swords with a will and taking their vengeance with dour satisfaction. Lord Satoris' orders would be obeyed. Elsewhere, the axes of the Gulnagel rose and fell, severing spinal columns as easily as blades of grass. They had no difficulty in dispatching the wounded.

Riderless horses milled, whinnying.

"Let them be." Tanaros raised one hand. "This day is no fault of theirs."

"And the Men?" Vorax asked grimly.

"We leave them for Haomane's Allies to find," Tanaros said. "And leave a warning. It shall be as his Lordship willed."

There had been no casualties in their company. A shrewd commander, Tanaros had planned wisely and well. There were wounded, and they were tended in the field. But the dead . . . it would fall to the wives and daughters of the Staccian traitors to number them. With the aid of the Fjel, they piled the dead, headless body upon headless body. It made a considerable heap, all told. Tanaros set Krolgun to ranging the plains until he found a chunk of granite that would serve as a marker. When it was set in place, Tanaros drew his dagger and used its point to scratch a message in the common tongue on the grey surface.

To Malthus the Counselor, who led these men into betrayal; mark well how they are served by your deeds. Do you assail Satoris the Sower, Third-Born among Shapers, expect no less.

In the day's dying light, the scratched lines shone pale against the dull grey rock. Behind the stone lay the heaped dead.

"Is it well done?" Tanaros asked Vorax.

"It is." The Staccian's voice rumbled deep in his chest. His gilded armor, kindled to mellow brightness by the setting sun, was splashed with blood. He spared Tanaros a heavy glance. "Do you think it will dissuade them?"

Tanaros shook his head. "No," he said gently. "I do not."

"So be it." Vorax gave a slight shrug, as if to adjust a weight upon his shoulders, then lifted his chin. His bearded profile was silhouetted against the dying sun. "Our task is finished!" he bellowed. "Let us leave this place!"

Tanaros, swinging into the saddle, did not gainsay him; he merely raised one hand to indicate his agreement, signifying to Men and Fjel alike to make ready to leave. There was time, still. The long, slanting rays of the setting sun would allow them leagues before they rested.

The plains of Curonan rang with thunder as they departed.

Behind them, the heaped dead kept their silence.

❖

THE GREEN GRASS OF NEHERINACH, still damp with the night's rain, sparkled in the afternoon sun. The ivy that covered the burial mounds twined in rich profusion, nourished by the rainfall. Birds flitted among the trees, hunting insects that seemed to have multiplied overnight. Overhead, the sky had cleared to a deep autumnal blue.

It was a lovely day, despite the bones that lay buried here.

Skragdal had chosen to make his stand before the largest of the burial mounds. Since the Kaldjager were driving the smallfolk here, let them see. Let them hear of how Haomane's Allies had slain unarmed Fjel by the thousand. Let them grasp the greater meaning of their quest. Let them understand why they met their death in this green and pleasant place, where ancient blood soaked the earth.

He felt at peace for the first time since leaving Darkhaven. It would have been terrible to fail at this task. Field Marshal Hyrgolf had recommended him; Hyrgolf, who was trusted by General Tanaros himself, Lord General of the Army of Darkhaven, right hand of Lord Satoris. Since Osric's death, Skragdal had been carrying the entire trust of Darkhaven on his shoulders. Broad though they were, it was a mighty weight. It would be good to have done with it.

"Today is a good day," he said to Thorun.

The other Tungskulder nodded. "A good day."

One of the Kaldjager emerged from the tree line, loping alongside the sparkling river. Catching sight of them, he veered across the field. It was Glurolf, one of those sent from Darkhaven to join them.

"Boss." He saluted Skragdal. "They're on their way."

Skragdal nodded. "How long?"

"Not long." Glurolf grinned. "A bit. They're moving slow. We ran them hard."

They waited with the steady patience of Fjel. Skragdal was glad to have Thorun at his side. Tungskulder understood one another. On either side of them, the Nåltannen were arrayed in a long line. Their hands rested on their weapons, steely talons glinting in the bright sun. It did not seem possible that two bone-weary smallfolk could prove dangerous, but Skragdal was not minded to take any chances.

In a little while, other Kaldjager began emerging from the tree-covered slopes. They paused, waiting. Skragdal counted them and nodded in satisfaction. There were three yet afield. They must have the smallfolk well in hand. He widened his nostrils, trying to catch the scent of their prey. Men called them the Charred Ones. He wondered if they would smell of smoke.

They didn't.

There it was; a tendril of scent, one that did not belong in this place of Neheris' Shaping. It was the scent of Men—the yeasty odor of their flesh, their living blood, warm and salty. It was the reek of fear, a bitter tang, and of stale sweat. But there was something else, too, elusive and haunting. Skragdal parted his jaws, tasting the odor with his tongue. It was familiar, and not.

He turned to Thorun. "Do you know?"

"Water," the other Tungskulder said. "*Old* water."

Skragdal saw them, then.

It was as Lord Vorax had said; there were two of them. They emerged from the cover of the trees, walking slowly. When they saw Skragdal and his lads waiting, they stopped. They looked very small, and very, very tired.

"Neheris!" Thorun snorted. "Mother of us all! *This* is what we've been searching for?"

"Do not judge in haste." Skragdal fingered his carved *rhios* uneasily, thinking about the crater at the northern end of Neherinach where the Galäinridder had burst from the earth. He had been there in the Ways when the wizard expelled them from the Marasoumië, his gem blazing like a terrible red star. "Perhaps it is a trick."

"Perhaps," Thorun said.

There was no trick. Three more Kaldjager emerged from the trees to come behind the smallfolk. On either side, the others began to close in upon them. The Kaldjager were in high spirits, baring their teeth and showing their pointed tongues. It had been a good hunt. One of them pointed toward Skragdal and spoke. Weary and resigned, the smallfolk began trudging across the field.

Skragdal folded his arms and watched them come, slow and halting. It was true they were dark-skinned, though not so dark as a Mørkhar Fjel. The bigger one moved as though he were bowed beneath a great weight. Skragdal understood the feeling. There were tears on that one's haggard face, and he no longer reeked of fear, but of despair.

The smaller one held one arm clamped to his side. With his other hand, he clutched at a small clay flask strung about his neck on a braided vine. For all that, his head was erect, and his dark eyes were watchful and grave.

"Not much more than a pup," Thorun observed.

"No," Skragdal said. "Bold, though."

By the time the smallfolk reached the burial mound, they were wavering on their feet. The bigger one tried to shield the smaller. Aside from belt knives and a tattered sling at the little one's waist, they weren't even armed. They did not belong in the place. And yet, there was the flask, as Lord Vorax had said it would be. The smell of water, of *old* water, was stronger. If everything else was true, it was more dangerous than a sword; than a thousand swords. Skragdal shook his head, frowning down at them.

"Do you know where you are?" he asked in the common tongue. They gaped at him in astonishment. "This place." He indicated the field. "Do you know it?"

"You *talk*!" the smaller one said in wonderment.

One of the Nåltannen made a jest in his own tongue; the others laughed. "Enough." Skragdal raised his hand. "We do not make jests in this place. Smallfolk, this is Neherinach, where Haomane's Allies killed many thousand Fjel. We carried no arms. We sought only to protect Satoris, Third-Born among Shapers, who took shelter among us. Do you understand? You will die here to avenge those deaths."

The bigger one rested his hands on the shoulders of the smaller, whispering to him. The smaller shook him off. "Why?" he asked simply.

Anger stirred in Skragdal's belly, and his voice rose to a roar as he answered. "You would carry the Water of Life into Darkhaven and you ask *why*?"

The small one flinched, clutching his flask, but his gaze remained steady on Skragdal's face. "Why did you protect Satoris?"

Skragdal gave a harsh laugh, a sound like boulders rolling down a mountainside. "Does it matter to you, Arahila's Child? Ah, no." He shook his head. "Haomane gave *you* the Gift of thought, not us. You have come too far to ask that question. Better you should have asked it before you began. Perhaps you would not be dying here today. Perhaps your people would not have been slain for your actions."

"*What?*" Blood drained from the small one's face, turning his skin the color of cold ashes. He stared at Skragdal with stricken eyes. The bigger one made a choked sound and dropped to his knees. "Uru-Alat, no! *No!*"

"Aye, lad. Did you not expect his Lordship to strike against his enemies?" It was hard not to pity the boy; no more than a pup, truly. How could he have understood the choices he'd made? Skragdal signaled to the others. The Kaldjager moved in close behind the smallfolk. Thorun and the nearest Nåltannen slipped axes from their belts, nodding readiness. "It will be swift, I promise you." Skragdal held out his hand for the flask. Lord Vorax had told him to spill it on barren ground. "Give me the Water, and we'll be done with it."

The boy closed his eyes, whispering feverishly under his breath. It was no language Skragdal knew; not the common tongue, but something else, filled with rolling sounds. He was clutching the flask so hard that the lines on his knuckles whitened. Skragdal sighed, beckoning with his talons.

"Now, lad," he said.

With trembling hands, the boy removed the cord from about his neck. His eyes, when he opened them, glistened with tears. They were as dark and deep as Skragdal thought the Well of the World must be. The boy cupped the flask in both hands, then held it out, his skinny arm shaking. It was a simple object to have caused so much trouble; dun-colored clay, smoky from its firing. A cork carved from soft desert wood made a crude stopper, and the braided vine lashed around its neck looked worn and mended. It couldn't possibly hold much water; no more than a Fjel mouthful.

"Here," the boy whispered, letting go.

Skragdal closed his hand on the clay vial.

It was heavy; impossibly heavy. Skragdal grunted. A bone in his wrist broke with an audible snap as the weight bore him to the ground. The back of his hand hit the earth of Neherinach with shuddering force.

There, the flask held him pinned.

It was absurd, more than absurd. He was Skragdal, of the Tungskulder Fjel. He got his feet under him, crouching, digging his talons into the soil. Bracing his injured wrist with his other hand, he set his shoulders to the task, heaving at the same time he thrust hard with his powerful haunches, roaring.

He could not budge his hand. There was nothing, only a pain in his wrist and a deeper ache in the center of his palm. And water, the smell of water. *Old* water, dense and mineral rich, the essence of water. It rose like smoke from a dragon's nostrils, uncoiling in the bright air and filling him with alarm. All around, he could hear his lads milling and uncertain, unsure how to proceed without orders. And beneath it, another sound. It was the boy, chanting the same words. His voice, ragged and grief-stricken, gained a desperate strength as it rose.

With an effort, Skragdal pried his fingers open.

The flask, lying on his palm, had fallen on its side. Worse, the cork had come loose. Water, silver-bright and redolent, spilled over the rough hide of his palm, trickling between his fingers, heavy as molten iron, but cool. It sank into the rich, dark soil of Neherinach and vanished.

The vines on the burial mound began to stir.

"Thorun!" Skragdal scrabbled at the flask with his free hand, tugging and grunting. This was not a thing that could be happening. His talons broke and bled as he wedged them beneath the flask's smooth surface. "Blågen, lads . . . *help me!*"

They came, all of them; obedient to his order, crowding round, struggling to shift the flask from his palm, struggling to lift him. Fjel faces, familiar and worried. And around them the vines crawled like a nest of green serpents. Tendrils grew at an impossible rate; entwining an ankle here, snaring a wrist there. Fjel drew their axes, cursing and slashing. Skragdal, forced to crouch, felt vines encircle his broad torso and begin to squeeze, until the air was tight in his lungs. Snaking lines of green threatened to obscure his vision. No matter how swiftly his comrades hacked, the vines were faster.

He turned his head with difficulty. There was the smallfolk boy, the stricken look in his eyes giving way to fierce determination. His lips continued to move, shaping words, and he held both hands before him, cupped and open. Odd lines in his palms met to form a radiant star where they met.

It seemed the Bearer was not so harmless as he looked after all.

"Forget me." Unable to catch his voice, Skragdal hissed the words through his constricted throat. *"Kill the boy!"*

They tried.

They were Fjel; they obeyed his orders. But there were the vines.

The entire burial mound seethed with them, creeping and entangling. And there was the older of the smallfolk, finding his courage. He had caught up a cudgel one of the Nåltannen had dropped, and he laid about him, shouting. If not for the vines, Skragdal's lads would have dropped him where he stood; but there were the vines, surging all about them in green waves.

It wasn't right, not right at all. This place marked the Fjel dead. It was a terrible and sacred place. But the Water of Life was older than the Battle of Neherinach. That which was drawn from the Well of the World held no loyalties.

Skragdal, pinned and entwined, watched it happen.

There was Thorun, who had never forgiven himself his error on the plains of Curonan where he had slain his companion Bogvar. Green vines stopped his mouth, engulfing him, until he was gone. No more guilt for him. There were the Nåltannen, casting aside their axes to slash with steel talons, filled with the fury of instinctive terror, the rising reek of their fear warring with the Water's scent. But for every severed vine that dropped, two more took its place, bearing the Nåltannen down, taking them into the earth and stilling their struggles. The largest burial mound on the field of Neherinach grew larger, and its vines fed upon the dead.

There were the Kaldjager, disbelieving. Nothing could stand against the Cold Hunters. Yellow-eyed and disdainful, they glanced sidelong at the creeping tide of vines and shook their hands and kicked their feet, contemptuous of the green shackles, certain they would wrest themselves free.

They were wrong.

It claimed them, as it had claimed the others.

Skragdal wished the vines had taken him first. It should have been so. Instead, they left him for the end. Neherinach grew quiet. He was crouching, enshrouded; a statue in green, one hand pinned to the earth. It ached under the terrible weight. He panted for air, his breath whistled in his constricted lungs. A wreath of vine encircled his head. The loose end of it continued to grow, wavering sinuously before his eyes. Pale tendrils deepened to green, putting out leaves. Flowers blossomed, delicate and blue. It would kill him soon.

A hand penetrated the foliage, thin and dark. Skragdal, rolling his eyes beneath the heavy ridge of his brow, met the smallfolk's gaze. He wished, now, he had answered the boy's question.

"I'm sorry," the boy whispered. "You shouldn't have killed my people."

His hand, quick and darting, seized the flask, plucking it from Skragdal's palm. He lifted it effortlessly and shook it. A little Water was left, very little. He found the cork and stoppered it.

Then he was gone and there was only the vine.

It struck hard and fast, penetrating Skragdal's panting jaws. He gnashed and spat at the foliage, clawing at it with his freed hand, but vines wound around his arm, rendering it immobile as the rest of his limbs. In his mouth, vine proliferated, still growing, clogging his jaws. A tendril snaked down his throat, then another. There was no more air to breathe, not even to choke. Everything was green, and the green was fading to blackness. The entangling vines drew him down toward the burial mound.

In his last moments, Skragdal thought about Lord Satoris, who had given the Fjel the gift of pride. *Did Neheris-of-the-Leaping-Waters not Shape her Children well? This I tell you, for I know: One day Men will covet your gifts.*

He wondered if the boy would have understood.

Dying, Skragdal lived in the moment of his death and wondered what the day would be like when Men came to covet the gifts of the Fjel. He wondered if there would be Fjel left in the world to see it.

With his dying pulse thudding in his ears, he hoped his Lordship would know how deeply it grieved Skragdal to fail him. He wondered what he had done wrong, where he had gone astray. He smelled the reek of fear seeping from his vine-cocooned hide and thought of the words of a Fjel prayer, counting them like coins in his mind. Words, precious and valued.

Mother of us all, wash away my fear.

Dying, he wondered if it was true that Neheris-of-the-Leaping-Waters would forgive the Fjel for taking Lord Satoris' part in the Shapers' War, if she would understand that Satoris alone upon the face of Urulat had loved her Children, whom she had Shaped with such care, tuning them to this place where she was born; to stone and river and tree, the fierce, combative joy of the hunt. The clean slash of talons, the quick kill and hot blood spilling. The warm comfort of a

"I am sorry," he said in the common tongue. "We do not speak your language. We are lost. We will go." Moving cautiously, he tapped his chest then pointed into the forest. "We will go, leave."

"No." She shook her head, gesturing toward the Keep with the point of her arrow. Her brow furrowed as she searched for words. "Go *there*."

Dani glanced at his uncle.

"Go *there*!" The arrow gestured with a fierce jerk.

"I don't think she means to give us a choice, lad," Uncle Thulu said.

If his skin had prickled in the forest, it was nothing to what he felt here, crossing open territory with the point of a drawn arrow leveled at his back. The Keep loomed before them, grey and ominous. A reek of charred wood was in the air, as though a hundred campfires had been extinguished at once.

As they drew nearer, Dani saw the source. There was a wooden building in the courtyard, or had been, once. Where the foundation had stood, there was nothing but a heap of ash and debris, strewn with scorched beams. He touched the vial at his throat for reassurance, glancing over his shoulder at the woman. "What happened here?"

She stared at him. "Fjeltroll."

At the tall doors of the Keep, she rapped for entry, speaking in Staccian to the woman who opened the spy-hole to peer out at her. The spy-hole was closed, and they waited. Dani eyed the doors. They were wrought of massive timbers, wood from the forest. Here and there, pale gouges showed where Fjel talons had scored them.

"I thought the Fjeltroll and the Staccians were allies," he whispered to his uncle.

"So did I," Uncle Thulu whispered back. "Keep quiet, lad; wait and see."

The doors were unbarred and flung open with a crash. Dani jumped and felt the point of an arrow prod his back. Their captor repeated her words, mangling the syllables with her thick accent. "You go there!"

They entered the Keep.

Inside, a dozen women awaited them, hands grasping unfamiliar weapons. Dani glanced about him. Women, all women. Where were the men? There were only women. From what little he knew of life outside the desert, the genders did not dwell apart any more than they did within it. On each of their faces, he saw the same emotions manifested: a resolute anger, belying the shock and horror that lay beneath it.

He knew that look. It plucked a chord within him, one that had sounded at the Fjeltroll's terrible words, one that was only beginning to settle into his flesh in the form of fearful knowledge.

Something bad, something very, very bad had happened here.

At their head was a woman of middle years, holding a heavy sword aloft in a two-handed grip. She had brown hair, parted in the center and drawn back on either side, and her face was a study in grim determination.

"Who are you?" She spoke the common tongue, spitting the words in distaste. "What seek you here?"

"Lady." Uncle Thulu spoke in a soothing voice. "Forgive us. We are travelers, far from home. What is this place?"

"Gerflod," she said grimly. "It is Gerflod, and I am Sorhild, who was wed to Coenred, Earl of Gerflod. Darklings, dark of skin; you do not come from Staccia, and I do not believe you come lost. What do you want?" Holding the sword aloft, she gritted her teeth. "Did *Darkhaven* send you?"

"No, lady." Dani spoke before his uncle could reply. He met Sorhild's blue-grey gaze, holding it steadily. "It is Darkhaven we seek, but Darkhaven did not send us. We are Yarru, from the place you call the Unknown Desert."

"Dani!" Uncle Thulu's protest came too late. The damage, if it were damage, was done.

Sorhild's eyes widened and something in her expression shifted; hope, painful and tenuous, entered. The sword trembled in her hands. "The Unknown Desert?"

Dani nodded, not trusting his voice.

" 'When the unknown is made known . . .' " Sorhild quoted the words of Haomane's Prophecy and gave a choked laugh, covering her face with both careworn hands. Her sword clattered against the marble flagstones as it fell. "Let them enter," she said, half-stifled. "It is the Galäinridder's will they serve."

At her insistence, Dani and Thulu spent the night in Gerflod Keep and learned what had transpired there. They heard the tale of the Galäinridder, who had come upon Gerflod in terror and splendor; of his white robes and his pale horse, of the blazing gem upon his breast, and the horrible warning he bore. War was coming, and Haomane would fall in his wrath upon all who opposed him; those who did were already marked for death. They heard how the Galäinridder, the Bright Paladin, had changed the hearts of the Staccians who beheld him, charging their spirits with defiance.

"Was it Malthus?" Dani whispered to his uncle. "Why didn't he come for us?"

"Who can say, lad?" Thulu shrugged. "The ways of wizards are deep and strange."

They learned of dissension in Staccia, and how the lords along the Galäinridder's route had gathered themselves for battle, making ready to ride to the plains of Curonan to await the coming war, filled with the fire of their changed hearts. And they learned how Earl Coenred had stayed, reckoning he guarded a more important thing.

Vesdarlig Passage.

It was a tunnel, a very old tunnel, leading to Darkhaven itself. Staccians and Fjel had used it from time out of mind. And from it, a company had come; Men and Fjel. Earl Coenred had seen them emerge and knew they were bound for his estate. He had sent away the women and children of Gerflod, bidding them take shelter at a neighboring manor house.

"There was a slaughter." Sorhild, wife of Coenred, told the story sitting at the head of the long table in the Great Hall, her eyes red-rimmed from long nights of weeping. "It is all we found upon our return. Bodies stacked like cordwood, and bloody Fjel footprints upon the floor, everywhere." She smiled grimly. "My husband and his men fought bravely. There were many human dead among those Darkhaven had sent. But they were no match for the Fjel."

"No," Dani murmured. "They would not be."

In the small hours of the night, her words haunted him. It was too easy, here, to envision it; it was written in the grieving visages of the women, in the bloodstained cracks of the floors. And if it was real here, it was real at home, too. He thought about Warabi, old Ngurra's wife, always scolding to hide her soft heart. It was impossible to think she was not there in the Stone Grove, awaiting their return. And Ngurra, ah! Ngurra, who had tried to teach him all his life what it meant to be the Bearer, patient and forbearing. Dani had never understood, not really.

Now, he wished he didn't.

"We cannot linger here," he whispered, hearing his uncle toss restlessly on the pallet next to him. "If there is pursuit, we would lead the Fjel to their doorstep."

"I know, lad." Uncle Thulu's voice was somber. "We'll leave at first light. What do you think about this *tunnel* she spoke of?"

"I don't know." Dani stared at the rafters overhead, faintly visible in the moonlight that filtered through the narrow window. It made him uneasy, all this wood and stone above him. The thought of being trapped beneath the earth for league upon league made his throat feel tight. "Are there more Fjel hunting us, do you think?"

"We cannot afford to assume otherwise," Thulu said. "But from which direction?"

"If they come from the north, the tunnel is the last place they would think to look for us. But if they come from Darkhaven . . ." Dani rolled onto his side, gazing in his uncle's direction.

Uncle Thulu's eyes glimmered. "We'd be trapped like rabbits in a burrow."

"Aye." Dani shuddered. "Uncle, I am afraid. You must choose. You are my guide, and I trust you. Whichever path you choose, I will follow."

In the darkness, Thulu nodded. "So be it. Leave me to think upon it, and I'll name my choice come dawn."

ELEVEN

MEARA REACHED FOR THE SOUP ladle.

"Not that one." Thom, who cooked the soups, didn't look up from the turnip he was chopping. "The Lady's is in the small pot. Mind you don't confuse them."

Despite the sweltering heat of the kitchen, Meara shivered as though an icy finger had run the length of her spine. "What are you saying?" she whispered. "What are you doing, Thom?"

"What is best." He worked the knife at blurring speed, thin, pale slices of turnip falling away from the blade.

"On whose orders?"

The knife went still then, and he did look at her. "By our lord's will."

He meant Ushahin, who was *theirs*. Who summoned them and gave them succor, who made a place for those who had no place. He had listened to the words she had spoken. There was a bitter taste in Meara's mouth, and she was afraid to swallow. "He is one of the Three! He cannot gainsay his Lordship's will!"

"No." Thom regarded her, lank hair falling over his brow. "But we can do it for him." He nodded at the door. "Hurry. Lord General Tanaros returns soon."

She filled the tray in haste, ladling soup from the small pot into a clay crock. It was of Dwarfish make, simple and fine. The soup was a clear broth with sweet herbs. It steamed innocently until Meara placed the lid on the crock, sealing in its heat. She selected three pieces of white bread, wrapping them in a linen napkin, then hurried out of the kitchen.

In her haste, she almost ran into Lord Ushahin.

"Meara!" He steadied her. "Is your errand so urgent, child?"

"I don't know, my lord." She lifted her gaze to meet his eyes; the one with its pale, splintered iris, the other solid pupil. In its dilated blackness was that understanding beyond understanding of all the spaces between, all the lost souls who had been thrust into them and forgotten. It was beautiful to her, and comforting. "Is it?"

He saw the tray then and understood that, too. Ushahin Dream-spinner shook his head gently, releasing her. "Do not speak to me of what you carry, Meara. Whatever it is, I may not know it for certain."

"I'm . . . I'm not certain, my lord. But whatever it is, is it worth . . ." She swallowed, tasting the bitter taste. "Defying his Lordship?"

"Out of loyalty, yes." A somber expression settled over his uneven features. "Do not fear. Whatever you do, I will protect you. Betimes it falls to madness to preserve sanity, child. Too many things have transpired, and now, in Neherinach, something further. An entire company of Fjel is missing." He shook his head once more, frowning into the unseen distance. "I sent my ravens too far afield, seeking the Bearer, and there were none that saw. It was an error. Yet there are too few of them for all of Haomane's Allies afoot, and the Bearer's pace swifter than I reckoned. How was I to know?"

"My lord?" Meara was confused.

"Never mind." Lord Ushahin smiled at her. "Serve the Lady her supper, Meara."

The halls had never seemed so long. She would have taken the secret ways, but General Tanaros had barred from within the entrances that led into the Lady's chambers. He was wary of her safety. Meara's rapid footfalls echoed, setting off a series of endless reverberations. She caught glimpses of her reflection in the shining black marble with its glimmering striations of marrow-fire; a hunched figure, scuttling and fearful. She remembered the might-have-been that the Lady Cerelinde had shown her: a pretty woman in an apron kneading dough, her hands dusty with flour. A man had entered the kitchen, embracing her from behind, whispering something in her ear that made her laugh. He was tall and handsome, with dark hair.

It was a fierce hurt to cling to. The Lady Cerelinde should never have shown her something that *nice*. It hurt too much. Kindness was not always kind, even when people begged for it.

A pair of Havenguard were posted outside the Lady's door; Mørkhar Fjel, black and bristling. They were loyal to General Tanaros. Meara held her breath as they examined her tray, lowering their massive heads, sniffing at it with flared nostrils. She kept her head low, tangled hair hiding her face. She knew they could smell her fear, but the Fjel would not think it strange, not in one of Darkhaven's madlings, who were prey to all manner of terror. She did not know if they could smell poison; or if, indeed, there *was* poison.

There must be poison.

If there was, it was nothing the Fjel could detect; nothing that was deadly to *them*. Little could harm the constitution of a Fjeltroll. They unbarred the door and granted her admittance into the Lady's chamber.

Maybe there was no poison.

And then she was inside, and there was the Lady Cerelinde, tall and shining. All the light in the room seemed to gather around her, clinging to her as though it loved her. It shimmered down the length of her golden hair, clung to her silken robes, rested on her solemn, beautiful face in loving benison. Unfair; oh, unfair! It filled her with a terrible yearning for all the lost beauty of the world, all that might have been, and was not. No wonder General Tanaros' face softened when he gazed upon her. Meara ducked her head and ground her teeth, remembering how he had spurned her advances.

She was a fool; no, *he* was a fool. She would have been content with a little, with so little. Was there madness in it, or a desperate sanity? She could no longer tell. Love, soup, poison, loyalty, folly. Which was which?

The Lady smiled at her as she placed the tray upon the table. "Thank you, Meara."

What did it cost her to be gracious? It was all the same in the end. She was one of the Ellylon. They had turned their back on Lord Ushahin when he was no more than an innocent babe, because he was not good enough, though their blood ran in his veins. Tainted by violence, tainted by the seed of Arahila's Children, who had accepted Lord Satoris' Gift. No one was good enough for them. For *her*.

Not Meara, who was only to be pitied.

Not General Tanaros, who protected her.

Not even his Lordship, no; Lord Satoris, who turned no one away. Whose Shaper's heart was vast enough to embrace *all* of them, even though he bled. Who saw in Ushahin Dreamspinner something rare and wonderful, who understood his pain and respected it. Who offered all of those whom the other Shapers had abandoned this sanctuary, who gave them a reason to live and to serve, who valued the least of their contributions.

Meara loved him; she did.

And still her tongue cleaved to the roof of her mouth as the Lady of the Ellylon lifted the lid from the crock, steam escaping. Was it right? What was right? Did it matter? The thought made her uneasy, setting a tide of gibberish rising in her mind, the words she had spoken echoing in the vault of her skull.

You should kill her, you know. It would be for the best.

The Lady Cerelinde lowered her silver spoon, filling it with broth, and lifted it to her lips, blowing gently across the steaming surface. Meara would have done the same. It wasn't fair. Were they so different, Arahila's Children and Haomane's? Thought chased itself around her mind, mingling with her words, her shattered visions and fragmented memories, until a dark pit opened before her. It was as it had been since she was a child of twelve. The world tilted and her thoughts spiraled helplessly, sliding into a chaos of repetition and babble, seeking to give voice to a pattern too vast to compass.

The spoon halted on its journey. "Meara?"

She clutched her head, seeking to silence the rising tide within it.

Be for the best for the best of the rest for the best for the blessed beast for the rest the beast blessed for the beaten breast of the blessed rest be eaten lest the breast be wrest for the quest of the blessed for the best beast that blessed the rest . . .

Words, slipping between her clutching fingers, slipping onto her seething tongue, sliding between her clenched teeth.

. . . eaten lest the blessed beast be beaten lest the beaten rest be left bereft lest the breast bereft be cleft lest the blessed be wrest . . .

Words and words and words crawling like insects in her mind, dropping from her lips, a rising tide of them; and somewhere, more words, *other* words, resonant and ringing, words as bright and straight and orderly as the blade of a sword.

The Lady Cerelinde was standing, was speaking; Ellylon words, words of power and ancient magics, words like a sword, bright and blazing. Each syllable rang like a bell, driving back the dark tide of madness, and Meara wept to see it go, for the awful remorse that came in its stead was worse.

In the silence that followed, the Lady turned back to the table. Droplets of broth had spattered the white linen. In a slow, reluctant gesture, she extended one hand above the steaming crock and whispered a soft incantation. There was a ring on her finger, set with a pale and glowing moonstone. Even as Meara watched, the stone darkened, turning a remorseless shade of black.

If it could have spoken, it would have uttered a single word: *Poison*.

"Oh, Meara!" The Lady's voice was redolent with sorrow. "Why?"

"Lady, what is it?" Meara scuttled forward, despising herself for her flinching movements, for the remorse she felt. She clapped the lid on the crock, making the poison vanish. "Is it not to your liking, the soup?" she asked, feigning anxiety. "Thom did but try a new recipe. If you do not like it, I will bring another."

"Meara." A single word, breathed; her name. All the gathered light in the room, all the gathered light of Darkhaven, shone in the Lady's eyes. She sighed, a sigh of unspeakable weariness, bowing her head. "What must I do?"

"I don't know," Meara whispered, sinking to her knees. "Lady . . ."

"Perhaps I should drink it." Cerelinde regarded the blackened gem upon her finger. "Do you say so, Meara? It is the simplest solution, after all. If I were no more, all of *this* would cease to be." Her gaze settled on Meara. "Would it be for the best, Meara of Darkhaven?"

"I don't know!" The words burst from her in agony; she raised her head to meet the terrible beauty of the Lady's gaze. "I don't know."

"Perhaps I should, after all," the Lady said softly. She lifted the lid from the crock and picked up the spoon.

"No!" Meara darted forward, snatching away the tray. The Lady touched her cheek. The skin of her hand was soft, impossibly soft, and her touch burned with cool fire. A bottomless pity was in her luminous eyes.

"Ah, Meara!" she said. "See, there is goodness in you yet, despite the Sunderer's corruption. Would that I could heal you. I am sorry I have only this poor Rivenlost magic to offer, that affords but a moment's respite. But take heart, for all is not lost. While goodness exists, there is hope. What I cannot do, Malthus the Wise Counselor may. He could heal you, all of you. He could make you whole, as Urulat itself could be made whole."

There were words, more words, spinning into skeins of answers, filling Meara's head until the pattern of her thoughts was as tangled as the webs in the Weavers' Gulch. She wanted to tell the Lady that it was too late, that Malthus should have cared for them long ago instead of letting them be lost and forgotten. That they had chosen the only love anyone ever offered them, that Ushahin Dreamspinner understood them, for he was one of them; yes, and so was Lord Satoris, in all his wounded majesty. That all pride was folly; the pride of Ellylon, of Men, yes, even of Shapers. That they had chosen the folly they understood best. Mad pride; a madling's pride, broken, but not forgotten.

There were words, but none would come.

Instead, something else was coming; fury, rising like a black wind from the bowels of Darkhaven. Lord Satoris knew; Lord Satoris was angry. The touch of Ellylon magic had alerted him. Beneath the soles of her feet, Meara felt the floor vibrate. His fury rose, crawling over her skin, making her itch and tremble. The lid on the crock rattled as she held the tray in shaking hands.

"Dreamspinner!"

The roar shook the very foundations of Darkhaven. It blew through Meara's thoughts, shredding them into tatters, until she knew only terror. The promise of Lord Ushahin's protection held little comfort.

The Lady Cerelinde felt it. Meara could tell; her face was bloodless, as stark and white as the new-risen moon. And yet she trembled only slightly, and the pity in her gaze did not fade. "So it is Ushahin the Misbegotten who wishes me dead," she murmured. "He uses his servants cruelly, Meara."

There were footsteps in the hall, coming at a run. It would be Speros, the Midlander. General Tanaros trusted him. Meara glanced involuntarily at the closed door, thinking of the Havenguard beyond it. Her actions would be reckoned a betrayal.

In a swift, decisive movement, the Lady Cerelinde yanked aside the tapestry that concealed the hidden passage into her quarters, throwing back the bolts that barred the door and opening it. "Fly," she said. "Fly and be gone!"

Meara wanted to stay; wanted to explain. Did not want to be indebted to the Lady of the Ellylon, to whom she had served a bowl of poisoned broth. But the Lady's face was filled with compassionate valor, and terror was at the door.

"I told him you would break our hearts," Meara whispered, and fled.

VINES CRAWLED DOWN THE FACE of the rock, concealing the entrance to the Vesdarlig Passage. The sight of them made Dani feel queasy. He swallowed hard, tasting bile as the women of Gerflod parted the dense curtain of vine to expose the dark, forbidding opening. He would feel better if they weren't touching the vines.

Uncle Thulu whistled between his teeth. "We'd never have found *that* on our own, lad!" He scanned the ground with a tracker's eye. "Fjel have been here, but not since the rains. I'd not have seen any sign if I hadn't known to look."

"That's good." Dani's voice emerged faint and thready.

Uncle Thulu gave him a hard look. "Are you sure you've got the stomach for this, Dani?"

He touched the clay vial at his throat, but there was no comfort in it; not with the women's careworn hands clutching the vines, patiently waiting. There was only the memory of writhing barrows and green death. He drew strength instead from their faces, from their terrible grief and the fierce, desperate hope to which they clung. Taking a deep breath, he answered, "I'm sure."

His uncle's look softened. "Then we'd best not delay."

Dani nodded, settling his pack on his shoulders. It held a warm blanket and as much food as he could carry; dried and salt-cured provender, laid up for the winter. They were dressed in sturdy, clean attire; warm woolens from the clothing-chests of men whose blood had stained the flagstones of Gerflod Keep. A fresh sling had been tied around his arm, giving respite to his still-aching shoulder. Their water-skins were full. In his pack, Uncle Thulu carried a bundle of torches soaked with a rendered pitch that burned long and slow.

The women of Gerflod had been generous.

"Thank you, Lady." Dani bowed to the Lady Sorhild. "We are grateful for your kindness."

She shook her head. "It is very little. I pray it is enough, and not too late. Still, I am grateful to have had this chance. We have many years of which to repent." Tears were in her blue-grey eyes. With a choked laugh, she gave him the traveler's blessing. "May Haomane keep you, Dani of the Yarru!"

"Come, lad." Uncle Thulu touched his arm.

Together they went forward, passing beneath the vine curtain. Dani glanced at the face of one of the women holding the vines. It was the young woman who had captured them, the one who had reminded him of Fianna. There were tears in her eyes, too, and the same desperate hope. She was whispering something in Staccian, the words halting on her lips. A prayer, maybe.

It had been a long time since anyone had prayed to Haomane First-Born in Staccia.

He wanted to tarry, to ask her name, to ask what it was the Galäin-ridder had said to make her so certain of the rightness of their quest, despite the fearful consequences. But they did not speak the same tongue, and there was no time. Already Uncle Thulu was moving past him, taking one of the torches from his bundle. There was a sharp, scraping sound as he struck the flint, a scattering of sparks, and then the sound of pitch sizzling as the torch flared to life.

Yellow torchlight danced over the rocky surfaces. It was a broad tunnel and deep, sloping downward into endless darkness. Beyond the pool of light cast by the torch, there was only black silence.

If they were lucky, that would hold true.

"Shall we go?" Thulu asked quietly.

"Aye." Dani cast one longing glance behind him. The vines were still parted, and he could see the Lady Sorhild holding up one hand in farewell. The hope in her face, in all their faces, was a heavy burden to carry. He sighed, setting his face toward the darkness, hearing the soft rustling of the vine curtain falling back into place. "Lead me to Darkhaven, Uncle."

"HE DID *WHAT*?" LIGHT-HEADED WITH fury, Tanaros grasped the front of Vorax's doublet, hurling the old glutton against the wall and pinning him there. "Is he *mad*?"

"Peace, cousin!" the Staccian wheezed, trying to pry Tanaros' grip loose. His bearded face was turning red. "As to the latter, need you ask?"

A cry of agony thrummed through the stones of Darkhaven, wordless and shattering; once, twice and thrice. It sounded raw and ragged, a voice that had been screaming for a long time. Somewhere, Ushahin Dreamspinner was suffering the consequences of having attempted to circumvent Lord Satoris' will.

Tanaros swore and released Vorax, who slumped to the floor, rubbing his bruised throat. "What did you have to do with it?"

"Nothing!" The Staccian scowled up at him. "Did we not just ride together, you and I? Did we not do his Lordship's bidding? Vent your anger elsewhere, cousin!"

Tanaros drew his sword, touching the point of it to Vorax's chest. The hilt throbbed in his grip, resonating to the anger of Lord Satoris, in whose blood its black blade had been tempered. The same beat throbbed in his chest, the scar over his heart pulsing with it. "Poison deadly enough to slay one of the Ellylon is not obtained with ease. Don't lie to me . . . cousin."

Vorax raised his hands. "Ask your Lady, since you value her so much."

Tanaros nodded once, grimly. "So I shall."

He sheathed the sword before he strode through the halls of Darkhaven. It didn't matter. His fury, Lord Satoris' fury, beat from him in waves, white-hot and searing. No one would stand in its way. Madlings and Havenguard alike fell back before it; the former scuttling to hide, the latter falling in at his back, exchanging glances.

The door to her quarters was ajar.

That alone was enough to fill him with rage. Tanaros flung the door wide open, striding through as it crashed. The sight of Cerelinde in all her beauty speaking to Speros rendered him momentarily speechless.

"General Tanaros."

"Lord General!"

They both rose to their feet to greet him. Cerelinde's face was grave and guarded; Speros' was open and grateful. Tanaros struggled for control. Somewhere, there was the scent of vulnus-blossom.

No.

It was imagination, or memory. Once, he had come upon them thusly; not these two, but others. Calista, his wife. Roscus Altorus, his lord. Not these two.

"What happened here?" Tanaros asked thickly. "Tell me!"

"It was one of the Dreamspinner's madlings, boss." Speros watched his face warily, standing clear of his sword; the blade Tanaros had no memory of having drawn since he had left Vorax. "Tried to poison her, near as I can figure. His Lordship's in a proper fury. The Lady says she doesn't know which one it was that brought the poison."

With an effort, Tanaros brought his breathing under control, pointing the tip of his blade at Cerelinde. "Who was it?"

Her chin rose. "I cannot say, General."

She was lying; or as near to a lie as the Ellylon came. She knew. She would not say. Tanaros stared at her, knowing it. Knowing her, knowing she would seek to protect those she perceived as lesser beings, loving her and hating her at once for it. His wife had offered him the same lie, seeking to protect her unborn child, but he had seen the truth in the child's mien and read it in her gaze. He could do no such thing with the Lady of the Ellylon.

"So be it." He pointed his sword at Speros. "Keep her safe, Midlander. It is his Lordship's will."

"Lord General." Speros gulped, offering him a deep bow. "I will."

"Good." Tanaros shoved his sword back into his scabbard, turning on his heel and heading in the direction of the cry. It had come from the Throne Hall. Whether or not his Lordship had summoned him, he could not have said; it was where his fury compelled him to go. His armor rattled with the swiftness of his strides, its black lacquered surface reflecting light cast by the veins of marrow-fire in a fierce blue-white glare. For once, the Havenguard had to hurry to keep pace with him.

Even as he approached the massive doors depicting the Shapers' War, the pair of Mørkhar Fjel on duty opened them. A slender figure stumbled between the doors, crossed the threshold, and fell heavily to its knees, head bowed, clutching its right arm. Lank silver-gilt hair spilled forward, hiding its features.

"Dreamspinner," Tanaros said drily.

Ushahin lifted his head with an effort. His face was haggard, white as bone. When he spoke, his voice was hoarse. "Cousin."

The hilt of the black sword pulsed under Tanaros' hand. He did not remember reaching for it a third time. Breathing slowly, he made himself release it. If Ushahin was alive, it meant his Lordship did not want him dead. He stared at the half-breed's pain-racked face, concentrating on breathing and willing himself to calm. "This was very foolish. Even for you."

One corner of Ushahin's mouth twisted. "So it would appear."

"What did he do to you?"

Moving slowly, Ushahin extended his right arm. Nerves in his face twitched with the residue of pain as he held his arm outstretched, pushing up the sleeve with his left hand. His right hand was clenched in a fist, nails biting into the palm. He opened his stiff fingers, a sheen of sweat appearing on his brow.

The arm was whole and perfect; more, it was beautiful. Strength and grace were balanced in the corded muscle, the sleek sinews. His skin was milk-white and flawless. A subtle pool of shadow underscored the bone hillock of his wrist, unexpectedly poignant. His hand was a study in elegance; a narrow palm and long, tapering fingers, only the bloody crescents where his nails had bitten marring its perfection.

"His Lordship is merciful," Ushahin said tautly. "He allows me to bear his punishment that my madlings might be spared it."

Tanaros stared, bewildered. "This is punishment?"

Ushahin laughed soundlessly. "He healed my sword-arm that I might fight at your side, cousin." A bead of sweat gathered, rolling down the side of his face. "You'll have to teach me how to hold a sword."

Tanaros shook his head. "I don't understand."

"Oh, he broke it, first." Ushahin licked lips parched from screaming. "Inch by inch, bone by bone. He ground them into fragments, and then he Shaped them anew, as slowly as he destroyed them. Does that help make it clear for you?"

"Yes." Tanaros swallowed against a wave of nausea. "It does."

"Good." Ushahin closed his eyes briefly. "You were right, it was foolish. Not the attempt, but its aftermath." He opened his eyes. "He drew on Godslayer's power to do this, Tanaros, and spent his own in the bargain. I shouldn't have taken the risk of provoking such a thing. He's precious little to spare."

"Dreamspinner." Somewhere, the anger had drained from Tanaros. He considered Ushahin and sighed, extending his hand. "Get up." Despite the tremors that yet racked Ushahin, Tanaros felt the strength of the half-breed's new grip through his gauntleted hand as he helped him to his feet. "After a thousand years, why does he want *you* to wield a sword?"

"Ah, that." Ushahin exhaled hard, clutching Tanaros' shoulder for balance. "It is so that I may be of some use in the battle to come, since

I am to be denied the Helm of Shadows." Their gazes locked, and Ushahin smiled his crooked smile. "You've worn it before. I may bring a greater madness to bear, but you bring the purity of your hatred and a warrior's skill. Wield it well, cousin; and ward it well, too. There is a prophecy at work here."

. . . and the Helm of Shadows is broken . . .

Tanaros took a deep breath. "It is a heavy burden."

"Yes." Ushahin relinquished his grip, standing on wavering feet. He flexed his newly Shaped sword-arm, watching the muscles shift beneath the surface of his pale skin. "I gambled, cousin, and lost. We will have to make do." He nodded toward the Throne Hall. "As you love his Lordship, go now and deliver news he will be glad to hear."

It was thrice a hundred paces to walk the length of the Throne Hall. The torches burned with a fierce glare, sending gouts of marrow-fire toward the rafters, casting stark shadows. His Lordship sat unmoving in his carnelian throne. Godslayer shone in his hands, and upon his head was the Helm of Shadows.

The sight of it struck Tanaros like a blow. It was never easy to bear, and hardest of all when Lord Satoris wore it, for it was tuned to the pitch of his despair—of the knowledge he alone bore, of the role he was fated to play. Of the anguish of a brother's enmity, of the loss of a sister's love. Of immortal flesh seared and blackened, of Godslayer's prick and his unhealing wound. Of generation upon generation of mortal hatred, eroding the foundations of his sanity.

There was a new pain filling the dark eyeholes: the agony of betrayal, the whirlwind of fury and remorse bound inextricably together, tainted with self-loathing. Tanaros felt tears sting his eyes, and his heart swelled within the constraint of his brand.

"Tanaros Blacksword." Lord Satoris' voice was low and weary.

"My Lord!" He knelt, the words bursting fiercely from him. "My Lord, I swear, I will never betray you!"

Beneath the shadow of the Helm, the Shaper's features shifted into something that might have been a bitter smile. "You have seen the Dreamspinner."

"He should never have defied your will." Tanaros gazed up at the aching void. "He should never have added to your pain, my Lord."

The Shaper bowed his head, studying Godslayer as the shard pulsed between his hands, emitting a rubescent glow. "It was not without reason," he mused. "And yet . . . ah, Tanaros! Is there no way to survive without becoming what they name me? I have fought so hard for so long. Ushahin Dreamspinner sought to take the burden on himself, but there is no escaping the pattern of destiny. Oh, loving traitor, traitorous love!" He gave a harsh echoing laugh, making the torches flare. "It is always the wound that cuts the deepest."

Tanaros frowned. "My Lord?"

"Pay me no heed." Lord Satoris passed one hand before his helm-shadowed eyes. "I am in darkness, my faithful general. I am surrounded by it. It is all I see, and it grows ever deeper. Pay me no heed. It is your time that is coming, the time of the Three. It is for this that I summoned you, so many years ago. I wonder, betimes, which one . . ." Glancing at Godslayer, he paused and gathered himself. "Vorax reports that it was done and the Staccian traitors dispatched. Have you ensured that the tunnels have been sealed?"

"Aye, my Lord." Tanaros touched the hilt of his sword for comfort, feeling its familiar solidity. "I pray you, know no fear. Darkhaven is secure."

"That is good, then." The Shaper's head fell back onto his carnelian throne as though it cost him too much to keep it upright. His shadowed eyes glimmered in the uptilted sockets of the Helm. He held Godslayer loosely in his grip. "Tell me, my faithful general. Did I ask it, did I return Godslayer to the Font, would you swear your oath anew?"

Tanaros stared at the beating heart of the dagger; the rough knob of the hilt, the keen edges, ruby-bright and sharp as a razor. The scar on his chest ached at the memory. It had hurt when his Lordship had plucked the dagger from the marrow-fire and seared his flesh with the pact of binding—more than any mortal fire, more than any pain he had ever known. He raised his gaze. "I would, my Lord."

"Loyal Tanaros," Lord Satoris whispered. "It is to you I entrust my honor."

"My Lord." Tanaros bowed his head.

The Shaper gave another laugh, weary and edged with despair. "It is no boon I grant, but a burden. Go, now, and tend to your duties. I must . . . I must think." He glanced once more at Godslayer, a bitter resentment in his gaze. "Yes, that is it. I must think."

"Aye, my Lord." Rising to his feet, Tanaros bowed and made to take his leave.

"Tanaros." The whisper stopped him.

"My Lord?"

Beneath the Helm, the Shaper's shadowed features shifted. "Teach the Dreamspinner to hold a blade," he said softly. "He may have need of the knowledge before the end."

TWELVE

DAYS PASSED IN MERONIL.

One, Lilias discovered, was much like the other. Sometimes the days were clear and the sun outside her tall windows sparkled on the Aven River far below. Betimes it rained; a gentle rain, silvery-grey, dappling the river's surface.

Little else changed.

There was no news; or if there was, no one did her the courtesy of telling her. Still, she did not think there was. It was too soon. Somewhere to the north, Haomane's Allies would be converging, gathering to march across the plains of Curonan and wage their great war. But in the west, the red star still rose in the evenings, a harbinger unfulfilled. It seemed so very long ago that she had watched it rise for the first time.

What does it mean, Calandor?

Trouble.

She had been afraid, then, and for a long time afterward. No longer. Everything she had feared, every private terror, had come to pass. Now there was only waiting, and the slow march of mortality.

She wondered what would happen in the north, but it was a distant, impersonal curiosity. Perhaps Satoris Banewreaker would prevail; perhaps he would restore her to Beshtanag. After all, she had kept their bargain. Perhaps he would even return into her keeping the Soumanië that she had wielded for so long, although she suspected not. No, he would not give such a gift lightly into mortal hands.

It didn't matter. None of it mattered without Calandor.

How was it that in Beshtanag, days had passed so swiftly? Days had blended into weeks, weeks into months, months into years. A decade might pass in what seemed, in hindsight, like the blink of an eye. Ah, but it was a dragon's eye, slow-lidded and amused, filled with amusement born of fathomless knowledge, gathered since before Shapers strode the earth.

Here, the days passed slowly.

Meronil was filled with women. There were a few men of the Rivenlost; an honor guard, rudimentary and sparse. Lilias watched them from her window as they passed, riding astride without need for saddle or reins. They looked stern and lovely in their bright armor. She wondered at their being left behind; wondered if they had volunteered, if they had been injured in previous battles. Perhaps they were reckoned too young to be on the front lines of a dire war; it was hard to gauge their age.

Mostly, though, there were women.

No children, or none that she saw. Few, precious few, children had been born to the Rivenlost in the last Age of Urulat. Few children had *ever* been born to the Ellylon; Haomane's Children, created by the Lord-of-Thought, who had rejected the Gift of his brother Satoris Third-Born.

And for that he was worshipped.

The thought made Lilias shake her head in bemusement. She did not understand—would *never* understand. How was it that Men and Ellylon alike refused to see that behind their endless quarrels lay the Shapers' War? It was pride, nothing but pride and folly; two things she had cause to know well.

The women of Meronil spoke seldom to her. There were handmaidens who tended to her needs; Eamaire and others, who brought food, clean water to bathe, linens for her bed. They no longer bothered with disdain, which in some ways was even harder to bear. Captive and abandoned, her power broken, Lilias was beneath their notice; a burden to be tended, nothing more.

When her heart was at its bleakest, Lilias imagined Meronil beset by the forces of Lord Satoris. She envisioned a horde of rampaging Fjel, besmirching its white towers and bridges with their broad, horny feet; bringing down its very stones with their powerful taloned hands, while Tanaros Kingslayer, the Soldier, sat astride his black destrier and watched and the Ellylon women fled, shrieking in disbelief that it come to this at the last.

Betimes, there was a fierce joy in the vision.

At other times, she remembered Aracus Altorus, with his wideset gaze; trusting, demanding. She remembered Blaise, dark-eyed Blaise, in all his fierce loyalty. They had treated her fairly, and in her heart of hearts she no longer wished to see them slain, lying in a welter of their own gore. It would not bring Calandor back, any more than Lord Satoris' victory. When all was said and done, they were her people; Arahila's Children. And yet both of them *believed*, believed so strongly. A hope, a vision, a world made whole; a faint spark nurtured and blown into a careful flame by Malthus the Wise Counselor, who was Haomane's Weapon.

Those were the times when Lilias leaned her forehead against the lintel of her window and wept, for she had too little belief and too much knowledge.

One day alone was different, breaking the endless pattern of tedium. Long after Lilias had assumed such a thing would never happen, an Ellyl noblewoman paid a visit to her quarters. It was the Lady Nerinil, who had sat in at Malthus' Council, who represented the scant survivors of the House of Numireth the Fleet, founder of Cuilos Tuillenrad, the City of Long Grass.

She came announced, filling the tower chamber with her unearthly beauty. Lilias had grown accustomed to the handmaidens; the Lady Nerinil was something else altogether. How was it, Lilias wondered, that even among the Rivenlost, one might outshine another? Perhaps it was a form of glamour, a remnant of the magics they had lost when the world was Sundered. She was glad she had asked the handmaidens to remove all mirrors from her room.

"Sorceress of the East!" Nerinil paced the chamber, unwontedly restless for one of her kind. Her tone was bell-like and abrupt. "There is a thing that troubles me."

Lilias laughed aloud. "Only one, Lady?"

The Lady Nerinil frowned. It was an expression of exceeding delicacy, the fine skin between her wing-shaped brows creasing ever so slightly. "In the Council of Malthus, I asked a question of you; one to which you made no reply."

"Yes." Lilias remembered; the sweet, ringing tones filled with anger and incomprehension. *Why would you do such a thing?* She looked curiously at her. "I answered with a question of my own. It was you who did not wish the conversation furthered, Lady. Why, now, do you care?"

Nerinil's luminous eyes met hers. "Because I am afraid."

Lilias nodded. "You have answered your question."

"Fear?" The Ellyl noblewoman gave a short, incredulous laugh. "Only fear? I am afraid, Sorceress, but I do not condemn thousands to death because of it."

"Yes," Lilias said wearily. "You do. You, and all of Haomane's Allies. What do you think will happen when they march upon Darkhaven?"

The Lady Nerinil shook her head, her dark hair stirring. Tiny diamonds were woven into it, and it gleamed like the Aven River reflecting stars at night. "Your question was asked and answered, Sorceress. You know our plight and our dream. We march upon Darkhaven despite our fear, and not because of it."

Lilias shrugged. "Doubtless that will prove great comfort to the wives and mothers of the slain. I'm sure they will be pleased to know a Midlander farmer's son died so that the Rivenlost may behold the face of Haomane once more."

A flash of anger crossed the Lady Nerinil's features. "You are swift to condemn Haomane's Allies for leading soldiers to take arms against the Sunderer, Sorceress. And yet you deceived us and sought to lead us into the Sunderer's trap to be slaughtered. Is this not hypocrisy? The Rivenlost had done nothing to threaten or harm you."

"No," Lilias agreed, gazing out the window. "But I would have been next."

There was silence, then. For a long time, the Lady Nerinil said nothing, for the Ellylon were incapable of lying. "Perhaps," she said at last, and her voice was low and melodious. "Like the Sunderer, you were a dragon-friend."

"I was that." Lilias swallowed, tasting the salt of her tears. *Oh, Calandor!*

"And your life was worth the lives of thousands?"

"It was to me." Lilias turned her gaze on the Ellyl noblewoman. "As you say, Lady, I had done nothing to threaten or harm you. I wished only to be left in peace. Did Beshtanag deserve to be destroyed because of it?"

"For that, no," the Lady Nerinil said quietly. "But the Soumanië was never meant to be yours to wield, and never in such a manner. You set yourself against Haomane's will when you did so. Surely you must have known such defiance could not go unanswered forever."

"Ah, Haomane." Lilias curled her lip. "We spoke of *fear*, Lady. What is it Haomane fears? Why is he so jealous of his power that he will not share even the smallest portion of it with a mortal woman?" She paused. "Or is it *knowledge* the Lord-of-Thought fears? Even Haomane's Allies seem passing fearful of the wisdom of dragons. Perhaps it is *that* he sought to extinguish."

"No." The Ellyl spoke tentatively, then frowned and repeated the word more strongly. "*No.*" Scintillant points of light danced around the room as she shook her head once more. "I will not fall prey to your sophistry and lies. You seek but to justify your actions, which served only your own ends."

"Can Haomane First-Born claim otherwise?" Lilias laughed shortly, feeling old and haggard, and wishing the Ellyl would depart. "At least, unlike the Lord-of-Thought, I know it. Have I ever denied as much?"

The Lady Nerinil looked at her with a fathomless expression in her dark, lambent eyes. "It seems to me that you spoke true words in the Council of Malthus, Sorceress. You are a proud woman, and a vain one."

"Yes," Lilias said. "I know."

"Arahila the Fair bids us to be compassionate," the Lady Nerinil mused. "May she in her infinite mercy forgive me, for I cannot find it in my heart to pity you, Lilias of Beshtanag."

The words carried a familiar sting. "I do not want your pity," Lilias murmured.

"I know." The Lady Nerinil of the House of Numireth the Fleet inclined her head with grace. "But it is all that you deserve."

THE TUNNEL WENT ON FOREVER.

After the unforgiving terrain of the northern Fjel territories, it should have been easy. Beyond the initial descent, the tunnel was level. Its floor was worn almost smooth by the passage of countless generations; broad Fjeltroll feet, the booted feet of Men, even horses' shod hooves, for it was vast enough for two Men to ride abreast. It was warmer beneath the earth than it was above it, out of the elements of wind and rain. They had food and water, and torches to light their way.

Set against that was a sense of stifling fear, and Dani would have traded all of the comforts the tunnel afforded to be rid of it. In the desert, one could see for leagues all around. Here, there was only the endless black throat of the tunnel. Stone below and stone above, ton upon ton of it. They used the torches sparingly, a tiny pool of firelight moving through the darkness.

Once, Dani had watched an enormous blacksnake swallow a hopping-mouse. Its hind legs were still twitching as it disappeared into the snake's gullet. Afterward, it made a visible lump as it moved through the long, sinuous body.

That was what it felt like.

The tunnel smelled of Fjeltroll; musky, faintly rank. Old or fresh? There was no way of knowing. They could see nothing beyond the edge of the torchlight. Every step forward was fraught with tension. If they could have done without the torches, they would have, but it was impossible. They would have been bumbling into the walls with every other step; or worse, wandered into one of the smaller side tunnels.

From time to time, they came upon ventilation shafts cut into the ceiling high above. When they did, they would pause, breathing deeply of the clean air and gazing upward at the slanting rays of daylight filtering into the tunnel. Uncle Thulu would snuff his torch, and for a precious span of yards they would continue by virtue of the faint illumination, no longer an excruciatingly visible target.

Then the air would grow stale and darkness thicker, until they could no longer see their hands before their faces, and they would pause again, straining their ears for any sound of approaching Fjeltroll. The sound of the flint striking, the violent spray of sparks as Uncle Thulu relit the torch, always seemed too loud, too bright.

There was no way of marking the passage of days. Although they tried counting the ventilation shafts, they had no idea how far apart they were. When they grew too weary to continue, they rested, taking turns sleeping in shifts, huddled in one of the side tunnels. Sometimes in their endless trudging, they felt a whisper of cool air on their faces though the darkness remained unalleviated. When that happened, Dani reckoned it was night aboveground.

In the tunnel, it made no difference.

They found resting-places where the forces of Darkhaven had made camp; broad caverns with traces of old campfires. There they found supply-caches, as Sorhild of Gerflod had told them. At the first such site they reached, Dani lingered beneath the ventilation shaft, studying marks scratched onto the cavern wall above the cold ashes of an abandoned campfire.

"Can you read what it says, Uncle?" he asked.

Uncle Thulu shook his head. "No, lad. I don't have the art of it."

Dani traced the markings with his fingertips, wondering. "Is it a spell, do you think? Or a warning?"

His uncle gave them a second glance. "It looks like clan markings as much as anything. Come on, let's be on our way."

Afterward, they did not linger in these places, for the scent of Fjeltroll was strongest where they had eaten and slept, but took aught that might be of use and hurried onward. Dani found himself thinking about the marks; wondering who had written them, wondering what they meant. It was true, they did look like clan markings. Among the Six Clans of the Yarru-yami, it was a courtesy to leave such signs in territories they hunted in common, letting others know where a new drought-eater had taken root, when a waterhole had silted closed, where a patch of *gamal* might be found. Or it could simply be a sign to let Lizard Rock Clan know that the Stone Grove had already passed through, hunting such prey as might be found.

It hurt to think of home.

He wondered what would be worth marking in the endless tunnel. Caches, perhaps; or perhaps it was notes about the other tunnels, the side tunnels Sorhild had warned them not to venture far into. Maybe it was nothing, only marks to show someone had passed this way. It was easy, in the tunnels, to believe the outside world could forget you ever existed.

He wondered if there was anyone *left* in the outside world to remember him. Surely the Fjeltroll could not have slain *all* of the Yarru-yami, not unless all of the Six Clans had remained at the Stone Grove. The desert was vast and Fjeltroll were not suited to traveling in an arid clime. Perhaps some of the Yarru lived.

Or perhaps they did not. Who, then, would remember Dani of the Yarru and his fat Uncle Thulu if they died beneath the earth? Blaise?

Fianna? Hobard? Peldras, the Haomane-gaali? Carfax, who had saved him after all? He held out little hope that any of them had survived. There had been too few of them, and the Were too swift, too deadly. Even Malthus had deemed it imperative to flee.

There was Malthus, if it was true, if he was the Galäinridder after all. Dani thought he must be, even though the gem was the wrong color. But the Galäinridder had gone south without looking for them. He must think they were dead already, or lost forever in the Ways.

He was still thinking about it when they broke for a rest, laying their bedrolls a short, safe distance inside one of the side tunnels. It took a bit of searching to find a stone with a sharp point that fit nicely in the hand.

"What are you doing, lad?" Uncle Thulu, rummaging through their packs, eyed him curiously. "We're in enough danger without leaving a sign to point our trail."

"With the two of us marching down the tunnel plain as day, I don't think we need to worry about it, Uncle." Scratching on the tunnel wall, Dani drew the marking of the Stone Grove clan, five monoliths in a rough circle. He frowned, settling back to squat on his heels, then leaned forward to sketch a small vessel with a cork stopper in it, adding a digging-stick for good measure. "There."

Against his will, Uncle Thulu smiled. "There we are."

"Aye." Dani set down the stone and met his uncle's gaze. "It's just . . . if we fail, if we're caught and slain out of hand, maybe some-day someone will find this; Malthus, or one of the Haomane-gaali; they have long memories. Or maybe a Staccian from Gerflod who remembers the Lady Sorhild's stories. And they will say, 'Look, the Bearer was here and his Guide was with him. Two Yarru-yami from the Stone Grove clan. They made it this far. They tried. Can we not do as much?'"

"Ah, lad!" Thulu's voice was rough. "I wish I had my digging-stick with me now. There may be no waterways to trace down here, but I hated to leave it in that Fjeltroll."

"You'll make another," Dani said. "I'll help you find it. After we go home. We'll rise before dawn and chew *gamal* together, then when the stars begin to pale, we'll go to the baari-grove and watch the dew form and pick just the right one." He smiled at his uncle. "One with a thirst for water, straight and strong, that peels clean as a whistle and fits firm in the hand, so you can lean on it once you've grown fat again."

Thulu laughed softly, deep in his chest. "Do you think so?"

"No." Dani's smile turned wistful. "But we can pretend."

"Then we shall." Thulu stroked the clan markings on the wall with his strong, blunt fingertips. "And, aye, lad, I promise you. Whatever happens, one day the world will say, 'Dani the Bearer was here, and his fat Uncle Thulu, too. They did their best. Let us do the same.'"

USHAHIN DREAMSPINNER SAT CROSS-LEGGED ON a high crag overlooking the plains of Curonan, squeezing a rock in his right hand. The heavy sheepskin cloak he wore cut the worst of the wind, but his bones still ached in the cold.

All except his right arm.

It felt strange; a foreign thing, this straight and shapely limb that moved with effortless grace. This finely made hand, the fingers capable of nimble manipulation and a powerful grip alike. Gone was the familiar stiffness of joint and bone-deep ache that plagued the rest of his body. In its place was an easy, lithesome strength and the memory of an agony that surpassed any pain the rest of his body had known, living like a phantom beneath the surface of his skin. The bones did not merely ache. They remembered.

Tanaros had told him to squeeze the rock. It would strengthen the new sinew and muscle, toughen the soft skin of his palm and fingers. It seemed unnecessary to Ushahin, but it gave a focal point to the pain; to the memory of pain. So he squeezed, and each time his hand constricted around the rock, it sent a pulse through fiber and bone that remembered its own slow pulverization. There was a macabre comfort in it; and irony, too. Another memory, an image that lay over him like a shadow, and it, too, carried a pain his bones remembered. Now, a thousand years later, here he was, a rock clenched in his fist. It was strange the way time brought all things full circle. Ushahin wished he could speak to Calanthrag about it. The Eldest would have understood.

But time itself was the problem, for there was none to spare. Not for him, not for any of them. His ravens were streaking across the face of Urulat. Ushahin sat, squeezing a rock in his right hand, and gazed through the fragmented mosaic of their myriad eyes. He could not say which filled him with the most fear: that which they saw, or that which they did not.

Hoofbeats sounded on the winding, treacherous path behind him, drawing him out of his distant reverie. "Lord Dreamspinner?"

"Speros of Haimhault." Ushahin acknowledged him without looking.

"General Tanaros has asked me to take you to the armory." Although he was doing his best to conceal it, the Midlander's voice held a complex mixture of emotions. Ushahin smiled to himself.

"Do you wonder that I still live?" he asked, dropping the rock and getting to his feet. "Is that it, Midlander? Would you see me dead for defying his Lordship's wishes?"

"No, my lord!" Speros' brown eyes widened. He sat astride the horse he had ridden during their flight to Darkhaven; the ghostly grey horse Ushahin had lent him. Behind him was the blood-bay stallion, its head raised and alert. "I would not presume to think such a thing."

"No?" Ushahin made his way to the stallion's side. Its once rough hide was glossy with tending, a deep sanguine hue. He felt it shudder beneath his touch, but it stood without flinching and let him mount, slewing around one wary eye. It was much easier to pull himself astride with one strong right arm. "How is it, then? Are you, like our dear general, ensorcelled by the Lady of the Ellylon's beauty?"

Speros kneed his horse around to face Ushahin, his jaw set, a flush creeping up his cheeks. "You do me an injustice," he said through gritted teeth, "and a greater one to the Lord General."

Ushahin gazed at him without answering, reaching out to sift through the Midlander's thoughts. Ignoring Speros' jolt of horror at the invasion, he tasted the deep and abiding awe with which the young man had first beheld the Lady of the Ellylon, weighing it judiciously against his fierce loyalty to Tanaros, born of their travail in the desert and his own inner demons. "So," he said softly. "It is loyalty that wins. Or need I search further? Shall I tell you your deepest fears, your darkest nightmares?"

"Don't." Speros choked out the word. The blood had drained from his face, and his wide-stretched brown eyes were stark against his pallor. "Please don't, my lord! It hurts."

Ushahin sighed and released him. "Then speak truth to me, Speros of Haimhault. What troubles you?"

Speros shuddered, tucking his chin into the collar of his cloak; heavy sheepskin like Ushahin's own. "You betrayed him," he said in a low voice. "Lord Satoris."

"No." Ushahin shook his head, gazing past the Midlander toward the plains. "I defied him, which is a different matter altogether." He looked back at Speros. So young, and so mortal! Why was it that he seemed so much more vulnerable than his own madlings? He had come here unwelcome, had braved far worse than his madlings, who were admitted unharmed. And yet. There was something touching about it; his fear, his loyalty. "Do you know what is coming, child?"

"War." Speros lifted his chin defiantly, the color returning to his face. "I'm not a *child*, Lord Dreamspinner."

"War," Ushahin echoed. "War, such as the world has not seen since the Fourth Age of the Sundered World." He pointed to the east. "Do you know what I have seen today, Midlander? Dwarfs, on the march. An entire company, following a column of Vedasian knights."

Speros laughed. "Dwarfs, my lord?"

"You laugh," Ushahin murmured. "Yrinna's Children have broken their Peace, and you laugh. You should not laugh, Midlander. They are strong and stubborn, as sturdy as the roots of an ancient tree. Once, long ago, before the world was Sundered, they made war upon the Ellylon."

"They are very . . . short," Speros said cautiously. "Or so it is said."

Ushahin gave him a grim smile. "We are all smallfolk to the Fjel, and yet they can be defeated. Do you know what I have not seen? An entire company of Fjel sent to hunt a pair of smallfolk. Not today, nor yesterday, nor for many days now. So, yes, Midlander, I defied his Lordship. I am uneasy at the signs converging upon us. I do not have a Shaper's pride; no, nor even a Man's, to scruple at a dishonorable course. If there was another chance to avert Haomane's Prophecy at a single stroke, I would take it."

For a long moment, Speros was silent. "I understand," he said at length.

"Good." Ushahin turned his mount. "Then take me to the armory."

They rode in single file along the path, and the Tordenstem Fjel on sentry duty saluted them as they passed. Speros glanced at the fortifications he had built at the edge of the Defile; the wooden ricks laden with boulders, levers primed and ready. "Darkhaven *is* well-guarded, Lord Dreamspinner," he said. "I do not discount your fears, but we are prepared for any army, whether it be Men, Ellylon, or Dwarfs."

"What of Shapers?" Ushahin inquired.

Speros shot him an alarmed look. *"Shapers?"*

"To be sure." Ushahin laughed mirthlessly. "Who do you think we are fighting, Speros of Haimhault? Aracus Altorus? Malthus the Counselor? The Lord of the Rivenlost?" He shook his head. "Our enemy is Haomane First-Born."

"I thought the Six Shapers would not leave Torath!"

"Nor will they," Ushahin said. "Not while his Lordship holds Godslayer. But make no mistake, this war is of Haomane's making. It is the wise man who can name his enemy."

The Midlander was quiet and thoughtful as they made their way back to within Darkhaven's walls and rode toward the armory. Alongside the Gorgantus River, the waterwheel built at Speros' suggestion creaked in a steady circle, powering the bellows. Grey-black smoke was churning from the smelting furnaces, and nearby, the forges were going at full blast, sending up a fearful din and clatter. Teams of Fjel handled the work of heating and reheating cast-iron rods and plates, beating and folding them back onto themselves until the iron hardened. Elsewhere, red-hot metal was plunged into troughs of water, sending up clouds of acrid steam, and grinding wheels shrieked, scattering showers of sparks. The Fjel worked heedless amid it all, their thick hides impervious. A Staccian smith clad in a heavy leather apron strolled through the chaos, supervising their efforts.

In the presence of so much martial clamor, Speros' spirits rose visibly. "Come, my lord," he shouted. "We'll find you a weapon that suits!"

Inside the armory, the thick stone walls diminished the racket outside. Weapons were stacked like firewood; piles of bucklers and full-body shields, racks of spears, bits and pieces of plate armor on every surface. Whistling through his gapped teeth, Speros strode toward a row of swords, hefting one and then another, pausing to eye Ushahin. At last he nodded, satisfied, and offered one, laying it over his forearm and extending the hilt. "Try this one, my lord."

It was strange to watch his hand, his finely made hand, close on the hilt. Ushahin raised the sword, wondering what he was supposed to discern from it, wondering what his Lordship expected him to do with it.

"Very nice!" Speros grinned at him. "Shall I teach you a few strokes, my lord?"

"I have seen it done," Ushahin said wryly.

"Ah, come now, Lord Dreamspinner." Speros plucked another blade from the row and tossed aside his sheepskin cloak, taking up an offensive stance. "If I were to come at you thusly," he said, aiming a slow strike at Ushahin's left side, "you would parry by—"

Ushahin brought his blade down hard and fast, knocking the Midlander's aside. "I have seen it done, Speros!" The impact made every misshapen bone in his body ache. He sighed. "This war will not be won with swords."

"Maybe not, my lord." The tip of Speros' sword had lodged in the wooden floor. Lowering his head until his brown hair spilled over his brow, he pried it loose and laid the blade back in its place. "But it won't be lost by them either."

"I pray you are right," Ushahin murmured. "You have done your duty to Tanaros, Midlander. I am armed. Go, now, and leave me."

After a moment's hesitation, Speros went.

Ushahin gazed at the blade in his right hand. The edges were keen, gleaming blue in the dim light of the armory. He wished, again, he knew what his Lordship expected of him. Since he did not, he found a scabbard for the blade and a swordbelt that fit about his waist and left the armory.

Outside, the blood-bay stallion was waiting, its reins looped over a hitching rail. Beneath the murky pall of smoke that hung over the place, its coat glowed with dark fire, as though it had emerged molten from the furnace and were slowly cooling. It stood unnaturally still, watching him with its wary, intelligent gaze.

"Have we come to a truce, you and I?" Ushahin asked aloud. "Then we are wiser, in our way, than our masters."

Perhaps it was so; or perhaps Ushahin, who had been abjured by the Grey Dam, no longer carried the taint of the Were on him like a scent. It grieved him to think it might be so. The horse merely gazed at him, thinking its own abstruse equine thoughts. He did not trouble its mind, but instead stroked its mane, wondering at the way his fingers slid through the coarse, black, hair. It had been a long time since he had taken pleasure in *touch*, in the sensation of texture against his skin.

"All things must be as they must," he said to the stallion, then mounted and went to tell Lord Satoris that the Dwarfs had broken Yrinna's Peace.

THIRTEEN

"Lady." Tanaros bowed. "Are you well?"

She stood very straight, and her luminous grey eyes were watchful and wary. Her travail in Darkhaven had only honed her beauty, he thought; paring it to its essence, until the bright flame of her spirit was almost visible beneath translucent flesh.

"I am," she said. "Thank you, General Tanaros."

"Good." He cleared his throat, remembering how he had burst into the room and feeling ill at ease. "On behalf of his Lordship, I tender apologies. Please know that the attempt upon your life was made against his orders."

"Yes," Cerelinde said. "I know."

"You seem very certain."

Her face, already fair as ivory, turned a paler hue. "I heard the screams."

"It's not what you think." The words were impulsive. Tanaros sighed and ran a hand through his hair. "Ah, Cerelinde! His Lordship did what was necessary. If you saw Ushahin's . . . punishment . . . you would understand."

Her chin lifted a notch. "The Ellylon do not condone torture."

"He healed his arm," Tanaros said abruptly.

Cerelinde stared at him, uncomprehending. "Forgive me. I do not understand."

"Slowly," Tanaros said, "and painfully. Very painfully." He gave a short laugh. "It matters not. Ushahin understood what he did. He bore his Lordship's punishment that his madlings might not. He did not want them to suffer for serving his will." A stifled sound came from the corner; turning his head, Tanaros saw Meara huddled there. A cold, burning suspicion suffused his chest. "Do you have something to say, Meara?"

She shook her head in frantic denial, hiding her face against her knees.

"*Let her be.*" Cerelinde stepped between them, her face alight with anger. "Do you think I would permit her in my presence did I not trust her, Tanaros?"

"I don't know," he said quietly. "*Do* you trust her?"

The Ellylon could not lie. She stood close to him, close enough to touch, her chin still lifted. He could feel the heat of her body; could almost smell her skin. Her eyes were level with his. He could see the pleated irises, the subtle colors that illuminated them; violet, blue, and green, and the indeterminate hue that lies in the innermost curve of a rainbow.

"Yes," Cerelinde said, her voice steady and certain. "I do."

There was a sob, then; a raw sound, wrenched from Meara's throat. She launched herself toward the door with unexpected speed, low to the ground and scuttling. Taken by surprise, Tanaros let her go. He caught only a glimpse of her face as she passed, an accusatory gaze between strands of lank, untended hair. Her hands scrabbled at the door, and the Mørkhar Fjel beyond it allowed her passage.

"What passes here, Lady?" Tanaros asked simply.

"You frighten her." Cerelinde raised her brows. "Is there more?"

"No." He thought about Meara; her weight, straddling him. The heat of her flesh, the touch of her mouth against his. Her teeth, nipping at his lower lip. The memory made him shift in discomfort. "Nothing that concerns you."

Cerelinde moved away from him, taking a seat and keeping her disconcerting gaze upon him. "You do not know me well enough to know what concerns me, Tanaros Blacksword."

"Lady, I know you better than you think," he murmured. "But I will not seek to force the truth you are unwilling to reveal. Since I am here in good faith, is there aught in which I may serve you?"

Yearning flared in her eyes and she took a deep breath, letting it out slowly. Her voice trembled as she answered, "You might tell me what passes in the world beyond these walls."

Tanaros nodded. "I would thirst for knowledge, too, did I stand in your shoes, Cerelinde. Never say I denied you unkindly. Yrinna's Children are on the march."

"What?" Yearning turned to hope; Cerelinde leaned forward, fingers whitening on the arms of the chair. There were tears in her bright eyes. "Tanaros, I pray you, play no jests with me."

He smiled sadly at her. "Would that I did."

"Yrinna's Children have broken her Peace!" she marveled. "And . . ." Her voice faltered, then continued, adamant with resolve. "And Aracus?"

"He is coming." Tanaros sighed. "They are all coming, Cerelinde."

"You know it is not too late—"

"No." He cut her off with a word. It hurt to see such hope, such joy, in her face. When all was said and done, it was true; he was a fool. But he was a loyal fool, and his loyalty was to Lord Satoris; and to others, who trusted him. Tanaros fingered the *rhios* that hung in a pouch at his belt. "Save your words, Lady. If you have need of aught else, send for me, and I will come."

With that he left her, because it was easier than staying. The Mørkhar Fjel at her door gave him their usual salute. Tanaros stared hard at them. Too much suspicion and longing was tangled in his heart.

"See to it that no one passes unnoted," he said. "Even the Dreamspinner's madlings, do you understand? It was one such who served the Lady poison."

"Lord General." It was Krognar, one of his most trusted among the Havenguard, who answered in a deep rumble. "Forgive us. One looks much like another."

"Do they *smell* alike?" Tanaros asked sharply.

The Mørkhar exchanged glances. "No," Krognar said. "But you did not ask us to note their scent. They are Lord Ushahin's madlings. You never troubled at them before."

"I'm asking you now."

The Mørkhar bowed. "It will be done," said Krognar.

Leaving them, Tanaros paced the halls. His heart was uneasy, his feet restless. He half-thought to track down Meara and question her, but there was no telling where she might be in the maze of corridors behind the wall. And did it matter? She was Ushahin's creature. If it had been her, she had only been doing his bidding. He had paid the price for it; for all of them. His Lordship was content. Could Tanaros be less?

Since he had no answers, he went to see Hyrgolf instead.

There was always merit in inspecting the barracks. Tanaros exited Darkhaven proper, making his way to the Fjel delvings north of the fortress. He strode through tunneled corridors, pausing here and there to visit the vast, communal sleeping chambers. They were glad of his visit, proud of their preparations, showing him armor stacked in neat readiness, weapons honed to a killing edge. Word traveled ahead of him, and he had not gone a hundred paces before the Fjel began spilling into the corridors, baring eyetusks in broad grins and beckoning him onward.

"Hey, Lord General!"

"Hey, boss!"

"Come check *our* weapons!"

"When are we going to war?"

The sheer weight of their enthusiasm settled his nerves and made him smile. The Fjel, who had the most to lose in accordance with Haomane's Prophecy, were with him. No sign of faltering there; their loyalty was unswerving. "Soon enough, lads!" he shouted to them. "I'm off to see Marshal Hyrgolf."

They cheered the mention of his name. One of theirs, one of their own.

And then there was Hyrgolf, standing in the entryway of his private chamber, his broad shoulders touching on either side of it. His leathery lips were curved in a smile of acknowledgment, but the squinting eyes beneath the heavy ridge of his brow held a deeper concern.

"General Tanaros," he rumbled. "Come."

Vorax walked along the northeastern wall of the auxiliary larder, touching items stacked alongside it; kegs of Vedasian wine, vast wheels of cheese wrapped in burlap piled into columns. Sacks of wheat, bushels of root vegetables; so much food it could not be stored within the confines of Darkhaven proper, but space must be found outside its walls. The towering cavern was filled to bursting with them.

All his, all his doing.

He was proud of it. There was no glamour in it; no, nor glory. There was something better: sustenance. Glutton, Haomane's Allies called him. Let them. He had earned his appetite, earned his right to indulge it. For a thousand years, Vorax had provided *sustenance*. Food did not fall on the plate and beg to be eaten, no matter who you were; peasant, Rivenlost lord, or one of the Three.

No, it had to be obtained; somehow, somewhere. In Staccia, they had always understood it. Precious little could be grown in the northern mountains. Neheris had not Shaped her lands with Men in mind. There was fish and game, and sheep and goats were tended. Never enough, not for as many Men dwelled in Staccia. For aught else, they had to trade; and they had little with which to trade. There was proud living in the mountains, but it was hard living, too. It had made them hungry, and it had made them shrewd.

And Vorax was the hungriest and shrewdest of them all. He had made the bargain to end all bargains—and he had kept it, too. Staccia had done naught but profit by it, and Darkhaven done naught but prosper. The betrayal of the Staccian lordlings incited by the Galäin-ridder was the only blot on his record, and that had been dealt with swiftly and irrevocably. He had earned the right to be proud.

"Do you see this, Dreamspinner?" He slapped a wheel of cheese with one meaty hand. It made a resounding echo in the vaulted cavern. "We could feed the Fjel for a month on cheese alone!"

"I don't imagine they'd thank you for it," Ushahin muttered, wrapped in his sheepskin cloak. Darkhaven's larders were built into the mountains of Gorgantum, deep enough that they remained cool even in the warmth of summer; not Fjel work, but older, part of the tunnel system that lore held was dragon-made.

"They would if their bellies pinched," Vorax said pragmatically. "And it may come to it, does this siege last. Meanwhile, who procured the flocks that keeps them in mutton?"

"Would you have me sing your glory?" The half-breed shivered. "I would as soon be done with it, Staccian."

"As you will," Vorax grumbled, and went back to counting kegs. "Third row, fifth barrel . . . here." He reached between the wooden kegs, grunting, and drew forth a parcel thrice-wrapped in waxed parchment, which he tossed onto the stony floor. "I had to bargain dearly for it, Dreamspinner. Are you sure we ought to destroy it?"

"I'm sure." Ushahin squatted next to the packet, bowing his head. The ends of his pale hair trailed on the ground; he glanced upward with his mismatched eyes. "We had our chance and took it. The time has passed. Do you want to risk Tanaros finding it? He is asking questions, cousin, and in time he may think of your outermost larder, or learn it from my madlings. Do you want his Lordship to know your involvement? Would you risk *that?*"

"No." Vorax shook his head and shuddered. "No, I would not."

"So." With his newly deft right hand, Ushahin unfolded the parcel. A scant pile of herbs lay in the center of the creased parchment. There had been more, once. He inhaled, his nostrils flaring. "All-Bane," he murmured. "Sprung from the death-mound of a Were corpse. I have not smelled it since I dwelled in the forests of Pelmar."

"Aye," Vorax said. "Or so the Rukhari swore. I demanded it in compensation for our aborted bargain. They were loath to part with it." He shrugged. "Do you think it would have killed her?"

"Yes," the half-breed said. "Oh, yes, cousin. All-Bane, Oronin's Foil. To taste of it is to hear the Glad Hunter's horn call your name. Death rides in his train, and not even the Ellylon are exempt from its touch." He regarded the herbs with his twisted smile. "Would that Oronin Last-Born had protected his Children as well in life as he does in death. The Lady would have died had she sampled the broth."

"Pity," Vorax said, reaching for a torch. "It was a noble effort."

"Yes." Ushahin straightened and rose. "It was."

Vorax touched the torch to the parcel. The waxed parchment ignited with a flare. Fire consumed it, and soon the dried herbs were ablaze. Tendrils of smoke arose, dense and grey, with a faint violet tint, more smoke than one would have thought possible from such a scant handful. It coiled along the floor, rising where it encountered living flesh.

"It smells . . . almost sweet," Vorax said in wonder. "No wonder the Fjel did not recognize it as a poison." A pleasant lassitude weighted his limbs and his eyelids felt heavy. He inhaled deeply. "What is the aroma? Like vulnus-blossom, only . . . only the memory it evokes is pleasant. It reminds me of . . . of what, Dreamspinner?" He smiled, closing his eyes and remembering. "Childhood in Staccia, and goldenrod blooming in the meadows."

"Out. *Out*, cousin!"

The words came to him filtered through a haze; a gilded haze of swimming light, violet-tinged, the air filled with pollen. Vorax opened his eyes and frowned, seeing Ushahin Dreamspinner's face before him, skin stretched taut over the misshapen cheekbones. "What troubles you, cousin?" he asked in a thick voice.

Pale lips, shaping a curse in the tongue of the Were; he watched with mild interest, watched the shapely right arm swing back, then forward, tendrils of smoke swirling in its wake. It all seemed so slow, until it was not. Vorax rocked on his heels at the impact of the half-breed's palm against his bearded cheek.

"Enough!" he roared, anger stirring in his belly. "Do not try my patience!"

Ushahin's eyes glittered through the smoke. One was black, drowning-black, swallowed by pupil; the other was silver-grey, fractured into splintered shards, like a mirror broken into a thousand pieces of bad luck, with a pinprick of black at the center. His hand, his right hand, fell upon the Staccian's shoulder with unexpected strength, spinning him. "Vorax of Staccia, *get out of this place!*"

There was a shove, a powerful shove between the shoulder blades, and Vorax went, staggering under the impetus, placing one foot after the other until he reached the outermost opening with its narrow ledge. There the air was cold and clean and he breathed deeply of it, gazing at Darkhaven's holdings until his head began to clear. There was edifice; there was the encircling wall, vanishing to encompass them. There was the Gorgantus River. There, in the distance, were the pastures and the mines; there, nearer, were the furnaces and forges, beneath their pall of smoke.

It made him glance involuntarily behind him; but the smoke of the All-Bane had not followed him. There was only Ushahin, huddled in his sheepskin cloak, looking raw with the cold.

"Are you well, cousin?" he asked in a low voice.

"Aye," Vorax said roughly. With his chin, he pointed at the Dreamspinner's hidden right arm. "Who would have thought there was such strength in that wing of yours. So is . . . *that* . . . what you might have been?"

"Perhaps." Ushahin gave a terse laugh. "I am the Misbegotten, after all."

"Ah, well. You would have made a doughty warrior, cousin." There was nothing else in those words he wanted to touch. Vorax breathed slow and steady, watching the sluggish flow of the Gorgantus River below them. The waterwheel Tanaros' Midlander protégé had built turned with excruciating slowness, murky water dripping from its paddles. Still, it did its job, powering the bellows. "Is it done?" he asked presently.

Ushahin shrugged his hunched shoulders. "Let us see."

They did, returning step by step, side by side. There was the larder, lined with kegs and loaves and wheels. There, on the floor, a tiny pile of ashes smoldered, no longer smoking. Side by side, they stared at it.

"Is it still dangerous?" Vorax asked.

"I do not believe so." Ushahin glanced into the darkness at the rear of the larder, where the chamber narrowed into a winding tunnel. "There is no one there to heed Oronin's Horn. The passages are too low, even for my madlings." He shrugged again. "Even if they were not, the tunnels leading from here link to the Vesdarlig Passage, and it is blocked, now. No one travels to or from your homeland, cousin."

"I pray you are right." Vorax stamped on the smoldering pile with a booted heel, grinding the remnants into harmless powder until nothing remained but a faint sooty smear. "There," he said with satisfaction. "All evidence of our conspiracy is gone."

Ushahin considered him. "Then we are finished?"

"Aye." Vorax met his gaze unflinching. "I lack the courage of your madness, Dreamspinner. Already, you have shielded me from his Lordship's wrath. I will not risk facing it a second time." He shook his head. "Haomane's Prophecy is no certain thing. His Lordship's fury is. Do you cross his will again, there will be no mercy. I would sooner die in his name than at his hands."

Ushahin nodded. "As you will, cousin."

"Uru-Alat!" Dani whispered. "A rockfall?"

There was a sick feeling in the pit of his stomach. Beside him, Uncle Thulu was silent, staring in disbelief. By the wavering torchlight, the pile of boulders before them reached all the way to the ceiling.

"No." Thulu spoke at last, his voice heavy. "No, this was done on purpose. There's no damage to the tunnel itself." He gave a hollow laugh. "Of course it was. Why wouldn't they block it? One less entrance to guard."

It was too much to encompass. How many days had they been traveling beneath the earth? Weeks, at least; it may have been longer. Each step filled with fear and trepidation, each curve in the tunnel harboring the potential of a Fjel attack. All for nothing. There had been no Fjel. There was no egress. The tunnel was blocked.

"Can we move them?" Dani asked. "Or climb over it?"

Uncle Thulu squared his shoulders, shaking off the yoke of despair. "I don't know, lad. Let's try."

They wedged the torches into the pile and began working, shifting the smaller rocks and digging out around the larger, concentrating their efforts on one several feet off the tunnel floor that appeared to be supporting the weight of others.

"Ready, lad?" Uncle Thulu asked, once he could wrap his arms around it.

Dani nodded grimly, taking hold of the boulder. "Ready."

On a count of three, they hauled together, tipping it. The massive stone's weight did the rest, rolling loose. As they leapt clear of its path, a small section of the pile shifted, other boulders settling in a cascade of smaller rocks.

Otherwise, it was unchanged.

"No good." Thulu shook his head. "This is Fjeltroll work. It may go on for yards; scores of them, is my guess. After all, they're trying to keep an army out, not just a couple of weary Yarru-yami."

Dani took a deep breath. "I'll see if we can climb over it."

He went slowly, testing each hand- and foothold with care. The boulders, disturbed by their efforts, shifted beneath his weight. For once, he was glad that he was unshod, feeling the subtle movement of the rocks beneath the soles of his bare feet. Although he no longer needed the sling, his left shoulder was imperfectly healed and ached with the strain. The muscles of his legs quivered; partly with effort, and partly with nerves. The clay vial strung around his neck had never seemed so vulnerable. One wrong step, and he would set off a rockslide. Whether or not Dani survived it, he doubted the fragile vessel would.

Endless as it seemed, he eventually reached the top.

"What do you see, lad?" Uncle Thulu called from the base of the pile, holding his torch as high as possible.

"Nothing." Dani braced his palms on the ceiling of the tunnel and sighed. The pile was solid. There was no gap at the top; or at least, only inches. "We could *try* making a passage from here." He reached forward with one hand to pry a few stones loose and tried to imagine it. Moving through the darkness, shifting rocks a scant few at a time, wriggling back and forth on their bellies, pinned against the ceiling. It was not a hopeful prospect.

"It might be quicker to walk back to Staccia," Thulu said dourly. "And safer, too. Come down, Dani. We'll find another way."

"Wait." There was something; a faint current of air, moving. Dani went still, holding his outspread hand over the rocks. He could feel it, a whisper against his skin. "There's an air shaft."

"Are you sure?"

"I'm sure." Taking a better stance, Dani slid the vial around and tucked it under his collar at the back of his neck. "Stand clear, Uncle!"

It felt good, after days and days of grinding sameness, to be *doing*. He burrowed steadily into the pile, working with both hands, grabbing rocks and tossing them to either side. Those at the uttermost top were smaller, easier to move. They bounced down the rockpile in a rattling, satisfying procession. The larger ones were trickier. The first one he managed to expose was at chest height, twice as large around as his head. Whispering a swift prayer to Uru-Alat, Dani worked it loose.

Unbalanced, the pile shifted. His footholds vanished, sending him sliding and scrabbling downward on his belly, nails clinging ineffectually to stone. Bruised and banged, he fetched up hard, jarring one hip against a solid, immobile boulder.

"Dani!"

"I'm all right!" He checked the clay vial and found it safe, then peered upward. The hole had widened considerably. He could feel the air on his face now. Dani inhaled deeply. "Uncle! I smell *grass*!"

The light cast by Thulu's torch flickered wildly. "Dani, lad, I'm coming up."

It was painstaking. Once Thulu completed the treacherous journey, laden with packs and torches and moving with infinitesimal care, they set to work in tandem. They worked as swiftly as they dared, widening the hole one rock at a time, working in the direction of the air current.

Torchlight aided, but it posed a hazard, too. Every time the rock-pile settled and their balance slipped, there was the added risk of setting themselves ablaze.

"All this work, and I don't suppose we've any idea how big the shaft is," Uncle Thulu observed. "It will be a hard blow if we don't fit."

Covered in rock dust, Dani grinned at him. "Maybe it's a good thing you're not so fat anymore!"

After further hours of labor, there was no jest left in either of them. Feeling with careful fingertips, they found the bottom of the ventilation shaft, clearing around and beneath it. There was no sign of daylight, which hopefully meant nothing worse than that night had fallen while they worked. The shaft was wide enough, barely; a scant three feet across. Whether it narrowed and how high it went was another matter.

"You found it," Thulu said somberly. "You look."

"All right." Returning the flask to its customary place at his throat, Dani eased himself onto his back and ducked his head under the opening. At first, his eyes grown used to torchlight, he saw only blackness and his heart sank. But gradually, his vision cleared, and he laughed aloud. The shaft was deep, but it cut an unswerving path through the solid rock. And far, far above him . . .

"What do you see?"

"Stars!" A patch of starlight, faint and distant. He ducked back out, eyes shining. "We can do this, Uncle. It's a long climb, but we can do it."

Uncle Thulu gave him a worried smile. "We'll try."

Squatting atop the rock-pile, they sorted through their gear, paring down supplies to the barest of essentials. A parcel of food and a waterskin apiece lashed around their waists, belt daggers, and the warm Staccian cloaks the Lady of Gerflod had given them. Dani kept his slingshot, and Thulu his flint striker. Everything else, they would leave.

"I'm smaller and lighter," Dani said. "I'll go first."

Thulu nodded, fidgeting with his pack. "You know, lad, a drop of the Water—"

"No." Dani shook his head, touching the flask. "We can't, Uncle. I don't dare. I don't even know if there's enough left for . . . for what I'm supposed to do. Will you at least try? If I can do it, you can."

Uncle Thulu sighed. "Go on, then."

There was only one way to do it. Squirming under the opening,

Dani stood up inside the ventilation shaft. If he craned his head, he could see the stars. It seemed a longer way up than it had at first glance. Setting his back firmly against one wall of the shaft, he braced his legs on the opposite wall and began to inch his way upward.

It was torturous going. He had underestimated; underestimated the distance, the difficulty, the sheer exhaustion of his muscles. Within minutes, his legs were cramping and his breath was coming hard. It made him thirsty, and he could not help but think about the Water of Life and the scent of it, the scent of all life and green growing things. Three drops, and Uncle Thulu had healed almost as completely as though he had never been injured, had gained the energy to run and run and run without tiring, carrying Dani on his back. It wouldn't take that much to make this climb infinitely easier.

One drop. How much harm would it do to take one drop of the Water? To restore vigor to his weary body, to uncramp his painful muscles, to quench his parched tissues, to erase the plaguing ache near his collarbone.

The temptation was almost overwhelming. Gritting his teeth, Dani remembered how much had spilled in Neherinach, where the Fjeltroll had caught them. Rivulets of water, gleaming silver in the sunlight, trickling over the Fjel's horny palm. If it hadn't . . . perhaps. But it had, and there was too little left to waste; not unless it was a matter of life or death. It wasn't, not yet.

He forced himself to keep inching upward, to remember instead the look of stark disbelief in the eyes of the last Fjel to die, the one who had spoken to him. The Water of Life was not to be taken lightly; never, ever. Old Ngurra had told him that many times. In the womb of the world, Life and Death were twins. To invoke one was to summon the other's shadow.

Inch by inch, Dani of the Yarru resisted temptation and climbed.

He had not known his eyes were clenched shut until he felt the tickle of grass upon his face and a cold wind stirring his hair and realized he had reached the top of the shaft. An involuntary cry escaped him as he opened his eyes.

"Dani!" Uncle Thulu's voice sounded ghostly far below. "Are you all right?"

"Aye!" He shouted down between his braced legs. "Uncle, it's beautiful!"

In a final surge of strength, he wriggled upward a few more inches and got his arms free of the shaft, levering his body out and onto solid earth. For a moment, Dani simply lay on his back, willing his muscles to uncramp. The sky overhead seemed enormous, a vast black vault spangled with a million stars, and Arahila's moon floating in it like a pale and lovely ship. In the distance there were mountains, tall and jagged, but all around there was nothing but grass; a sea of grass, sweet-smelling, silvery in the moonlight, swaying in waves.

"All right, lad!" Thulu's words echoed faintly from the shaft. "My turn."

Dani rolled onto his belly and peered down. "One inch at a time, Uncle." Reaching to one side, he tore out a handful of grass. "Just keep moving."

It was impossible, of course. He had known that before he'd made it halfway up the shaft. Uncle Thulu, he suspected, had known it all along. He was thin enough to fit in the shaft, but too big to make the climb. His longer limbs would be too cramped. His muscles, support-ing his greater weight, would begin to quiver. He would be forced to give up and tell Dani to continue on his own. Dani should have given him a drop of the Water of Life. Now, it was too late.

Sitting upright, Dani began plaiting grass.

It was not as sturdy as thukka-vine, but it was strong and pliant. Head bowed, he worked feverishly. Over and under, fingers flying. It was one of the earliest skills the Yarru learned. From time to time he paused, wrenching up more handfuls of the tough, sweet-smelling plains grass, weaving new stalks into his pattern. Arahila's moon con-tinued to sail serenely across the sky, and a length of plaited rope emerged steadily beneath his hands.

"Dani." Uncle Thulu's voice, low and exhausted, emerged from the shaft. "Dani, lad."

"I know." He peered over the edge and saw his uncle's figure lodged in place. Thulu had not quite made it halfway. "Stay where you are." Kneeling, he paid out the rope, hand over hand. It dangled, a few inches too short. "Can you hold on a little while longer?"

"Dani, listen to me . . ." Angling his head, Thulu saw the rope and fell silent. Moonlight caught the glimmer of tears in his eyes. "Ah, lad!"

"Hold on," Dani repeated, coiling the rope. "A little while."

The words of the Song of Being whispered through his mind as he worked. Although his lips were silent, he spoke them with his finger-tips, plaiting grass into rope; each strand, each loop, each growing inch a prayer to Uru-Alat. He did not measure a second time. The rope was a prayer. It would be as long as the prayer. That was the length that was needed.

When it was done, he knelt beside the shaft and lowered the rope. Wedged between the walls, Uncle Thulu braced himself in place with his legs and lashed the rope around his waist, tying it securely.

"Ready?" Dani called.

Thulu nodded. "Ready."

Dani got to his feet. He could feel the words of the Song of Being beneath his hands, chanting in his veins. As he hauled, slowly and steadily, hand over hand, he listened to them. There was wisdom in them, old Ngurra had said; the secrets of Life and Death, twined to-gether in the death of Uru-Alat the World God and the birth of the world. Dani was not wise enough to understand them. But he was trying.

It was part of the Bearer's burden.

Arahila's moon was riding low when Thulu clambered clear of the shaft. As Dani had done, he could do no more than roll onto the grass and stare at the stars. For his part, Dani dropped where he stood and sat heavily in the grass. He felt as though his limbs were made of stone. It was a long time before he could summon the strength to speak. "Where are we, Uncle?"

Thulu sat up with an effort, rubbing the aching, cramped muscles of his legs and glanced around him. "The plains of Curonan, lad."

"And Darkhaven?"

Thulu pointed westward across the plains, toward the distant moun-tains that rose, black and jagged, blotting out the stars. "There."

THE CANDLES BURNED LOW IN Hyrgolf's chamber, until the rocky niches held little more than blue flames dancing above puddles of tallow. For long hours, they had conferred on matters regarding the defense of Darkhaven; the posting of sentries, scouting parties of Gulnagel, in-spections of the tunnels, manning of the fortifications, battle-tactics useful against Men and Ellylon and Dwarfs. The night was already old when Hyrgolf rummaged in a corner, bringing forth a half-empty skin of *svartblod*.

"General," he said, holding it forth in one enormous hand. "Drink."

Tanaros hesitated, then accepted it. Uncorking the skin, he took a deep swig. It burned all the way down to his belly, and the foul taste made his eyes water. "My thanks!" he gasped, handing it back.

The Tungskulder Fjel studied him. "I have never smelled fear on you before."

"Fear." Tanaros gave a harsh laugh, his throat seared by the *svartblod*'s heat. "Hyrgolf, my skin crawls with it. There is too much I mislike afoot in this place."

"The Dreamspinner's betrayal troubles you," Hyrgolf said.

"Yes." Tanaros met his eyes; the Fjel's familiar gaze, small as a boar's and steady as a rock. "More than I can say, for I fear there is reason in his madness. Would you do such a thing, Hyrgolf? Would you defy his Lordship's will and betray his wishes if it would avert Haomane's Prophecy at a single stroke?"

"No," Hyrgolf said simply. "I do not have the wisdom to meddle in the affairs of Shapers. The Fjel made their choice long ago, General. Haomane's Prophecy binds us to it." He smiled with hideous gentleness. "How did you tell me it went? *The Fjeltroll shall fall.*"

"Yet you do not fear," Tanaros murmured.

"Death in battle?" Hyrgolf shook his massive head. "No, not that. Lord Satoris . . ." He paused, raising the skin to drink. "He made us a promise, once. He said one day Men would covet our gifts." Lowering the skin, he handed it back to Tanaros. "He said Neheris-of-the-Leaping-Waters Shaped us well."

"She did." Tanaros took another scalding swig. "She did at that, Marshal." He wiped his lips and sighed. "Do you think we are so different in the end, Hyrgolf? You and I, Haomane's Allies?"

"No." The Fjel shrugged his heavy shoulders, gazing past Tanaros at the crudely carved *rhios* in a niche behind one of the dwindling candles. His boy's first effort. *Not bad for a mere pup, eh?* "Not in the end, General." He smiled ruefully, a shadow beneath the dense ridge of his brow. "Problem is, we seem to be somewhere in the middle, don't we?"

"Aye." Tanaros got unsteadily to his feet, returning the skin to

Hyrgolf. He clapped one hand on the Fjel's shoulder, reassured by the solid warmth of it, the unwavering loyalty. "His Lordship has the right of it, Hyrgolf. Even now, I envy you."

"General." Hyrgolf heaved his massive body upright. His taloned hands were surprisingly delicate as they closed around Tanaros' arm. "Go, and sleep. You have need of it. His Lordship has need of you."

"He entrusted me with his honor," Tanaros whispered.

"Aye." Hyrgolf nodded. "He is wise that way. And you entrust us with yours."

Tanaros shivered. "At what price, Hyrgolf?"

The Fjel smiled one last time, sad and slow. "I do not think that is ever given to us to know, General. We rejoice in it, for it is all we have, all we have chosen." He gave Tanaros a gentle shove, and the advice given to the rawest of recruits. "Go now, and sleep. You will feel better once the battle is joined."

Tanaros went, stumbling slightly. Outside, the cold air struck like a blow, diminishing the intoxicating effects of the *svartblod* he had drunk. He gazed at the horizon, where Arahila's moon swam low, a tarnished silver coin, and remembered the night his Lordship had first called them to the tower to see the red star that had arisen. His soft words, the pain in his voice.

Oh, Arahila!

"Why didn't you stay at his side?" Tanaros, wavering on his feet, addressed the moon. "You, any of you! Neheris, whom the Fjel still worship! Were you frightened? Is that it? Was Haomane Lord-of-Thought that powerful? What did you know that his Lordship did not?"

There was no answer, only a pair of Mørkhar Fjel on patrol, confirming his identity and giving him a wide berth.

Tanaros laughed softly. The air was cold, but the *svartblod* in his veins insulated him from it. Although he was not drunk, his flesh felt warm. "Or what did *he* know that Haomane First-Born did not?" he asked the moon. "Tell me that, O my Shaper!"

Light, only light; the light of the Souma, a lesser light, but no less lovely for it. It shed its silent benison. Things grew by it; things that blossomed in his Lordship's gardens. Tanaros sighed and set his feet on a homeward course.

"He loves you still," he informed the moon, glancing over his shoulder. "But he has made his choices. As I have made mine, as the Fjel have made theirs. The difference is, we made them freely. And *he* allowed us to do it. The Lord-of-Thought would not have done as much."

The moon, the beautiful moon, made no reply.

FOURTEEN

DAWN BROKE OVER THE PLAINS of Curonan, a glorious and terrifying sight. The sun's red orb crept slowly over the eastern horizon, staining the waving grass until it resembled a sea of blood. To the west, the mountains of Gorgantum threw up a defiant challenge, their implacable peaks shrouded in darkness.

At night, drenched in silvery moonlight, the plains had been a safe and magical place. It was different by daylight, with the eye of Haomane's Wrath opening in the east and the baleful shadow of Gorgantum to the west. Caught between the two on the vast, open space of the plains, Dani felt horribly conspicuous.

"Which way, lad?" Uncle Thulu asked quietly.

Grasping the clay flask that hung about his neck, Dani bowed his head. Sunlight, he knew. Haomane's Wrath could be terrible and impersonal, but he knew it. He was Yarru, and he understood. Darkness was another matter. Darkness, in which the Sunderer awaited; Satoris Banewreaker, who had slain his people, who wanted nothing more than for Dani to die so he could spill the Water of Life upon barren ground.

And more than anything else, Dani did not want to enter the shadow of those mountains. But he was the Bearer, and the burden of choice was upon him.

"Darkhaven," he said. "We go toward Darkhaven."

Uncle Thulu nodded. "So be it."

They set out at a steady walk, the sun at their backs, trampling their shadows into the sweet-smelling grass. They did not speak of how entrance might be gained into the Vale of Gorgantum. For the moment, the journey alone sufficed.

Hours later, the mountains scarcely seemed closer. Distances were as deceiving on the plains as they were in the desert. What it was that made Dani glance over his shoulder toward the eastern horizon, he could not have said. Regret, perhaps, or simple longing. It had crossed his mind that if the plains were not so immense, they might find Malthus in the east; Malthus, whose wisdom could guide him.

What he saw made him shudder.

"Uncle." His nails bit into Thulu's arm. "Look."

Ravens; a flock of ravens. A long way off, a smudge of darkness against the bright sky, but coming fast. Dani remembered how a trio of ravens had found them in the marshy land on the outskirts of Vedasia, circling high above them. How Malthus' voice had risen like thunder, giving warning. *The eyes of the Sunderer are upon us!* How Fianna had leapt from the saddle; the Archer of Arduan, the longbow singing in her hands. One, two, three, and her arrows had streaked skyward, striking down the Sunderer's spying eyes.

Not here.

"Run," said Thulu, and they ran without thought, sprinting over the plains, the long grass lashing their legs. There was no cover, not so much as a shrub. Nowhere to hide. Once the ravens spotted them, there would be Fjeltroll; hundreds of them. Thousands. And the Slayer, the man on the black horse, who had drawn his black blade to kill Malthus in the Marasoumië. Dani's heart pounded in his chest. In the forests of Pelmar, he had watched mice scurry beneath the shadow of a hunting owl's wings. Perhaps it was a swifter death than being swallowed by a snake, but the terror was worse.

If there was any chance he survived this ordeal, he decided, he would never hunt hopping-mice again.

The thought made him careless; his foot struck something hard and stony, hidden by the thick grass, and he fell headlong. Both hands rose instinctively to protect the clay vial as he struck the ground hard, the impact jarring the breath from him. He fumbled at the vial. It was unbroken, but the cork stopper had been knocked partially loose, and moisture gleamed on its exposed surface. With frantic fingers, Dani shoved it back in place. Only then did the constriction in his chest ease, and his breath returned in a sobbing gasp.

He could smell the Water of Life in the air, its clean, mineral essence rising like a beacon.

"Are you all right?" Uncle Thulu's voice was taut.

"Aye." Dani glanced down at the object that had tripped him. It was the lip of a ventilation shaft. He felt for the grass rope he had woven, coiled in his pack. "Uncle. Surely we must have cleared the blockage."

Their eyes met, a spark of hope leaping between them; then Thulu shook his head. "Without the rockpile beneath us, the rope's too short," he said wearily. "The fall from the shaft would kill us. Even if it wasn't"—he gestured around—"there's naught to anchor the rope, lad."

Dani bowed his head, stroking the rope's plaited length. A trace of moisture glistened on his fingertips. His pulse quickened, and he began to chant the Song of Being under his breath.

"Lad," Thulu began, then fell silent as the rope began to grow beneath Dani's fingertips, stalks seeding and sprouting, stretching and growing in ever-lengthening plaits, young and strong and green. One end sprouted roots, pale tendrils questing in the open air.

Still chanting, Dani risked a glance toward the east. The ravens were coming; no longer a smudge, but a wedge-shaped cloud, soaring and wheeling, mighty enough to cast a shadow on the plains. It rode before them on the grass, darkness moving over the waves, veering in their direction. Something had caught their attention; perhaps movement, perhaps the scent of the Water of Life itself, faint and rising.

His voice faltered, then continued. There was no other avenue of escape. In one swift gesture, he stabbed the rope's end into the cold soil, feeling the tendrils take root, sending their shoots into the dark earth. The plaited stalks continued to lengthen and twine, whispering like a snake's coils between his palms. He tugged once, experimentally. The rope was firmly rooted.

"It will never hold us," Uncle Thulu said flatly.

"It will," Dani said. "It has to."

He did not offer this time, but simply went, clearing away the overgrown grass and clambering into the shaft. The rope felt sturdy in his hands, though he could hear the hoarse, dry rustle of its growth echoing in the shaft.

Hand over hand, Dani lowered himself into darkness.

It was a narrower shaft than the other. His elbows scraped the sides, and he prayed Uncle Thulu would fit. It was a relief when he cleared the shaft, dangling in the empty darkness. Ignoring his aching shoulder for the hundredth time, he went as quickly as he dared, fearful despite his assurance that the rope would end before his feet touched the floor of the tunnel.

It didn't.

"Uncle!" he called. "Hurry!"

What faint light the shaft admitted was blocked by Thulu's body. Muffled sounds of scraping and banging ensued, accompanied by a muttered stream of Yarru invective. Dani clutched the rope to hold it steady, his heart in his throat until he saw daylight once more and, at the apex of the tunnel, his uncle's battered figure clinging to the rope, lowering himself at a dangerous pace.

Then he was down, a broad grin visible on his dark face. "Think I left half my skin on that damned rock, lad!"

"Did they see us?" Dani asked anxiously.

Thulu shook his head. "I don't think so. Uru-Alat, boy! You were as quick as a rabbit. I followed as best I could." He touched Dani's shoulder. "Well done, Bearer."

"I'm glad you're safe." He hugged Uncle Thulu, wrapping both arms around his solid warmth, feeling his embrace returned. For a moment, the world was a familiar place, safe and loving.

"So am I, Dani." Thulu's breath stirred his hair. "So am I." Squeezing Dani's arms, he released him. "You know it only gets harder, don't you?" His expression had turned somber. "We left the torches in the other tunnel. In a dozen paces, we'll be traveling blind into Darkhaven. And I do not know the way, or what branchings lie along it."

"I know. And I am afraid. But you are my guide, and I trust you to guide me." Dani laughed softly, stroking the grass-plaited rope that hung beside him. "I have been traveling blind from the beginning, Uncle. It is only now I begin to see, at least a little bit."

The plaited rope shivered beneath his touch. It was dwindling, the sere grass stalks crackling as they returned to their natural length. There had not been enough of the Water of Life to sustain its impossible growth, not with winter's breath at their necks. Dani released it, and the Yarru watched in silence as it shrank, the loose end retreating into the dimly lit shaft high above their heads.

There it hung, brittle and useless. There would be no pursuit from that quarter—and no escape.

Thulu shuddered. "I told you it wouldn't hold us!"

"Aye." Dani grasped the flask at his throat, feeling at the cork to ensure it was firmly in place. "But it did." He squared his shoulders beneath the burden of the Bearer's responsibility and set his face toward the unknown. "Let's go."

Together, they set out into the impenetrable dark.

THEY WERE COMING.

In the swirling, gleaming darkness that encircled the Tower of Ravens, it was all the Ravensmirror showed.

It was nothing they had not seen before, in bits and pieces. And yet here it was in its entirety. The promise of the red star had come to fruition. Upon the outskirts of Curonan, Haomane's Allies had converged into an army the likes of which had not been seen since the Fourth Age of the Sundered World.

And perhaps not even then, Tanaros thought, watching the images emerge. *Dwarfs*. Yrinna's Children, who had maintained her Peace since before the world was Sundered. They had turned their back on Lord Satoris' Gift, refusing to increase their numbers, refusing to take part in the Shapers' War, tending instead to the earth's fecundity, to the bounty that Yrinna's Gift brought forth.

No more.

He gazed at them in the Ravensmirror; small figures, but doughty, gnarled and weathered as ancient roots, trudging through the tall grass alongside the gleaming knights of Vedasia. Their strong hands clutched axes and scythes; good for cutting stock, good for shearing flesh. What had inspired them to war?

"*Malthus*," Lord Satoris whispered, his fists clenching. "What have you done?"

Malthus the Wise Counselor was there, the clear gem ablaze on his breast, the Spear of Light upright in his hand; he was there, they all were. Aracus Altorus, riding beneath the ancient insignia of his House; Blaise Caveros beside him, steady and loyal. There was the Borderguard of Curonan, with their dun-grey cloaks. There were all the others; Pelmarans in forest-green, Duke Bornin of Seahold in blue and silver, a motley assortment of others. Midlanders, Free Fishers, Arduan Archers. Ah, so many! Ingolin the Wise, and his Rivenlost Host, shining in stern challenge. There was no attempt to hide. Not now, no longer. Even the archers paid the circling ravens no heed; conserving their arrows, concealing nothing.

They were coming, parting the tall grass as they rode.

"Come," Lord Satoris crooned. *"Come."*

The Ravensmirror turned and turned, and there was a reflection of ravens in it; a twice-mirrored image of dark wings rising in a beating cloud, carried on a glossy current of dark wings. Tanaros frowned and blinked, then understood. They had been feasting on the pile of Staccian dead he had left on the plains for Haomane's Allies to find. There were the headless bodies, heaped and abandoned. There were Haomane's Allies, reading the message he had scratched onto the marker stone. A ripple ran through their ranks. There was Malthus, bowing his head in sorrow, grasping his gem and murmuring a prayer, white light blazing red between his fingers. There was Aracus Altorus, turning to face them, drawing his sword and speaking fierce words; an oath of vengeance, perhaps.

Vorax licked dry lips and glanced sidelong at Tanaros. "How long?"

"A day's ride," Tanaros said. "At their pace, perhaps two." He watched fixedly, trying to decide which of them he despised the most. Aracus Altorus, with his arrogant stare and Calista's faithless blood running in his veins? Malthus the Counselor, Haomane's Weapon, the architect of this war? Or perhaps Ingolin the Wise, Lord of the Rivenlost. What an honor it was he had deigned to lead his people into battle, how conscious he was of it!

And then there was Blaise of the Borderguard; his own kinsman, many generations removed. How proud he was to be at the right hand of the Scion of House Altorus! How determined he was to make amends for his ancestor's treachery! Tanaros narrowed his eyes, studying the Borderguardsman's seat, the way his hand hovered near his hilt, gauging his skills.

"You're better than he is, aren't you?" Tanaros murmured. "I was always better than Roscus, too. But we must keep the positions to which we were born, mustn't we?" Hatred coiled like a serpent in his entrails. "All things in their place," he said bitterly. "Order must be preserved as the Lord-of-Thought decrees."

"Haomane." The Shaper's low voice made the stones vibrate. In the center of the Tower, he gave a mirthless laugh. "Enough! I have seen enough."

The Ravensmirror dispersed.

"You know your jobs." Lord Satoris turned away. "Prepare."

A weight settled on Tanaros' shoulder; he startled, seeing Fetch's eye so near his own, black and beady. There had been none of the disconcerting echo of doubled vision he had experienced before. "Fetch!" he said, his heart gladdening unexpectedly. "I did not know you were here."

The raven wiped its beak on his doublet. Its thoughts *nudged* at his own. Grass, an ocean of grass, the swift, tilting journey across the plains of Curonan to report . . . and, what? A stirring, a tendril of scent wafting on the high drafts. Water, all the fresh water the raven had ever seen; the sluggish Gorgantus, the leaping flume of the White, the broad, shining path of the Aven. A hidden Staccian lake, a blue eye reflecting sky; a water-hole in the Unknown Desert. Rain, falling in grey veils.

Water, mineral-rich, smelling of life.

Green things growing.

Tanaros swallowed. "What do you seek to tell me?"

The raven's thoughts flickered and the plains rushed up toward him, stalks of rustling grass growing huge. Rustling. Something was sliding through the grass; a viper, sliding over the edge of a stone lip. No. A length of braided rope, vanishing.

Then it was gone and there was only the wind and the plains, and then that too was gone, and there was only Fetch, his claws pricking Tanaros' shoulder. His Lordship had gone, and Vorax, too. Ushahin alone remained in the Tower of Ravens with them, his new sword awkward at his side, a glitter of fear in his mismatched eyes.

"You saw?" Tanaros asked hoarsely.

"Yes."

Tanaros pressed the heels of his hands to his eyes. "Do we tell his Lordship?"

"It is for you to decide, cousin." Ushahin's voice was quiet. "You know well the course I would advocate."

"No." Tanaros lowered his hands. On his shoulder, Fetch chuckled

uneasily deep in his throat. "She has nothing to do with this, Dream-spinner."

Ushahin shrugged and said nothing.

"All right." Tanaros took a deep breath. "I will tell him."

He made his way through the fortress, following his Lordship's path. To his surprise, Fetch remained with him, riding his shoulder with familiar comfort. Where the Shaper had passed, his presence hung in the air, the copper-sweet tang of his blood mixed with the lowering sense of thunder. Approaching the threefold doors to the Chamber of the Font, Tanaros felt as though he were swimming in it, and his branded heart ached with love and sorrow. Through the door, he heard his Lordship's summons.

"Come, Blacksword."

The Font's brilliance hurt his eyes. Facing away from it and squinting, he told Lord Satoris what he had sensed in Fetch's thoughts. In the Tower, it had seemed a fearful concern with which to burden his Lordship, but as he spoke the words, they began to sound foolish.

"A scent," the Shaper said thoughtfully. "A rope."

"My Lord, I believe it was the odor of the Water of Life," Tanaros said, remembering the Well of the World. "And the rope . . . the rope was of Yarru making. I have seen its like before." He was grateful for the slight weight of the raven on his shoulder, steadying him. "My Lord, I fear the Bearer is making his way toward Darkhaven."

"Yes." In the darkness beyond the Font, the Shaper sighed and the shadows seemed to sigh with him. "He is coming, Tanaros Blacksword. They are all coming, all my Elder Brother's little puppets."

"My Lord?"

"They are always coming, and they have always been coming, since long before the world was Sundered, since before there was a world to dream of Sundering. I have always known. It is only the when of it that remains uncertain; even here, even now. But they are mistaken if they believe this is the end. This time, or any other time. There is no end, save in beginning. Even the Lord-of-Thought cannot change this pattern." The Shaper drew near, waves of power emanating from him. "Curious little raven," he said to Fetch. "Whose thoughts have *you* been thinking?"

Fetch chuckled.

"Ah." A long, silent moment passed between them. The dark ghost of a smile crossed Lord Satoris' ruined visage. "Thank you, loyal Tanaros, for bringing me this small guest." He inclined his head. "For this small kindness."

"My Lord?" Tanaros repeated, confused and fearful that his Lordship was succumbing to madness after all.

"It comes and goes, my general, the way of all things." The Shaper raised one hand in a gesture of dismissal. "As you, now, shall go."

"What of the Bearer, my Lord?"

"Malthus' spell hides him even from the eyes of the Souma." Lord Satoris shook his head. "There is nothing *I* can do. Would you have me tell you your business, Blacksword? Double your patrols in the tunnels between here and the blockage."

"My Lord." Bowing carefully, mindful of Fetch, Tanaros took his leave.

Aboveground once more, he made his way to the great entrance, where the Havenguard admitted him passage through the tall doors. It was another cold, clear night. Standing in the courtyard, he moved Fetch to his forearm and stood for a moment, thinking about the oncoming army, about a length of plaited rope, old Ngurra's face beneath the shadow of his sword, and the dark-skinned boy he had seen in the Ways, the questioning look on his face. He thought about Cerelinde in her chambers, praying for rescue, and his Lordship's strange mood, and about Fetch.

"Whose thoughts *have* you been thinking?" he asked the raven, stroking him with one finger. Fetch ducked his head, shifting from foot to foot. "What happened to you before you found me in the desert?"

For an instant, Tanaros saw himself once more through the raven's vision: a stark, noble figure with haunted eyes, mantled in passions that flickered like dark fire around the edges of his being, a doom he carried like embers in his cupped hands. Scarred hands and a scarred heart, capable of tenderness or violence, and behind him stars falling endlessly, lovely and dying.

Somewhere, a dragon roared.

"So be it," Tanaros whispered. "Go, little brother, and find shelter from the coming storm." Lifting his arm, he watched the raven take flight, black wings glossy in the starlight. "Good-bye, Fetch."

A small kindness.

His eyes stung; touching them, he found them wet with tears. Hyrgolf was right, he would feel better once the battle was joined. Gathering himself, Tanaros went to rouse Speros and give him new orders.

IN THE SMALL HOURS OF the night, Malthus the Wise Counselor sat silently on a narrow folding stool in a corner of Aracus Altorus' tent, watching the pupil he had taught for so many years pace its confines, restless and unable to sleep.

"Out with it," he said at last. "You cannot afford to ride into battle already weary, Aracus."

Aracus' gaze lit, as it had many times that night, on the coffer that held the tourmaline stone linked to the Bearer of the Water of Life. "It was dimmer," he said. "Not by much, but a little. Others did not notice, but I did. I saw it, Malthus."

"Yes." The Counselor folded his hands in his sleeves. "I know."

"Does it mean the Bearer is failing?" His tone was harsh. *"Dying?"*

"I cannot say, Aracus," Malthus replied quietly. "No more than I could before. I lack the knowledge, for this is a thing that has never been done. But if you would ask what thought is in my heart, it is that the Water of Life dwindles as the Bearer perseveres. Dani used it in Malumdoorn to answer the Dwarfs' challenge of the Greening. He knows its power."

"Dwindles," Aracus repeated, following a path worn by his restless feet. He shot a glance at the Counselor. "By how much, Malthus? How much is required to extinguish the marrow-fire? How much remains? Enough?"

Malthus shook his hoary head. "I know not, and cannot say."

"No?" Aracus eyed him. "How many times have you withheld the fullness of your knowledge from me, Malthus? Your plots have ever been deep-laid. I wonder, betimes, what you fail to tell me now."

"There is nothing." Malthus touched the gem on his breast. Its clear blaze underscored the deep lines graven on his features. "Forgive me, Son of Altorus. The Lord-of-Thought's will is set in motion, and I, like this Soumanië I bear, will soon be spent. There is some service I may yet do to lure the Sunderer's minions from his lair. But I have no more knowledge to conceal." He smiled sadly. *"The unknown is made known.* There is nothing more I may tell you."

"Would that there was!" The words burst from Aracus. He fetched up before Malthus and flung himself to his knees, his face pale and strained. "Wise Counselor, I am leading men, good men, unto their deaths; Men, aye, and Ellylon and Dwarfs. Whatever else happens, this much is certain. And they are trusting me to do it because I was born to it; because of a Prophecy spoken a thousand years before my birth." He gave a choked laugh, his wide-set eyes pleading. "Tell me it is necessary, Malthus! Tell me, whatever happens, that it is all worthwhile."

A man's face, holding the phantom of the boy he had been, reckoning the cost of youth's dreams. How many generations had it taken for one such as him to come? Malthus the Counselor reached out, cupping the cheek of the boy he remembered, speaking to the man he had become.

"All things," he said gently, "must be as they are."

Aracus bowed his head, red-gold hair falling to hide his expression. "Is that all the comfort you have to offer?"

"Yes," Malthus said, filled with a terrible pity. "It is."

"So be it." Aracus Altorus touched the hilt of his sword; the sword of his ancestors, a dull and lifeless Soumanië set in its pommel. "Strange," he murmured. "It seems to me I have heard those words before, only it was the Sorceress who spoke them. Perhaps I should have listened more closely."

"We all choose our paths," Malthus said. "Unless you wish to follow hers, soaked in innocent blood, it is the better part of wisdom to pay her words scant heed; for such truth as they held, the Sorceress twisted to justify her own deeds. Yet there was more folly in her than evil, and even one such as she may have a role to play in the end. Do not discount Lilias of Beshtanag."

"You counsel hope?" Aracus lifted his head.

"Yes," said Malthus. "Always." He smiled at Aracus. "Come. Since sleep evades you, let us review the ways in which the Soumanië's power may be invoked and used, for it is my *hope* that such knowledge may yet be needful."

With a sigh, Aracus Altorus began to repeat his mentor's teaching.

FIFTEEN

THE GULNAGEL WERE IN HIGH spirits, and Speros' lifted accordingly. He was grateful for the assignment, grateful for the show of trust on General Tanaros' part. And truth be told, he was grateful to be away from Darkhaven and the presence of the Lady Cerelinde. It made him feel at once awestruck and insignificant, vile and ashamed, and between the General's fierce glare and Ushahin Dreamspinner's insinuations, it was altogether too unnerving.

This, now; this was more the thing. The camaraderie of the Fjel and a purpose to achieve. A warrior's purpose, serving Darkhaven's needs. He'd had only a small glimpse of the tunnels underlying Uru-lat when they'd traveled through the Ways. The Vesdarlig Passage was bigger than he could have imagined; wide enough for two Fjel to run abreast, tall enough for Speros to ride his tall grey horse.

Ghost, he had named her, because of her coloring. She moved like one, smooth and gliding. After his first mount had been lost in the Ways, Speros had thought he might never be given another such to ride, but the General had let him keep Ghost for his own. She bore him willingly, though Speros was uncertain whether she liked him. She had a trick of gazing at him out of the corner of one limpid eye as if wondering how he would taste, and her teeth were unnaturally sharp.

That was all right. He didn't know whether he liked her. He was, however, quite certain that he loved her.

They moved swiftly, the Gulnagel at their steady lope, with one pair scouting ahead and Ghost keeping pace with the others at a swift canter. Streaking torchlight painted the walls with a shifting fresco of light and shadow, and it felt strange and exciting, a little like the unforgettable ride through the Midlands when Ushahin Dreamspinner had led them along the paths between waking and dreaming.

How odd it was to think that the plains of Curonan were above them. In another day, Haomane's Allies might be riding over their heads and never even know it.

If there had been more time, Speros mused, perhaps it would have been better to *use* the tunnels rather than block them. How long would it take to move the army in a narrow column? He calculated in his head, trying to estimate how large an opening it would require to allow them egress, how far away it would have to be to enable them to assemble unseen, yet close the distance and fall upon the enemy before they could rally.

A sound from the darkness ahead broke his reverie. For an instant, it sounded like a hound baying, and Speros was confused, remembering a dusty road and a small farmstead, trying to steal horses with the General.

But no, there were Ghost's tireless muscles surging beneath him, and there was one of the Fjel grinning upward, eyes reflecting torchlight, and the sound was deep, far too deep and resonant to issue from any hound's throat. It was the hunting-cry of the Gulnagel Fjel.

"Quarry, boss!"

Speros whooped aloud in triumph, setting his heels to Ghost's flanks. She surged forward, and the Gulnagel quickened their pace. They burst down the tunnel like a wave, prepared to sweep away everything before them.

"There, boss!" A taloned finger, pointing down a side tunnel. Speros wrenched Ghost's head, and she sank onto her haunches like a cat, skidding and turning, her iron-shod hooves sparking against the stones while the Gulnagel bounded ahead.

He followed them, their torches bobbing like fireflies, while the tunnel grew steadily narrower. Here and there it branched, then branched again, doubling back toward Darkhaven. The air grew hot and close. The feeling of triumph gave way to unease. As the walls closed in upon them and the ceiling lowered, he slowed Ghost to a trot, then a walk, slower and slower, until the walls of the tunnel were brushing his knees.

When he could ride no farther, Speros dismounted and felt along the wall until he found a crevice into which he could jam Ghost's reins. He continued on foot, stumbling over the tunnel's floor. Unlike the main passage, worn smooth over centuries, it was rocky and uneven. Sweat beaded on his brow, and he wondered why he had bothered to wear full armor in pursuit of a pair of Charred Folk.

Ahead, the torches swarmed and separated, growing more distant. The sound of baying had ceased. It was hard to breathe, and harder to see. Speros fought back a spasm of panic. How many branchings had he taken? He hadn't kept track. If the Gulnagel left him, he wasn't sure he could find his way back.

"Hold up, lads!" he shouted.

To his relief, a pair of torches lingered unmoving. He made his way down the tunnel, forced to walk bent and doubled under the sloping ceiling. The Gulnagel were crouching, resting their weight on the knuckles of one hand, torches held awkward in the other. As Speros arrived, other Fjel were returning from farther tunnels, some nearly crawling. The narrow space was crammed with flesh and hide, rife with the acrid tang of smoke, the musty odor of Fjel, and something faint and sweet beneath it.

"Any luck?" Speros asked grimly.

"Sorry, boss." It was Krolgun who answered, blinking. His eyes looked bleary. "Our mistake. Thought we scented Man-prey close at hand, but it's gone."

"You're sure?" Craning his bent neck, Speros tried to peer past the hulking forms. There was nothing but tunnels and more tunnels, a maze of tunnels, each one narrowing like a funnel into the darkness beneath the mountains.

"Sure enough." Krolgun shrugged. "Can't smell prey, and the tunnels are too small to go farther." He chuckled low in his throat. "Maybe it *is* you we caught a whiff of."

"What *is* that smell?" Speros sniffed the air, trying to identify the underlying odor. It reminded him of his boyhood, long ago; before he had ever filched a coin or borrowed an untended horse, before his father had disavowed his name. A heady odor, like ripe, sun-warm strawberries in the fields of Haimhault.

Krolgun gave another shrug. "Sheep?"

"No, not sheep." Speros frowned, then shook himself. The torches were guttering for lack of air and his thoughts were doing the same. "Never mind. Let's get out of here before we suffocate, lads. We'll double back, retrace our steps. Maybe it was a trick."

If it was a trick, it was well-played. The Fjel searched every turn and blind alley and found nothing. Speros made his way back through the smoke-wreathed air to where Ghost stood awaiting him with unnatural patience, baring her teeth at his return. He took care to avoid them as he mounted. There was no room to turn her and he had to back her down the tunnel, watching uneasily as the dark maze before him receded.

Surely, no living thing could survive in such a place.

The remainder of their search was uneventful. They traveled at a more moderate pace until they reached the massive rock-pile that blocked the Vesdarlig Passage. The Gulnagel glanced at one another and shrugged.

Speros sighed. "Back toward Darkhaven, lads. Slow and careful, eyes and ears! Aye, and noses, too."

There was nothing to be found. Hours later they emerged to murky daylight in the Vale of Gorgantum. Speros relayed orders regarding doubled patrolling of the tunnels, then rode toward the fortress to stable Ghost before reporting to General Tanaros. Despite the futility of his mission, open air and Ghost's smooth, gliding pace cheered him. He wished the news were better, but perhaps it had been a fool's errand after all, chasing after something a raven had not quite seen. A plaited rope? It may have been, or it may have been the wind in the tall grass. Like as not, it had been. At least he could set the General's mind at ease. Soon, battle would be upon them and there would be no more need for mucking about after bits and pieces of Haomane's cursed Prophecy.

Riding toward Darkhaven, Speros of Haimhault smiled and dismissed from his memory the scent of strawberries ripening on the sun-warmed earth.

"GO!" THULU HISSED BETWEEN HIS teeth. "Go, lad, *go!*"

On his hands and knees, Dani scrambled as fast as he could, heedless of the rocks bruising and tearing his skin, horribly aware of the pounding feet and baying voices of the Fjeltroll that pursued them.

Attempting to navigate the Vesdarlig Passage in darkness had been a fearful task, but they had worked out a system. He had taken one wall, and Uncle Thulu the other. As long as each of them kept one hand on their respective walls, they could warn the other of gaps and confer, pooling their knowledge to avoid straying into the side tunnels.

Ominous though the darkness had been, it had saved their lives; or at least prolonged them. With their dark-accustomed eyes, they had seen the torches of the oncoming Fjel in enough time to hide deep in the very side tunnels they had been avoiding.

But the Fjel had caught their scent, and there was nothing for it but to flee and flee and flee, racing ahead of the pursuing torches, the howling Fjel, twisting and turning, deeper into the narrowing maze, running bent, then doubled, then forced to crawl in single file as the tunnels closed in upon them, too small to allow the Fjel to enter.

It was the chance fate afforded them, and they took it.

For what seemed like hours, Dani crawled blindly, scurrying. Terror fueled his flight. He chose at random unseen branches, head lowered and shoulders hunched, protecting the clay vial hanging from his throat, never certain when he would collide headfirst with a wall. Sometimes it happened. His head throbbed, his knees ached, and his hands were slick with blood.

And then there was silence, broken only by the sound of their ragged breathing. There was no sign of pursuit. They had entered a blackness so absolute, it seemed all the light in the world—every candle, every spark, every distant, glimmering star—had been extinguished. Dani slowed, then halted. Like a hunted animal, he crouched in his burrow.

"Do you hear anything?" he whispered.

"No," his uncle whispered back. "I think we've lost them."

"I think we've lost *us*." The words were not as frightening as they should have been. Wriggling, Dani maneuvered his body into a sitting position. If he drew his knees up tight to his chest and scrunched low, he could rest his back against the tunnel wall. Just a rest to catch his breath, he thought. It was a relief to have his weight off his bruised knees. The enfolding blackness was reassuring, warm and familiar. And why not? Dying was like being born, after all; so the Song of Being told. Inside the womb there was perfect blackness, although Dani did not remember it.

He remembered his mother, who had died before he was two years old. He remembered warm flesh, soft and dusky, smelling sweetly of milk. In the darkness, Dani smiled. Mother's milk, the odor of *love*. She had loved him very much. He remembered his father telling him so, and afterward, after his father was gone, Warabi and old Ngurra, who had raised him, the scent of mother's milk and warmed flesh, the sharp tang of a wad of well-chewed *gamal*.

Truly, the blackness was not so terrible.

"Do you smell that, lad?" Uncle Thulu said dreamily. "It's like the scent of baari-wood, newly peeled, slick with morning dew. Nothing like it, is there?" He laughed softly. "I must have been about your age when I cut my first digging-stick. 'Learn to follow the veins of the earth,' old Ngurra told me. 'The Bearer will have need of your skills.'" Another soft laugh. "Even the wise are wrong sometimes."

A faint sense of alarm stirred in Dani. "Baari-wood?"

"Peeled clean as a whistle, sweet as dawn." Uncle Thulu squirmed into place and slumped back against the wall beside him, their shoulders brushing companionably in the darkness. "You'll see, we'll go to the grove together, and you'll see." He inhaled deeply, then yawned. "You can almost see it now, if you try."

It was wrong, all wrong. There was no scent of baari-wood in the tunnels, only mother's milk and desert-warm flesh, and that was wrong, too, because his mother was long dead and his father, too, and there was nothing here save stone and darkness.

"Uncle." Dani shook Thulu's unresponsive shoulder. "Something's not right. We've got to keep moving. Please, Uncle!"

"To where, lad?" Thulu asked, peaceable and sleepy. "Back where the Fjel are waiting? That path is gone. Onward to starve in darkness? There's no way out of here. Better to rest, and dream."

"*No.*" Gritting his teeth, Dani wiped the blood from his sticky hands and fumbled for the clay flask, trying to work the cork loose. It was tight; he had made sure of it after his fall had jarred it loose on the plains. His palms burned, his fingers felt thick and clumsy, and it was hard to get a grip on the cork. For a moment he thought, why not rest? Uncle is right, we are lost forever, it's better to rest and dream.

Then the cork gave way and the scent of the Water of Life arose, and it was clear and clean and potent, heavy with minerals, almost a weight on the tongue, shredding the veils that clouded his mind. With his head heavy and low, Dani took a deep breath, tasting life, verdant and alive, and understood anew how precious and precarious it was, and how tenuous their grasp upon it here in the bowels of the earth.

"Here." He thrust blindly into the blackness, shoving the flask in the vicinity of his uncle's nose. "Breathe, Uncle. Breathe deep."

Thulu did, and shuddered as though awaking from a dream. "Dani?" he murmured. "Dani, lad?"

"I'm here, Uncle." Retracting the flask, Dani felt for the lip and replaced the cork, banging it in tight with the heel of his wounded palm, repressing a wince. All around them was blackness, and there was no longer any comfort in it. "It's time."

"Time?"

"Time to follow the veins of the earth," Dani said gently. He felt for Thulu's arm and squeezed it. "We're under the mountains, Uncle; at least, I think we are. You're right, there's no going back, but there's still forward. Somewhere, these tunnels must emerge, and somewhere there is a river, the Gorgantus River."

"Yes." In the blackness, Thulu's voice was muffled, hands pressed to his face. "Perhaps. Ah, Dani! It's hard, so hard, buried alive beneath the earth. I wish I had my digging-stick to sense the way. Maybe then . . ."

"You don't need it." Beneath his fingertips, Dani felt the sinews of his uncle's arm shifting, the blood pulsing steadily under his skin. "Please, Uncle! You can do it, I know. It is what you trained all your life to do. Guide us."

For a time, an endless time, there was only silence. And then, faint and ragged, a tuneless song. It rose from his belly, rumbling deep in his lungs. In the black bowels of the earth, Thulu of the Yarru-yami sang of water, closing his blind eyes and tracing the veins of the earth, singing the song of its course through the stony flesh of the World God, Uru-Alat. And his voice, at first uncertain and desperate, slowly grew in strength, syllables rolling from his lips like cataracts leaping from a mountain ledge.

"Forward," he said at last. "You'll have to lead, lad; there's not enough room for me to pass you. Forward, and when the path forks, bear to the right."

Eyes open onto utter blackness, Dani got back onto his hands and knees and began to crawl.

"His Lordship wishes to see you."

In the doorway of her chambers, Cerelinde took a step backward, but having delivered his message, the Havenguard remained waiting in silence, huge and impassive, three of his fellows behind him. Cerelinde glanced behind her at the tapestry with its hidden door.

"It is his Lordship's custom to send a madling at such times," she said, temporizing. The prospect of being accompanied solely by the Fjel filled her with deep unease. Damaged and unpredictable though the madlings were, they were not without reverence for the Lady of the Ellylon.

The Havenguard's features creased, his leathery upper lip drew back to reveal the tips of his eyetusks. "No more since one tried to kill you, Lady."

On another race, the expression might have passed for a smile. Cerelinde studied him, wondering if it was possible that the Fjeltroll was amused. "What does his Lordship desire?"

The Havenguard shrugged, indicating the irrelevance of the question. He was Mørkhar Fjel, with a dark, bristling hide beneath the gleaming black armor. Whatever his Lordship ordered, he would do. "You."

Cerelinde fought back a surge of fear and inclined her head. "As he commands."

They led her through the halls of Darkhaven, along corridors of gleaming black marble, laced with the blue-white veins of the marrow-fire. Their heavy weapons, polished to a bright shine, rattled against their armor. She found herself wishing Tanaros was there, for the Fjel respected and obeyed him. They had no reverence for the Lady of the Ellylon, no awe. Other races among the Lesser Shapers held the Ellylon in high regard. Not so the Fjel, for whom they held little interest.

It was not that she felt it her due, but it was familiar; understood. There was a measure of comfort was in it.

What a terrible thing it was, Cerelinde thought, to be deprived of Haomane's Gift, the gift of thought. She pitied the Fjel insofar as she was able. It was difficult to pity the pitiless, and the fierce Fjel seemed to her lacking in all sympathy, even for their own plight. It was Satoris' doing, she supposed, but it made the Fjel no easier to comprehend.

Envy, she understood. All of the Lesser Shapers envied Haomane's Children, for the Chain of Being bound them but loosely and the light of the Souma was their birthright.

Disinterest was another matter, and incomprehensible.

She walked amid the Havenguard, feeling uncommonly small and insignificant. The least among them topped her by head and shoulders, and the Ellylon were a tall folk. Why had Neheris-of-the-Leaping-Waters seen fit to make her children so huge?

Such thoughts, while not comforting, were a welcome distraction, for altogether too soon they emerged through the middle of the threefold doors and descended the spiral stair into the Chamber of the Font. There it was, close and hot, reeking of ichor; the glittering Font, the beating ruby heart of Godslayer, the shadows crowding the corners. There *he* was, a shadow among shadows, speaking to the Fjel in their own guttural tongue, in a voice so low and resonant it lent a harsh beauty to the words. There were the Fjel, saluting and withdrawing. And then there was only Cerelinde and the Shaper.

"Cerelinde." He said her name; only that. The shadows sighed.

"My Lord." She lifted her chin and sought not to tremble.

Satoris, Third-Born among Shapers, laughed, and the shadows laughed with him. It was a low laugh, insinuating. "Are you so afraid, Lady of the Ellylon? Have I been such a poor host?" He gestured toward a chair, shadows wreathing his arm. "Sit. I mean you no harm. I would but converse with you upon the eve of battle. Who understands it as do we two?"

Cerelinde sat stiffly. "Do you jest?"

"Jest?" His eyes gleamed out of the shadows, twin coals. "Ah, no, Daughter of Erilonde! I made you an offer, once. Do you recall it?"

She remembered the garden by moonlight, the Sunderer's hand extended, its shadow stark upon the dying grass. *What if I asked you to stay?* Her own refusal, and the shivering sound of the sorrow-bells. "I do, my Lord."

"We reap the fruits of our pride, Cerelinde." He sighed. "And it is a bloody harvest. I ask again; who understands as do we two?"

"It is not pride, my Lord." Cerelinde shook her head. "It is *hope*."

"Hope?" he echoed.

"Hope." She repeated the word more firmly. "For a world made whole, healed. For the Souma, made whole and glorious, and order

restored. For the Lesser Shapers to become our better selves." The
words, the vision, gave her strength. She remembered a question Meara
had posed her, and wondered if she dared to ask it after all. "What is
it you are afraid to confront, my Lord?" Cerelinde asked, feeling the stir
of ancient Ellylon magics creeping over her skin, the scant remnant of
gifts the Rivenlost had ceded to the Sundering. "I, too, posed you a
question. I do not believe you answered it."

"Did I not?" the Shaper murmured.

What might-have-been . . .

Unexpectedly, Cerelinde found tears in her eyes. She swallowed.
"Your crossroads, my Lord. There have been many, but only one is
foremost. Three times, Haomane Lord-of-Thought asked you to withdraw your Gift from Arahila's Children. I asked why you refused him,
and you did not answer. Do"—she hesitated—"do you wish to know
what might have been if you had acceded?"

Satoris lowered his head, and the shadows roiled. His shoulders
hunched, emerging like dark hills from the shadowy sea. His hands
knotted into fists, sinew crackling. There was another sound, deep and
hollow and bitter, so filled with anger that it took Cerelinde a moment
to recognize it as laughter.

"Ah, Cerelinde!" He raised his head. The embers of his eyes had
gone out; they were only holes, empty sockets like the Helm of Shadows, filled with unspeakable sorrow. "Do *you?*"

"Yes." She made herself hold his terrible gaze. "Yes, my Lord. I do
wish to know. I am Haomane's Child, and we do not thrive in darkness and ignorance."

"Nothing," the Shaper said softly. "*Nothing*, is the answer. I need
no trifling Ellyl gift to tell me what I have known for far, far too long."

"My Lord?" Cerelinde was perplexed.

"Not immediately." He continued as though she had not spoken,
turning his back upon her and pacing the confines of the chamber.
"Oh, the world would have gone on for a time, Daughter of Erilonde;
Urulat, rigid and fixed. An echelon of order in which Haomane's Children reigned unchallenged, complacent in their own perfection. A
sterile world, as sterile as I have become, ruled by the Lord-of-
Thought, in which nothing ever changed and no thing, no matter what
its passions, no being, no *creature*, sought to exceed its place. And so
it would be, on and on and on, generation upon generation, age upon

age, until the stars fell from the sky, and the earth grew cold, and died." His voice raised a notch, making the walls tremble. *"Is that what you wish?"*

"No," she whispered. "Yet—"

"Look!" Rage thundered in the air around him. He drew near, looming over her, smelling of blood and lightning. "Do you not believe me? Use your paltry Rivenlost magics, and *see.*"

Shrinking back in her chair, Cerelinde stared into his eyes and saw a barren landscape of cold stone, a dull grey vista stretching on endlessly. There were no trees, no grass, not even a trickle of water. Nothing moved. Nothing breathed. Nothing lived. Overhead there was only a void; perfect blackness, the space between the stars, aching with the pressure of emptiness. Cold, so cold! Her teeth chattered, her flesh like ice, her bones aching to the marrow.

"Please," she got out through a clenched jaw. "Please!"

"Life *quickens*, little Ellyl." Granting her mercy, he turned away. "Quickens unto death, quickens into *generation*. Living and dying, giving birth unto ourselves. Everything. Even Shapers," he added in a low voice. "Even worlds."

Cerelinde rubbed her arms, trying to restore warmth to her flesh. "Is this the famous wisdom of dragons, my Lord? They twist truth into lies and they are not to be trusted."

"They are older than the Lord-of-Thought, you know." His head averted, the Sunderer laughed softly. "Ah, Haomane! We are but parts, scattered and broken; heart and head, limbs and organs. None of us perceives the whole, not even you, my Elder Brother. They do. What they think, what they feel . . . I cannot say. But they *know*. And I, I spoke to them, and I am cursed with knowledge for it. Skeins of lies, woven with threads of truth; that is the world we have Shaped. You need me. *Urulat* needs me; Urulat, Uru-Alat that was, that will be again. I did not choose this role. I do what I must. All things, in the end, must be as they are. Is it not so?"

Uncertain whether he spoke to her or to the specter of Haomane First-Born, Cerelinde gazed at the Shaper's back; the taut sinews, the wrath-blackened flesh. "Forgive me, but I do not understand."

"No," he said. "No, I suppose not. And yet it is in the *striving* that understanding begins, and that is the seed of generation that begets worlds." Again, Satoris gave his soft, dark laugh. "You should strive, little Ellyl; as all of us should. He made you too well, my Elder Brother did. Mortality serves a purpose. Oronin's Horn blows seldom for Haomane's Children. No urgency quickens your flesh, no shadow of exigency spurs your thoughts. What would you have to *strive* for, were it not for me?"

"You pretend you do us a service," Cerelinde murmured.

"No." The Shaper's shoulders hunched, rising like stormclouds. "I do the *world* a service. By my very existence, by this role not of my choosing."

"The world," Cerelinde echoed, feeling weariness settle upon her. She was tired; tired of fear, tired of lies. Lies, piled upon lies; half-truths and evasions. Some things were known. Some things were true. "My Lord, if you cared so much for the world, why did you Sunder it?"

"I DID NOT SUNDER THE WORLD!"

Satoris Banewreaker's fist crashed against the wall of the chamber; shadows roiled and sinews cracked, and Darkhaven shuddered from its foundation to its towers. The Font leapt, spewing blue-white fire, shedding sparks on the stone floor. Within its flames, Godslayer pulsed. He stood, breathing hard, his back to her. Ichor ran in rills down his inner thigh, black and oily.

"I did not Sunder the world," he repeated.

And Haomane smote the earth with his sword, and the earth was divided and the heat of Uru-Alat severed from the body. And in accordance with Meronin's will, the Sundering Sea rushed in to fill the divide, and so it was done.

"You shattered the Souma," Cerelinde said in a small voice.

"Not alone." Satoris Third-Born, who was once called the Sower, sighed. Lifting his head, he gazed toward the west, as though he could see through the stone walls of Darkhaven to the isle called Torath, the Crown, where the Six Shapers dwelled in the broken glory of the Souma. "Never alone." He shivered, lowering his head. "Go, little Ellyl, Daughter of Erilonde. I was wrong to summon you here. There is no hope, no hope at all."

"There is always hope," Cerelinde said.

"Will you ever harp upon it?" Satoris pitted his furrowed brow with his fingertips. "For your kind, perhaps. My Gift, the Gift my Elder Brother refused . . . it lies awaiting you in the loins of the Scion of Altorus. There are ways and ways and ways. Perhaps, then; perhaps not.

It is your sole chance. Why else do you suppose Haomane's Prophecy is as it is?" He smiled grimly. "For me, there is nothing. And yet you are all my Children in the end. Make no mistake, I have sown the seeds of my own regeneration. In one place or another, they will take root."

"My Lord?"

"Go." He waved one hand. "Go, and begone from my sight, for you pain me."

Summoned by arcane means, the Havenguard appeared at the top of the spiral stair. There they waited, impassive in the flame-shot darkness.

The Sunderer pointed. *"GO!"*

Cerelinde climbed the stair slowly, her limbs stiff with the residue of fear and bone-deep cold. Below, Satoris Banewreaker resumed his pacing, disturbing the shadows. He glanced often toward the west and muttered to himself in a strange tongue, filled with potent, rolling syllables; the Shapers' tongue, that had not been heard on Urulat since the world was Sundered. One word alone Cerelinde understood, uttered in a tone of anguish and betrayal.

"Arahila!"

And then the Fjel led her away and the threefold door closed behind her, and Cerelinde of the House of Elterrion was escorted back to her chambers to await the outcome of the war that would decide her fate.

In the empty garden, beneath Arahila's moon, sorrow-bells chimed unheard.

SIXTEEN

HAOMANE'S ALLIES HAD GONE ON the march under cover of darkness.
Dawn broke over the plains to find them encamped a short distance
from the foot of the Gorgantus Mountains. The mountains trembled at
the roars of the Tordenstem sentries, summoning the Three and their
chosen companions.

"By the Six!"

Tanaros heard Speros' shaking oath behind him. Another time, perhaps, he might have reprimanded the Midlander for it. In Darkhaven,
one did not swear by the Six Shapers. Today it seemed meet.

The army covered the plains of Curonan, armor gleaming in the
bloody light of dawn. Nothing glimpsed in the Ravensmirror had prepared him for the sight. Even from the overlook high atop the crags, it
was immense.

Side by side by side, the Three gazed at the army.

So many companies! There they were, gathered at last in one place,
arrayed for battle. The Rivenlost formed the vanguard. It surprised
Tanaros, a little; but then, it was the Lady of the Ellylon over whom
this war was waged. Perhaps it was a matter of honor.

"Well," Vorax said. "There they are."

"Indeed," Ushahin said drily.

Vorax leaned over in the saddle and spat. "And there they can sod-
ding well stay, as far as I'm concerned. Maybe they'll go home when
they begin to starve." At his rear, a pair of Staccians chuckled.

Tanaros said nothing, squinting, trying to pick out individuals. The
companies were still milling and unsettled. Yes, there; glint of red-gold,

a rider moving among the disparate companies, gesturing, giving orders, attempting to stitch them into a cohesive whole. Some of them had fought together at Beshtanag, but many of them had not. Coordination would be difficult in the field.

"You look like you're sizing them up for battle, cousin." Ushahin's remark sounded casual. "Do you lack faith in our fortifications?"

"No." Tanaros wondered why Haomane's Allies had bothered to waste a precious hour or two of sleep to arrive at dawn. He exchanged a glance with Hyrgolf, who shrugged. There was no element of surprise to be gained. Did they imagine the sight would shock Darkhaven into surrendering? He frowned, studying the army. There, there was another figure he knew, riding to the forefront as the ranks parted to allow him passage. White-robed and white-maned, the tip of his spear shining like the last star of the morning, a spark of brightness nestled in his snowy beard. He rode astride a horse as white as foam, with an arched neck and hooves that fell with deft precision.

"Is that . . . him?" Speros asked in a low voice.

"Malthus the Counselor." Tanaros confirmed it absently, still frowning. "What did you *do* to my horse, damn you?"

As if in answer, the figure of Malthus spread his arms wide. The clear Soumanië on his breast burst into a blaze of light, bathing him in white radiance. On either side of him, Rivenlost heralds in bright armor raised horns to their lips and blew long blasts, high and clarion, shivering and silvery in the dawn.

On the plains of Curonan, Malthus the Wise Counselor lifted his voice, and whether it was through some vestigial magic of the Soumanië or the wizard's own arts, given to him by Haomane himself, his voice carried above the plains, as powerful and resonant as any Tordenstem Fjel; as his Lordship himself.

"Satoris Third-Born, whom Men and Ellylon have named Sunderer and Banewreaker, we have come in answer to your challenge! In the name of Haomane First-Born, Lord-of-Thought, I command you to face us, or be forever branded a coward!"

His words broke like a thunderclap over the mountains, accompanied by a blinding wash of brilliant white light. Tanaros rocked back in the saddle as though he had been struck. It felt like it. Fury flooded his veins, drowning rational thought; for an instant, he nearly spurred his mount over the edge of the crag into thin air. He found he was laughing,

his teeth bared in a grimace of defiance, one hand on the hilt of his
black sword. The Fjel were roaring, Vorax was roaring, the Staccians
and Speros were shouting promises of bloody death. Tanaros shook
his head, trying to clear it. There was only one way down to the
plains; back, back to Darkhaven and down through Defile's Maw. Yes,
that was the way.

"Tanaros! *Tanaros!*"

A hand was on his arm; Ellyl-fair, tangling his reins and detaining
him as he sought to turn his mount. Impatient, he tried to shake it off,
but there was unexpected strength in the grip.

"You were right." Ushahin's voice was taut. "There is as much danger in the power to Shape spirit as matter."

The words penetrated slowly. Tanaros took a shaking breath, aware
of his heart threatening to burst from his branded chest, of hungering
for the scent of blood. Ahead of him, Fjel and Men alike were scrambling along the path toward Darkhaven. "Malthus' Soumanië," he said
thickly, understanding. "Why should *you* be immune?"

"To this?" Ushahin Dreamspinner gave his bitter smile. A vein
throbbed in his dented temple and his dilated eye was black as a void,
seeping meaningless tears at the painful onslaught of light. "It is only
another form of madness." He nodded down the path. "You had better halt your troops."

Cursing, Tanaros lashed his mount's haunches with his reins. He
rode them down, plunging amid them, shouting. "Turn back, turn
back! Hyrgolf! Vorax! Speros! Turn back!"

Hyrgolf heeded him first, coming to himself with a mighty shudder.
He waded through the milling troops to plant himself in their path, setting his shoulders and roaring orders until the headlong rush stalled
into aimless chaos.

"What was that?" Speros sounded confused, half-awake.

"That," Tanaros said grimly, "was Malthus."

The Midlander blinked befuddled brown eyes at him. "What happens now?"

They were all gazing toward him for an answer. Tanaros shook his
head, wordless. Behind and beyond them, above the looming edifice
of Darkhaven's fortress, stormclouds were gathering; black and roiling.
One atop another they piled, bruise-colored and furious, until the air

was heavy with tension. Wind blew in every direction, cold and cutting as a knife.

A peal of thunder answered Malthus' challenge. It began deep and
low, so low it was little more than a tremor felt in the pit of the belly,
then built in burgeoning fury, built and built in rolling peals, culminat-
ing in a booming crack, the likes of which had not been heard since the
foundation of the world was Sundered. Even the horses of Darkhaven
staggered, and Men and Fjel lifted their hands to cover their ears.

A fork of lightning split the dirty clouds, blue-white as the marrow-
fire, and its afterimage was as red as the beating heart of Godslayer.

Then there was silence, until it was broken again by the silvery
horns of the Rivenlost, casting their tremulous, valiant challenge aloft
on a surge of light, sowing fresh unrest in their enemies' souls.

"What *now*?" Speros of Haimhault's voice broke. "Ah, Shapers!
What now?"

"War." Ushahin Dreamspinner rode up the path with shoulders
hunched against the biting winds. Under the lowering skies and their
murky light, the mount that consented to bear him was the color of old
blood, spilled and drying. Tanaros watched him come; half-breed, half-
healed, his gilt hair lank with disdain. Ushahin met his eyes, but it was
Speros he answered. "It is what it has always been, Midlander. War."

"We will give them *war*!" Vorax growled, and the Staccians echoed
assent. "Supplies be damned! We will fall upon them and make them
wish they had never been born."

Tanaros raised his hand, halting them. "It is for his Lordship to
decide."

"It is in my heart that he has already decided," Ushahin murmured
to him. "The Soumanië is persuasive, and his Lordship was not unwilling to be persuaded in the matter. I hope you took their measure well,
cousin."

Tanaros glanced back toward the plains, longing to answer the
horns' call. "Well enough, cousin, if it comes to it." He steeled himself.
"We'd best make haste. The fortress is likely to be in an uproar. Can I
trust you all to hold firm?"

There were grim nods all around. Bloodlust itched in all of them,
but the initial madness of Malthus' spell had been broken. What remained could be resisted.

It was well, for his prediction proved an understatement. They arrived at Darkhaven to find it boiling with battle-frenzy. Fjel poured from the barracks, abandoned their posts along the wall, streaming toward the Defile Gate. Only their sheer mass prevented them from passing through it and entering Defile's Maw. So many Fjel were pressed up against the Gate it was impossible to open it. Enraged and slavering, partially armed or not at all, they flung themselves against the stone walls.

"Shapers!" Speros looked ill.

"Marshal Hyrgolf." Tanaros kneed his mount forward, taking a position atop the high path where all could see him. He gazed down at the seething mass of bodies. "Get me one of the Tordenstem." There was a slight commotion behind him, and then one of the Tordenstem, the Thunder Voice Fjel, was at his side, squat and grey as a boulder, offering a steady salute. Tanaros nodded at him. "Tell them their General commands their attention."

The Tordenstem took a great breath, his barrel-shaped torso swelling visibly, and loosed his voice in a mighty roar. *"All heed the Lord General Tanaros! Tan-a-ros! Tan-a-ros! All heed the Lord General!"*

Stillness settled, slow and gradual. The long training of the Fjel had instilled the habit of obedience in them. They ceased flinging themselves at the impervious stone and gazed upward at Tanaros, a semblance of sanity returning to their features.

"Brethren!" Tanaros raised his voice; an ordinary Man's voice, possessed of no special might, but pitched to carry over battlefields. "Who is it that has ordered this assault?" There was no answer. The Fjel shuffled and looked at their horny feet. "No?" Tanaros asked. "Then I will tell you: Malthus. It is Malthus the Counselor who orders it, and Malthus alone you obey if you heed this madness!"

They looked shame-faced and Tanaros felt guilty at it. He, too, had been caught up in the frenzy. If not for the Dreamspinner's intervention, he would be down there among them. But it would avail nothing to confess it. Now was the time to provoke their pride, not assuage it.

"Listen to me," he said to the Fjel. "This"—he gestured—"this mayhem, this undisciplined ferocity, *this* is how Haomane's Allies see you. This is what they wish the Fjel to be; mindless, unthinking. Ravening beasts. Do you wish to prove them aright? Is that how Neheris Shaped her Children?"

A roar of denial rose in answer. Tanaros smiled and drew his black sword. Its hilt pulsed in his grip, attuned to the hatred that throbbed in his veins. It glowed with its own dark light under the shrouded skies.

"By this sword!" he called. "By the black sword, quenched in his Lordship's blood, I swear to you! We will obey his Lordship's orders and see his will is done. And if his will be *war*, Haomane's Allies will know what it means to face the wrath, and the might, and the *discipline* of Darkhaven!"

Their cheers drowned out the distant call of Ellylon horns.

Tanaros sheathed the black sword and turned to Hyrgolf. "Summon your lieutenants and restore some semblance of order. Tell the lads to remain on alert."

"Aye, General." Hyrgolf paused. "You think his Lordship means to do it?"

"I don't know." Tanaros leaned over in the saddle, clasping the Tungskulder's shoulder. "We shall see, Field Marshal."

LILIAS STARTLED AWAKE FROM A dream of Beshtanag.

She had been dreaming of the siege, the endless siege, watching her people grow starved and resentful, waiting for an army that would never come, hearing once more the silvery horns of the Rivenlost blow and the herald repeating his endless challenge. *Sorceress! Surrender the Lady Cerelinde, and your people will be spared!*

Waking, she found herself in her pleasant prison-chamber, sunlight streaming through the high windows. Beshtanag was far, far away. And still she heard horns, a faint and distant call echoing through Meronil's white bridges and towers.

For a terrified moment, she thought it was Oronin's Horn summoning her to death. In Pelmar it was said those of noble birth could hear it; of a surety, the Were could. But, no, those were Ellylon horns.

"Eamaire." Swallowing her pride, Lilias pleaded with the attendant when she arrived. "What passes in the world? Is Meronil besieged?"

"While Haomane's Children draw breath on Urulat's soil, Meronil stands, Lady." A cool disdain was in the Ellyl's leaf-green eyes, as though she had borne witness to Lilias' darkest fantasies of destruction. "The Lord of the Rivenlost travels with the Host. You do but hear their horns sounding in the distance."

Lilias took a sharp breath. "Darkhaven?"

The Ellyl hesitated, then shook her head. "It may be. We cannot know."

She departed, leaving Lilias alone with the memory of her dream and the awful knowledge that it was true, all true, that Beshtanag was lost, everything was lost, and she was to blame. The horns sounded again, reminding her.

Perhaps Oronin's Horn would not have been so terrible after all.

Lilias sat at her window seat and watched the broad silver ribbon of the Aven River unfurl far, far below, thinking about her dream. Perhaps, she thought, she would sleep and dream it again. As awful as it was, it was no worse than the reality to which she had awakened, the reality she was forced to endure. At least in the dream, Beshtanag had not yet fallen, Calandor still lived, and Lilias was immortal.

There were worse things than death and dreams.

THE THRONE HALL WAS ABLAZE with marrow-fire. It surged upward from the torches to sear the mighty rafters and laced the walls in stark blue-white veins; earth's lightning, answering to Lord Satoris' rage. The Shaper was pacing the dais in front of his carnelian throne, a vast and ominous figure, unknown words spilling from his lips.

The Three glanced at one another and approached.

"My Lord." Tanaros went to one knee, bowing his head. From the corner of his eye, he saw Vorax do the same. Ushahin, unaccountably, remained standing. "We come to learn your will."

"My *will*." Lord Satoris ground out the words. He ceased his pacing and his eyes flashed red as coal-embers. "Did you not hear the challenge Malthus raises? My *will*, my Three, is to take up Godslayer and split open the very earth beneath his feet until he is swallowed whole by Urulat itself, and my Elder Brother's allies with him!"

His words echoed throughout the Throne Hall, echoed and continued to echo. Tanaros kept his head bowed, feeling the Shaper's wrath beating in waves against his skin. The air was filled with the acrid odor of blood and thunder, so dense he could taste it in his mouth.

"Can you, my Lord?" It was Ushahin, still standing and gazing up at Satoris, who asked the question. There was a strange tenderness in his voice. "Can we yet delay this hour?"

The Shaper sighed. His shoulders slumped and his head lowered. A beast brought to bay; and yet no beast had ever stood so motionless, so still. The last echo of his words faded, until there was only the sound of the Three breathing, the crackle and hiss of the torches, and the slow, steady drip of ichor pooling on the dais.

"I cannot." Satoris whispered the words, turning out his empty hands. "Oh, my Three! I am not what I was. It is a terrible burden to bear. I have borne it too long and spent too much." A shudder ran through him. "Was I unwise? I cannot say."

"Not unwise." Ushahin wiped at his dilated eye, watering in the marrow-fire's painful glare. "Never that, my Lord."

"No?" Satoris laughed, harsh and hollow. "And yet, and yet. Ah, Dreamspinner! What did you *see* in the Delta? Too much, I think; too much. I destroyed the Marasoumië and I reckoned it worth the cost, for it would destroy Haomane's Weapon within it. And yet he lives, he places himself within my grasp, no longer able to Shape matter, and I . . ." He glanced at his empty hand. "I cannot seize him. I bleed, I diminish. Clouds I may summon; smoke and fire, signifying nothing. Godslayer beckons, but I cannot rise to its challenge. I cannot Shape the earth. I spent myself too soon."

"My Lord!" Unable to bear it any longer, Tanaros rose to his feet. "We are here to serve you," he said passionately. "Tell us your will, and we will accomplish it."

"My will." Lord Satoris glanced around him, surveying his creation. "These mountains, this fortress . . . oh, my Three! Years, it bought me, bought us; ages. How much of myself did I spend to erect them? What folly beckons me to betray them? Ah, Malthus! You are a formidable foe. And I . . . I am *tired*. Uru-Alat alone knows, I am tired." He heaved another sigh. "I would see it ended."

Tanaros bowed to the Shaper. "My Lord, you have not erected Darkhaven in vain. It can withstand this siege. But if it is your wish to give battle, my Fjel are eager and ready."

"Can we win?" Vorax asked bluntly. He glanced sidelong at Tanaros and clambered to his feet. "Folly, aye, there's no question it's folly. Less of one if we stand a chance of winning."

"Our chances are good." Tanaros pictured the army of Haomane's Allies in his mind. "They are many, but poorly coordinated. It is the effects of Malthus' Soumanië I fear the most."

"Malthus will not be so quick to assail your soul once you take to the field wearing the Helm of Shadows, cousin," Ushahin murmured. "He will be hard-pressed to quell the terrors in his own people."

"You are eager to do battle for one who can scarce wield a blade, Dreamspinner." Vorax shook his head. "No, there is too much risk, and too little merit. I like my flesh too well to offer it to the swords of Hao-mane's Allies when I have strong walls to protect it. That way lies madness."

"Madness," Ushahin said drily. "Not an hour ago, you were charging toward the Defile, willing to mount a single-handed assault. Whose madness was that?"

Vorax flushed brick-red. "Malthus', and you well know it!"

Ushahin shrugged. "It will come again, and again and again. The Counselor is powerful, and Haomane's will lends him strength. He will use the Soumanië to weaken our resolve." He smiled crookedly. "We have weapons to counter such an attack, but none to defend against it."

"It is his Lordship's choice," Tanaros said.

They looked to the dais and waited.

Lord Satoris sank into his throne. "Choice," he said bitterly. "What *choice* have I ever had? The pattern binds me fast, and I alone suffer the knowledge of it." He clutched his thigh, fingers digging deep into the wounded flesh. When he raised his hand, it dripped with black ichor, glistening wetly in the light of the marrow-fire. "Drop by drop, year by year, age upon age," he mused. "What will be left of me if I refuse this choice? For it will come again, and again and again, and there will be less of me to meet it. Did you know, Oronin Last-Born, when you planted Godslayer's blade in my flesh? Will you sound your Horn for me?" He laughed softly. "And what will happen when you do? Who will sound the Horn for *you*? For make no mistake, the day will come. Fear it, as you fear to cross the Sundering Sea. I will be waiting for it. I will be waiting for you *all*. I have placed my stamp upon the world, as I was meant to do."

"My Lord." Tanaros sought to return the Shaper's wandering thoughts to the present. "Your will?"

"You are insistent, my General." The Shaper lifted his hand, his ichor-wet hand, dragging his splayed fingertips down his face. Broad trails gleamed, black on black. "Malthus," he said in a calm voice, "wants a battle; so my Elder Brother bids him. It is my *will* that he shall have it, and I wish them all the joy of their desire." Lord Satoris met Tanaros' eyes. "Send an envoy. Let them retreat to a fair distance, and we will meet them in battle. And then . . ." He smiled. "Destroy them."

Tanaros bowed. "My Lord, it will be done."

NOT A MOUSE, BUT A worm.

A worm, a lowly worm, crawling blindly through the earth; that was what Dani felt himself to be. Only Thulu's intermittent directions whispered from behind reminded him otherwise. It was easier, in a way. It kept the terror at bay, the suffocating fear that stopped his throat when the walls closed in tight and he had to wriggle on his belly to keep going, never certain whether the tunnel would widen beyond, grow ever narrower, or end altogether.

At times it happened and they had to backtrack, slow and painful, to the last fork they had taken. And then Thulu had to pause, singing the veins of the earth in a ragged voice, reorienting himself toward distant *water.*

I am a worm, Dani thought, a worm.

There was air, though not much. It was close and stifling. They breathed in shallow breaths, trying to dole it out in precious lungfuls. Dani wondered how worms breathed as they inched through the black earth. Through their skin, perhaps.

Neither could have said how long their journey through the labyrinth of narrow tunnels lasted. At least a day; perhaps more. When seconds seemed to last minutes and minutes hours, it was impossible to say. It felt like an eternity. They crawled until they had the strength to crawl no farther, then they rested, sharing the last of their dwindling supplies; dry mouthfuls of food moistened by sparing sips of water.

They wasted no precious air in conversation. What was there to say? Either they would succeed or they would die, here beneath countless tons of rock, crawling in the pitch-black until the last of their supplies were gone and their strength failed and there was nothing left to do but lie down and die.

When the sound of human voices filtered into the tunnels, faint and distant, Dani thought at first that he had slipped into a waking dream; or worse, fallen into madness. Such a thing had been known to happen. Men had gone mad in the desert from an excess of sun, wandering dazed and speaking of things that did not exist. If light could cause such madness, surely darkness could do no less.

It was hard to make out words, but from the broad tone it seemed the voices were speaking the common tongue, which was irksome. Not since Gerflod had he used the hard-learned language, and after days upon days with only Uncle Thulu's company, Dani found it hard to comprehend. If he were going mad, he thought, he would prefer to do it in Yarru. Even a worm deserved that much.

He crawled toward the voices, a vague notion in mind of complaining to them.

"Dani!" Behind him, Uncle Thulu called his name. "Slow down, lad."

Dani paused, touching the clay vial dangling from his throat. It was solid and reassuring beneath his abraded fingers. What was he doing? "Uncle." He tried his voice, finding it hoarse and strange. He had not spoken in *any* tongue since they had first begun crawling, however long ago it was. "Listen."

They listened, breathing quietly. "Voices," Uncle Thulu said. "I hear voices."

In the blackness, Dani wept with gladness. "You hear them, too!"

"Aye, lad." His uncle's hand touched his ankle. "Go toward them, but slowly, mind. Whoever it is, they're not likely to be a friend."

Dani crept forward forgetting his aching knees and torn hands, the lingering pain in his shoulder. The tunnel continued to twist and turn, forking unexpectedly. He followed the sound of the voices, backtracking when they grew fainter. The path sloped upward, emerging gradually from the bowels of the earth. Turn by turn, the sound grew steadily louder.

Voices, a symphony of voices. As the tunnel widened, he could hear them; some high, almost flittering, some low, a bass rumble. Most were speaking in the common tongue, but here and there were Staccian tones he had heard among the women at Gerflod Keep, and there, too, was the Fjeltroll tongue, which sounded like rocks being pulverized.

The words in the common tongue had to do with food.

It was enough to make Dani wonder anew at his sanity; but then something else changed. The impenetrable blackness lessened. From somewhere, from wherever the voices spoke, *light* was seeping into the tunnels. He saw the dim outline of his own hands before him as he crawled, and kept going. He would have crawled into a den of Fjeltroll if it meant seeing the sun once more.

The light grew stronger; torchlight, not sunlight. It was enough to make him squint through eyes grown accustomed to utter blackness. When he could make out distant shadows moving across the rocky floor, Dani regained sense enough to freeze.

The tunnel, still low, had widened enough for Uncle Thulu to squirm alongside him. They lay on their bellies, watching the shadows move.

"Do you reckon we dare look?" Thulu whispered presently.

"I'll go," Dani whispered back.

He wriggled forward, inch by frightening inch. The tunnel sloped upward. The voices had grown clear as day, accompanied by scuffling and thudding, a steady series of grunts. Narrowing his eyes to slits, Dani peered over the crest of the incline.

The tunnel emerged onto a vast cavern, its walls stacked with foodstuffs. A throng of figures filled the space, Men and Fjeltroll alike, engaged in a concerted effort to shift the supplies. A steady stream were coming empty-handed and going laden, and an imposing figure, burly and bearded, directed their efforts. "An army travels on its belly!" he roared, slapping his own vast belly, clad in gilded plate-armor, for emphasis. "Come on, lads, *move!* I've more important matters on my plate!"

Dani winced and wriggled backward into the safety of the deep shadows, careful not to let the clay vial bang against the stony floor. In a soft whisper, he told Uncle Thulu what he had seen.

"Darkhaven's larder." Thulu gave a soundless chuckle. "Ah, lad! Time was I could have put a dent in it."

"What should we do?" The thought of retreating into the tunnels made Dani shudder all over his skin. "Try to find another route to the river?"

"We wait." Thulu nodded toward the cavern. "The river lies a distance beyond. No point tempting fate; I don't know if there *is* another route. Whatever they're doing, it can't take forever. Wait for silence and darkness, and then we'll see."

Once, Dani would have thought it a bleak prospect; lying on cold, hard stone for untold hours, hungry and thirsty. With fresh air to breathe, the tunnels behind him, and Darkhaven before him, it seemed like bliss. "And after that?" he asked.

Uncle Thulu glanced at him. "I don't know." He shook his head. In the dim light, his eyes were wide and dark in his worn face. "After that it's up to you, lad."

SEVENTEEN

THE THREE QUARRELED ABOUT IT, but in the end, Vorax won. He would serve as his Lordship's envoy. It had to be one of the Three; on that, they agreed. No one else could be trusted with a task of paramount importance. They did not agree it should be Vorax.

It was the logical choice, though Tanaros Blacksword and the Dreamspinner refused to see it, arguing that he was needed in Dark-haven, that they could ill afford the delay. Vorax listened until he could abide no more of their foolishness, then brought his gauntleted fists crashing down upon the table in the center of the Warchamber.

"We are speaking of driving a *bargain!*" he roared. "Have either of you an ounce of skill at it?"

They didn't, of course, and his outburst made them jump, which made him chuckle inwardly. It wasn't every day any of the Three was startled. There was menace in the old bear yet. In the end, they relented.

He spent the morning supervising the creation of a supply-train, shifting most of the contents of the larder, arranging for it to be carted down the Defile. Meat was a problem, but it could be hastily smoked; enough to provide for the Fjel, at least. There was food aplenty. Vorax had prepared for a siege of weeks; months. As long as it took. A battle on open ground, that was another matter.

It was folly, but it was his Lordship's folly. And in truth, although his head was loath, the blood in his veins still beat hard at the thought of it, remembering the maddening call of the Ellylon horns.

Still, it would take a cool head to negotiate the matter. That ruled out Blacksword, who was like to lose his the moment he clapped eyes on Aracus Altorus, and the Dreamspinner . . . well. The half-breed could be cool enough when he chose, and betimes he spoke sense in his foolhardy madness, but he was as unpredictable as spring weather in Staccia.

No, it had to be Vorax.

When the matter of supplies had been dealt with to his satisfaction, he retired to his chambers and ate a hearty dinner, enough to give him ballast for the task to come. He kissed his handmaids good-bye and fancied he saw a shadow of concern in the eyes of the youngest. An old bear was entitled to his fancy. It heartened him when he went to speak to the Ellyl bitch.

Cool heads; now, there was one. She didn't bat a lash at his query, just stared at him with those unsettling eyes and said, "Why should I assist you, Lord Vorax? It is not in my interest to give you tools with which to bargain."

He shrugged. "Lady, your only chance lies in this battle. If I'm not satisfied with the negotiations, it will not happen. Do you want to take that chance?"

She turned her head. What thoughts were passing beneath that smooth white brow, he could not have said. "Is Lord Ingolin in the field?"

"Your Rivenlost Lord?" Vorax scratched his beard. He hadn't picked him out from atop the crag, but the Ravensmirror had shown him leading the Host of the Ellylon. "Aye, Lady. He's there."

"Then tell them I said Meronil must have rung with the sound of horns this morning." She spoke without deigning to look at him. "By that token, they will know I live."

"Ladyship." He bowed with an ironic flourish. "My thanks."

He took his leave of her, accompanied by a pair of Havenguard. Tanaros had insisted upon it. The General might be hotheaded, but he was cautious of the Ellyl bitch's safety. Wisely enough, since Vorax would as lief see her dead.

His escort was waiting at the Defile Gate; ten of his Staccians, a company of thirty Fjel including a pair of Kaldjager scouts, and the young Midlander Speros. Vorax had his doubts about the lad—he was untried, desert travail or no—but he knew when to hold the line and when to quibble. It was what made him a shrewd bargainer; that, and the fact that he didn't *look* shrewd.

It felt strange to pass through the Gate, to abandon the safety of the thick walls and unscalable heights and enter the narrow Defile. There was little danger here—the Defile was well guarded from above—but it brought home the reality of the folly of his Lordship's decision; aye, and the excitement, too. His skin crawled at the same time he found himself humming battle-paeans.

"If it be folly, let it be a glorious one," he said aloud.

"Sir?" The Midlander glanced at him.

"Battle, lad. This battle."

They passed through the Weavers' Gulch without incident, the Kaldjager striding ahead to part the sticky veils. Vorax regarded the scuttling spiders with distaste. The Dreamspinner was fond of them, finding some arcane beauty in the patterns they wove. Small wonder he was mad, though it was a madness he shared with Lord Satoris. One of several, perhaps.

For the remainder of the descent, they spoke little, paying close heed to the dangerous trail. The Kaldjager had vanished, but Vorax could hear their sharp, guttural cries and the answer of the Tordenstem sentries above, low and booming. He wished they had more Kaldjager. The Cold Hunters were tireless in the chase, and if there was any weakness in their enemy's rearguard that could be exploited, they would find a way to circle around and sniff it out.

Too many lost in the northern territories, chasing down a rumor, a whisper of prophecy. Vorax would have given up his youngest handmaid to know what had truly happened there. Some trick of Malthus', like as not. There was simply no way a pair of desert-bred Charred Folk could have evaded the Kaldjager and defeated an entire company of Fjel.

The Kaldjager were waiting at the last bend, before the Defile opened its Maw, crouched like a pair of yellow-eyed boulders. They nodded at him, indicating the way was clear.

"All right, lads." Vorax settled his bulk more comfortably in the saddle and pointed with his bearded chin. "Let's drive a bargain."

They filed ahead of him, rounding the bend. Eigil, his Staccian lieutenant—the last one so appointed—carried their banner, the black banner of Darkhaven with the red dagger of Godslayer in the center. He was young for the task, but what else was Vorax to do? He had lost his best man, Carfax, in the decoy flight to Beshtanag; Osric had fallen to Staccian treachery. His blood still boiled when he thought about it. Speros of Haimhault carried the parley-banner; a pale blue oriflamme, unadorned. He took his job seriously, knuckles white on the banner's haft.

A silvery blast of horns sounded the instant they were seen. Vorax scowled into his beard. Trust the damned Ellylon to make a production of war. He waited for Eigil's answering shout.

"Lord Vorax of Darkhaven will entertain a delegation!"

He rode around the bend, traversing the final descent, lifting one hand in acknowledgment. It was a shock to see Haomane's Allies at close range. There were so *many*, covering the plains, arrayed no more than fifty yards from the Maw itself. His company was clustered at its base, the Fjel with their shields held high, prepared to defend his retreat if necessary.

Haomane's Allies stirred, conversing among themselves. He watched figures gesticulating, wondering if they argued as did the Three.

They knew the protocol. Three figures relinquished their arms with ceremony and rode forward, accompanied by an escort of forty Men and Ellylon. Half wore the dun-grey cloaks of the Borderguard; half the bright armor of the Rivenlost. There were no archers among them. If it came to a fight, it would be fair.

Vorax waited.

Malthus, Ingolin, Aracus; Haomane's Counselor, the Lord of the Rivenlost, and the Scion of Altorus. Vorax took their measure as they approached, riding from sunlight into the mountain's shadow. Their escort fanned out in a loose circle. His remained where they stood; shields high, bristling with weapons. The pale blue oriflamme in Speros' hands trembled, then steadied.

"Vorax of Staccia!" Aracus Altorus' voice was hard and taut. One hand rested on the hilt of his ancestral sword, drawing attention to the dull red gem set in its pommel. "We have come to demand that the Lady Cerelinde be restored to us."

Vorax laughed. "Why, so you have, little Man. Will you go if she is?"

It made the would-be King of the West uncertain; he frowned hard, staring. Malthus the Counselor exchanged a glance with Ingolin the Wise and shook his white-maned head.

"Vorax." His voice was gentle; almost kind. The clear Soumanië on his breast sparkled. "Do not insult us with false promises. Your Dark Lord knows what we are about. Why does he send you? What is his will?"

Vorax smiled. It was always good to establish the principal agent in any bargain. "One that should please you, wizard. For a small price, it is his Lordship's *will* to give you what you desire."

"Cerelinde!" Aracus Altorus breathed.

"War," the Rivenlost Lord said gravely.

"War," Vorax said, agreeing with the latter. Broadening his smile, he opened his arms. "What else have you courted so assiduously? You have swayed him, wizard; you have swayed us all! His Lordship is willing to meet the forces of Haomane's Allies upon the plain. And yet, we must have certain assurances."

Aracus Altorus raised his brows. "Why should we bargain with you?"

"Ah, little Man!" Vorax bent a benign glance upon him. "Do you see these heights?" He pointed toward the Gorgantus Mountains. "They cannot be scaled. There is but one passage, and believe me, if you believe nothing else I say, when I tell you it is well guarded. You have no leverage here."

"What is the Sunderer's price?" Malthus asked.

"Fall back." Vorax shrugged. "As I said, it is a small one. You seek battle; his Lordship is willing to give it. Fall back . . . half a league, no more. Allow our forces to assemble and meet yours in fair combat upon the plains. No attack shall begin until the signal is given."

The Counselor nodded. "And if we do not agree?"

"Look around you." Vorax indicated the plains with a sweep of his hand. "Can you fill your bellies with grass, like horses? I think not, Haomane's Counselor. Darkhaven can outwait you. Darkhaven *will* outwait you."

Malthus smiled, wrinkles creasing his face. The Soumanië nestled in his beard brightened, starry. "Will you?" he asked. "Oh, I think not, Vorax of Staccia. The Sunderer's will is fixed."

Vorax squinted sidelong at the Soumanië, feeling the urge to battle quicken his blood. "You're handy with that, Counselor," he observed. "Makes me pity my countrymen, those you led into betrayal. I trust you found them waiting, as promised. Doubtless Haomane is pleased." Bloodlust thickened his tongue, and he nodded at the gem. "Have a care. I come to bargain in good faith."

"And yet you perceive your weakness," Malthus said gently.

"Mine, aye." With an effort, Vorax tore his gaze from the Soumanië. "Funny thing, Counselor. Seems your pretty brooch doesn't work on the Dreamspinner." He forced his lips into a smile. "Something in his nature renders him proof against its folly, and he's right eager to see the Lady Cerelinde dead, is Ushahin Dreamspinner. He doesn't mind defying Lord Satoris to do it. He's quite mad, you know."

Aracus Altorus swore; Malthus passed his hand over the Soumanië, quenching its light.

Ingolin of the Rivenlost, who had sat motionless in the saddle, stirred. "You touch upon my fears, Vorax of Staccia. You are quick to use the Lady Cerelinde's life as a bargaining chip, yet it is in my heart that the Sunderer has little reason to have spared it to date."

"Oh, aye, she lives." Breathing easier, Vorax laughed. "For now, El-lyl lordling. His Lordship," he added contemptuously, "has staked his *honor* upon it."

Ingolin's melodious voice deepened. "I put no trust in the honor of Satoris Banewreaker. Let her be brought forth, if you would have me believe. Let us see with our own eyes that the Lady Cerelinde lives!"

"See, I thought you might ask that." Vorax scratched at his beard. "Problem is, Ingolin my friend, she's our safeguard. I don't put a great deal of trust in *your* word." He gave the Lord of the Rivenlost a friendly smile. "Why, you might break it, if you reckoned it were for the greater good!"

"I would not," the Ellyl Lord said stiffly. "The Ellylon do not lie."

"Maybe, maybe not." Vorax shrugged. "Someone else might break it for you, eh? The Lady stays in Darkhaven. But I asked her for a token, whereby you might know she lives. She asked me if you were in the field. When I said you were, she said, 'Tell them Meronil must have rung with the sound of horns this morning.' Does that suffice?"

Ingolin bowed his head, silver hair hiding his features. "Cerelinde," he whispered.

"Cerelinde," Vorax agreed. "Whose life hangs by this bargain, and your ability to honor it to the word. Shall we strike it?"

"How do we know you will keep your word?" Aracus Altorus' eyes blazed. "Perhaps this bargain is but a mockery. What safeguard do *you* offer, Glutton?"

Vorax glanced around, his gaze falling on the Midlander. "Speros of Haimhault." He beckoned. "Are you willing to serve?"

"My lord!" The Midlander looked ill. "Aye, my lord."

"Here you are, then." Vorax clapped a hand on his shoulder. "He's the architect of Darkhaven's defense. Try the Defile, and see what he's got in store for you! Word is he engineered the means to let General Tanaros fill in that pesky Well in the Unknown Desert, though you might know more of it than I. Any mind, he's been Tanaros Blacksword's right-hand Man for some time. Will he suffice?"

They looked shocked; all save Malthus. Did nothing on the face of Urulat shock the damned Counselor? He inclined his head, white beard brushing his chest.

"He will suffice," Malthus said somberly.

"Good." Vorax glanced at the sky, gauging the angle of the sun. "You'll withdraw your troops by dawn on the morrow, on pain of the Lady's death?"

"We will."

"Then we will meet you ere noon. You'll know our signal when we give it." He grinned. "Gentlemen, I will see you anon!"

His Staccians closed in tight, following as he turned his mount and headed into Defile's Maw, the Fjel guarding their retreat, step by backward step, shields held high. Below them, Speros of Haimhault sat on his ghost-grey mount and watched them go with desperate eyes.

It was, Vorax thought, a well-struck bargain.

SILVER HOARFROST SPARKLED ON THE sere grass in the moon-garden, shrouded its plants and trees in cerements of ice. No drops fell from the pale pink blossoms of the mourning-tree, and the corpse-flowers' pallid glow was extinguished. The mortexigus did not shudder in the little death, shedding its pollen, and the shivering bells of the clamitus atroxis waited in silence. Even the poignant scent of vulnus-blossom had been stilled by the cold.

Tanaros wrapped his cloak tighter and wondered if Cerelinde would come. He could have gone to her, or he could have ordered her to come. In the end, he had chosen to ask. Why, he could not have said.

Overhead, the stars turned slowly. He gazed at them, wondering if Arahila looked down upon Darkhaven and wept for her brother Satoris' folly, for the bloodshed that was certain to follow. He wondered if poor Speros, unwitting victim of Vorax's bargain, was watching the same stars. He was angry at Vorax for his choice, though there was no merit in arguing it once it was done. Other matters were more pressing; indeed, even now, he wasted precious time lingering in the garden. Still, his spirit was uneasy and an ache was in his heart he could not name.

After a time, he became certain she would not come; and then the wooden door with the tarnished hinges opened and she was there, flanked by the hulking figures of the Havenguard. They remained behind, waiting.

Her gown was pale, its color indeterminate in the starlight. A dark cloak enfolded her like green leaves enfolding a blossom's pale petals. Its sweeping hem left a trail in the frosted grass as she approached him.

"Tanaros," she said gravely.

"Cerelinde." He drank in the sight of her. "I didn't know if you would come."

"You have kept your word of honor, and I am grateful for the protection you have given me." She studied his face. "It is to be war, then?"

"Yes. On the morrow. I wanted to say farewell."

She laid one hand on his arm. "I wish you would not do this thing."

He glanced at her hand, her slender, white fingers. "Cerelinde, I must."

"No." She shook her head. "You have a choice, Tanaros. Even you, even now. Perhaps it is too late to stem the tide of battle, but it need not be, not for you. There is goodness in you; I have seen it. It is yours to reclaim."

"And do what?" Tanaros asked gently. "Shall I dance at your wedding, Cerelinde?"

The matter lay between them, vast and unspoken. She looked away. In that moment, he knew she understood him; and knew, too, that unlike his wife, the Lady of the Ellylon would never betray the Man to whom she was betrothed. The ache in his heart intensified. He laid his hand over hers, feeling for a few seconds her smooth, soft skin, then removed her hand from his arm.

"I'm sorry," he said. "I cannot."

"There are other things!" She looked back at him and starlight glimmered on her tears. "The world is vast, Tanaros. You could . . . you could help Staccia rebuild its ties to the rest of Urulat, or the Beshtanagi in Pelmar, or hunt Were or dragons or Fjeltroll—"

"Cerelinde!" He halted her. "Would you have me betray what honor I possess?"

"*Why?*" She whispered the word, searching his face. "Ah, Tanaros! What has Satoris Banewreaker ever done that he should command your loyalty?"

"He found me." He smiled at the simplicity of the words. "What has he not done to be worthy of my loyalty, Cerelinde? When love and fidelity alike betrayed me, when the world cast me out, Lord Satoris found me and summoned me to him. He understood my anger. He bent the very Chain of Being to encompass me, he filled my life with meaning and purpose."

"*His* purpose." Her voice was low. "Not yours."

"Survival." He spread his hands in a helpless gesture. "He seeks to survive. What else do any of us seek? Because he is a Shaper, the stakes are higher. I tell you this, Cerelinde. His Lordship is *here*. Wounded and bleeding, but *here*. And he has given shelter to all of us, all whom the world has bent and broken, all who yearn for a Shaper's love, all whom the world has despised. He demands our loyalty, yes, but he allows us the freedom to question the order of the world, to be who and what we are. Can you say the same of Haomane Lord-of-Thought?"

"You do not understand." Cerelinde's voice trembled. "He is . . . everywhere."

"For you, perhaps." Tanaros touched her cool cheek. "Not for me."

For a time, they stood thusly; then Cerelinde, Lady of the Ellylon, shuddered like the petals of the mortexigus flower and withdrew from his touch. Wrapped in her dark cloak, she gazed at him with her glorious eyes.

"Tanaros," she said. "I will not pray for your death on the morrow."

"Lady." He bowed low and said no more.

The Havenguard reclaimed her, and she went.

Speros of Haimhault found sleep difficult.

It had all happened so *fast*. One moment, he had been concentrating on acquitting himself bravely, holding the parley-flag and assessing the forces of Haomane's Allies to report to the General; the next, he was agreeing to be a hostage.

At least they had been civil.

They were that; he had to admit. Back in the old days, when he was but a piddling horse-thief, he had never been treated with such care. The architect of Darkhaven's defense! It was a prodigious title, even if Lord Vorax had invented it.

To be honest, their triumvirate of leaders seemed to sense it; *they* were dismissive. Once they returned to the campsite, white-bearded Malthus made it clear he had greater concerns on his mind, which was just as well. Speros had no desire to find the wizard's attention focused on him. Aracus Altorus merely looked him up and down as if gauging his worth and finding it wanting. As far as Ingolin, Lord of the Rivenlost, was concerned, Speros might as well not exist.

But others were at the campsite; hangers-on, no doubt. Blaise Caveros, the Borderguard commander with an unsettling look of the General about him, took Speros to be a legitimate threat. He assigned a pair of guards fitting to his purported station to him; some minor El-lyl lordling and an Arduan archer. They took turns keeping watch over him. A woman, no less! She had a strange bow made of black horn, which she cosseted like a babe. At nightfall she brought him a bowl of stew from the common kettle. After he had eaten, Speros grinned at her, forgetful of the gaps where he was missing teeth.

"Very nice," he said, nodding at her weapon. "Where did you get it?"

She stared blankly at him. "This is Oronin's Bow."

"Oh, aye?" He whistled. "So where did you get it?"

The archer shook her head in disgust. "You tend to him," she said to the Ellyl, rising to survey the campsite.

"Did I say somewhat to offend her?" Speros asked the Ellyl, who smiled quietly.

"Fianna the Archer slew the Dragon of Beshtanag with that bow," he said. "Surely the knowledge must have reached Darkhaven's gates."

"It did." Speros shrugged. "I was in the desert at the time."

"Indeed." The Ellyl, whose name was Peldras, laced his hands around one knee. "Your Lord Vorax spoke of your efforts concerning a certain Well when he offered you into the keeping of the Wise Counselor."

"You know it?" Speros repressed a memory of the General's black sword cleaving the old Yarru man's chest, the dull thud of the Gulnagels' maces.

"I do." Peldras regarded him. "You seem young and well-favored to have risen high in the Sunderer's service, Speros of Haimhault."

He shrugged again. "I've made myself useful."

"So it seems." Peldras raised his fair, graceful brows. "Although I fear you may have outlived your usefulness, or Vorax of Staccia would not have been so quick to surrender you. Did I stand in your shoes, young Midlander, I would find it a matter of some concern. The Sunderer's minions are not known for their loyalty."

Speros thought of Freg, carrying him in the desert; of the General himself, holding water to his parched lips. He laughed out loud. "Believe as you wish, Ellyl! I am not afraid."

"You were not at Beshtanag," Peldras murmured. "I witnessed the price the Sorceress of the East paid for her faith in Satoris Banewreaker, and the greater toll it took upon her people. Are you willing to pay as much?"

"That was different." Speros shook his head. "I was in the Ways when your wizard Malthus closed them upon us. We would have aided her if we could."

"The Sunderer could have reopened the Ways of the Marasoumië if he chose." The Ellyl glanced westward toward the shadowy peaks of the Gorgantus Mountains. "With the might of Godslayer in his hands, not even Malthus the Counselor could have prevented it. He chose instead to destroy them."

"Aye, in the hope of destroying Malthus with them!" Speros said, exasperated. "You forced this war; you and all of Haomane's Allies! Will you deny his Lordship the right to choose his strategies?"

"No." Peldras looked back at him. Under the stars, illuminated by the nearby campfire, his features held an ancient, inhuman beauty. "Ah, Speros of Haimhault! On another night, there is much I would say to you. But I fear sorrow lies heavy on my heart this night, and I cannot find it in me to speak of such matters when on the morrow, many who are dear to me will be lost."

"Did I ask you to?" Speros muttered.

"You did not." Rising, the Ellyl touched his shoulder. "Forgive me, young hostage. I pray that the dawn may bring a brighter day. Yet the world changes, and we change with it. It is in my heart that it is Men such as you, in the end, who will Shape the world to come. I can but pray you do it wisely."

Speros eyed him uncertainly, trying to fathom what trickery lay in the words. "Me?"

"Men of your ilk." Peldras gave his quiet smile. "Builders and doers, eager for glory, willing to meddle without reckoning the cost." Tilting his head, he looked at the stars. "For my part, I wish only to set foot upon Torath the Crown, to enter the presence of Haomane First-Born, Lord-of-Thought, and gaze once more upon the Souma."

Since there seemed to be no possible reply, Speros made none. The Ellyl left him then, and the Arduan woman Fianna returned. She pointed out a bedroll to him and then sat without speaking, tending to her bowstring. The scent of pine rosin wafted in the air, competing with the myriad odors of the campsite.

Speros wrapped himself in the bedroll and lay sleepless. The frost-bitten ground was hard and uncomfortable, cold seeping into his bones. Oronin's Bow gleamed like polished onyx in the firelight. He wondered what sound it made when it was loosed, if echoes of the Glad Hunter's horn were in it.

At least the Ellylon horns were silenced by night, although one could not say it was *quiet*. The vast camp was filled with murmurous sound; soldiers checking their gear, sentries changing guard, camp-fires crackling, restless horses snuffling and stamping in the picket lines. He could make out Ghost's pale form against the darkness, staked far from the other cavalry mounts. Haomane's Allies gave her a wide berth, having learned to be wary of her canny strength and sharp bite.

There was a tent nearby where the commanders took counsel; too far for Speros to hear anything of use, but near enough that he saw them coming and going. Once, he saw it illuminated briefly from within; not by ordinary lamplight or even the diamond-flash of Malthus' Soumanië, but something else, a cool, blue-green glow. Afterward, Blaise Caveros emerged and spoke to Fianna in a low tone.

"Haomane be praised!" she whispered. "The Bearer lives."

At that, Speros sat upright. Both of them fell silent, glancing warily at him. It made him laugh. "He knows, you know," he said conversationally. "Lord Satoris. The Charred Folk, the Water of Life. There is no part of your plan that is unknown to him."

"Be as that may, Midlander," Blaise said shortly. "He cannot prevent Haomane's Prophecy from fulfillment."

"He can try, can't he?" Speros studied the Borderguardsman. "You know who you've a look of? General Tanaros."

"So I have heard." The words emerged from between clenched teeth.

"He says you're better with a sword than Aracus Altorus," Speros remarked. "Is it true?"

"It is," Blaise said in a careful tone, "unimportant."

"You never know." Speros smiled at him. "It might be. Have you seen the Lady Cerelinde? She is . . . how did the General say it? We spoke of her in the desert, before I'd seen her with my own eyes. 'She's beautiful, Speros,' he said to me. 'So beautiful it makes you pity Arahila for the poor job she made of Shaping us, yet giving us the wit to know it.' Is it not so? I think it would be hard to find any woman worthy after her."

Blaise drew in his breath sharply and turned away. "Be watchful," he said over his shoulder to Fianna. "Say nothing in his hearing that may betray us."

She nodded, chagrined, watching as the Borderguardsman strode away. Speros lay back on his bedroll, folding his arms behind his head. "Do you suppose he harbors feelings for his lord's betrothed?" he wondered aloud. "What a fine turn of events that would be!"

"Will you be *silent!*" the Arduan woman said fiercely. Her nervous fingers plucked at the string of Oronin's Bow. A deep note sounded across the plains of Curonan, low and thrumming, filled with anguish. Speros felt his heart vibrate within the confines of his chest. For a moment, the campsite went still, listening until the last echo died.

"As you wish," Speros murmured. Closing his eyes, he courted elusive sleep to no avail. Strangely, it was the Ellyl's words that haunted him. *Men of your ilk, builders and doers.* Was it wrong that he had taken fate in his own hands and approached Darkhaven? He had made himself useful. Surely the General would not forget him, would not abandon him here. Speros had only failed him once, and the General had forgiven him for it. His mind still shied from the memory; the black sword falling, the maces thudding. The old Yarru folks' pitiful cries, their voices like his grandmam's. His gorge rising in his throat, limbs turning weak.

But the General had not wanted to do it, any more than Speros had. The Ellyl was wrong about that. He did not understand; *would* not understand. Though Speros did not want to remember it, he did. The General's terrible sword uplifted, the cry wrenched from his lips. *Give me a reason!*

Opening his eyes, Speros blinked at the stars and wondered why so many questions were asked and went unanswered, and what the world would be like if they were not.

TOTAL DARKNESS HAD FALLEN BEFORE Dani and Thulu dared venture from the tunnels. They crept blindly, bodies grown stiff with long immobility, parched with thirst and weak with hunger, fearful of entering a trap.

But no; by the faint starlight illuminating the opening, the larder appeared empty of any living presence. The supplies stacked within it had been diminished, but not stripped. They fell upon what remained, tearing with cracked and broken nails at the burlap wrapping on a wheel of cheese, gnawing raw tubers for the moisture within them. They stuffed their packs with what scraps and remnants remained. The kegs of wine alone they left untouched, fearing that breaching one would leave evidence of their presence behind.

Only after they had assuaged their hunger and the worst of their thirst did they dare peer forth from the opening of the cavern onto the Vale of Gorgantum.

"Uru-Alat!" Dani felt sick. "*That's* Darkhaven?"

The scale of it was unimaginable. For as far as the eye could see, the Vale was encircled by a massive wall, broken by watchtowers. It vanished somewhere behind them, blocked by the swell of the slope, reemerging to encompass a small wood of stunted trees. A broad, well-trodden path led from the larder-cavern to the rear gates of the fortress itself. It was huge; impossibly huge, a hulking edifice blotting out a vast segment of the night sky. Here and there, starlight glinted on polished armor; Fjeltroll, patrolling the gates.

"Aye," Uncle Thulu said. "I don't suppose they're likely to let us in for the asking. Any thoughts, lad?"

Dani stared across the Vale. He could make out the Gorgantus River by the gleam of its tainted water. Other lower structures squatted alongside it, lit within by a sullen glow. He could smell smoke, thick and acrid in the air. "What are those?"

"Forges, I think. For making weapons and armor."

"Do you reckon they're guarded by night?"

"Hard to say." Thulu shook his head. "They're not in use or we'd hear the clamor. But the fires are still stoked, so they're likely not unattended. It's a long scramble, and there are guards on the wall, too."

"Aye, but they're looking outward, not inward. If we don't make any sound, move slowly, and keep to the shadow, they'll not spot us. It's the armor that gives them away. At least it would get us closer." Dani studied the fortress. Darkhaven loomed, solid and mocking, seemingly impenetrable. He wished he knew more about such matters. "There has to be another entrance *somewhere*, doesn't there?"

"I don't know." Uncle Thulu laid one hand on Dani's shoulder. "But truth be told, I've no better ideas. This time, lad, the choice is yours."

Dani nodded, touching the clay vial at his throat for reassurance. "We can't stay here forever. Let's try. We'll make for the river and follow it."

It was a nerve-racking journey. They emerged from the mouth of the cavern, abandoning the broad path to clamber down the mountain's slope where the shadows lay thickest. Both of them moved slowly, with infinite care. One slip of the foot, one dislodged pebble, and the Fjel would come to investigate.

If it had done nothing else, at least their long travail had prepared them for this moment. The inner slopes of the Gorgantus Mountains were gentler than the unscalable crags that faced outward, no more difficult to traverse than the mountains of the northern territories. They had learned, laboring atop the rock-pile, how to place their feet with the utmost care, how little pressure it took to shift a loose stone. Their night vision was honed by their time in the tunnels.

Once they reached level ground, it was another matter. Atop the incline to their right, they could see the curving shoulder of the encircling wall. The distant spark of torches burned in the watchtowers. Dani pointed silently toward the wood. Inching along the base of the slope, they made toward it. From time to time, the low tones of Fjeltroll drifted down from above.

The wood was foreboding, but the gnarled trees would provide cover and allow them to leave the wall. Dani breathed an inaudible sigh of relief when they reached the outskirts. Tangled branches, barren of leaves, beckoned in welcome. He entered their shadow and stepped onto the hoarfrosted beech-mast, grimacing as it crackled faintly beneath his feet.

Uncle Thulu grabbed his arm, pointing.

Dani froze and squinted at the trees.

There, a short distance into the wood; a ragged nest. There were others beyond it, many others. He thought of the dark cloud that had winged toward them on the plains, so vast it cast a shadow, and his heart rose into his throat.

Uncle Thulu pointed toward the left.

There was nowhere else to go. Step by step, they edged sidelong around the wood. The trick was to do it slowly, lowering their weight gradually with each step until the warmth of their bare soles melted the hoarfrost and prevented it from crackling. It seemed to take forever, and with each step Dani feared the woods would stir to life. He imagined a beady eye in every shadow, a glossy black wing in every glimmer of starlight on a frosted branch. He kept an anxious eye on the sky, fearing to see the pale light of dawn encroaching.

It seemed like hours before they had covered enough ground to put the wood between them and the wall. They backed away from it, away from the danger of sleeping ravens and waking Fjeltroll, and made for the river.

Here was open territory, unguarded. They crossed it as swiftly as they dared. The Gorgantus River cut a broad, unnatural swath through the Vale. Once, it had flowed southward down the Defile, where only a trickle remained. Lord Satoris had diverted it to serve his purposes, but it flowed low and sluggish, resentful despite untold ages at being deprived of its natural course.

And for other reasons.

They crouched on the bank, staring at the water. It looked black in the starlight, moving in slow eddies, thick as oil. An odor arose from it; salt-sweet and coppery.

"Do you reckon we can drink it?" Dani whispered.

Uncle Thulu licked his parched lips. "*I* wouldn't." He glanced at Dani. "You mean for us to get in that filth, lad?"

"Aye." He touched the flask, steeling his resolve. "The banks will hide us."

"So be it." Thulu slid down the bank.

Dani followed, landing waist deep in the tainted water. Cold mud squelched between his toes. Here, at least, they would be invisible to any watching sentries; merely a small disturbance on the river's oily surface. Lowering their heads, shivering against the water's chill, they began to make their way downstream. For all their efforts at caution, they slipped and slid, until they were wet, mud-smeared, and bedraggled, all the supplies they carried spoiled by the tainted water.

The sky *was* beginning to pale by the time they reached the buildings where the forges were housed; not dawn, not yet, but the stars were growing faint and the unalleviated blackness between them was giving way to a deep charcoal. And other obstacles, too, forced them to halt. Ahead of them on the river, a strange structure moved; a mighty wheel, turning steadily, water streaming from its broad paddles. Beyond it lay the low array of buildings; furnaces and forges, and a ramshackle structure that seemed to have been erected in haste. Despite the fact, it was the site of the greatest activity. Smoke poured from it, dim figures moving in its midst, going to and fro.

For the first time since the tunnels, Dani knew despair.

"What do you suppose that is?" Thulu whispered, leaning on the muddy bank. He sniffed the air. "Smells like . . . like a *meal*."

"I don't know," Dani murmured. With an effort, he stilled his chattering teeth and studied the buildings. The nearest one seemed the most abandoned. He nodded at it. "We'll make for there. It may be we can find a place to hide."

"Aye, lad." Thulu extricated himself from the sucking mud. "Come on."

It was hard to move, cold as he was. Dani took his uncle's strong hand, bracing his feet against the bank and hauling himself out of the river. They shook themselves, wringing the foul water from their clothes. There was nothing to be done about the mud.

The entire place was wreathed in smoke. It did, Dani realized, smell like a meal; like roasting flesh, at once greasy and savory. His belly rumbled. Attempting to lead the way, he found himself stumbling.

"Hey!" A figure emerged from the smoke, soot-blackened and filthy, with unkempt hair and wild, red-rimmed eyes. It clutched a haunch of meat. "Lord Vorax says it's done enough for Fjel," it said in the common tongue, freeing one smeared hand to point. "Hurry, we've got to get it all moved!"

Tensed for flight, Dani stared in bewilderment as the figure—man or woman, he could not tell beneath the grime—beckoned impatiently. The slow realization dawned on him that in the dark, covered in filth as they were, no one could tell a Yarru from an Ellyl. He exchanged a glance with his uncle.

"You heard him, lad." Thulu wiped his forearm over his face, leaving a muddy smear that further obscured his features. "Lord Vorax said to hurry!"

Dani nodded his understanding. Keeping their heads low, they plunged into the billowing smoke to follow the beckoning madling.

Darkhaven had invited them inside after all.

EIGHTEEN

THE ARMY OF DARKHAVEN ASSEMBLED at dawn.

Tanaros scanned the scene before him with a seasoned eye. What he saw pleased him. Tens of thousands of Fjel were arrayed in orderly ranks, awaiting his command. They were eager, but contained. Vorax's Staccians, five hundred strong, were mounted and ready.

There was chaos in the rearguard where the supply-wagons were still being loaded, but he trusted Vorax would see all was in order. Beside him sat Ushahin Dreamspinner astride his blood-bay stallion, the leather case containing the Helm of Shadows wrapped in his arms.

Together, they waited.

The orange rim of the sun rose above the easternmost peaks of the Gorgantus Mountains to meet the enshrouding cloud cover above the Vale of Gorgantum, and the sound of Ellylon horns rent the air, uttering their silvery summons. The ranks stirred. Tanaros raised one gauntleted hand.

They waited.

A distant Tordenstem roared, then another.

Haomane's Allies were withdrawing.

Tanaros clenched his hand into a fist, and Hyrgolf bawled an order to the Fjel maintaining the Defile Gate. The bar was lifted. Two teams of Fjel put their backs into the task, and the massive doors, depicting the Battle of Neherinach, creaked slowly open.

"To war!" Tanaros shouted.

The long column began its descent into the Defile.

SPEROS OF HAIMHAULT, THE ARCHITECT of Darkhaven's defense, was acutely aware that he was little more than baggage.

For all their unwieldy composition, the myriad companies of Haomane's Allies executed their withdrawal with a disturbing precision. Dawn broke, the horns sounded, and they were on the move.

Much of it, loath though he was to admit it, was due to Aracus Altorus. Somehow, he managed to be *everywhere* on the field; conferring with the Lord of the Rivenlost, with the Pelmaran Regents, with Duke Bornin of Seahold, with whoever commanded the knights of Vedasia and the company of Dwarfs. He was tireless. Everywhere Speros looked, there he was; a red-gold needle, stitching the army together with the thread of his will.

It was an orderly withdrawal. Companies of infantry—Midlanders, Dwarfs, Free Fishermen, Arduan archers, Pelmarans—marched stolidly, trampling the plains grass. The mounted companies—the Borderguard of Curonan, the Vedasian knights, the Host of the Rivenlost—rode at a sedate jog.

Speros rode with them, watched by his minders, the Ellyl Peldras and the Arduan woman Fianna. He was glad to be astride Ghost, whose snapping teeth kept the others at bay. He thought more than once of turning her head and fleeing, giving her free rein across the plains. No mount here could catch her, unless it was Malthus'. But if he did, it would give Haomane's Allies cause to break their bargain.

So he went with them, casting glances over his shoulder as he rode.

His heart rose when he first caught sight of Darkhaven's army, worming its way down the Defile. It was *vast*. Rank upon rank of Fjel, marching in twos. High above them, Tordenstem sentries perched on the peaks, roaring out the signal for all clear.

The vanguard reached the plains and spread out, aligning themselves to reform in precise configurations and making ready to accommodate others, who kept coming and coming. Aye, and there were the Staccians; a crack troop of five hundred, all mounted on the horses of Darkhaven, taking the left flank. There was Lord Vorax coming from the supply-train at the rear to take his place at their head, gilded armor flaming in the morning light.

And there—there was General Tanaros, astride his black mount, still and dark and ominous. *He* did not need to ride herd on a divided force. He sat tall in the saddle, bare-headed, giving orders and watching them obeyed with alacrity.

Speros grinned.

"Something pleases you, Midlander?" Blaise Caveros swerved near him.

"How not?" Speros spread his arms. "It is a fine day for a battle!"

Blaise eyed him grimly. "Haomane willing, you shall have one."

At a distance of some half a league, Haomane's Allies turned and made their stand. Speros, mere baggage, was relegated to the rearguard. Ghost was taken from him and picketed once more by wary handlers. It frustrated him, for he could see little but an sea of armor-clad backsides as the troops moved into formation.

His minders were going into battle, leaving Speros under the undignified watch of the attendants and squires who composed the rearguard. It seemed they would not fight together; Blaise was to lead the Borderguard, while Peldras would join the Host of the Rivenlost, and Fianna the Arduan force. He watched as they made a solemn farewell, standing in a circle with their right hands joined in the center. There was a story there; he wondered what it was.

The Bearer lives. . . .

Speros thought about the chase through the tunnels leading from the Vesdarlig Passage, the scent the Fjel had lost, the scent of sun-warmed strawberries he had all but forgotten. He glanced uneasily toward Darkhaven and wondered what manner of guard the General had left in place. Surely, one that would suffice; the General was no fool. Still, Speros wished he could speak to him.

There was no time. Across the plains a mighty din arose; a howl uttered by tens of thousands of Fjel throats, the clangor of tens of thousands of Fjel beating their weapons upon their shields. The horns of the Ellylon blew in answer, high and clear.

The battle was beginning.

"IT IS TIME."

Tanaros nodded to Ushahin Dreamspinner, who opened the leather case he held. The Commander General of the Army of Darkhaven lifted forth the Helm of Shadows and donned it.

Darkness descended like a veil over his vision. The sun yet shone, but it was as though it had been wrapped in sackcloth. Everything around him stood out vividly on a shadowy background. A throbbing pain seared his groin; a ghostly pain, the Helm's memory of Lord Satoris' burden. Inside his armor, Tanaros could feel ichor trickling down his thigh. Such was the price of the Helm of Shadows.

The ranks of Fjel parted to allow him passage. They were silent now, watching him from the corners of their eyes. Hyrgolf, solid, blessed Hyrgolf, met his gaze, unafraid. He saluted. Tanaros returned the salute, touching the little pouch that hung at his belt, containing the *rhios* Hyrgolf had given him.

A small kindness.

Vorax's Staccians averted their eyes. It was harder for Men. But they were astride the horses of Darkhaven, who watched him with fearless, gleaming eyes. There was Vorax at their head, saluting. The bulk of his work was done; the bargain struck, the supply-train in place. This was Tanaros Blacksword's hour.

He jogged his mount to the forefront of the army. There could be no leading from the rear, not wearing the Helm of Shadows. The black moved smoothly beneath him, untroubled by the added burden of armor it bore; armor that echoed his own, lacquered black and polished until it shone like a midnight sun. Madlings had tended to it with love. Corselet and gorget, cuisses and greaves and gauntlets for the Man. Glossy plate at the horse's chest, flanks, and neck, covering its crupper, a demi-chaffron for the head.

Black horse, black rider.

Black sword.

It glowed darkly in his vision as he drew it; a wound in the morning sky. A shard of shadow, the edge glittering like obsidian. It had been quenched in the blood of Lord Satoris himself and was strong enough to shatter mortal steel.

Tanaros drew a deep breath; past the ache in his branded heart, past the phantom pain of his Lordship's wound. He had given speeches on the training-field, rousing his troops. Now that the hour had come, there was no need. They knew what they were about. When the air in his lungs burned, he loosed it in a shout.

"Forward, Darkhaven!"

With a second roar, his army began to advance. Across the plains, the Ellylon horns answered and Haomane's Allies moved forward to meet them.

Tanaros kept the pace slow, gauging his enemy's forces. Aracus Altorus had rearranged them, placing the Arduan archers in the vanguard ahead of the Rivenlost. The move was to be expected. Darkhaven had no archers; it was not a skill to which the Fjel were suited, and Staccians disdained the bow for aught but hunting. He signaled to Hyrgolf, who barked out an order. His bannermen echoed it with sweeping pennants. A company of fleet Gulnagel shifted into place on either side of him, the muscles in their thighs bunched and ready. They bore kite-shaped shields that covered their whole bodies, and they had trained for this possibility.

What else?

Aracus had put the Vedasian knights on his right, in direct opposition to Vorax's Staccians. They formed a solid block, clad from head to toe in shining steel, their mounts heavily armored. Well-protected, but slow to maneuver. Tanaros nodded to Vorax, who nodded back, grinning into his beard. Let the Vedasians see what the horses of Darkhaven were capable of doing. No need to worry about them.

The Host of the Rivenlost was clustered behind the archers, in their midst a starry glitter that made his head ache. Malthus? Tanaros squinted. Yes, there he was among them; clad in white robes, disdainful of armor. He carried the Spear of Light upright, and the clear Soumanië shone painfully on his breast, piercing the darkness. Behind him was the Borderguard of Curonan, with Aracus Altorus and Blaise Caveros, and massed behind them, countless others; Seaholders, Midlanders, Pelmarans.

Behind the Helm of Shadows, Tanaros smiled.

Let him come, let them all come. He was ready for them. He had a legion of Fjel at his back. Ushahin Dreamspinner was among them; protected, he hoped, by Hyrgolf's Tungskulder Fjel. He was not worried. The Dreamspinner would find a way to ward himself.

The gap between them was closing. On the far side of the plains, an order was shouted. The Arduan archers went to one knee.

"Shields up!" Tanaros cried, raising his own buckler.

The air sang with the sound of a hundred bowstrings being loosed at once, and amid them was surely the sound of Oronin's Bow, a deep, belling note of sorrow. A cloud of arrows filled the sky, raining down upon their raised shields. The clatter was horrible, but the armor of Darkhaven was well-wrought and the arrows did little harm.

"Left flank, hold! Right flank, defensive formation!" Tanaros shouted. "Center, advance at my pace! All shields up!"

He could hear Hyrgolf roaring orders, knew his lieutenants and bannermen were echoing them. Tanaros nudged the black into a walk. On either side of him, the Gulnagel tramped forward behind their shields.

Slowly and steadily, the center began to advance.

This was the true test of his army's mettle; indeed, of his own. At close range, the arrows of the Arduan archers could pierce armor, foul their shields. If they kept their heads, they would hold until the last possible moment. Tanaros watched the Arduan line through the eye-slits of the Helm of Shadows. They could see it now, he could see their fingers trembling on their bowstrings. Still, any closer and he would be forced to halt.

The archers' nerve broke. A second volley of arrows sang out, ragged and discordant. Tanaros heard a few howls of pain, felt an arrow glance off his buckler. "Gulnagel, go!" he shouted. "Strike and wheel!"

On either side the Gulnagel surged forward, bounding on powerful haunches. They came together in a wedge; a difficult target, tight-knit and armored, driving toward the line of kneeling archers, closing the distance too swiftly for them to loose a third volley. There was shouting among Haomane's Allies as they scrambled to part ranks and allow the Arduans to fall back.

Too late. They had not anticipated so swift an attack. The wedge of Gulnagel split, wheeling along both sides of the Arduan line. They struck hard and fast, lashing out with mace and axe at the unprotected archers. Flesh and bone crunched, bows splintered. As quickly as they struck, they turned, racing back toward the formation.

A lone archer stood, loosing arrow after arrow at the retreating Fjel. The sound of Oronin's Bow rang out like a baying hound; one of the Gulnagel fell, pierced from behind. Tanaros gritted his teeth. "Left flank, on your call! Right flank, ward! Center, advance and strike!"

The horns of the Ellylon answered with silvery defiance.

Haomane's Allies had begun to regroup by the time Darkhaven's forces fell upon them; the advance of the Tungskulder and the Nåltannen was plodding, not swift. But it was steady and inevitable, and it was led by Tanaros Blacksword, who wore the Helm of Shadows.

This was not the battle he would have chosen; but it was his, here and now. Tanaros felt lighthearted and invulnerable. *I will not pray for your death on the morrow.* At twenty paces, he could see the faces of the enemy; Ellylon faces, proud and stern, limned with a doomed brightness in the Helm's vision.

Her kin; his enemy. Not the one he wanted most to kill, no. The time of the Rivenlost was ending; so the Helm whispered to him. But beyond them were the Borderguard of Curonan in their dun-colored cloaks. *He* was in their midst; Roscus' descendant, proud Aracus.

Malthus, with the Spear of Light.

At twenty paces, Tanaros gave a wordless shout and charged.

The Rivenlost gave way as he plunged into their ranks. They beheld the Helm of Shadows, and there was horror in their expressions. He broke through their line, dimly aware of them reforming behind him to meet the onslaught of the Fjel, that his charge had carried him into the thick of Haomane's Allies.

White light blazed, obliterating his Helm-shadowed vision. Tanaros turned his mount in a tight circle, striking outward with his black sword, driving down unseen weapons. He clung grimly to the pain of his phantom wound, to the pain that filled the Helm; the hatred and anguish, futile defiance, the bitter pain of betrayal. The scorching torment of Haomane's Wrath, the impotent fury, the malice fed by generation upon generation of hatred. He fed it with his own age-old rage until he heard the cries of mortal fear around him and felt Malthus' will crumble.

Darkness slowly swallowed the light until he could see.

The battle had swirled past him, cutting him off from his forces. A ring of Pelmaran infantrymen surrounded him, holding him warily at bay. Malthus the Counselor had ceded the battle in favor of the war; there, a bright spark of white-gold light drove into the ranks of Fjel.

Somewhere, Hyrgolf was roaring orders. The right flank of Fjel was swinging around to engage Haomane's Allies. Ignoring the Pelmarans, Tanaros stood in his stirrups to gaze across the field.

"Ah, no!" he whispered.

VORAX OF STACCIA PATTED HIS armor-clad belly. When all was said and done, there was nothing like the excitement of a battle to work up a man's appetite. He was glad he could rest content in the knowledge that the army was well-supplied. If nightfall came with neither side victorious, they'd all be glad of it.

At the moment, it bid fair to do just that. He watched Tanaros' charge carry him into the midst of enemy ranks and shook his head. Better if his Lordship had given the Helm of Shadows to the Dreamspinner.

The battlefield was getting muddled. In the center, Rivenlost and Borderguard were fighting side by side, pressing Marshal Hyrgolf's line in a concerted effort. The right flank was a mess, with two companies of Nåltannen Fjel wreaking havoc among hapless Midlanders.

And in front of him, the damned Vedasian knights were holding their ground. They were arrayed in a square, smirking behind their damned bucket-size helmets as though their armor made them invincible. On your call, Tanaros had ordered. Vorax sighed. If he waited any longer, he'd be faint with hunger.

"All right, lads!" he called in Staccian. "On my order. Nothing fancy; fan out, circle 'em, strike fast and regroup. Speed's our ally. Once they break formation, we'll pick off the bucket-heads one at a time." Raising his sword, he pointed at the Vedasians. "Let's go!"

Vorax set his heels to his horse's flanks. A Staccian battle-paean came to his lips as he led the charge. Five hundred voices picked it up, hurling words in challenge. Vorax felt a grin split his face. If Haomane's Allies thought their wizard had pulled Staccia's teeth, they were about to find they were sore mistaken.

Behind him, his lads were fanning out; each one astride a horse swifter, more foul-tempered, more glorious than the next. Vorax picked himself a likely target, a tall Vedasian knight with the device of an apple-tree on his surcoat.

Even as he was thinking it was considerate of the Vedasians to provide such an immobile target, the front line of their square folded inward to reveal a second company concealed within their ranks.

The Dwarfs, Yrinna's Children.

They ran forward to meet Vorax's Staccians, long spears clutched in their sturdy hands. Not spears, no; scythes, pruning hooks.

Some of the Staccians swerved unthinking. Others attempted to plow onward. Neither tactic worked. Everywhere, it seemed, there were Dwarfs; small and stalwart, too low to be easy targets, dodging the churning legs of the horses of Darkhaven and swinging their homespun weapons to terrible effect.

Horses foundered and went down, squealing in awful agony. Men who could stand struggled to gain their feet and combat the unforeseen menace. Others moved weakly, unable to rise. The Vedasian knights began to move toward the field, ponderous and inexorable.

In the midst of the impossible carnage, Vorax roared with fury, leaning sideways in the saddle, trying to strike low, low enough to reach his nearest assailant. He could see the Dwarf's face, grim and resolute, silent tears gleaming on the furrowed cheeks. Yrinna's Child, aware of the awful price of breaking her Peace in such a manner.

Too far, out of reach.

And then he was falling; overbalanced, he thought. Too fat, too damned fat. But, no, it was his mount collapsing beneath him. Hamstrung, one knee half-severed.

They went down hard, the impact driving the breath from Vorax's body. He was trapped beneath the horse's flailing weight, unable to feel his legs. On the field, the Dwarfs were laying down their arms, bowing their heads. Here and there, overwhelmed Staccians fought in knots. A handful of Vedasian knights were dismounting to dispatch the wounded.

Vorax felt his helmet removed. He squinted upward at the faceless figure above him. It was brightness, all brightness; sunlight shining mirror-bright on steel armor. The figure moved its arms. He felt the point of a sword at his throat and tried to speak, but there was no air in his lungs.

No more bargains.

No more meals.

The sword's point thrust home.

No more.

ON THE PLAINS OF CURONAN, Ushahin-who-walks-between-dusk-and-dawn was present and not present.

His Lordship's will had placed him here for the sin of his defiance;

his Lordship's will had placed a blade in Ushahin's right arm. And so he rode onto the battlefield for the first time in his long immortal life and beheld the pathways between living and dying, casting his thoughts adrift and traveling them.

Present and not present

A squadron of Tungskulder Fjel formed a cordon around him. Twice, Rivenlost warriors broke through their line. Ushahin smiled and swung a sword that was present and not present, cutting the threads that bound their lives to the ageless bodies. What a fine magic it was! He watched them ride dazed away to meet their deaths at Fjel hands. One day, Oronin's Horn would sound for him, as it had sounded long ago when he lay bleeding in the forests of Pelmar. Today he whispered what the Grey Dam had whispered to him, *Not yet.*

There were things to be learned, it seemed, upon the battlefield.

And then death came for Vorax of Staccia, Vorax the Glutton, and the shock of it drove Ushahin into the confines of his own crippled body. One of the Three was no more.

The horns of the Rivenlost sounded a triumphant note.

Over the Vale of Gorgantum, an anguished peal of thunder broke.

TANAROS FLUNG BACK HIS HEAD and shouted, "Vorax!"

There were no words to describe his fury. It was his, all his, and it made what had gone before seem as nothing. There was no need to hold it, to feed it. It was a perfect thing, as perfect in its way as beauty and love. It filled him until he felt weightless in the saddle. The Helm of Shadows, his armor, the black sword; weightless. Even his mount seemed to float over the field of battle as he broke past the Pelmarans and plunged into the ranks of Haomane's Allies.

His arm swung tirelessly, a weightless limb wielding a blade as light as a feather. Left and right, Tanaros laid about him.

Wounded and terrified, they fell back, clearing a circle around him. What sort of enemy was it that would not engage? He wanted Aracus Altorus, wanted Malthus the Counselor. But, no, Haomane's Allies retreated, melting away from his onslaught.

"General! *General!*"

Hyrgolf's voice penetrated his rage. Tanaros leaned on the pommel of his saddle, breathing hard, gazing at his field marshal's familiar face, the small eyes beneath the heavy brow, steady and unafraid. He had regained his army.

Across the plains, combatants struggled, continuing to fight and die, but here in the center of the field a pocket of silence surrounded him. The battle had come to a standstill. Hyrgolf pointed past him without a word, and Tanaros turned his mount slowly.

They were there, arrayed against him, a combined force of Rivenlost and Borderguard at their backs. Ingolin, shining in the bright armor of the Rivenlost. Aracus Altorus, bearing his ancestor's sword with the lifeless Soumanië in the pommel. Malthus the Counselor, grave of face. Among them, only Malthus was able to look upon the Helm of Shadows without flinching away. The Spear of Light was in his grasp, lowered and level, its point aimed at Tanaros' heart.

"Brave Malthus," Tanaros said. "Do you seek to run me through from behind?"

The Counselor's voice was somber. "We are not without honor, Tanaros Kingslayer. Even here, even now."

Tanaros laughed. "So you say, wizard. And yet much praise was given to Elendor, son of Elterrion, who crept behind Lord Satoris to strike a blow against him on these very plains, ages past. Do you deny it?"

Malthus sat unmoving in the saddle. "Does Satoris Banewreaker thus accuse? Then let him take the field and acquit himself. I see no Shaper present."

"Nor do I," Tanaros said softly. "Nor do I. And yet I know where my master is, and why. Can you say the same, Wise Counselor?"

"You seek to delay, Kingslayer!" Aracus Altorus' voice rang out, taut with frustration. "You know why we are here. Fight or surrender."

Tanaros gazed at him through the eyes of the Helm of Shadows, seeing a figure haloed in flickering fire; a fierce spirit, bold and exultant. Still, his face was averted. "I am here, Son of Altorus." He opened his arms. "Will you stand against me? Will you, Ingolin of Meronil? No?" His gaze shifted to Malthus. "What of you, Counselor? Will you not match Haomane's Spear against my sword?"

"I will do it."

The voice came from behind them. Blaise Caveros rode forward, unbuckling his helm. He removed it to reveal his face, pale and resolute. With difficulty, he fixed his gaze upon the eyeholes of the Helm of Shadows and held it there. Beads of sweat shone on his brow. "On one condition. I have removed my helm, kinsman," he said thickly. "Will you not do the same?"

Malthus the Counselor lifted his head as though listening for a strain of distant music. The tip of the Spear of Light rose, wreathed in white-gold fire, and the Soumanië on his breast sparkled.

Aracus Altorus drew a sharp breath. "Blaise, stand down! If this battle belongs to anyone, it is me."

"No." Blaise looked steadily at Tanaros. "What comes afterward is your battle, Aracus. I cannot wed the Lady Cerelinde. I cannot forge a kingdom out of chaos. But I can fight this . . . creature."

Tanaros smiled bitterly. "Do you name me thus, kinsman?"

"I do." Blaise matched his smile. "I have spent my life in the shadow of your infamy, Kingslayer. If you give me this chance . . . an *honorable* chance . . . to purge the world of its blight, I will take it."

Tanaros pointed toward Malthus with his blade. "Do you speak of honor, kinsman? Let the Counselor relinquish yon Spear."

"Tanaros," a voice murmured. He turned his head to see Ushahin Dreamspinner, his mismatched eyes feverish and bright. "There is madness in this offer."

"Madness, aye," Tanaros said quietly. "Madness to risk the Helm; madness, too, for Malthus to surrender a weapon of Haomane's Shaping while Ushahin-who-walks-between-dusk-and-dawn is afoot."

The half-breed shivered. "I do not know. Vorax's death—"

"—cries for vengeance. Let us provide it for him." Tanaros reached up to unbuckle the Helm of Shadows. Even through his gauntlets, its touch made his hands ache. Behind him, the Tungskulder Fjel murmured deep in their throats. "What say you, Counselor?"

Malthus' hand tightened on the Spear of Light. With a sudden move, he drove it downward into the earth. "Remove the Helm and lay it upon the ground, Kingslayer," he said in his calm, deep voice. "And I will release the haft and honor this bargain, if it be your will to make it."

A bargain was a fitting way to honor the death of Vorax of Staccia. Tanaros glanced around. Word had spread, and stillness in its wake. Across the plains, weary combatants paused, waiting. Some of Haomane's Allies were using the respite to haul the wounded from the field; behind their lines, figures hurried to meet them. The sturdy

Dwarfs aided, carrying wounded Men twice their size. The dead lay motionless, bleeding into the long grass. There were many of them on the left flank, clad in Staccian armor.

There were no wounded Fjel to be tended. Wounded Fjel fought until there was no more life in them. There were only the living and the dead.

"Marshal Hyrgolf." Tanaros beckoned. "Order the Nåltannen to regroup, and move the second squadron of Gulnagel in position to harry the Vedasians. Tell them to hold on your orders. Give none until provoked."

"Aye, Lord General, sir!" Hyrgolf saluted.

Tanaros smiled at him. "Once I remove this Helm, I want your Tungskulder lads to guard it as though their lives depended on it. Does any one of Haomane's Allies stir in its direction, strike them down without hesitation or mercy. Is that understood?"

Hyrgolf revealed his eyetusks in a broad grin. "Aye, Lord General, sir!"

"Good." Tanaros offered a mocking bow to Blaise Caveros. "Shall we meet as Men, face-to-face and on our feet? Men did so once upon the training-fields of Altoria, before I razed it to the ground."

Color rose to the Borderguardsman's cheeks; with an oath, he dismounted and flung his head back. "Come, then, and meet me!"

Tanaros sheathed his sword and dismounted. Six Tungskulder stepped forward promptly to surround him. With careful hands, he lifted the Helm of Shadows from his head. He blinked against the sudden brightness, the disappearance of the phantom pain in his groin, the ache in his palms. Astride his foam-white horse, the Wise Counselor watched him, still gripping the planted shaft of the Spear of Light.

"What did you do to my horse, Malthus?" Tanaros called to him.

"All things are capable of change," Malthus answered. "Even you, Kingslayer."

"As are you, Counselor; for we are Lesser Shapers, are we not? Change is a choice we may make." Stooping, Tanaros laid the Helm on the trampled grass. "And yet I do not think you gave such a choice to my horse."

There was a moment of fear as he straightened; if Haomane's Allies were to betray their bargain, it would be now. But, no; Malthus had kept his word and released the Spear of Light. There it stood, gleaming, untouched by any hand, upright and quivering in a semicircle of Hao-mane's Allies. The eyeholes of the Helm of Shadows gazed upward from the ground, dark with pain and horror. Beyond the Tungskulder, Ushahin nodded briefly at him, his twisted face filled with sick resolve.

"So." Tanaros stepped away. A cold breeze stirred his damp hair, making him feel light-headed and free. His world was narrowing to this moment, this hard-trodden circle of ground. This opponent, this younger self, glimpsed through the mirror of ages. He gave the old, old salute, the one he had given so often to Roscus; a fist to the heart, an open hand extended. *Brother, let us spar. I trust my life unto your hands.* "Shall we begin?"

Blaise Caveros drew his sword without returning the salute. "Do you suggest this is a mere exercise?" he asked grimly.

"No." Tanaros regarded his gauntleted hand, closing it slowly into a fist. He glanced up to meet the eyes of Aracus Altorus; fierce and de-manding, unhappy at being relegated to an onlooker's role. Not Roscus, but someone else altogether. "No," he said, "I suppose not."

"Then ward yourself well," Blaise said, and attacked.

NINETEEN

DARKHAVEN'S KITCHENS WERE FILLED WITH a fearsome clatter.

That was where Dani and Thulu found themselves herded once the long work of loading half-smoked sides of mutton onto the endless supply-wagons was done. It had been a long nightmare, filled with blood and smoke, the both of them staggering with laden arms along the stony trails. It seemed impossible that no one should notice them, but amid the horde of toiling madlings, they might as well have been invisible. Back and forth, back and forth, until the work was done and the army departed for the plains below.

And when it was, they were herded into the kitchens under the careless eye of a pair of Fjeltroll guards, who had larger matters on their minds. Darkhaven was buzzing like a hornets' nest; no one paid heed to a pair of filth-blackened Yarru huddled in a corner. The kitchens swarmed with such figures, swarthy with smoke and pitch and dried blood from the long night's labors.

Madlings.

Dani heard the word without understanding. In the kitchens, he understood. The inhabitants—the *human* inhabitants—of Darkhaven were mad. They had no way to cope with what transpired. It was clear to him, and to Thulu, that the bulk of Darkhaven's forces had abandoned the premises. Still, the madlings must cook; must prepare, must tend and be useful.

Pots boiled on stoves. Dishes roasted in ovens. It did not matter that there was no one to eat them. There was a kind of fearful safety amidst the mayhem, but it was not one that could last.

"Where to, lad?" Uncle Thulu whispered.

Dani, who had sunk his head onto pillowed arms, raised it with an effort. "I don't know," he said dully. "I would ask . . . I would ask . . ." He shook his head. "I'm tired."

Thulu regarded him. "Would you ask, lad, or *do*?"

"I don't know." Dani raked his hands through his lank black hair. "Before . . . ah, Uncle! I wanted to *ask*. What has the Sunderer done to the Yarru that I should seek to destroy him? And yet . . ." He was still, remembering. *Perhaps your people would not have been slain for your actions.* "I fear perhaps we have passed such a point, and Malthus the Counselor had the right of it all along."

"Hey!" A figure shouted at them, glowering, brandishing a ladle in one hand. "What idleness is this? Does it serve his Lordship?" A platter was thrust forward, a silver salver with a dish-dome upon it. "Here," the figure said roughly. "Take it to her Ladyship. She's been near forgotten in the uproar. Few enough folk want to take the risk of waiting on her now, but you'll do in a pinch."

Dani rose to his feet and took it unthinking, hunching his shoulders and ducking his head; Uncle Thulu was a step behind him.

"Well?" The cook's figure loomed. "What are you waiting for? Go!"

They went.

Darkhaven's halls made its kitchens seem a haven of comfort. They were massive and windowless, wrought entirely of gleaming black stone. No gentle lamplight alleviated the darkness; only veins of blue-white fire glittering in the walls. Cradling the tray against his hip, Dani laid one hand upon one wall and found it warm.

"Marrow-fire," he murmured. "It must be."

"Aye, but where's the Source?"

"I don't know." Dani shook his head. *"Below,* Malthus said. Somewhere in the depths of the earth, below Darkhaven's foundation."

"I've seen no stair." Thulu sighed. "We'll have to search, Dani. Best we find a place to hide that tray and ourselves before our luck runs out."

"The tray." Dani glanced at it. "For her Ladyship, he said. Do you suppose . . ."

"The Lady Cerelinde?" Uncle Thulu whistled softly.

"She would know what to do," Dani said, for it seemed to him it

must be true. The Haomane-gaali Peldras had been wise; not as wise
as Malthus, but wise and gentle, filled with the knowledge of his long
years. Surely the Lady of the Ellylon must be no less! The thought of
laying the burden of decision on the shoulders of someone wiser than
he filled him with relief. "All we have to do is find her."

The task proved easier than they reckoned. After a few more turns,
they rounded a corner to see a quartet of Fjeltroll posted outside a
door halfway down the hall. They were hulking Fjel with black, bristling hides and gleaming black armor. A madling was speaking to
them; a woman.

Dani stopped with a mind to retreat. It was terrifying enough to
have passed to and fro under the noses of the Fjeltroll amid a reeking
crowd. This was too dangerous.

And too late.

The woman caught sight of them and raised her voice. "Time and
more you came! Would you have her Ladyship starve?" She beckoned,
impatient, as they stood frozen and staring. "Well, come on!"

Dani and his uncle exchanged a glance, then proceeded slowly.

For a moment, a brief moment, he thought they would get away
with it. The madling woman snatched the tray from his hands, giving
it to the Fjeltroll to inspect. One lifted the domed cover, and another
leaned down to smell the dish. Dani began to back away unobtru-
sively, Thulu behind him.

"Wait." One of the Fjel guards spoke. They froze where they stood.
It sniffed the air, broad nostrils widening. "These two are new," it said
in its low, guttural voice. "What did the General say to do?"

Dani wished they had run, then; had run, had hidden, had never
tried to find the Lady Cerelinde. The madling came toward them. Her
eyes glittered with an unholy glee as she drew near, near enough that
he could smell her, rank and unwashed.

"Who are you?" she asked. "Has General Tanaros been looking
for *you?*"

Neither of the Yarru answered.

Slow and deliberate, the madling held up one hand and licked her
forefinger, then swiped it down the side of Dani's face. He held himself still and rigid, staring at her. A layer of soot and river mud came
away, revealing the nut-brown skin beneath it.

"If I were you," the madling said almost kindly, "I would run."

They took her advice, pelting down the hall. Behind them came the clamor of a laden tray falling, and the deep roar of Fjel pursuit.

MEARA WATCHED THE CHARRED FOLK run. The sight made her laugh as few things did in these dire times. Lord Ushahin Dreamspinner would be proud if he were here; even *Tanaros* himself would be proud. She took a moment to imagine it—his hands on her shoulders, his dark eyes filled with fondness, a rare smile on his lips as he said, "Meara, today your deeds fill me with pride."

Of course, the Fjel had to catch them first. The thought caused her laughter to falter and vanish, replaced by a frown. She shouldn't have told them to run. She hadn't thought they really would. The Mørkhar Fjel of the Havenguard were tireless, but not swift, not like the Gulnagel.

But then, if the Charred Folk hid, the madlings could find them. Meara brightened at the thought. There was nowhere in Darkhaven anyone could hide that the madlings could not find them. Her smile was quite restored by the time the Lady opened the door.

Suddenly, Meara did not feel proud anymore.

The Lady Cerelinde looked at the silver dishes, the remains of her meal spattered over the gleaming marble floor of the hall. "Meara, what has happened here?" she asked in her gentle voice.

"Danger, Lady." She ducked her head and mumbled. "Strange Men. The Fjel will find them."

"What Men?" The Lady's voice rose when Meara remained silent. It was not harsh, no, it could never be harsh, but it held an edge as keen and bright as a sword. "Meara, what Men?"

"Charred Folk," Meara whispered, lifting her head.

The Lady Cerelinde took a sharp breath, and something in her face changed. A connection was made, a piece of the puzzle falling into place at last. It was nothing Meara understood, and yet she bore witness to it. "The Unknown Desert!" The Lady's slender fingers closed on Meara's arm, unexpectedly strong. "Come inside."

Meara followed, helpless and obedient. Behind closed doors, the Lady laid her hands on Meara's shoulders. It was just as she had imagined, only it was wrong, all wrong. No General Tanaros, no warm glow of pride. Only the Lady Cerelinde, her face filled with bright urgency. The world seemed to tilt and sway as she spoke. "Tell me about these Men. Did they come bearing anything that you might have noted? Waterskins? Vessels?"

Meara gaped at her. "No, Lady! They were . . . Men, dirty Men!"

The Lady's face changed again as hope went out of it, and it was as though someone had blown out all the lamps in the room. "Thank you, Meara," she said, releasing her.

"I'll go see about your dinner, Lady," Meara said humbly. Everything was normal and the world was no longer tilting; and yet it seemed as though something precious had been lost. A memory came unbidden and she offered it up. "The younger one did have a flask, Lady. A little one made of clay, tied on a thong around his neck."

There was a long pause, a not-daring-to-hope pause. "You're certain of this, Meara?"

She nodded, miserable. She should not have spoken.

The world spun crazily as hope returned in a blaze; brightness, brightness in the room, brightness in the Lady Cerelinde's face. The Lady was speaking, more words that rang like swords, bright and terrible, and Meara longed for the black pit to open, for the tide of gibberish to rise in her head, silencing words she did not want to hear. Anything, anything to drown out the awful charge. But no black pit opened, no tide arose. The voices were silent, driven into abeyance by the Lady's fierce glory.

". . . must find them, Meara, seek them out and find them, hide them from the Sunderer's minions! Give them what aid you may, for unless I am sore mistaken, the fate of the world rests upon their shoulders." She stooped to gaze into Meara's face. "Do you understand?"

Meara freed her tongue from the roof of her mouth to answer. "No," she whispered.

"I speak of healing the world," the Lady Cerelinde said gravely. She touched Meara, cupping her head in her fair, white hands. "All the world, Meara; Urulat and all that lies within it. Even you. All that might have been may yet be."

Fire, cool fire. Why did Haomane have to Shape such majesty into his Children? Why must it be given to us to know, to compare? No wonder Tanaros ached for her; and he did, he did. Meara knew he did. *I told him you would break our hearts.* She felt tears well in her eyes, her nose running. Ugly, unglamorous; a filthy madling, no more. She longed to wipe it, longed to break away from the horrible burden of trust in the Lady's glorious eyes.

"I can't!" she gasped. "I can't!"

"You can." Still stooping, the Lady Cerelinde touched her lips to Meara's damp brow. An oath, a promise, a lance of cool fire piercing her fevered brain. "Haomane's Prophecy is at work here. And there is goodness in you, Meara of Darkhaven. In that, I believe."

She staggered when the Lady loosed her; staggered and caught herself, staring dumbfounded as the Lady went to the tapestry that concealed the hidden passage, drawing back its bolts. So she had done once before, saving Meara from certain discovery. A debt had been incurred, returning threefold. She had not wanted it, had not wanted any of it. And yet, still it was.

Cerelinde, Lady of the Ellylon, stood upright and tall, shining like a candle in the confines of Darkhaven. She breathed a single word; but all the pride, all the hope, all the terrible, yearning beauty of the Rivenlost lay behind it.

"Please."

Stumbling and numb, wiping her nose, Meara went.

TWENTY

BEHIND THE LINES OF HAOMANE'S Allies, no one was paying attention to the abandoned piece of baggage that was Speros of Haimhault.

On the battlefield, a strange hiatus had occurred; the armies had fallen back, regrouping, their attention centered on a knot of disturbance at its core. What it was, Speros could not have said. He knew only that he was forgotten. There were wounded incoming; scores of them, hundreds. Men, Men like him, and women, too, injured and groaning, carried on makeshift stretchers wrought out of spears, carried over the shoulders of hale comrades. Arduan's archers, limbs pulped by Fjel maces; Midlanders with crushed skulls, splintered ribs protruding from their pale flesh.

Such was war.

The sight made him sick and uneasy; and yet, and yet. War was war. Where did the true battlefield lie?

The smell of strawberries ripening in the sun . . .

He had promised the Lord General that he would not fail him again, and he believed he had kept his word. He had built the waterwheel, improved the furnaces, created the carefully balanced defenses above the Defile. General Tanaros had not asked him to do any of those things, but he had done them anyway and done them well. Still, he had failed anyway. Some enchantment had been at work that day in the tunnels. The Fjel had been right the first time around; the Bearer had been there.

He might still be there; or worse, seeking entry into Darkhaven.

Speros paced restlessly behind the lines, glancing over at Ghost.

No one was paying her any heed, either. She met his gaze, her wicked eyes calm and bright. The picket stakes that held her were pounded loosely into the plains. A thought took shape in his mind. He drifted closer to her, waiting for one of his minders to shout at him, to order him back.

No one did.

There was no further need for him to serve as a hostage. Haomane's Allies had kept their word and withdrawn; the battle was engaged, his usefulness was ended. There would be no repercussions for Darkhaven if he failed in the attempt. The Ellyl Peldras was wrong; the General *would* come for him. Still, how much more impressed would he be if Speros proved himself in no need of rescue? And moreover, with a valuable warning to give.

I will not fail you again.

Speros took a deep breath. It would need to be done swiftly, but that was all right. He had stolen horses before. This wouldn't be much different, except that Ghost was *his* horse. He wished he had a dagger to cut the picket lines, but Haomane's Allies had taken his weapons. That was all right, too. Ghost was not an ordinary horse. She wouldn't panic.

It was a piece of luck that they had not bothered to remove her bridle; too fearful of her snapping teeth. Speros sidled close, watching her eye roll around at him. "Be sweet, my beauty," he murmured, low and crooning. "For once in your life, as you love his Lordship, be gentle."

Her ears pricked forward. With two quick yanks, Speros dragged the picket stakes from the earth. Ghost had already begun to move when he grasped her mane and hauled himself astride.

They were ten strides away from the encampment before an alarm was shouted. Speros laughed and flattened himself against Ghost's grey hide, feeling her muscles surge beneath him as she accelerated. Her neck stretched out long and low, coarse mane whipping his face. They were all shouting now, Haomane's Allies, shouting and pointing. Too late. Ghost's hooves pounded the tall grass, haunches churning, forelegs reaching, heedless of the dangling picket lines bouncing in her wake.

The plains rolled by beneath him. Speros' eyes watered. He blinked away the wind-stung tears and saw the rearguard of Haomane's Allies turning their attention toward him. A lone Ellyl horn wailed a plangent alarm. He sent Ghost veering wide around them, around their attendants still carting the wounded from the field. No hero's charge, this; no fool, he. He only wanted to warn General Tanaros. If he could get behind Darkhaven's lines, he could send word. *Something is wrong, very wrong. Let me investigate. I will not fail you again.*

Or better yet, he would return directly to Darkhaven. There was no need to ask the General's permission. It would be better if he went himself in all swiftness. After all, if the Bearer had managed to penetrate Darkhaven's walls, there was only one place he would go—to the very Source of the marrow-fire itself. General Tanaros admired his initiative, he had told him so. He would still send word, so the General would know.

What a wondrous thing it would be if Speros of Haimhault were to avert Haomane's Prophecy!

The thought made Speros smile. He was still smiling when one of Haomane's Allies, kneeling beside a wounded Arduan archer, rose to her feet and unslung her bow, nocking an arrow. Speros' smile broadened to a grin. He reckoned he was too far away and moving too fast to be within range.

Of a surety, he was too far away to see that the archer was Fianna and the bow in her hands was wrought of black horn, gleaming like onyx. It was no mortal weapon, and its range could not be gauged by mortal standards.

Oronin's Bow rang out across the plains; once, twice, three times.

Speros did not feel the arrows' impact, did not feel the reins slip from his nerveless fingers. The earth struck him hard, but he didn't feel that, either. He blinked at the sky overhead, filled with circling ravens. He wondered if Fetch, who had saved them in the desert, was among them. He tried to rise and found his body failed to obey him. At last, he understood, and a great sorrow filled him.

"Tell him I tried," he whispered to the distant ravens, then closed his eyes. He did not reopen them, nor ever would.

Whickering in dismay, a grey horse raced riderless across the plains.

THE FIGHT FILLED TANAROS WITH a stark, pitiless joy.

There was a purity in it, one that no one who was not born and raised to the battlefield could understand. Two men pitted against one another; weapon to weapon, skill against skill. The world, with all its burdens and paradoxes, was narrowed to this circle of trampled grass, this single opponent.

He would win, of course. The outcome was not in question, had never been in question. Haomane's Allies were fools. They were so blinded by the terror the Helm of Shadows invoked that they had overlooked the other weapon he bore: the black sword, tempered in the marrow-fire and quenched in his Lordship's blood. It could shear through metal as easily as flesh, and it would do so when Tanaros chose.

Blaise Caveros was good, though. Better than his liege-lord, yes; better than Roscus had been, too. It was in his blood. He circled carefully, trying to get the sun in Tanaros' eyes; it worked, too, until a flock of ravens careened overhead, blotting out the sun like a vast black cloud. He kept his shield high, prepared to ward off blows at his unprotected head. He stalked Tanaros with patience, striking with deft precision. Tanaros was hard-pressed to strike and parry without using the edge of his blade and make a believable job of it.

The fight could not end too soon. If Ushahin had any chance of claiming the Spear of Light, it would have to last awhile. From the corner of his eye, Tanaros could see that the Dreamspinner was not where he had been; where he was, he could not say. Only that it was necessary to delay.

It helped that his skills were rusty. Tanaros had a thousand years of practice behind him, but it had been centuries since he had engaged in single combat in the old Altorian fashion. Only a single sparring match with Speros, shortly after the Midlander's arrival. He hoped the lad was well. It was a foul trick Vorax had played him, though Tanaros could not find it in his heart to fault the Staccian. Not now, while his grief was raw. After all, there had been merit in the bargain, and Haomane's Allies would not harm the lad. Their sense of honor would not permit it. Other things, oh, yes! They saw the world as they wished to believe it and thereby justified all manner of ill deeds. But they would not kill a hostage out of hand.

There was a dour irony in it, Tanaros thought, studying his opponent. There was nothing but hatred and determination in Blaise Caveros' face; and yet they looked alike, alike enough to be near kin.

His son, if his son had been his, might have resembled this Man who sought his life. Quiet and determined, dark and capable.

But, no, his *son*, his wife's child, had been born with red-gold hair and the stamp of the House of Altorus on his face. Speros of Haimhault, with his irrepressible gap-toothed grin and his stubborn desire to make Tanaros proud, was more a son than that babe had ever been to him.

Blaise feinted right, and Tanaros, distracted, was almost fooled. He stepped backward quickly, catching a glancing blow to the ribs. Even through his armor and the layers of padding beneath it, the impact made him grimace. Behind him, the Fjel rumbled.

"You grow slow, Kingslayer," Blaise said. "Does the Sunderer's power begin to fail you?"

Tanaros retreated another pace, regaining his breath and his concentration. Beneath the armor, his branded heart continued to beat, steady and remorseless, bound to Godslayer's pulse. "Were you speaking to me?" he asked. "Forgive me, I was thinking of other matters."

The Borderguardsman's dark, familiar eyes narrowed; still, he was too patient to be baited. He pressed his attack cautiously. Tanaros retreated before it, parrying with sword and buckler, trying to catch a glimpse of the Spear of Light. Was there a rippling disturbance in the air around it? Yes, he thought, perhaps.

Somewhere, toward the rear of Haomane's Allies, there was shouting. Their ranks shifted; a single Ellyl horn sounded. The sound made him frown and parry too hastily. Blaise Caveros swore as his blade was notched, an awful suspicion beginning to dawn on his face.

Overhead, the ravens of Darkhaven wheeled and veered.

Three times over, Oronin's Bow sang its single note of death and anguish.

For a fractured instant, Tanaros' sight left him, taking wing. In an urgent burst, Fetch's vision overwhelmed his thoughts. Tanaros saw the plains from on high; saw the tall grass rippling in endless waves, the small figures below. Saw the lone horse, grey as smoke, her brown-haired rider toppling, pierced by three feathered shafts. Saw his lips move, his eyes close, a final stillness settle.

First Vorax, now Speros.

"Damn you!" Blinded by grief and visions, Tanaros lowered his guard. The injustice of the Midlander's death filled him with fury. *"He wasn't even armed!"*

Haomane's Allies—Haomane's Three—were looking to the south, seeking to determine what had transpired. Unwatched, unguarded, Blaise Caveros moved like a flash, dropping his sword and snatching the Spear of Light from the earth with one gauntleted hand. With a faint cry, Ushahin Dreamspinner emerged from nothingness; on his knees, his face twisted with pain, his crippled left hand clutched to his chest. He had been reaching for the Spear with it.

Too late, too slow.

Tanaros flung up his buckler, heard Hyrgolf roar, saw the Fjel surge forward. On the frozen ground, the Helm of Shadows stared with empty eyeholes. Blaise Caveros never hesitated. Hoisting the Spear like a javelin, he hurled it not at Tanaros, but at the empty Helm, hard and sure.

Light pierced Darkness.

The world exploded. Tanaros found himself on his hands and knees, deafened. He shook his head, willing his vision to clear.

It did, showing him the Helm of Shadows, cracked clean asunder, its dark enchantment broken. As for the Spear of Light, it was gone, vanished and consumed in the conflagration.

Tanaros climbed to his feet, still clutching his sword-hilt. "For that, you die," he whispered thickly, "kinsman." He nodded at the ground. "Pick up your sword."

Blaise obeyed.

There was a peaceful clarity in the Borderguardsman's dark eyes as he took up a defensive pose. He held it as Tanaros struck; a long, level blow, swinging from the hips and shoulders, the black sword shearing through metal and flesh. Cleaving his blade, slicing through his armor. Blaise sank to his knees, holding his shattered weapon. His face was tranquil, almost glad. Blood, bright blood, poured over his corselet.

He was smiling as he folded and quietly died.

Word was spreading; through the ranks of Haomane's Allies, through the Army of Darkhaven. Holding his dripping sword before him, Tanaros backed away. He stood guard over Ushahin Dreamspinner, who rose to retrieve the two halves of the broken Helm. Aracus Altorus stared at him as though made of stone, tears running down his expressionless face. Malthus the Counselor had bowed his head.

Word spread.

In its wake came wild cheers and cries of grief.

"Go," Tanaros said harshly, shoving Ushahin. "Take what remains of the Helm back to Darkhaven, Dreamspinner! You will do more good there than here." He found his mount without looking, mounted without thinking. He reached out his hand, and someone placed a helm in it. A mortal helm, made of mere steel. He clapped it on his head, his vision narrowed but unchanged.

Four Borderguardsmen had dismounted. One removed his dun-colored cloak, draping it over the body of Blaise Caveros. Together, they lifted him with care and began walking from the field. Tanaros let them go unmolested.

Aracus Altorus pointed at Tanaros with his sword. "You seal your own fate, Kingslayer. Haomane help me, I will kill you myself, enchanted blade or no."

Tanaros gave his bitter smile. "You may try, Scion of Altorus. I will be coming for you next."

Malthus the Counselor lifted his head, and the sorrow in his eyes was deep, deep as the Well of the World. But from a scabbard at his side, he drew forth a bright sword of Ellylon craftsmanship. The clear Soumanië on his breast blazed and all the horns of the Rivenlost rang forth in answer at once. Against the silvery blare of triumph a lone horn sounded a grieving descant, the tones intermingling with a terrible beauty.

From Darkhaven, silence.

When the Helm of Shadows is broken . . .

Tanaros exchanged a glance with Hyrgolf, saw the same knowledge reflected in his field marshal's gaze. He thought of the crudely carved *rhios* in Hyrgolf's den. *Not bad for a mere pup, eh, General?*

Hyrgolf smiled ruefully, extending one hand. "For his Lordship's honor, Lord General?"

Tanaros clasped his hand. "For his Lordship's honor."

On his order, the army of Darkhaven charged.

MERONIL WAS FILLED WITH THE sound of distant horns.

Lilias of Beshtanag stood before the tall windows in her tower chamber, opening them wide onto the open air to catch the strains of sound. Throughout the day, it seemed they blew without cease.

The clarion call of challenge she heard many times over; and the undaunted call of defiance. Once, there was a peal of victory, brief and vaunting; but defiance and a rallying alarum followed, and she knew the battle was not ended.

This was different.

Triumph; a great triumph, resonant with joy, and a single note of sorrow threaded through it. Haomane's Allies had won a great victory, and suffered a dire loss.

Lilias rested her brow on the window-jamb, wondering who had died.

She had been a sorceress, once; the Sorceress of the East. It was the Soumanië that had lent her power, but the art of using it she had mastered on her own merit, guided by Calandor's long, patient teaching.

It could not be Aracus Altorus who had fallen. Surely, she would sense it through the faint echo of the bond that remained, binding her to the Soumanië he bore. What victory had Haomane's Allies won, and at what cost?

A longing to *know* suffused her. Lilias clenched her fists, lifting her head to stare out the window. Below her the Aven River flowed, serene and unheeding. Around the tower, the sea-eagles circled on tilted wings, mocking her with their freedom. She hated them, hated her prison, hated the rotting mortal confines of the body in which she was trapped, bound tight in the Chain of Being.

Closing her eyes, Lilias whispered words of power, words in the First Tongue, the Shapers' Tongue, the language of dragons.

For a heartbeat, for an exhilarating span of heartbeats, her spirit slipped the coil of flesh to which it was bound. She was aware, briefly, of the Soumanië—Ardrath's Soumanië, *her* Soumanië—set in the pommel of Aracus Altorus' sword, the hilt clenched tight in his fist. She saw, briefly, through his eyes.

Blaise, dead.

The Helm of Shadows, broken.

And war; carnage and chaos and war, Men and Fjel and Ellylon swirling and fighting, and in the midst of it Tanaros Blacksword, Tanaros Kingslayer, the Soldier, looming larger than life, coming for Aracus astride a black horse, carrying a black blade dripping with Blaise's blood, a blade capable of shearing metal as easily as flesh.

No longer did it last, then Lilias was back, huddled on the floor, exhausted and sickened, trapped in her own flesh and weary to the bone. She saw again Blaise Caveros' body, limp and bloodied; felt Aracus' terror and determination, the desperate love that drove him. She remembered how Blaise had told her to look away when they passed what remained of Calandor, how he had forbidden the Pelmarans to desecrate the dragon's corpse. How Aracus had shown her Meronin's Children aboard the Dwarf-ship and treated her as an equal.

It was hard, in the end, to hate them.

"Calandor," she whispered. "Will you not guide me once more?"

There was no answer; there would never be an answer ever again. Only the echo, soft and faint, of her memory. *All things musst be as they are, little sssister.*

All thingsss.

Lilias rose, stiff and aching. The horns, the horns of the Rivenlost were still blowing, still rising and falling, singing of victory and loss, of the glory of Haomane's Prophecy and the terrible price it exhorted. And yet it seemed to her that beneath it all another note sounded, dark and deep and wild, filled with a terrible promise. It reminded her of her childhood, long, long ago, in the deep fastness of Pelmar, where Oronin the Glad Hunter had once roamed the forests, Shaping his Children to be swift and deadly, with keen jaws and amber eyes.

It sang her name.

Over and over, it sang her name.

"So be it," Lilias whispered. A weary gladness filled her. The stories that were told in Pelmar were true after all. That was his Gift; Oronin Last-Born, the Glad Hunter. She was mortal, and she was his to summon.

She could resist his call, for a time. Hours, perhaps days. She was the Sorceress of the East and her will was strong. It might be enough to tip the outcome on the battlefield . . . and yet, in her heart, she no longer believed it. The Helm of Shadows was broken. The things that Calandor had shown her were coming to pass, and while the world that followed might not be the one that Haomane's Allies envisioned, surely it would be one in which there was no place for Lilias of Beshtanag.

It would be a relief, a blessed relief, to slip the coil of mortality forever. She had tried. She had cast her die and lost, but it did not matter. Not in the end. Whether Haomane's Prophecy was fulfilled or thwarted, there was no winning for mortals in the Shapers' War.

And on the other side of death, Calandor awaited her.

There were things even the Shapers did not know.

Lilias embraced that thought as she climbed onto the window seat. She swayed there, leaning forward and spreading her arms. It was a clear day in Meronil, the white city sparkling beneath the sun. The wind fluttered her sleeves, her skirts. A sea-eagle veered away with a harsh cry, making her laugh. Far, far below, the silvery ribbon of the Aven River beckoned, flowing steadily toward the sea.

It was a relief, a blessed relief, to lay down the burden of choice.

"Calandor!" Lilias cried. "I am coming!"

She stepped onto nothingness and plummeted.

TWENTY-ONE

DANI RACED DOWN THE HALLS of Darkhaven, his bare feet pounding the marble floors. Behind him, he could hear Uncle Thulu, breathing hard as they ran, accompanied by the blurred rush of their dim reflections in the glossy black walls, fractured by blue-white fire.

The sound of the pursuing Fjeltroll was like a rockslide at their backs; roaring, thudding, jangling with weaponry. But they were slow, thanks be to Uru-Alat, they were *slow*! Massive and ponderous, not like the Fjel who had hunted them in the north, driving them like sheep to the slaughter.

Still, they kept coming, tireless.

And they summoned others.

At every third corner Dani rounded, it seemed another squadron was advancing, grim and determined, forcing him to backtrack and pick another route. There were Fjel at entrances, guarding doors, joining the slow hunt. Soon, there would be no avenues left down which to flee . . . and he still had no idea how to find the marrow-fire.

Sheer desperation led him to the alcove. They had passed it once already; a tall, arched niche inset with a sculpture in high relief. He glimpsed it briefly, caught a vague impression of two vast figures struggling. When more Fjel were around the next corner, Dani doubled back, nearly colliding with Thulu, only to hear the clamor of pursuit coming from the other end of the hall.

"Here!" he gasped. "Hide!"

Suiting actions to words, he flung himself toward the alcove in a slide, skidding feet-first on the slippery floor, passing beneath the locked arms of the grappling figures, between their planted legs into the shadowy recess behind them.

There he found a small, hidden doorway, one that opened to his tug.

Scrambling onto his bruised knees, Dani grabbed Thulu's arm and hauled him into the alcove, into the narrow, hidden passage he had found. There was no time to close the door. He clamped one hand hard over his uncle's mouth, stifling his panting breath.

Together they huddled motionless, peering out of the shadows and watching the horny, taloned feet and the thick, armor-clad legs of the Fjel churn past. The parties met, with a sharp, frustrated exchange. Orders were barked and the Fjel separated, trotting back toward opposite ends of the hall, intent on further search.

When all was silent, Dani closed the door carefully and pointed farther down the passage. Thulu nodded. Clambering to their feet, they began to explore behind the walls of Darkhaven.

The air was hot and close, growing hotter the farther they progressed. The narrow, winding path, rubble-strewn, slanted downward in a shallow slope. Where it branched, Dani took the lowermost path. From time to time, he heard skittering, scrabbling sounds in the other passages, but they saw nothing. Periodic nodes of marrow-fire, emerging in thick, pulsing knots from the walls, illuminated only darkness.

Below, Malthus had said.

Surely, this was below.

Dani touched the clay vial at his throat, glancing uneasily at the walls. So much marrow-fire! If what permeated the fortress and its foundation was any indication, he could not imagine what lay at its Source. And he could not imagine how the scant mouthful of the Water of Life that remained in the vessel could have even the slightest impact upon it, beyond raising a brief puff of steam.

Your courage will be tested, young Bearer, beyond anything you can imagine.

Malthus had said that, too. At the time, Dani had accorded it little weight. It was the sort of tiresome warning Elders used to scare foolish boys into being cautious when there was an opportunity to do something worth doing, an opportunity for glory.

Later, in the barren reaches, when he had come to understand something of the true nature of the Bearer's burden, he had thought he understood it better. In the northern forests, in the terrible tunnels, he had been sure of it.

In the bowels of Darkhaven, he realized he had not even begun to grasp it.

Malthus had spoken truly. It was beyond anything he could imagine. In the stifling heat, Dani shivered to the bone. He had not expected to survive this journey, not for a long time. Still, the nearer he came to its end, the harder it was to continue.

The path grew level, the passage wider. Rounding a bend, Dani froze.

Ahead of him was a cavern; a rough-hewn chamber, enlarged by the crude efforts of many generations of human hands. Everywhere, lit candles flickered; butt-ends wedged into crevices. Writing was scratched and scrawled upon the walls, and scraps of carpet were strewn about.

In the center of the room, the madling woman who had bid them to run sat waiting for them on an overturned crate. Her hands were folded in her lap, her skirts tucked around her ankles. Beneath her lank hair, her brow shone with sweat and her gaze was fever-bright.

"You have found our place," she said to them. "I thought you would. After all, you must be a little bit mad to have come here."

Dani took a step backward, bumping into Uncle Thulu.

The madling woman shook her head. "No, not now. It's not time to run, now. Behind the walls, they are all around you. They are coming. Do you not hear?" Her mouth twisted in a rictus of a smile. *"They. We.* Will you come hither or be taken?"

"What do you want?" Dani asked cautiously.

She laughed, a harsh and terrible sound, and he realized tears were in her eyes. "Me? *Me?* Does it matter?"

"I don't know." Dani gazed at her. "Does it?"

"Yes." She whispered the word as though it hurt. "I think maybe it does. I think maybe it matters a great deal."

In the passages all around them, the sounds Dani had heard before were growing louder, drawing nearer. Scrabbling sounds, skittering sounds. Madlings, madlings behind the walls, coming for them. It didn't matter. There had never been a way back, not after coming this far. There was only forward. The madling woman beckoned. Dani took a deep breath. Reaching behind him, he found the solid warmth of his uncle's hand and clasped it hard.

Together, they entered the chamber.

MEARA WATCHED THE CHARRED FOLK enter.

What do you want?

Oh, she could have laughed, laughed and laughed, while the tears streamed down her face. Such a grimy little youth! What did she want? She wanted to raise an alarm, to summon the other madlings to hurry, hurry, take them now. She wanted to whisper in the Charred lad's ear, tell him Darkhaven's secrets.

He was gazing at her with wide, dark eyes; liquid-dark, desert eyes. They should have been filled with innocence, but they weren't. There was too much sorrow, too much knowledge. If he had been a boy once, he was no longer.

The madlings could take them, take them both.

General Tanaros would be proud, so proud . . . but he had never trusted her, never *seen* her. She had offered herself to him; her heart, her body, the passion that was his Lordship's Gift to Arahila's Children. But Tanaros was a Man and a fool, wanting what he could never have. What would he do once the burst of pride faded? Turn away, forgetting Meara, longing after *her.*

The Lady Cerelinde's kiss burned on her brow.

Please, she had said.

The other Charred One watched her warily, holding the lad's hand. He looked as battered and exhausted as the lad. Clearly, they had been through much together. It was a pity. She did not want to betray them. She did not want to save them, either.

Give them what aid you may . . .

Not both of them, no. It was too much. Her head ached at the thought, splitting. She shook it hard and rose, approaching them. They stood fast, though the older tried to shield the younger. Meara ignored him, concentrating on the lad.

"You're a mess, you know," she said, trying on a tone of tenderness, a tone she might have used on a lover or a child, if things had been otherwise. Lifting a corner of her skirt, she scrubbed at the lad's face. They were almost exactly the same height. He stood very still, his narrow chest rising and falling. Dropping her skirts, she touched the clay vial that hung about his throat. It was an unprepossessing thing, crudely made, tied with a greasy thong. "Is this what his Lordship desires?"

"Yes," he said softly. "I reckon it is."

"Dani," the other said warningly.

"Dani." Meara touched his face. His skin was soft and warm, and though he was afraid, it was not her that he feared. "Is that your name?"

"Yes. What's yours?"

"Meara. Do you like it?"

He smiled. "I do."

"Why are you here, Dani?" she asked curiously.

He let go the other's hand, raising both of his and cupping them, palms together. The skin was pale, paler than the rest of him. It was marred by dirt and calluses, a myriad of scrapes and half-scabbed wounds. Still, she could discern radiating lines creasing his palms. They met, converging on the joined edges, forming a starburst.

"I am the Bearer," he said simply. "It is mine to do."

Meara nodded. She did not understand, not really; and yet, she did. Madlings heard things. The Charred lad was a piece of a puzzle, a terrible puzzle that should never be assembled. For the second time in her life, she wished the tide of madness would arise, the black pit would open.

Again, it did not happen. The Lady's kiss burned on her brow, a silvery mark, keeping the tide at bay. She had branded Meara as surely as his Lordship had branded his Three, but there was no gift in it. There was only this moment, this crux, and Meara balanced upon it as if on the edge of a blade. The splitting pain in her head intensified, until it felt as though it would cleave her very skull in twain. She wished it would.

The others were drawing nearer. Shuddering, Meara spoke.

"You are going to have to choose." The words came quickly, spilling from her lips. It was the only way to make the pain stop. "I cannot do this, not all of it. *Please*, the Lady said. And I owe her, I owe her, but I owe his Lordship, too. His Lordship and Lord Ushahin, who has always understood what we are." They did not understand, but it didn't matter. Like her, they understood enough. Meara pointed toward the far end of the chamber. "What you seek lies beyond. And in a moment, I am going to scream and betray you. One of you." She felt her face twist into a smile. "One may flee. One must stay. Do you understand?"

The Charred Folk exchanged a glance, silent.

Meara's voice rose. *"Do you understand?* Now, now, or I betray you both! You will die, the Lady will die, all of you, all of Haomane's Allies, dead, you should be dead." She swiped angrily at her weeping eyes. "Do you understand? I am breaking, broken, I cannot do this!"

The older one laid his hands upon the shoulders of the younger, speaking urgently in their tongue. His face was somber, filled with pride. So much love there! It twisted in Meara's guts like a serpent. She hated them both; hated them, hated Tanaros, hated the Lady, hated the very world that had brought her to such an impasse. Ah, what-might-have-been! She might have been elsewhere, might have been a pretty woman in an apron, kneading dough, while a handsome man embraced her, laughing. It would have been a good life, her life, but it was not to be. It never had.

"Go," she said, grinding out the word. "Go!"

The Charred lad sent her a single glance, and fled.

Meara drew in her breath, filling her lungs. The other, the older Charred One, stood braced with his legs astraddle, waiting for what would come. There was a calm acceptance in his dark eyes.

Loosing her breath, Meara screamed.

BLINDED BY TEARS, DANI RAN.

It felt like leaving a piece of himself behind. It *was* leaving a part of himself behind. He felt the rocks of the passage tear at his skin, scraping away patches. It seemed only fair, having left the better part of himself to the madlings' mercy. He heard Meara's scream arise, awful and piercing, filled with all the pain of her divided soul. He heard the shrieks descend, the sound of shouting and struggling.

Uncle Thulu!

A thousand memories crowded his thoughts; Uncle Thulu, guiding and protecting him; Uncle Thulu, teaching him to hunt; Uncle Thulu, still fat, laughing as he tried to mount a horse for the first time, floundering so badly even Malthus laughed, too; Uncle Thulu, fighting Fjeltroll by the river; Uncle Thulu, carrying him on his back in the dry reaches.

What would the madlings do to him?

Better not to know, better not to think. The path sloped sharply downward. Dani navigated it blindly, feeling the way with both hands. It was hot, so hot. He dragged his forearm across his brow, clearing his vision.

There was a fissure in the earth.

It was impossibly, unfathomably deep. It had broadened and grown despite efforts to seal it. The remnants of charred beams and broken slabs of rock clung to its sides. Blue-white light blazed upward, casting stark shadows on the ceiling. Dani fell to his hands and knees, crawling forward to peer over the edge.

The marrow-fire roared. He had found the Source.

He felt faint and rolled onto his back, clutching the clay vial. His lips moved as he murmured the Song of Being.

There was no turning back. There had never been a way back, only forward. The drop was jagged and raw, but it would afford hand- and footholds, provided the heat did not kill him. It shouldn't. He was the Bearer, desert-born, Dani of the Yarru, whose people had endured Haomane's Wrath and learned the secrets of Uru-Alat.

Uncle Thulu had sacrificed himself for this.

Still praying, eyes clenched tight, Dani began to descend.

TWENTY-TWO

THE BATTLE WAS JOINED ONCE more.

For all his fury, Tanaros kept his wits about him. The Helm of Shadows was broken. His army was one of the last things standing between Haomane's Allies and fulfillment of the Prophecy, and he would take no careless risks. With deliberate forbearance, he let the Fjel charge precede him and sow chaos in the ranks of Haomane's Allies. The Tungskulder waded among them, roaring, laying about with axe and mace.

Men and Ellylon alike fell beneath their onslaught; unhorsed, wounded, trampled. Tanaros smiled grimly. On the left flank, his Gulnagel essayed sorties against the Vedasian knights, striking and wheeling as he had taught them. On the right flank, the Nåltannen were wreaking havoc amid the motley infantry.

But Aracus Altorus was no fool. Wheeling his mount, he shouted orders. His troops rallied, changing tactics. On the front line, fleet riders of the Rivenlost and the Borderguard dodged and swerved, striking at the slow Tungskulder with quick, slashing blows until Hyrgolf was forced to order his Fjel to regroup in a tighter defensive formation. The Dwarfs had retired from the field, but a handful of archers remained in the fray, and these Aracus moved to his right, slightly behind the front lines, setting them to picking off stray Gulnagel. Malthus the Counselor was everywhere, his white Soumanië a beacon of hope.

Still, Tanaros thought, the edge was his.

Darkhaven's army was too strong, too well trained. The Borderguard and the Host of the Rivenlost might stand against them, but the others—the Seaholders, the Midlanders, the Free Fishermen—were slowly being slaughtered. Even the Pelmarans, flush from victory in Beshtanag, and the Vedasian knights in their heavy armor, had not reckoned with the awesome might of the Fjel.

They fought so beautifully! The sight of them filled Tanaros with fierce pride. They kept their shields high, they held their formations, pressing forward, slow and inexorable. What a thing it would be, what a glorious thing, if Haomane's Prophecy were yet to be averted—by this, by strength of arms, by dint of long training. Lord Satoris had not *sought* this war. Haomane's Allies had pressed it upon him the moment Cerelinde agreed to wed Aracus Altorus. But he had prepared for it for many long years.

As had Tanaros. And though there was little room in his heart for hope, he meant to try nonetheless. He owed Lord Satoris no less.

If Aracus Altorus died, there could be no victory for Haomane's Allies. Not now, nor ever. There would be no Son of Altorus left living to wed a Daughter of Elterrion. No more royal Altorian bloodline tainted with the betrayal of Tanaros Caveros' faithless wife.

The sun was high overhead, moving toward the west. How long had the battle lasted? Hours, already. And yet, Tanaros felt no weariness. His mind was clear and keen, as though all his anger, all his grief, had been distilled into a single point of brightness. All he needed was an opening, a single opening.

Tanaros watched his enemies tire as the euphoria of their brief victory faded. The Rivenlost showed no sign of slowing, but the battle was taking its toll on the Men. Their faces were white with exhaustion, their horses lathered. The battlefield stank of blood and ordure.

When the Borderguard began to falter, Tanaros signaled to Hyrgolf.

His field marshal roared orders in the Fjel tongue, and his lieutenants and bannermen conveyed them. On the right flank, a banner rose and dipped in acknowledgment. Two squadrons of Nåltannen abandoned their careful discipline and plunged into the ranks of Haomane's Allies, cutting a swath through the infantry to mount a rear attack on the combined forces of the Borderguard and the Rivenlost.

Tanaros saw Aracus Altorus turn to meet this new threat and signaled again. With a mighty roar, the Tungskulder forged forward, and Tanaros with them.

In this new surge of chaos, it was all hand-to-hand fighting. The battle lines had crumbled. The black sword sang as Tanaros cut his way through the Rivenlost vanguard. An Ellyl warrior was in his path, his shining armor smeared with mud and gore. Tanaros swung his blade, felt it bite deep, and continued without pausing, letting the black horse carry him past, deeper into the fray.

Pennants were all around him; not signal-banners, but the standards of the Rivenlost, carried high above the mayhem, still proud, still glittering. Tanaros ignored them, keeping his gaze fixed on one that lay beyond: no Ellyl badge, but a gilt sword on a field of sable, the arms of the ancient Kings of Altoria.

"Aracus!" he shouted. "Aracus!"

The pennant turned in his direction.

More Ellylon, seeking to assail him on either side. Tanaros slashed impatiently at the one on his right, took a sharp blow to the shoulder from the other, denting his spauldron; and then one of the Tungskulder was there, dragging the Ellyl from the saddle by sheer force. The Tungskulder grinned at his General, then grunted as the unhorsed Ellyl lunged upward, his blade piercing a gap in his armor.

No time for sorrow. Tanaros plunged onward; toward the Altorian banner, toward the dun-grey cloaks of the Borderguard of Curonan.

"Aracus Altorus!"

And he was there, waiting, his standard-bearer beside him. His Men had turned back the Nåltannen attack. It had been a costly diversion, but worthwhile. Tanaros reined his mount, saluting with his sword. "Aracus."

"Kingslayer." The word was filled with unutterable contempt. Behind the eyeslits of his helm, Aracus Altorus stared at him. The sword in his hand echoed the one on his standard; his ancestor's sword. Once upon a time, Tanaros had known it well. The only difference was the lifeless Soumanië in its pommel. "You come at last."

"As I promised, Son of Altorus," Tanaros said softly.

Aracus nodded, taking a fresh grip on his sword-hilt. Beneath the contempt, he looked tired and resolute. It seemed like a very long time since they had first laid eyes on one another in the shattered nuptial ceremony in Lindanen Dale. "Shall we put an end to it?"

Tanaros inclined his head. "Nothing would please me more, Son of Altorus."

There should have been more to say, but there wasn't.

Settling their shields, they rode at one another.

They struck at the same instant, both catching the blows on their bucklers. Tanaros felt the impact jar his arm to the shoulder. He felt, too, Aracus' buckler riven beneath the force of his blow, metal plate giving way, wood splitting. Tanaros laughed aloud as the would-be King of the West was forced to discard his useless shield.

"Shall it be now?" Tanaros asked, and without waiting for a reply, struck another blow.

Aracus Altorus parried with his ancestral sword, the sword Altorus Farseer had caused to be forged, the sword Roscus Altorus had borne before him long ago. A symbol, nothing more. It shattered in his grip, leaving him clutching the useless hilt with its curved tangs and dull Soumanië, a few jagged inches of steel protruding from it.

He lifted his bewildered gaze. He had believed, somehow, it would not happen.

Tanaros had thought to taunt him, this Man who sought to wed the Lady of the Ellylon, who sought to destroy Lord Satoris. He had thought to find satisfaction in this moment; and yet, having reached it, he found none. Aracus' gaze reminded him too much of Roscus' at the end; dimly surprised, uncomprehending.

He hadn't found it in killing Roscus, either.

"I'm sorry," he said, raising the black sword for the final blow. There was no choice here, only duty. "But you brought this upon yourself."

At that moment, the Soumanië in the pommel of Aracus Altorus' shattered sword blazed wildly into life.

HALFWAY UP THE DEFILE PATH, Ushahin felt it happen.

The world gave a sickening lurch and his mount staggered beneath him. An unaltered Soumanië, with the power to Shape matter, had passed to a new owner. Ushahin's vision veered crazily, and he saw the Defile loom beneath him, pebbles skittering beneath his blood-bay stallion's scrabbling hooves, bouncing down the crags toward the riverbed below.

He righted himself with an effort that made every ill-set bone in his body ache, twisting in the saddle to glance behind him.

It was bad.

The tide of battle was shifting, surging against them. The horns, the damned Ellylon horns, were raised in their clarion call, echoing and insistent. Everywhere, figures were reeling; the very *earth* was in motion, the plains lifting in a vast, slow surge, rippling like a wave.

Ushahin tasted bile.

"Oh, my Lord!" he whispered. "You should have let me kill her!"

It was not too late, not yet. Lashing the blood-bay stallion with his reins, Ushahin raced toward Darkhaven.

TANAROS' FINAL BLOW NEVER LANDED.

For the space of a few heartbeats, they simply stared at one another, wide-eyed and astonished, the Soumanië blazing between them. Then Aracus Altorus whispered a word and the world erupted in rubescent light.

The earth surged and Tanaros found himself flung backward, losing ground, half-blinded and lurching in the saddle as his mount squealed in rage and fought to remain on its hooves. In some part of him, Tanaros understood what must have happened. Somehow, somewhere, the Sorceress Lilias had died; the Soumanië's power was passing to its wielder: Aracus Altorus, who had been mentored by Malthus the Counselor, whose reserves of inner strength the Soumanië required had never been tapped.

In that instant, everything changed.

Haomane's Allies knew it. The horns of the Rivenlost rang out joyously, maddeningly. New vigor, new *hope* infused them, gave them strength. They had a new ally. The very plains themselves rose up in rebellion against the Army of Darkhaven; churning, fissuring.

And in the center of the battlefield, Aracus Altorus sat astride his mount, untouchable, both hands clasped around the hilt of his shattered sword. He had removed his helm to afford a clearer field of vision, and in the wash of ruby light pouring from the Soumanië, his face was at once agonized and transcendent. Malthus had reached his side in a flurry of white robes, was lending him strength and counsel.

And Ingolin, Lord of the Rivenlost, was rallying his troops.

All the hatred Tanaros had been unable to summon on the verge of dealing Aracus his death blow returned tenfold. With no thought in his mind but finishing the job, he spurred his mount back toward Aracus.

It was to no avail. His Lordship's brand afforded protection against the Soumanië itself, but the earth rose against him in waves, softened beneath him. At twenty paces away, his mount floundered, sunk to its hocks.

Malthus the Counselor gazed at him, grave and implacable.

Tanaros could draw no closer.

With a curse, he wrenched his mount's head around; and cursed again to see what transpired on the battlefield. The surging earth favored Haomane's Allies, bore them up. The infantry massed against his Nåltannen, whose numbers had been decimated by the charge Tanaros had ordered. Somewhere, Oronin's Bow was singing; mired Gulnagel twisted futilely, raising their shields as the archers circled. Riding the crest of its waves, the Rivenlost fell upon the Tungskulder. Still floundering, Tanaros was forced to watch as the Host of the Ellylon rode down his beloved Fjel.

"Hyrgolf!"

The word escaped him in a raw gasp. Hyrgolf knew what had happened, what *was* happening. He had chosen to meet the charge and buy time for his lads. He stood bravely, knee-deep in a sudden mire, baring his eyetusks in a fierce grin. It took four Ellylon to bring him down, and one was Lord Ingolin himself, who struck the final blow. With a peaceful sigh, Hyrgolf died, measuring his length on the trampled grass of the plains, the last ounces of his life bubbling from his slashed throat.

Tanaros swore, laying about him on either side with his black sword at the warriors who came for him. He gouged his mount's flanks with his heels, driving it mercilessly onto solid land. He rode unthinking, swerving to follow the shifting crests, killing as he went.

"Retreat!" he bellowed, seizing the nearest Fjel, shoving him toward home. "Retreat to Darkhaven!"

Overhead, the ravens screamed and wheeled.

Someone took up the call, then another and another. *"Retreat! Retreat! Retreat!"*

It was not in the nature of the Fjel to retreat. Some obeyed, the ragged ends of Tanaros' discipline holding true. Elsewhere, it frayed at last and Fjel stood, fighting until the end, dying with bitter, bloody grins. And then there were many, too many, trapped by the treacherous earth, who had no choice but to fight and die.

Tanaros wept, unaware of the tears trickling beneath the faceplate of his helm, mingling with his sweat. On the far outskirts of the battle-field, he took a stand, watching the staggering columns of Fjel file past. The earth was stable here; even with Malthus' aid, Aracus' strength extended only so far.

It had been far enough.

The horns of the Rivenlost sounded and a company detached to ride in pursuit of the fleeing remnants of Darkhaven's army. They came swiftly, carrying their standards high, armor glittering beneath the mire, dotted here and there with the dun-grey cloaks of the Bor-derguard. And at the forefront of them all was the argent scroll of the House of Ingolin the Wise, Lord of the Rivenlost.

"Go!" Tanaros shouted at the retreating Fjel. "Go, go, *go!*"

They went at a stumbling jog, slow and wounded, passing the supply-trains that Vorax of Staccia had so diligently mustered. Useless, now. Tanaros pushed the memory aside and glanced at the sky. "One last kindness," he whispered, trying to catch Fetch's winged thoughts. "One last time, my friend."

Turning his mount, he charged the oncoming company. The black horse of Darkhaven was not the mount he had trained for many years, but it had born him willingly into battle and it ran now with all the fearlessness of its proud, vicious heart.

A dark cloud swept down from the sky.

Wings, all around him, black and glossy. It was like being in the center of the Ravensmirror, save that the path before him was clear. In front of him, Tanaros saw alarm dawning on the faces of his enemies. And then the ravens were among them, clamoring, obscuring their vi-sion, wings battering, claws scrabbling.

In the chaos, Tanaros struck once, hard and true. Blue sparks flew and metal screeched as his black sword pierced bright Ellylon armor, sinking deep, deep into the flesh below.

"For Hyrgolf," he whispered, wrenching his blade free.

He did not linger to watch the Lord of the Rivenlost die, though the image stayed with him as he wheeled and raced toward the Defile; In-golin's eyes, fathomless and grey, widening in pain and sorrow, the light of Haomane's regard fading in them. Behind him, the horns went silent and a great cry arose from the Host, echoed mockingly by the rising ravens.

From Darkhaven, nothing.

Fear, true fear, gripped Tanaros, then. Beneath his armor, the brand on his chest felt icy. Worse blows even than this could be dealt against Darkhaven. He remembered his Lordship's voice, low and strange. *He is coming, Tanaros Blacksword. They are all coming, all my Elder Brother's little puppets. . . .*

At the base of Defile's Maw, he caught up with the Fjel and shouted, "Follow as swiftly as you can! I go to his Lordship's aid!"

They nodded wearily.

Tanaros glanced behind him. A handful of Ellylon warriors remained with their fallen Lord. The rest were coming, swift and deadly, with hearts full of vengeance. The Defile could be sealed against them; but it would take time for the slower Fjel to get clear, more time than their pursuers allowed. He looked back at his lads, stolid and loyal, even in defeat. "Defile's Maw must be held. Who among you will do it?"

Twelve Tungskulder stepped forward without hesitation, saluting him. "For as long as it takes, Lord General, sir!" one said.

"Good lads." Tanaros' eyes burned. "I'm proud of you."

Spurring his black horse, he plunged into the Defile.

THE HAVENGUARD WERE SLOW TO open the Defile Gate.

Ushahin shouted with rare impatience; to no avail, for it took two teams of Fjel to shift the gates and one team was absent. Something had passed within the fortress, something that had the Havenguard in an uproar.

A bitter jest, to be powerless before mere stone, while on the plains below, a Man, a stupid mortal brute of an Altorus, wielded the power to Shape matter itself. Ushahin shivered in the saddle, wrapping his arms around the case that held the sundered Helm of Shadows and waiting.

He saw the ravens return, pouring like smoke above the Defile. He knew, then, that the army would follow and prayed that Tanaros would stay with them, would be a good commander and remain with his troops.

But, no; Tanaros Blacksword was one of the Three. Like Ushahin, he knew too well where danger lay at the end. As the Defile Gate began to creak open at last, hoofbeats sounded. And then the General was there, blood-spattered, the black blade naked in his fist.

"Dreamspinner," he said. "There is a thing that must be done."

Ushahin raised his head, daring to hope. "The Lady—"

"Damn the Lady!" Tanaros' voice cracked. "She's a pawn, nothing more!" Removing his borrowed helm, he passed a vambraced forearm over his face. For an instant, Ushahin imagined that he wiped away tears. "You were right," he said in a low tone. "The foundation . . . the foundation is crumbling, and Ushahin, I think he's coming. The Bearer. It's all happened, piece by piece. And I need to stop him."

"All we *need* to do—" Ushahin began.

"They're *coming*, Dreamspinner!" Tanaros took a deep breath. "We have to seal the Defile. Rally the Tordenstem, get them to those ricks Speros built. They won't think to do it on their own, they'll need orders. My lads' lives depend on it, those that are left."

"Tanaros," Ushahin said, shifting the case in his arms. "With the Soumanië, Aracus Altorus can—"

"*Time,*" Tanaros said abruptly. "Aracus is a mortal Man, he can only do so much. It will purchase time, Ushahin! And lives, too; my *lads'* lives. I beg you, don't let all their sacrifices be in vain." A muscle in his jaw twitched. "And I pray you, do not make me do more than beg."

The Defile Gate stood open. They stared at one another.

"All right, cousin," Ushahin said gently. "You know well that I lack the strength to oppose you. For the moment, I will do your bidding. And afterward, in this *time* we have earned, you will heed my words."

"My thanks, Dreamspinner." Tanaros extended his free hand.

Ushahin clasped it with his right hand, his strong, healed hand. "Go, then, and protect the marrow-fire! I will see your Fjel home safely, all those who remain."

Together, they passed through the Defile Gate.

Ushahin watched Tanaros lash his mount, sprinting for the fortress. He shook his head as he turned the blood-bay stallion's course toward the high path along the Defile, thinking of the Grey Dam Sorash, who had raised him as her own, who had given her life to this venture.

It was folly, all folly. Yet he knew well, too well, the cost Tanaros bore this day.

Forgive me, Mother, he thought.

The Tordenstem were glad to see him; pathetic, bounding like dogs, squat, boulder-shaped dogs. Everything had gone wrong, confusing them. Ushahin sighed, riding to the verge of the crags where the easternmost rick was stationed and peering over the edge.

Tanaros' Fjel were coming, a straggling line of them. It shocked him to see how few they were, how slowly they moved. At the Defile's Maw, a scant dozen had made a stand, barring the path to Haomane's Allies, there where it was narrow enough to be defended. They were wielding maces and axes to deadly effect, roaring in defiance.

"Tan-a-ros! Tan-a-ros!"

It wouldn't last. A spark was moving on the plains; a red spark, a Soumanië, twinned with a diamond-brightness. Aracus Altorus was coming, and Malthus the Counselor with him. They were all coming, all of Haomane's Allies.

Ushahin sighed again. "How did it come to this?"

Levers in hands, the Tordenstem exchanged confused glances. "Boss?"

"Pay me no heed." Ushahin shook his head, impatient. "On my word, make ready to loose the first rockslide."

"Aye, boss!" They positioned their levers.

Ushahin watched, raising one hand. The Fjel were hurrying, hurrying as best they could. Aracus Altorus had arrived at the base of the Defile. He forged a swath through Haomane's Allies, his Soumanië flashing. Malthus the Counselor was at his side. The path began to crumble beneath the Tungskulder defenders' feet.

"Tell the others to hurry," Ushahin murmured to the Tordenstem.

One filled his lungs, his torso swelling. *"Snab!"* he howled. *"Snab!"*

The Fjel column hurried, even as the defenders began to fall and die, and Haomane's Allies to push past them. Not daring to wait, Ushahin let his hand drop. "Now!" he cried.

The Tordenstem heaved on their levers. Rocks tumbled, boulders fell, all in a great rumbling rush, bouncing down the crags, blocking the Defile.

For a time.

Below, the red spark of the Soumanië gleamed, and pebbles began to shift, slow and inexorable.

For a third time, Ushahin sighed. "Let us go to the next station. Perhaps this time we can manage to crush a few of Haomane's Allies."

There was scant consolation in the thought, but at least it would

take him a step closer to Darkhaven. Glancing uneasily toward the
fortress, Ushahin prayed that it would not be too late, that it was not
already too late. He remembered the Delta and the words of Calanthrag the Eldest.

Yet may it come later than sssooner for ssuch as I and you. . . .

In his heart, he feared it had not.

TWENTY-THREE

TANAROS STRODE THROUGH DARKHAVEN LIKE a black wind.

The shock of his arrival rippled through the fortress with a palpable effect. The Havenguard hurried from far-flung quarters of Darkhaven to meet him, falling over one another in their haste. His abrupt, awful news shocked them into momentary silence, and he had to shout at them twice before they were able to tell him what had transpired in his absence.

Two Men, Charred Folk, madlings caught one . . .

He wasted precious minutes hurrying into the dungeon, clattering down the slippery stair, hoping against hope to see the Man the madlings had caught. It gave him an unpleasant echo of the memory of Speros, hanging in chains, grinning crookedly with his split lips. Not Speros, no; not the Bearer, either. It was the other Yarru, his protector. Manacled to the wall, scratched and beaten and bloodied, he hung limp, lacking the strength to even stir. The Fjel had not been gentle. Only the slight rise and fall of his scarred torso suggested he lived.

"Where's the boy?" Tanaros asked, prodding him. *"Where's the boy?"*

Unable to lift his head, the prisoner made a choked sound. "Slayer," he said in a slow, thick voice. "Where do you think?"

Tanaros cursed and ran from the dungeon, taking the stairs two at a time.

He made his way behind the walls, through the winding passages, through the rising heat, to the chasm. To the place he had known he must go. The madlings had scattered, abandoning the places behind the walls, hiding from his fury, from the terrible news. There was only the heat, the light-shot darkness, and the chasm like a gaping wound.

There, he gazed over the edge.

Far below, a small, dark figure was descending laboriously.

Straightening, Tanaros shed his gauntlets. With deft fingers, he unbuckled the remainder of his armor, removing it piece by piece. When he had stripped to his undertunic, he replaced his swordbelt, then lowered himself into the chasm and began to climb.

It was hot. It was scorchingly, horribly hot. The air seared his lungs, the blue-white glare blinding him. Narrowing his eyes to slits, Tanaros willed himself to ignore the heat. It could be done. He had done it in the Unknown Desert. He was one of the Three, and it could be done.

Fear lent his limbs speed. Hands and feet moved swift and sure, finding holds. He took risks, careless risks, tearing and bruising his flesh. The worst thing would be to fail for being too *slow*, to be halfway down and find the marrow-fire suddenly extinguished.

It did not happen.

Reaching the bottom, Tanaros saw why.

The Source, the *true* Source, lay some paces beyond the chasm itself. It was not so large, no larger than the circumference of the Well of the World. Indeed, it was similar in shape and size; a rounded hole in the foundation of the earth itself.

But from it, the marrow-fire roared upward in a solid blue-white column. High above, at its core, a spit of flame vanished through an egress in the ceiling. The Font, Tanaros thought, realizing he was beneath his Lordship's very chambers. Elsewhere, the marrow-fire fanned outward in a blue-white inferno, flames illuminating the chasm, licking the walls, sinking into them and vanishing in a tracery of glowing veins.

And at the edge of the Source stood the Bearer.

It was the boy, the Charred lad he had seen in the Marasoumië. He had one hand on the clay vial strung about his throat and a look of sheer terror on his face. Even as Tanaros approached, he flung out his other hand.

"Stay back!" he warned.

"Dani," Tanaros said softly. He remembered; he had always been good with names, and Malthus the Counselor had spoken the boy's. So had Ngurra, whom he had slain. "What is it you think to do here, lad?"

Despite the heat, the boy was shivering. His eyes were enormous in his worn face. "Haomane's will."

"Why?" Tanaros took a step closer. The heat of the column was like a forge-blast against his skin. "Because Malthus bid you to do so?"

"In the beginning." The boy's voice trembled, barely audible above the roaring of the marrow-fire. "But it's not that simple, is it?"

"No." Something in the lad's words made Tanaros' heart ache, longing for what-might-have-been. In a strange way, it was comforting to hear them spoken by an enemy. It was true, after all was said and done, they were not so different. "No, lad, it's not." He drew a deep breath, taking another step. "Dani, *listen*. You need not do this. What has Haomane done that the Yarru should love him for it and do his bidding?"

The boy edged closer to the Source. "What has Satoris the Sunderer done that I should heed his will instead?"

"He left you in peace!" Tanaros said sharply. "Was it not enough? Until—" His voice trailed off as he watched the boy's expression change, terror ebbing to be replaced by profound sorrow. Somehow, the boy knew. The knowledge lay there between them. In the roaring marrow-fire, it seemed Tanaros heard anew the pleas and cries of the dying Yarru, the sound of Fjel maces crunching. And he knew, then, that whatever conversation he might have hoped to hold with the lad, it was too late.

"Did you kill them yourself?" Dani asked quietly.

"Yes," Tanaros said. "I did."

The dark eyes watched him. "Why? Because Satoris bid you to do so?"

"No." Gritting his teeth, Tanaros drew his sword and drew within reach of the boy. "I begged him. Old Ngurra, the old man. *Give me a reason!* Do you understand, lad? A reason to spare his life, his people; a reason, any reason! Do you know what he said?"

Dani smiled through the tears that spilled from his eyes, glittering on his brown skin. "Aye," he whispered. "Choose."

"Even so." Tanaros nodded. "And I am sorry for it, as I am sorry for this, but his Lordship did not ask for this battle and I have a duty to do. Now remove the flask, and lay it gently upon the stone, Dani. *Gently.*"

The boy watched the rising arc of the black sword and his dark eyes were like the eyes of Ngurra, filled with knowledge and regret. "I will ask you what you asked my grandfather," he said. "Give me a reason."

"Damn you, I don't *want* to do this!" Tanaros shouted at him. "Is your *life* not reason enough? Relinquish the flask!"

"No," Dani said simply.

With a bitter curse, Tanaros struck at him. The black blade cut a swathe of darkness through the blinding light. Loosing his grip on the flask, Dani flung himself backward, teetering on the very edge of the Source, almost out of reach. The tip of Tanaros' sword shattered the clay vessel tied around the lad's throat, scoring the flesh beneath it.

Fragments of pit-fired clay flew asunder.

Water, clear and heavy, spilled from the shattered flask; spilled, glistening, in a miniature torrent, only to be caught in the Bearer's cupped palms.

The Water of Life.

Its scent filled the air, clear and clean, heavy and mineral-rich, filled with the promise of green, growing things.

There was nothing else for it; no other option, no other choice. Only the slight figure of the Bearer silhouetted against the blazing column of blue-white fire with the Water of Life in his hands, his pale, scarred palms cupped together, holding the Water, the radiating lines joining to form a drowned star.

"I'm sorry," Tanaros whispered, and struck again.

And Dani the Bearer took another step backward, into the Source itself.

HE FELT THEM DIE, ALL of them.

So many! It should not have mattered, not after so long; and yet, he had imbued so much of himself in this place. This place, these folk, this conflict. An infinite number of subtle threads bound him to them all; threads of fate, threads of power, threads of his very dwindling essence.

Godslayer hung in the Font of the marrow-fire, pulsing.

It tempted him. It tempted him well nigh unto madness, which was a cruel jest, for he had been losing that battle for many a century.

One of the first blows had been the hardest. Vorax of Staccia, his

Glutton. One of his Three, lost. Oh, he had roared at that blow. The power that had stretched the Chain of Being to encompass the Staccian was broken, lost, bleeding into nothingness. Ah, he would miss Vorax! He was all the best and worst of Arahila's Children combined; tirelessly venal, curiously loyal. Once, long ago, Vorax of Staccia had amused him greatly.

He would miss him.

He would miss them all.

Their lives, the brief lives—Men and Fjel—blinked out like candles. So they did, so they had always done. Never so many at once. Many of them cried his name as they died. It made him smile, alone in his darkness, and it made him gnash his teeth with fury, too.

Godslayer.

He remembered the feel of it in his palm when he'd taken to the battlefield ages ago. Striding, cloaked in shadow, blotting out the sky. Pitting its might against Haomane's Weapons, his vile Counselors with their bloodred pebbles of Souma. There had been no Three, then; only the Fjel, the blessed Fjel.

And they had triumphed. Yet it had been a near thing, so near. Already, then, he had endured many long ages sundered from the Souma, wounded and bleeding. An Ellyl sword, stabbing him from behind. He had dropped the Shard. If the courage of Men had not faltered, if a Son of Altorus had not sounded the retreat too soon . . .

His hand was reaching for Godslayer. He made himself withdraw it.

It was the one thing he dared not do, the one thing he *must* not do. He was weaker now, far weaker, than he had been. If he risked it, it would be lost. The Counselor would reclaim it in his brother's name, and Haomane would Shape the world in his image. That was the single thread of sanity to which he clung. He made himself remember what had gone before. The Souma, shattering. Oronin's face as he lunged, the Shard glittering in his fist.

A gift for his Gift.

He had called the dragons, and they had come. Ah, the glory of them! All the brightness in the world, filling the sky with gouts of flame and winged glory. No wonder Haomane had Sundered the earth to put an end to it. But what a price, what a terrible price they had all paid for the respite.

There would be no dragons, not this time.

He waited to see who would come instead.

Outside, the story retold itself, writing a new ending. The Helm of Shadows, that once he had claimed and bent to his own ends, was broken. The Counselor's Soumanië was clear, clear as water. The Son of Altorus did not flee, but wielded a bloodred pebble of his own. A weary lad carried a grimy clay vessel into the depths of Darkhaven itself. His faithful ones, his remaining minions, raced desperately to prevent them.

They were coming, they were all coming.

And there was naught to do but wait; wait, and endure. Perhaps, in the end, it was as well. He was weary. He was weary of the endless pain, weary of meditating upon the bitterness of betrayal, weary of the burden of knowledge, of watching the world change while everything he had known dwindled and passed from it, while he diminished drop by trickling drop, stinking of ichor and hurting, always hurting; hurting in his immortal flesh, aching for his lost Gift, diminishing into madness and hatred, a figure of impotent, raging despite.

Still, the story was yet to be written.

It was always yet to be written.

The thought pleased him. There were things Haomane First-Born, the Lord-of-Thought, had never understood. He had not listened to the counsel of dragons. The death and rebirth of worlds was a long and mighty business.

"You are all my Children."

He whispered the words, tasting them, and found them true. So many lies, so few of them his! One day, perhaps, the world would understand. He was a Shaper. He had been given a role to play, and he had played it.

They were close now.

There was a sound; one of the threefold doors, opening. He lifted his heavy head to see which of them had arrived first.

It was a surprise after all; and yet there were no surprises, not here at the end. The Font burned quietly, spewing blue-white sparks over the impervious stone floor. Within it, Godslayer, the Shard of the Souma, throbbed steadily.

At the top of the winding stair, his visitor regarded him warily.

"My child," said Satoris Third-Born, who was once called the Sower. "I have been expecting you."

USHAHIN RODE BACK AND FORTH along the edge of the cliffs high above the Defile, gazing at the path far below.

The surviving Fjel had made a safe return to Darkhaven. If nothing else, his actions had accomplished that much. But Haomane's Allies had managed to clear the first rockslide; and worse, they had spotted the trap that would trigger the second one.

Now they waited, just out of range.

It was a maddening impasse. He wished Tanaros would return, wished Vorax was alive, or Tanaros' young Midlander protégé; anyone who would take command of the disheartened Tordenstem.

There was no one. It shouldn't have mattered; Darkhaven was a fortress, built to be defended. Time should be their ally, and a day ago, it might have been so. But now the army of Darkhaven was in tatters, the Helm of Shadows was broken, Haomane's Prophecy loomed over the Vale of Gorgantum, and Ushahin's very skin crawled with the urgent need to be *elsewhere*.

In the Weavers' Gulch, the little grey spiders scuttled across the vast loom of their webs, repairing the damage the Fjel had done in passing, restoring the pattern. Always, no matter how many times it was shredded, they restored the pattern.

Watching the little weavers, Ushahin came to a decision.

"You." He beckoned to one of the Tordenstem. "How are you called?"

The Fjel saluted him. "Boreg, sir!"

"Boreg." Ushahin pointed into the Defile. "You see Haomane's Allies, there. Watch them. At some point, they will begin to advance. When half their numbers have reached this bend in the path, I want you and your lads to trigger the rockslide."

"Aye, sir." The Tordenstem looked ill at ease with the command. "Will you not stay?"

"I cannot." Ushahin laid a hand on the Fjel's shoulder, feeling the rock-solid warmth of it. "General Tanaros trusts you, Boreg. Do your best."

"Aye, boss!"

Ushahin spared one last glance at Haomane's Allies. They were watching; a figure in the distant vanguard raised one hand, and the

Soumanië flashed like a red star in the gloomy depths. Ushahin smiled contemptuously, certain that Aracus Altorus dared not waste a precious ounce of strength on assailing him, not with another rockslide and the Defile Gate awaiting. He did not know by what magic the power of the Souma was invoked, but he knew it took a considerable toll.

His Lordship was proof of that, and he was a Shaper.

"Enjoy this taste of victory, Son of Altorus," he murmured. "I go now to do what should have been done long ago."

Ushahin turned his mount's head toward Darkhaven. The blood-bay stallion caught his mood, its hooves pounding an urgent cadence as they made for the fortress. The case containing the sundered Helm jounced, lashed haphazardly to the saddle behind him. His right hand, healed and hale, itched for the hilt of his sword. He remembered how it had felt to move *between* life and death on the battlefield, to sever the threads that had bound the ageless Ellylon to their immortal souls.

He wondered how it would feel to cleave the life from the Lady Cerelinde's flesh.

The inner courtyard was jammed with milling Fjel, wounded and dazed, bereft of orders. Ushahin dismounted and pushed his way through the throng of Fjel, carrying the Helm's case, ignoring their pleas for guidance. There was nothing he could do for them. He was no military strategist.

Inside Darkhaven proper, it was quieter. The Havenguard, oddly subdued, had restored some semblance of order. None of his madlings were about, which gave him a moment's pause. He thought briefly of summoning them, then shook his head. There was no time.

It had to be done. It should have been done long ago.

There was madness in it; oh, yes. His right arm ached with the memory of his Lordship's wrath, the merciful cruelty that had Shaped it anew, pulverizing fragments of bone, tearing sinews asunder, a scant inch at a time. Ushahin had no illusions about the cost he would bear for this action.

And he had no doubt about its necessity.

He strode the halls, reaching the door to the Lady of the Ellylon's quarters. A pair of Havenguard sought to turn him away. With the case containing the broken Helm under his arm, he quelled them with a single, furious glance.

Chastened, they unbarred the door.

Ushahin stepped inside, smiling his bitter, crooked smile. "Lady," he began, and then halted.

Over a hidden passageway, a tapestry hung askew.

The chamber was empty.

"EXPECTING ME?" CERELINDE WHISPERED THE words. "How so, my Lord? For I did not expect to find myself here."

Some yards beyond the base of the stair, Satoris Banewreaker gazed upward at her with terrifying gentleness. "Will you seek after my knowledge now, little Ellyl? I fear it is too late." He beckoned. "Come."

She had never thought to get this far. As she'd paced restless in her chamber, the certainty that she must *try* had grown upon her. The weight of the burden Haomane's Allies had placed upon the Bearer, the burden she had laid on Meara's shoulders, were too great. It was unfair to ask what one was unwilling to give.

Meara might fail her.

The young Bearer's task might consume him.

And it had come to her that perhaps, after all, it was Haomane's plan that had placed her here, where she alone among his Allies held the key to fulfilling his Prophecy. Cerelinde knew the way to the threefold door.

She had not expected it to open to her touch. Surely, it must be a trap.

"Come." The Sunderer gestured at Godslayer. "Is this not what you seek?"

From her vantage point atop the stair, Cerelinde glanced at the dagger, pulsing in the Font. "You mock me, my Lord," she said quietly. "Though my life is forfeit for this error, do not ask me to walk willingly onto the point of your blade."

"There is no mockery." The Shaper smiled with sorrow, the red glow in his eyes burning low. "Can you not feel it, daughter of Erilonde? Even now, the Bearer is beneath us. Even now, he dares to risk all. Do you dare to risk less?"

"I am afraid," Cerelinde whispered.

"Indeed. Yet I have given my word that I will not harm you." The Shaper laughed softly, and there was no madness in it. "You mistrust my word, Lady of the Ellylon; yet if I am true to it, will you dare to become the thing you despise? Will you take that burden on yourself for the sake of your foolish, unswerving obedience to my Elder Brother's will?"

She shuddered. "I know not what you mean, my Lord Satoris."

"Come, then, and learn it." Once more, he beckoned to her, and an edge of malice crept into his tone. "Or will you flee and leave the Bearer to fail?"

"No." Cerelinde thought of the unknown Charred lad and all he had risked, all he must have endured. Gathering every measure of courage she possessed, she pushed her fear aside and gazed at the Shaper with clear eyes. In the coruscating light of the Font, he stood without moving, awaiting her. "No, Lord Satoris," she said. "I will not."

And though her legs trembled, she forced herself to move, step by step, descending the stair into the Chamber of the Font and the Sunderer's presence.

USHAHIN GATHERED HIS MADLINGS.

They came, straggling, in answer to his summons; his thoughts, cast like a net over Darkhaven, gathering all of those who were *his*. They crowded, as many as could fit, into the Lady's chambers, others spilling into the hallways.

"What has happened here?" he asked.

They explained in a mixture of glee and terror; the hunt, the Charred Man, the Lord General's furious arrival, and how they had scattered before it.

"And the Lady?" he asked them. "How is it that she knew to flee?"

They exchanged glances, fell to their knees, and cried out to him, professing denial; all save one, who remained standing. And Ushahin's gaze fell upon her, and he knew what it was that she had done.

"Meara," he said gently. "How is it that I failed you?"

She shook her head, tears spilling down her cheeks. "Not you," she whispered. "Never you, my lord."

The others wailed.

Ushahin raised one hand. "No. I have failed you, all of you. I have been remiss in accepting my burden. But with your aid, it will end here."

The wailing continued; growing louder, interspersed with cries of fear and deeper, guttural shouts, the sound of pounding feet and jangling armor. Even as Ushahin opened his mouth to call for silence, one of the Havenguard burst into the room, forging a path through the kneeling madlings like a ship plowing through shallow waves. He was panting, the breath rasping harshly in the thick column of his throat. "Lord Dreamspinner!" He saluted. "Haomane's Allies approach the Defile Gate!"

"*What?*" Ushahin stared at the Fjel. "The rockslide—"

"Too late." The Havenguard shuddered. "The wizard, the white gem; I know not what he did, only that the lads were slow and the rocks fell too late." He paused, his small eyes beneath the heavy brow ridge bright with anxiety. "Will you come?"

They were gazing at him; all of them, his madlings, the Fjel, guilt-ridden Meara. Ushahin tasted despair.

"Listen," he said to them. "There is no time." He pointed toward the tapestried door. "The Lady of the Ellylon has passed behind the wall, and even now her kindred attempt a rescue." He paused, drawing his sword. "I go now in pursuit, for her death is our last hope, our only hope. My madlings, I charge you, all of you, with infiltrating every passage, every hidden egress in the fortress of Darkhaven. Do you come upon the Lady, halt her; kill her if you may. Any consequence that comes, I will accept. Do you understand?"

The madlings shouted their assent, leaping to their feet.

"Good." Ushahin pointed at the Havenguard with the tip of his blade. "Hold the Gate," he said grimly. "There is no other order I can give. Tell the lads they must resist if Malthus seeks to wield his Soumanië against them and sway their spirits. Bid them to cling to the thought of his Lordship's long suffering, bid them think of their fallen comrades. It may lend them strength. If it does not . . ." He glanced at Meara. "Bid them make ready to slay any comrade who seeks to betray us."

"Aye, boss!" Relieved to have orders, the Havenguard whirled to depart. The madlings went with him, surging out the door in a roiling, shouting mass. Ushahin watched them go.

Meara remained. "Will you not punish me?" she asked plaintively.

"What punishment will suit?" Ushahin asked. "Your penitence comes too late to aid his Lordship. I will deal with you anon, Meara of Darkhaven. Now go, and serve while you may."

Bowing her head, she went.

With a sword-blade naked in his strong right hand and the case containing the broken Helm tucked beneath his aching left arm, Ushahin thrust aside the tapestry and plunged into the passageways.

FOR A MOMENT, THE SOURCE continued to surge upward in a blazing column.

The Bearer, Dani the Bearer with his cupped hands, stood within it; stood, and lived. Through the sheets of blue-white flame, his gaze met Tanaros'. His lips, cracked and parched, whispered a word.

"Uru-Alat!"

And then his hands parted and the Water of Life fell, splashing, slow and glistening. The scent of water filled the cavern, sweet and clean and unbearable, as though all the water in the world was gathered in the Bearer's hands.

A handful; not even that, a scant mouthful.

It was enough.

The Source of the marrow-fire, the vast, roaring column of blue-white fire, winked out of existence. Tanaros, gaping, sword in hand, caught a final glimpse of the Bearer's figure crumpling to the ground.

And then he was trapped in darkness beneath the bowels of Darkhaven.

The Source was gone.

The marrow-fire had been extinguished.

For the space of a dozen heartbeats, Tanaros saw only blackness. He sheathed his sword, hands moving blindly. Slowly, his eyes adjusted to this new darkness, and when they did, he saw that traceries remained. The blue-white veins within the stony walls lingered, their light ebbing. *When the marrow-fire is quenched and Godslayer is freed . . .*

A new spasm of fear seized him. "Godslayer," Tanaros said aloud.

"URU-ALAT."

The word seemed to come from everywhere and nowhere, the World God's name whispered in every corner of the Chamber, all at once a prayer, a plea, a promise. It carried the scent of water, overwhelming for a moment the sweet charnel reek of ichor.

In the center of the room, Satoris Third-Born lifted his mighty head. "Now," he said. "It is now."

In the blink of an eye, the glittering Font vanished, plunging the Chamber into gloom. For the span of a breath, Godslayer seemed to hang in the darkling air above the hole where the Font had blazed, then it dropped, clattering off the stones that ringed the empty pit. There it lay, unharmed, its lucid crimson radiance beating vividly against the darkness.

An involuntary cry escaped Cerelinde's lips. As swiftly as thought, she moved, darting toward the extinguished Font. All around her, shadows seethed. It seemed a penumbra of darkness gathered as the Shaper, too, moved forward. But if her mother was born to the House of Elterrion, her father was a scion of Numireth the Fleet, capable of outracing the darkness. Stooping, Cerelinde seized the rounded haft of the dagger.

Godslayer.

It throbbed against her palm, singing a wordless song of power that made the blood surge in her veins; a Shaper's power, power she did not know how to use. It didn't matter. It was a Shard of the Souma, and it had another purpose. Cerelinde straightened and whirled, prepared to fend off the Sunderer.

He had not moved.

"You see," he murmured. "I kept my word." He took a step toward her, turning his hands outward. "Finish your task."

Although she could not have said for whom she wept, there were tears in her eyes, blurring her vision. Cerelinde tightened her grip on Godslayer's haft. "Why?" she asked, her voice ragged with grief. *"Why?"*

The Shaper smiled. "All things must be as they must, little sister."

He took another step forward and another, looming before her. The clean aroma of water had vanished, and the sweet, coppery scent of ichor filled her nostrils. A Shaper's blood, spilled many Ages ago. An unhealing wound. Cerelinde raised the dagger between them. The Shard's deadly edges glimmered with its own rubescent light. "Stay back!"

Satoris Third-Born shook his head. "One way or the other, you will

give me what is mine." He extended his hand as he had done once before, in the moon-garden. "How do you choose, daughter of Erilonde?"

Now, as then, there was no menace in the gesture; save that it
asked Cerelinde to betray all that she knew, all that she held dear. The
traceries of marrow-fire that illumed the walls of the Chamber dimmed
but slowly, revealing the Shaper's grave features. His empty hand was
outstretched and the vast expanse of his breast was before her, im-
maculate and vulnerable, marrow-lit obsidian flesh. Godslayer
throbbed in her hand, a reminder of the dream of the Rivenlost. The
Souma made whole and Urulat healed, a world no longer Sundered.

Will you dare to become the thing you despise?

"Arahila forgive me!" Cerelinde gasped.

Raising the dagger high, she plunged it into the Shaper's breast.

It sank with sickening ease, driving hilt-deep. Her clenched knuckles brushed his immortal flesh, immortal no more. He cried out; only
once, a cry of such anguish, terror, and relief that Cerelinde knew it
would echo in her ears for the remainder of her days. For a moment
they swayed, locked together; her hand on Godslayer's hilt, the
Shaper's hands rising to cover hers.

Cerelinde saw things.

She saw the dawning of the world and the emergence of the Seven
Shapers within it and understood that it was at once an ending and a
beginning; the death of Uru-Alat and the birth of a vast divergence.
She saw mountains arise and rivers burst forth. She watched the world
grow green and fruitful. She beheld the Shapers at their labor, crafting
their Children in love and pride. She saw Satoris Third-Born walking
alone and without fear in the deep places of the earth, conversing with
dragons.

And then she saw no more.

Godslayer's hilt slipped from her grasp. In the Chamber of the
Font, the Sunderer had fallen to his knees, was slumping sideways.
The shadow of a smile still hovered on his lips. In his breast, the dag-
ger pulsed like a dying star.

"So," he whispered. "It begins anew."

TANAROS WASTED NO TIME EXAMINING the inert form of the Bearer. The
lad's role was finished; it no longer mattered whether he lived or died.

Moving swiftly in the dim light, Tanaros made his way to the outer wall of the chasm and began to climb.

If fear had impelled his descent, no word was large enough for the emotion that hastened his ascent. He was dizzy and unfeeling, his body numb with shock. His limbs moved by rote, obedient to his will, hauling him up the harsh crags until he reached the surface.

The passages behind the walls were growing dimmer, the veins of marrow-fire fading to a twilight hue. Tanaros paused to catch his breath and regain his sense of direction.

Then, he heard the cry.

It was a sound; a single sound, wordless. And yet it held in it such agony, and such release, as shook the very foundations of Darkhaven. On and on it went, and there was no place in the world to hide from it. The earth shuddered, the floor of the passage grinding and heaving. Tanaros crouched beneath the onslaught of the sound, covering his ears, weeping without knowing why. Stray rocks and pebbles, loosened by the reverberations, showered down upon him.

Although it seemed as though the cry would never end, at last it did.

Tanaros found himself on his feet with no recollection of having risen. Drawing his black sword, he began running.

WITHIN TEN PACES, IT HAPPENED.

There was no warning, no sound; only a sudden dim coolness as the veins of marrow-fire that lit the passages dwindled in brightness and the temperature in the stifling passages plummeted. Elsewhere in the passageways, he could hear his distant madlings uttering sounds of dismay and fear. Somewhere, the horns of the Rivenlost were calling out in wild triumph. Above Darkhaven, the ravens wheeled in sudden terror.

Ushahin shivered and pressed onward.

He was halfway to the Chamber of the Font when he heard the cry. It struck him like a blow, piercing him to the core. It was like no sound ever heard before on the face of Urulat, and he knew, with a horrible certainty, what it must portend. Ushahin stood, head bowed as rubble pelted him from above, his branded heart an agony within his hunched torso, arms wrapped around the useless case, and waited it out as another might outwait a storm.

Too late, always too late. The enemy was at the gate. The little weavers had completed their pattern. Haomane's Prophecy hovered on the verge of fulfillment.

Everything he feared had come full circle.

Almost . . .

In the silence that followed, Ushahin Dreamspinner stirred his ill-set, aching limbs. Step by painful step, gaining speed as he went, he began to follow the faint echoes of his Lordship's cry to their source.

TWENTY-FOUR

ENTERING THE CHAMBER OF THE Font at a dead run, Tanaros halted, brought up short by the sight before him. "No," he said, uttering the word without thinking, willing it to be true, willing his denial to change what had happened and render it undone. "Ah, my Lord, *no!*"

It didn't change. Nothing changed.

Where the Font had burned for century upon century, there was nothing save a ring of scorched stone blocks surrounding an aperture in the floor of the Chamber. It seemed a small opening to have admitted such a gout of marrow-fire. Without the Font, the Chamber was dim-lit, the fading veins of marrow-fire that laced its walls filling it with a vague, subterranean twilight.

Lord Satoris lay supine upon the floor of the Chamber; shadows clustered the length of his awesome form. It seemed impossible, and yet it was so. Even fallen, he filled the space until it seemed little else could exist within it. The scent of blood that was not blood, of sweet, coppery ichor, was thick in the air.

The rough-hewn haft of Godslayer pulsed faintly, a ruby star, where it protruded from the bulwark of the Shaper's chest.

It moved, ever so slightly.

She stood in the far corner of the Chamber, beyond the ashen pit of the Font, shrinking away from it; from the Shaper, from her deed. Her eyes were stretched wide with horror, her hands upraised, sliding over her mouth as though to stifle a cry.

"Cerelinde," Tanaros said. The black sword was loose in his grip. *"Why?"*

Unable to answer, she shook her head.

Ignoring her, Tanaros went to his Lord. In the dying light of the marrow-fire, he knelt beside him. The flagstones were hard beneath his knees, tilted askew by the tremors that had shaken Darkhaven. Ichor puddled, soaking his breeches.

"My Lord," he said tenderly. "What must I do?"

At first there was no response, and he feared it was too late, that his Lordship was gone. And then the Shaper's head moved, as though his gaze sought the western horizon beyond the stone walls of his Chamber. "Arahila," he whispered, almost inaudible. "O my sister. What happens to *us* when we die?"

"My Lord, no!" Tanaros reached, touching the Shaper's vast breast, pressing the immortal flesh pierced by the glittering dagger, feeling ichor seep beneath his fingers. "Please, my Lord, what must I do to save you?"

Slowly, Satoris lifted one dragging hand, covering Tanaros', forcing his grip onto the dagger's burning hilt. "Draw it," he said with difficulty. "Let it be done."

Tanaros wept. "My Lord, no!"

In the corner, the Lady Cerelinde made an inarticulate sound.

"So it is not you, my General." With an effort, the Shaper turned his head. His eyes were dark and clear; clear as a child's, but far, far older. The red light of rage had faded in them, as though it had been extinguished with the marrow-fire. So they must have looked long ago, before the world was Sundered, when Satoris Third-Born walked in the deep places of the earth and spoke with dragons. His mouth moved in the faintest hint of a smile. "Not you, at the end."

With a crash, one of the threefold doors at the top of the spiral stair opened; the left-hand door, Ushahin's door. Even as he entered, wild-eyed, Tanaros was on his feet, the black sword in his hand.

"Dreamspinner," he said.

"Tanaros." At the top of the stair, Ushahin swayed and caught himself. "They are at the Gate." He gazed blankly around the Chamber. "My Lord," he said, his voice sounding strange and hollow. "Ah, my poor Lord!"

"He yet lives," Tanaros said roughly. "He bid me draw the dagger and end it."

Ushahin laughed, a terrible, mirthless sound. It held all the bitterness of his mad, useless knowledge, of the ending he had failed to prevent. "Are you not sworn to obey him in all things, cousin? Are you not Tanaros Blacksword, his loyal General?"

"Aye," Tanaros said. "But I think this task is yours, Dreamspinner."

They exchanged a long glance. For a moment, they might have been alone in the Chamber. The Shaper's words lay unspoken between them. They were of the Three, and some things did not need to be spoken aloud. "And her?" Ushahin asked at length, jerking his head toward Cerelinde. "Whose task is *she*?"

Tanaros raised his black sword. "Mine."

"So be it." Ushahin bowed his head briefly, then sheathed his blade and descended the stair. He crossed the crooked flagstones, dropping to his knees beside the Shaper's form, laying the leather case containing the broken Helm gently beside him.

"I am here, my Lord," he murmured. "I am here."

Sword in hand, Tanaros watched.

In the dusky light, the Shaper's body seemed wrought of darkness made manifest. Ushahin felt small and fragile beside him, his illformed figure a sorry mockery of the Shaper's fallen splendor; all save his right arm, so beautifully and cruelly remade.

It fell to him, this hardest of tasks. Somehow it seemed he had always known it would. When all was said and done, in some ways his lot had always been the hardest. He had seen the pattern closing upon them. He had spoken with Calanthrag the Eldest. It was fitting. Kneeling on the flagstones, Ushahin leaned close, the ends of his moon-pale hair trailing in pools of black ichor.

"What is your will, my Lord?" he asked.

The Shaper's lips parted. A terrible clarity was in his eyes, dark and sane, filled with knowledge and compassion. "Take it," he breathed in reply, his words almost inaudible. "And make an end. The beginning falls to you, Dreamspinner. I give you my blessing."

Ushahin's shoulders shook. "Are you certain?"

The Shaper's eyes closed. "Seek the Delta. You know the way."

With a curse, Ushahin raised his right hand. It had been Shaped for this task. It was strong and steady. He placed it on the Shard's crude knob of a hilt. Red light pulsed, shining between his fingers, illuminating his flesh.

It held the power to Shape the world anew, and he did not want it.

Even so, it was his.

"Farewell, my Lord," Ushahin whispered, and withdrew Godslayer.

Darkness seethed through the Chamber. The Shaper's form dwindled, vanishing as its essence coalesced slowly into shadow, into smoke, into a drift of obsidian ash. There was no outcry, no trembling of the earth, only a stirring in the air like a long-held sigh released and a profound sense of passage, as though between the space of one heartbeat and the next, the very foundation of existence had shifted.

Quietly, uneventfully, the world was forever changed.

Ushahin climbed to his feet, holding Godslayer. "Your turn, cousin," he said, hoarse and weary.

CERELINDE WEPT AT THE SHAPER'S passing.

It did not matter, in the end, who drew forth the dagger. She had killed him. He had stood before her, unarmed, and reached out his hand. She had planted Godslayer in his breast. And Satoris Third-Born had known she would do it. He had allowed it.

She did not understand.

She would never understand.

She watched as Ushahin rose to his feet, uttering his weary words. She saw Tanaros swallow and touch the raised circle of his brand beneath his stained, padded undertunic. Hoisting his black sword, he walked slowly toward her. Standing beneath the shadow of his blade, she made no effort to flee, her tears forging a broad, shining swath down her fair cheeks.

Their eyes met, and his were as haunted as hers. He, too, had sunk a blade into unresisting flesh. He had shed the blood of those he loved, those who had betrayed him. He understood the cost of what she had done.

"I'm sorry," he said to her. "I'm sorry, Cerelinde."

"I know." She gazed at him beneath the black blade's shadow. "Ah, Tanaros! I did only what I believed was needful."

"I know," Tanaros said somberly. "As must I."

"It won't matter in the end." She gave a despairing laugh. "There's another, you know. His Lordship told me as much. Elterrion had a second daughter, gotten of an illicit union. So he said to me. 'Somewhere among the Rivenlost, your line continues.'"

Tanaros paused. "And you believed?"

"No," Cerelinde whispered. "Such things happen seldom, so seldom, among the Ellylon. And yet it was his Gift, when he had one, to know such things." She shuddered, a shudder as delicate and profound as that of a mortexigus flower shedding its pollen. "I no longer know what to believe. He said that my mother prayed to him ere she died at my birth. Do you believe it was true, Tanaros?"

"Aye," he said softly. "I do, Cerelinde."

Ushahin's voice came, harsh and impatient. "Have *done* with it, cousin!"

Tanaros shifted his grip on the black sword's hilt. "The madling was right," he murmured. "She told me you would break all of our hearts, Lady." He spoke her name one last time, the word catching in his throat. "Cerelinde."

She nodded once, then closed her eyes. Whatever else was true, here at the end, she knew that the world was not as it had seemed. Cerelinde lifted her chin, exposing her throat. "Make it swift," she said, her voice breaking. "Please."

Tanaros' upraised arms trembled. His palms were slick with sweat, stinging from the myriad cuts and scrapes he had incurred in his climbing. He was tired, very tired, and it hurt to look at her.

Elsewhere in Darkhaven, there were sounds; shouting. His Lordship was dead and the enemy was at the gates.

A blue vein pulsed beneath the fair skin of Cerelinde's outstretched throat.

He remembered the feel of his wife's throat beneath his hands, and the bewildered expression on Roscus' face when he ran him through. He remembered the light fading in the face of Ingolin the Wise, Lord of the Rivenlost. He remembered the Bearer trembling on the verge of the Source, his dark eyes so like those of Ngurra, the Yarru elder.

I can only give you the choice, Slayer.

None of them had done such a deed as hers. Because of her, Lord Satoris, Satoris Third-Born, who was once called the Sower, was no more. For that, surely, her death was not undeserved.

"Tanaros!" Ushahin's voice rose sharply. *"Now."*

He remembered how he had knelt in the Throne Hall, his branded heart spilling over with a fury of devotion, of loyalty, and the words he had spoken. *My Lord, I swear, I will never betray you!*

Wherein did his duty lie?

Loyal Tanaros. It is to you I entrust my honor.

So his Lordship had said. And Ngurra, old Ngurra . . .

Choose.

Breathing hard, Tanaros lowered his sword. He avoided looking at Cerelinde. He did not want to see her eyes opening, the sweep of her lashes rising as disbelief dawned on her beautiful face.

She whispered his name. "Tanaros!"

"Don't." His voice sounded as harsh as a raven's call. "Lady, if you bear any kindness in your heart, do not thank me for this. Only go, and begone from this place."

"But will you not—" she began, halting and bewildered.

"No." Ushahin interrupted. "Ah, no!" He took a step forward, God-slayer still clenched in his fist, pulsing like a maddened heart. "This cannot be, Blacksword. If you will not kill her, I will."

"No," Tanaros said gently, raising his sword a fraction. "You will not."

Ushahin inhaled sharply, his knuckles whitening as his grip tightened. "Will you stand against Godslayer itself?"

"Aye, I will." Tanaros regarded him. "If you know how to invoke its might."

For a long moment, neither moved. At last, Ushahin laughed, short and defeated. Lowering the dagger, he took a step backward. "Alas, not yet. But make no mistake, cousin. I know where the knowledge is to be found. And I *will* use it."

Tanaros nodded. "As his Lordship intended. But you will not use it today, Dreamspinner." He turned to Cerelinde. "Take the right-hand door. It leads in a direct path to the quarters of Vorax of Staccia, who died this day, as did so many others. No one will look for you there." He paused, rubbing at his eyes with the heel of his left hand. "If you are fortunate," he said roughly, "you may live."

Her eyes were luminous and grey, glistening with tears. "Will you not come with me, Tanaros?"

"No." If his heart had not been breaking at his Lordship's death, at the death of all who had fallen this day, it might have broken at her beauty. "Lady, I cannot."

"You *can!*" she breathed. "You can still—"

"Cerelinde." Reaching out with his free hand, Tanaros touched her cheek. Her skin was cool and smooth beneath his fingertips, damp with tears. A Man could spend an eternity loving her, and it would not be long enough. But she had slain his Lordship. Arahila the Fair might forgive her for it, but Tanaros could not. "No."

She gazed at him. "What will you do?"

"What do you think?" He smiled wearily. "I will die, Cerelinde. I will die with whatever honor is left to me." He moved away, pointing toward the right-hand door with the tip of his sword. "Now go."

"Tanaros." She took a step toward him. "Please . . ."

"Go!" he shouted. "Before I change my mind!"

The Lady of the Ellylon bowed her head. "So be it."

Ushahin watched her leave.

As much as he despised her, the Chamber was darker for her absence. It had been a place of power, once. For a thousand years, it had been no less. Now it was only a room, an empty room with a scorched hole in the floor and an echo of loss haunting its corners, a faint reek of coppery-sweet blood in the air.

"What now, cousin?" he asked Tanaros.

Tanaros gazed at his hands, still gripping his sword; strong and capable, stained with ichor. "It was his Lordship's will," he murmured. "He entrusted me with his honor."

"So you say." Ushahin thrust Godslayer into his belt and stooped to retrieve the case that held the sundered Helm of Shadows. "Of a surety, he entrusted me with the future, and I would fain see his will done."

"Aye." Tanaros gathered himself. "Haomane's Allies are at the Gate?"

Ushahin nodded. "They are. I bid the Havenguard to hold it."

"Good." The General touched a pouch that hung from his sword-belt. His haunted gaze focused on Ushahin. "Dreamspinner. You can pass between places, hidden from the eyes of mortal Men. I know, I have ridden with you. Can you use such arts to yet escape from Haomane's Allies?"

"Perhaps." Ushahin hesitated. "It will not be easy. Not with the Host of the Rivenlost at our Gate, the Soumanië at work, and Malthus the Counselor among them."

Tanaros smiled grimly. "I mean to provide them with a distraction."

"It will have to be swift. If the Lady escapes to tell her tale, they will spare no effort to capture Godslayer." Unaccountably, Ushahin's throat ached. His words came unbidden, painful and accusatory. "Why did you do it, Tanaros? *Why?*"

The delicate traceries of marrow-fire lingering in the stone walls were growing dim. The hollows of Tanaros' eyes were filled with shadows. "What would you have me answer? That I betrayed his Lordship in the end?"

"Perhaps." Ushahin swallowed against the tightness in his throat. "For it seems to me you did love her, cousin."

"Does it?" In the gloaming light, Tanaros laughed softly. "In some other life, it seems to me I might have. In this one, it was not to be. And yet, I could not kill her." He shook his head. "Was it strength or weakness that stayed my hand? I do not know, any more than I know why his Lordship allowed her to take his life. In the end, I fear it will fall to you to answer."

A silence followed his words. Ushahin felt them sink into his awareness and realized for the first time the enormity of the burden that had settled on his crooked shoulders. He thought of the weavers in the gulch, spinning their endless patterns; of Calanthrag in her swamp with the vastness of time behind her slitted eyes. He laid his hand upon Godslayer's rough hilt, feeling the pulse of its power; the power of the Souma itself, capable of Shaping the world. The immensity of it humbled him, and his bitterness gave way to grief and a strange tenderness. "Ah, cousin! I will try to be worthy of it."

"So you shall." Tanaros regarded him affection and regret. "His Lordship bid me teach you to hold a blade. Even then, he must have suspected. I do not envy you the task, Dreamspinner. And yet, it is fitting. In some ways, you were always the strongest of the Three. You are the thing Haomane's Allies feared the most, the shadow of things to come." Switching his sword to his left hand, he extended his right. "We waste time we cannot afford. Will you not bid me farewell?"

Here at the end, they understood one another at last.

"I will miss you," Ushahin said quietly, clasping Tanaros' hand. "For all the days of my life, howsoever long it may be."

Tanaros nodded. "May it be long, cousin."

There was nothing more to be said. Ushahin turned away, his head averted. At the top of the winding stair, he paused and raised his hand in farewell; his right hand, strong and shapely.

And then he passed through the left-hand door.

TANAROS STOOD ALONE IN THE darkening Chamber, breathing slow and
deep. He returned the black sword to his right hand, his fingers curving around its familiar hilt. It throbbed in his grip. His blood, his Lordship's blood. The madlings had always revered it. Tempered in the
marrow-fire, quenched in ichor. It was not finished, not yet.

Death is a coin to be spent wisely.

Vorax had been fond of saying that. How like the Staccian to measure death in terms of wealth! And yet there was truth in the words.

Tanaros meant to spend his wisely.

It would buy time for Ushahin to make his escape; precious time in
which the attention of Haomane's Allies was focused on battle. And it
would buy vengeance for those who had fallen. He had spared Cerelinde's life. He did not intend to do the same for those who took arms
against him.

There were no innocents on the battlefield. They would pay for the
deaths of those he had loved. Tanaros would exact full measure for
his coin.

He touched the pouch that hung from his swordbelt, feeling the reassuring shape of Hyrgolf's *rhios* within it.

The middle door was waiting.

It gave easily to his push. He strode through it and into the darkness beyond. These were *his* passageways, straight and true, leading
to the forefront of Darkhaven. Tanaros did not need to see to know
the way. "Vorax. Speros. Hyrgolf," he murmured as he went, speaking
their names like a litany.

TWENTY-FIVE

THE PASSAGEWAY WAS LONG AND winding, and the marrow-fire that lit it grew dim, so dim that she had to feel her way by touch. But Tanaros had not lied; the passage was empty. Neither madlings nor Fjel traversed it. At the end, there was a single door.

Cerelinde fumbled for the handle and found it. She began to whisper a prayer to Haomane and found that the words would not come. The image of Satoris Banewreaker hung before her, stopping her tongue.

Still, the handle turned.

Golden lamplight spilled into the passage. The door opened onto palatial quarters filled with glittering treasure. Clearly, these were Vorax's quarters, unlike any other portion of Darkhaven. Within, three mortal women leapt to their feet, staring. They were fair-haired northerners, young and comely after the fashion of Arahila's Children.

"Vas leggis?" one asked, bewildered. And then, slowly, in the common tongue: "Who are you? What happens? Where is Lord Vorax?"

Tanaros had not lied.

It made her want to weep, but the Ellylon could not weep for their own sorrows. "Lord Vorax is no more," Cerelinde said gently, entering the room. "And the reign of the Sunderer has ended in Urulat. I am Cerelinde of the House of Elterrion."

"Ellyl!" The youngest turned pale. She spoke to the others in Staccian, then turned to Cerelinde. "He is dead? It is ended?"

"Yes," she said. "I am sorry."

And strangely, the words were true. Even more strangely, the three women were weeping. She did not know for whom they wept, Satoris

Banewreaker or Vorax the Glutton. She had not imagined anyone could weep for either.

The oldest of the three dried her eyes on the hem of her mantle. "What is to become of us?"

There was a throne in the center of the room, a massive ironwood seat carved in the shape of a roaring bear. Cerelinde sank wearily into it. "Haomane's Allies will find us," she said. "Be not afraid. They will show mercy. Whatever you have done here, Arahila the Fair will forgive it."

Her words seemed to hearten them. It should have gladdened her, for it meant that there was hope, that not all who dwelled within the Sunderer's shadow were beyond redemption. And yet it did not.

What will you do?

What do you think? I will die, Cerelinde.

A great victory would be won here today. She would take no joy in it.

HAVENGUARD WERE AWAITING WHEN TANAROS emerged from the passageway, crowding Darkhaven's entry. The inner doors were shuddering, battered by a mighty ram. The enemy was past the Gate, had entered the courtyard. They were mounting an offense, coming to rescue the Lady of the Ellylon, coming to fulfill Haomane's Prophecy.

They would succeed.

And they would fail.

Tanaros grinned at his Fjel, watching them respond to it like a deep draft of *svartblod*, relishing their answering grins, broad and leathery, showing their eyetusks.

"Well, lads?" he asked them. "Shall we give our visitors the welcome they deserve? I'll give the greeting myself!"

They roared in acclaim.

"Be certain of it, lads, for it means your deaths!" He touched his branded chest, clad only in his padded undertunic. His armor was lost, vanished in the darkness of the crumbling passageways where the chasm gaped. "In his Lordship's name, I go forth to claim mine. I ask no one to accompany me who does not seek the same!"

The Havenguard Fjel laughed. One of them shouldered past the others, hoisting a battle-axe in one hand and a shield in the other. "I stand at your side, General," he rumbled. "I keep my shield high."

"And I!"

"And I!"

"So be it." The words brought to mind an echo of Cerelinde's farewell. Standing before the great doors, Tanaros paused. He felt keenly the lack of his armor. He wondered about Cerelinde, bound for Vorax's chambers, and how she would live with her deeds afterward. He wondered about the Bearer, if he lived or died. He wondered about the Bearer's comrade, who hung in chains in Darkhaven's dungeons, unable to lift his head. Somewhere, Ushahin was making his way through the hidden passages, Godslayer in his possession.

An Age had ended; a new Age had begun. The Shapers' War would continue.

The thought made Tanaros smile.

In the end, it didn't matter.

Haomane's Allies would Shape this tale as they saw fit. What mattered, what mattered the most, was that the tale did not end here.

"Open the doors," Tanaros ordered.

The Fjel obeyed, as they had always obeyed, as they had obeyed since his Lordship had fled to take shelter among them, sharing with them his vision of how one day, Men and Ellylon alike would envy their gifts, fulfilling the promise of Neheris-of-the-Leaping-Waters, who had Shaped them.

Tanaros strode through the open doors, flanked by a stream of Fjel. The Men wielding the battering-ram dropped back, gaping at his sudden appearance, at the doors behind his back, unbarred and thrown wide open.

Brightness in the air made him squint. The sun, the symbol of Haomane's Wrath, had pierced the veil of clouds that hung over the Vale of Gorgantum. It was low and sinking in the west, but it had prevailed.

Tanaros opened his arms.

They were there; they were all there amid the ragged, dying remnants of his Fjel. All his enemies, gathered. Aracus Altorus, grey-faced and exhausted, barely able to hold his shattered hilt aloft, his Soumanië flickering and dim. Malthus the Counselor astride his pale mount, his white robes swirling. The Rivenlost, at once bereft and defiant. The Archer of Arduan, a bow wrought of black horn in her hands.

Behind them, a legion of Haomane's Allies.

They were silent, watching him.

Gazing at them, Tanaros smiled.

When the last of his strength failed, when arrows pierced his breast, when their sheer numbers bore down his sword-arm and the black sword fell at last from his nerveless fingers, one of them would kill him. It didn't matter which one. All that mattered, here at the end, was that he would die with his Lordship's name on his lips, his honor intact in his heart. He would fulfill his duty.

"I am Darkhaven," he said. "Come and take me."

USHAHIN'S MADLINGS CLUNG TO HIM.

They surrounded him in a ragged tumult, weeping and apologizing for their failure to find the Lady of the Ellylon, begging him not to leave them. Some of them crawled, gasping at the sight of Godslayer; others sought to touch the case that held the severed Helm of Shadows, keening at Lord Satoris' death.

"Hush," Ushahin said, gentling them as he went. "Hush."

They wept all the harder, grasping his hands and kissing them, the healed and the broken alike.

"All things must be as they must," he said to them. "And I must leave you. Do not fear. Haomane's Allies will treat you gently."

He hoped it was true. They had not bothered to do so when they were ordinary people living ordinary lives. But perhaps the burden of *right* they had taken so violently on themselves would impel them to kindness.

It crossed his thoughts to send them to Vorax's quarters. There was time, yet, for the Ellyl bitch to pay for her sins. It would be a fitting ending for her. But the memory of the shadowed pain haunting Tanaros' eyes forestalled him.

Was it strength or weakness that stayed my hand?

Ushahin did not know. The question begged an answer, and he had an immortality in which to find it . . . if he lived through the next hour. If he did not, nothing would matter. And vengeance was unimportant in comparison with fulfilling his Lordship's will and taking his place in the pattern that bound him.

"Do you know which mount is mine?" he asked instead. "Bring it round to the postern gate near the kitchens."

The silent madling boy, the one who loved horses, pelted away at a dead run. Ushahin let the others escort him. His people, his wailing, keening throng. It would hurt to leave them. They passed through the kitchens, the fires burned down to unbanked embers, untended for the first time in memory, crowding through the door after him, surrounding him at the postern gate.

There was the stablehand, holding the bridle of his blood-bay stallion.

It was time.

Ushahin lashed the Helm's case to his saddle. He touched God-slayer's hilt, making certain it was secure in his belt. He mounted his horse.

"Remember," he said to them. "Remember Satoris, Third-Born among Shapers. Remember he was kind to you when the world was not."

The wailing throng swirled and parted, then Meara was there, clutching his stirrup, her tearstained face lifted upward.

"Forgive me," she gasped. "Oh please, oh please, my Lord, forgive me!"

He gazed down at her, thinking what a piece of irony it was that his Lordship's downfall should have hinged in part on such a small matter. It was true, Ushahin had failed his madlings. He alone had understood their longings, their vulnerability. He had let himself grow overly concerned with great dangers, forgetful of the small ones. Did he not owe Meara compassion? It was a fit counterpoint to the act of vengeance he had forgone.

An act of honor; a small kindness. Things his enemies would never acknowledge.

Leaning down in the saddle, Ushahin laid his misshapen left hand upon her head. "Meara of Darkhaven. In Satoris' name, I do forgive you."

Her eyes grew wide. Ushahin smiled his crooked smile.

"Farewell," he said to them. "When you remember his Lordship, think of me."

Straightening, he invoked the dark magic taught to him long ago by the Grey Dam of the Were, letting his waking awareness drift. The world shifted in his vision, leached of color. The madlings' voices faded, and Meara's last of all.

He beheld the paths between and set out upon them.

THE COURTYARD WAS A PLACE of slaughter.

It was too small to contain Haomane's Allies in their entirety. The bulk of their warriors were trapped behind the walls flanking the broken Defile Gate. The rest had fallen back before their onslaught, unprepared for fierce resistance.

Tanaros plunged into the thick of battle, laying about him on all sides.

There was no strategy in it, no plan. Men and Ellylon swarmed him and he swung his black sword, killing them. The Havenguard Fjel struggled to protect him, their shields high. Still the enemy came with sword and spear, piercing his guard, his unarmored flesh. For every one he killed, another took his place. He bled from a half a dozen wounds; from a dozen, from a score.

Still he fought, light-headed and tireless.

The flagstones grew slippery with blood. Horses slipped; mounted warriors dismounted, only to stumble over the bodies of fallen comrades. There was no magic here, only battle at its ugliest. Oronin's Bow was silent, for there was no way for the Archer to take aim in the milling fray.

Aracus Altorus had expended his strength.

But he was a born leader. He gathered his Men instead; the Borderguard of Curonan. Set them to fighting their way around the outskirts of battle, making for the open inner doors. Set them on a course to rescue Cerelinde, to penetrate the secrets of Darkhaven.

"Havenguard!" Tanaros shouted. "Ward the doors!"

They tried. They fought valiantly. He watched them go down, struggling under numbers even a Fjeltroll could not withstand. He watched a handful of Borderguardsmen slip past them, vanishing into the depths of the fortress. He would have led them, once.

It was a long time ago.

In the courtyard, his ranks were thinning. Here and there, bowstrings sang. More of Haomane's Allies streamed past the Defile Gate. Tanaros took a deep breath and squared his shoulders, meeting them.

Someone's blade grazed his brow. A young Midlander, his expression terrified. Tanaros shook his head, blinking the blood from his eyes, and killed him. He stood for a moment, wavering on his feet, thinking of Speros.

Another bow sang out; Oronin's Bow. Its fading echoes called his name. Tanaros felt a sharp punch to his midriff. When he lowered his hand, he found the arrow's shaft, piercing the padded, blood-soaked tunic over his ribs.

He looked for the Archer.

She was staring at him, her face fixed with hatred and grief. Another arrow was nocked in her bow, Oronin's Bow. Her arms trembled. Malthus the Counselor had dismounted to stand beside her, an Ellyl sword in his hand, the clear Soumanië on his breast, his aged face grave.

Tanaros blinked again.

Something was wrong with his vision, for the world seemed dim and strange. They stood out brightly, those two; and behind them, another figure. One who rode astride, giving the battle a wide berth and making for a gap in the forces entering freely through the Defile Gate. A Shard of terrible brightness burned at his hip, red as blood and urgent as the rising sun. He glanced in Tanaros' direction, a glance filled with vivid emotion that had no name.

Overhead, ravens circled and cried aloud.

"Ushahin," Tanaros whispered. "Go!"

The Counselor's head tilted, as though to catch a distant strain of sound. He began to turn, his gaze already searching. Tanaros struggled to fill his lungs, hearing his breath catch and whistle, feeling the arrow's shaft jerk.

"Malthus!" he shouted. "I am *here*!"

The Counselor's gaze returned, fixing him. His Ellyl blade swept up into a warding position. To Tanaros' vision, it seemed limned with pale fire. He laughed aloud, raising his own sword. It burned with dark fire; a wound in the sky, quenched in black ichor. Step by halting step, Tanaros advanced on them.

Oronin's Bow sang out, over and over.

Arrows thudded into his flesh, slowing him. There was pain, distant and unrelated. The air had grown as thick as honey. Tanaros waded through it, shafts protruding from his left thigh, his right shoulder, clustering at his torso. Ellylon and Men assailed him; he swatted their blades away, his black sword shearing steel. One step, then another and another, until he reached the Counselor.

Tanaros raised the black sword for a final blow.

"Malthus," he said. "I am here."

Or did he only think the words? The echoes of Oronin's Bow made it hard to hear. Tanaros fought for breath, his lungs constricted. He felt his grip loosen on the hilt of his sword; his hands, his capable hands, failing him at last. The black sword fell from his hands. The Counselor's face slid sideways in his vision. Malthus' lips were moving, shaping inaudible words. The light of the clear Soumanië he bore struck Tanaros with the force of Haomane's Wrath.

It hurt to look at it, so Tanaros turned his head, looking toward the Defile Gate. The world was growing dark. He understood that he was on his knees, swaying. The flagstones were hard, and sticky with blood; most likely his own. Here at the end, the pain was intense. All his myriad wounds hurt, and his branded heart ached with loss and longing. He fumbled at his breast, finding the shaft of another arrow.

He understood that he was dying.

There was shouting, somewhere, joyous and triumphant. There were Fjel in isolated knots, battling and dying. And there, beyond the Defile Gate, was a bright specter, moving unseen among the wraithlike figures of the living, bearing a spark of scarlet fire. Only Tanaros, caught between life and death, could see it.

He watched it dwindle and vanish, passing out of sight.

It seemed Ushahin Dreamspinner took the light with him, for darkness fell like a veil over his eyes. Tanaros thought of the events that had brought him to die in this place and found he could no longer conjure the old rage. The memory of his wife, of his liege-lord, had grown dim. Had they mattered so much to him once? It seemed very distant. He thought of Cerelinde standing beneath the shadow of his blade, awaiting death; and he remembered, too, how she had smiled at him in the glade of the rookery, making his heart glad.

He wished he could see her face once more and knew it was too late.

The sounds of the courtyard faded. The light of Malthus' Soumanië diminished, until it was no more troublesome than a distant star. The bonds that had circumscribed his heart for so long loosened, falling away. He had kept his vow. His Lordship's honor was untarnished. Godslayer, freed, would remain in Ushahin's hands. Tanaros had spent the coin of his death wisely.

His heart, which had beat faithfully for so many centuries, thudded; once, twice. No more. It subsided into stillness, a long-delayed rest.

There was only the long peace of death, beckoning to him like a lover.

Tanaros met it smiling.

ARACUS' VOICE CUT THROUGH THE clamor of ragged cheers and shouts that greeted her appearance, filled with relief and joy.

"Cerelinde!"

She stood on the steps of Darkhaven, gazing at the carnage in silent horror. Everywhere, there was death and dying; Men, Ellylon, Fjel. Aracus picked his way across the courtyard, making his way to her side.

She watched him come. He looked older than she remembered, his face drawn with weariness. His red-gold hair was dark with sweat, his armor splashed with gore. In one hand, he held the hilt of a shattered sword, set with a dimly flickering gem. A pebble of the Souma, smooth as a drop of blood. Her palm itched, remembering the feel of Godslayer pulsing against her skin.

"Cerelinde." Aracus stood before her on the steps, searching her eyes. The Borderguardsmen who had found her in Vorax's quarters began to speak. He silenced them with a gesture, all his urgent attention focused on her. "Are you . . . harmed?"

"No." She fought the urge to laugh in despair. "I killed him."

For a moment, he merely gazed at her, uncomprehending. "The . . . Sunderer?"

"Yes," she whispered. "The Shaper."

His Men did speak, then, relating what she had told them. Behind them, others emerged from the depths of Darkhaven, escorting Vorax's handmaids and an unarmed horde of weeping, babbling madlings. Aracus listened gravely to his Borderguard. "Get torches. Find the lad and his uncle," he said to them. "And Godslayer; Godslayer, above all. It lies in the possession of the Misbegotten, and he cannot have gotten far. Search every nook and cranny. He *will* be found." He turned back to Cerelinde. "Ah, love!" he said, his voice breaking. "Your courage shames us all."

Cerelinde shook her head and looked away, remembering the way

Godslayer had sunk into Satoris' unresisting flesh. "I did only what I believed was needful."

Aracus took her hand in his gauntleted fingers. "We have paid a terrible price, all of us," he said gently. "But we have won a great victory, my Lady."

"Yes," she said. "I know."

She yearned to find comfort in his touch, in that quickening mortal ardor that burned so briefly and so bright. There was none. It had been the Gift of Satoris Third-Born, and she had slain him.

He had spoken the truth. And she had become the thing that she despised.

"Come," Aracus said. "Let us seek Malthus' counsel."

He led her across the courtyard, filled with milling warriors and dying Fjeltroll. They died hard, it seemed. A few of them looked up from where they lay, weltering in their own gore, and met her eyes without fear. They had seemed so terrifying, once. It was no longer true.

Malthus was kneeling, his robes trailing in puddles of blood. He straightened at her approach. "Lady Cerelinde," he said in his deep voice. "I mourn the losses of the Rivenlost this day."

"I thank you, Wise Counselor." The words caught in her throat, choking her. She had seen that which his kneeling body had hidden. "Ah, Haomane!"

"Fear not, Lady." It was a strange woman who spoke. In one hand, she held a mighty bow wrought of horn. Though her face was strained with grief, her voice was implacable. "Tanaros Kingslayer is no more."

Cerelinde nodded, not trusting her voice.

Though half a dozen arrows bristled from his body, Tanaros looked peaceful in death. His unseeing eyes were open, fixed on nothing. A slight smile curved his lips. His limbs were loose, the taut sinews unstrung at last, the strong hands slack and empty. A smear of blood was across his brow, half-hidden by an errant lock of hair.

The scent of vulnus-blossom haunted her.

We hold within ourselves the Gifts of all the Seven Shapers and the ability to Shape a world of our choosing. . . .

Cerelinde shuddered.

She could not allow herself to weep for his death; not here. Perhaps not ever. Lifting her head, she gazed at Aracus. He was a choice she had made. He returned her gaze, his storm-blue eyes somber.

There would be no gloating over this victory. His men had told her of the losses they had endured on the battlefield, of Blaise Caveros and Lord Ingolin the Wise, and many countless others.

She saw the future they would shape together stretching out before her. Although the shadow of loss and sorrow would lay over it, there would be times of joy, too. For the brief time that was alotted them together, they would find healing in one another, and in the challenge of bringing their races together in harmony.

There would be fear, for it was in her heart that neither Ushahin nor Godslayer would be found on the premises of Darkhaven. Haomane's Prophecy had been fulfilled to the letter, and yet it was not. Without Godslayer, the Souma could not be made whole, and the world's Sundering undone. The Six Shapers would remain on Torath, apart, and Ushahin would be an enemy to Haomane's Allies; less terrible than Satoris Banewreaker, for even with a Shard of the Souma, he would not wield a Shaper's power, capable of commanding the loyalty of an entire race. More terrible, for he did not have a Shaper's pride and the twisted sense of honor that went with it.

There would be hope, for courage and will had triumphed over great odds on this day, and what was done once might be done again.

There would be love. Of that, she did not doubt. She was the Lady of the Ellylon, and she did not love lightly; nor did Aracus. They would be steadfast and true. They would rule over Urulat with wisdom and compassion.

And yet there would be doubt, born out of her long captivity in Darkhaven.

Shouting came from the far side of the courtyard. More Borderguardsmen were emerging from Darkhaven, carrying two limp figures. The Bearer and his uncle had been found and rescued. One stirred. Not the boy, who lay motionless.

"Aracus." Malthus touched his arm. "Forgive me, for I know your weariness is great. Yet it may be that the Soumanië can aid him."

"Aye." With an effort, Aracus gathered himself. "Guide me, Counselor."

In the midst of slaughter and carnage, Cerelinde watched them tend to the stricken Yarru, their heads bowed in concentration. The young Bearer was gaunt and frail, as though his travail had pared him down to the essence.

She tried to pray and could not, finding herself wondering, instead, if this victory was worth its cost. She longed to weep, but her eyes remained dry. She watched as the Bearer drew in a breath of air, sudden and gasping, his narrow chest heaving. She longed to feel joy, but felt only pity at the harshness with which Haomane used his chosen tools. She listened to the shouts of Men, carrying out the remainder of their futile search, and to the horns of the Rivenlost, declaring victory in bittersweet tones.

And she knew, with the absolute certainty with which she had once believed in Haomane's unfailing wisdom and goodness, that no matter what else the future held, in a still, silent place in her heart that she would never share—not with Aracus, nor Malthus the Counselor, nor her own kinfolk—she would spend the remainder of her days seeing the outstretched hand of Satoris Third-Born before her, feeling the dagger sink into his breast, and hearing his anguished death-cry echoing in her ears.

Wondering why he had let her take his life; and why Tanaros had spared hers. Wondering if there was another scion of Elterrion's line upon the face of Urulat. Wondering if her mother had prayed to Satoris on her deathbed.

Wondering why the Six Shapers did not dare leave Torath, and whether a world in which Satoris prevailed would truly have been worse than one over which Haomane ruled, an absent father to his Children.

Wondering where lies ended and truth began.

Wondering if she had chosen wisely at the crossroads she had faced.

Wondering, and never daring to know.

What might have been?

EPILOGUE

A SHADOW PASSED THROUGH THE Defile, disturbing the shroud of web-bing that hung from the Weavers' Gulch in tattered veils. The little grey weavers chittered in dismay, scuttling furiously, setting about their endless work of rebuilding and repair.

No one else noticed.

Ushahin-who-walks-between-dusk-and-dawn rode the pathways between one thing and another; between waking and dreaming, be-tween life and death, between the races of Lesser Shapers, between a dying Age and one being born.

He rode a blood-bay stallion, its coat the hue of drying gore, its mane and tail as black as the spaces between the stars. Lashed to his saddle was a leather case that contained a broken Helm, its empty eye-sockets gazing onto darkness.

And at his belt he bore a dagger wrought from a single Shard of the Souma, the Eye in the Brow of Uru-Alat. It was red, pulsing with its own inner light, and it would have betrayed his presence had he not wrapped it in shadow, in a cloak of the vague ambiguities that lay be-tween victory and defeat, between pride and humility, between right and wrong.

Between all things.

He kept his thoughts shrouded as he rode, and no one challenged him as he passed beyond the Vale of Gorgantum.

Beyond him, the plains of Curonan stretched toward the east. He set out upon them, picking his way among the dead.

Overhead, there was a sound.

Glancing up, Ushahin-who-walks-between saw the raven circling and understood that it saw him in turn. He paused, waiting. It descended to land on his left shoulder, talons pricking. He sensed its sadness and looked into its thoughts as the Grey Dam of the Were had taught him long ago.

He saw death and knew he was the last of the Three.

The raven made a keening sound in its throat. He stroked its head, its errant tuft of feathers, with one crooked finger.

Soothed, the raven settled.

Ushahin-who-walks-between resumed his journey. He was pleased to have the raven's company. Later, he would give thought to vengeance, to the new pattern taking shape in the world, to the role that had befallen him, to the promise he had made to Lord Satoris, to the memory of the nameless child he had once been, before a rock in a stranger's fist had shattered his world.

Today, there was comfort in the simple communion of shared sorrow.

There would be time for the rest.

With his back to Darkhaven, Ushahin rode toward the Delta, where Calanthrag the Eldest awaited him.

In the Sundered World of Urulat, the sun set on an Age.

Tomorrow, a new one would dawn.